Hers to Have and to Hold

June Francis' sagas include *Step by Step*, *A Dream To Share*, *When Clouds Go Rolling By*, *Tilly's Story* and *Sunshine and Showers*. She had her first novel published at forty and is married with three sons. She lives in Liverpool.

GW00670437

Also by June Francis

Look for the Silver Lining
A Place to Call Home
The Heart Will Lead
Another Man's Child
Someone to Trust
Shadows of the Past
It's Now or Never
Love Letters in the Sand
Many a Tear Has To Fall
Memories Are Made of This
Walking Back to Happiness
Where There's a Will
For Better, For Worse
Friends and Lovers
Hers to Have and to Hold

The Victoria Crescent Sagas

Step by Step
A Dream to Share
When the Clouds Go Rolling By
Tilly's Story
Sunshine and Showers

JUNE FRANCIS

Hers to Have and to Hold

CANELO

First published in the United Kingdom in 2023 by

Canelo
Unit 9, 5th Floor
Cargo Works, 1-2 Hatfields
London SE1 9PG
United Kingdom

A CIP catalogue record for this book is available from the British Library.

Print ISBN 978 1 80436 314 0
Ebook ISBN 978 1 80436 313 3

Cover design by Rose Cooper

Cover images © Shutterstock, Arcangel

Look for more great books at www.canelo.co

Printed and bound in Great Britain by Clays Ltd, Elcograf S.p.A.

1

To my sons Iain and Timothy, for without their continuing help during their father's Alzheimers, this book would never have been completed.

PROLOGUE

Eliza Jones hurried along the pavement, desperate to reach home, while the warning wail of the air-raid siren accompanied her steps, even as she told herself she had to go carefully. In the near distance she could hear an aeroplane and her hand covered her swollen belly protectively, and she prayed that she and the baby would survive this night. Her foot caught on some debris left over from the raid the night before and she barely managed to prevent herself from falling, and her breath caught in her throat. She stopped. Her gaze managed to pierce the darkness of the late spring, which was not quite black, and she realised that she had arrived at the house where her apartment was situated, so she took her door key from the pocket of her jacket. She managed to insert it in the lock at her first attempt and stepped over the threshold as she heard an explosion some distance away, probably down by the docks, but that did not mean that the rest of the city escaped Hitler's plan to destroy Liverpudlians' morale. Their homes, factories, churches, hospitals and shops were targeted to disrupt the passage of vehicles, water and power supplies – the list was endless. She attempted to stem the terrifying thoughts, and turned this way and that, realising that the darkness inside was blacker than out on the street.

Then she froze in fear and clutched her handbag to her body. She heard several explosions, and felt small pieces of debris landing on her head and shoulders, but some fell on the floor and were alight. There were screams and shouts of anger coming from inside the building and she guessed that a fire incendiary – or maybe more than one – had gone through the roof and she had not seen the flames from outside. There would be no reaching her apartment upstairs, and she could not risk going outside again, as it was not unknown for people to be shot from the air as they fled their homes in terror. She had to find a place of safety: under the stairway. Blindly, with outstretched arms, she stumbled in what she thought was the right direction. She was aware of voices shouting out on the street and the noise of a vehicle, and then suddenly she felt an almighty whack on her head and tripped over something. All around her the floor was littered with broken and splintered lengths of wood, clumps of plaster and bricks, even items of furniture, which she could just make out now her eyes were accustomed to the darkness. She fought to stay conscious and realised she had fallen on a body, as it had moaned. She felt it all over and her hand came away with what she decided was blood, and her heart sank. She concluded by the clothing that the woman was the elderly widow, Mrs Gaskell, who lived on the first floor and that she must have fallen through a hole made by falling debris.

'Help me?' she mumbled, clinging to Eliza's sleeve.

'I will,' Eliza reassured her. 'We must get to the cupboard under the stairs. I will drag you by the shoulders and crawl if you could use your heels as if you were doing backstroke.'

'I never learned to swim, us girls didn't in my day. Mam thought it wasn't proper to appear half-naked in public.' The words were slurred.

Somehow Eliza managed to drag the old woman towards the cupboard under the stairs, despite her aching body and the fear that the ripples of pain, which felt like period pains, were alerting her to the possibility that her labour could have started, and her baby's life could be at risk. Fortunately, she was only a couple of feet from the cupboard but, to her dismay, the door, which was half-open, was blocked by a body. She was terrified that if she attempted to move it out of the way, it could put her baby and herself at further risk. A sob burst from her, and she collapsed on the floor, fighting back tears and praying for a miracle. She had no idea how long she lay there, hoping and praying in fear, with no thought for Mrs Gaskell, who was still and silent, as she attempted to force the door open wider. Then, through her fear, came the sound of wood splintering and men's voices, and she felt a draught of fresh air and the darkness was lightened by the flash of torches. She attempted to call out, but her throat was dry with dust and smoke. She sensed the men moving carefully about the room and one was coming closer. She attempted a cough to clear the dust and smoke. Then she felt a touch on her shoulder and despite the fogginess in her head, she was vaguely aware of a man calling urgently, 'Ben, there's one alive here. The other two are dead.'

'Baby coming. Ambulance!' Eliza managed to utter through another pain.

A different voice this time, telling the other rescuer to go and see to the ambulance. She felt arms slide beneath her and lift her up, and her fear lessened. She allowed herself to relax as the pain faded and she drifted into sleep.

PART ONE

MAY–OCTOBER 1941

CHAPTER ONE

Eliza moaned as pain surged through her – her stomach and her legs. Even her head and arms ached, and she was scared, not knowing what was happening to her or where she was, but through the fog in her head she told herself to open her eyes.

'Now come on, love. It'll soon be over,' said a kind calm voice.

'Where am I?' cried Eliza. 'I can't remember.'

'You're safe for now in Oxford Street Maternity Hospital. The All Clear has sounded and your baby will soon be here.'

Her baby! Eliza struggled with that thought, trying to remember the father's name – why couldn't she picture him? Then, unexpectedly, in her mind she heard a man's voice with a musical Welsh accent, saying, 'Come on, say yes, Eliza? You know you want to marry me before I go off and fight. We have less than a week to do the deed and spend time together.'

'But we hardly know each other,' she found herself murmuring.

'What was that you said, Mrs Jones?' asked the nurse.

So, we did get married, thought Eliza, and his name was Jones, a common enough name. One thing was for sure: he was not here because, if her memory wasn't playing tricks on her, he was away fighting in the army.

Suddenly, she was back in the present, as pain washed over her and she felt an urge to push, which she fought for a moment, but it was too strong and the midwife told her to take it easy. She felt confused, scared of making a mistake and harming her baby.

'I can see the crown,' said the midwife. 'Now push.'

She did as her body directed, felt a sharp pain and her baby was born.

'A handsome little fellow,' said the midwife.

She wanted to see him and attempted to sit up, but the effort was too much, and she flopped back. A boy, she thought, that should please his father, who if she remembered right wanted a son. She lay there, trying to work out how she had come to be here in this hospital, but thinking made her head throb and she felt muddled. 'I wasn't booked in to come to this hospital,' she said.

The other midwife looked up from where she was dealing with the afterbirth. 'No, but that had been bombed. You went into labour when the house where you lived was struck by an incendiary that set fire to the top floor. You were fortunate – apparently, you must have just entered the building. You were hit by falling debris, and that's most likely why you don't remember it happening.'

'Will my memory of what happened ever come back?'

'You can ask your doctor when he comes. You need a few stitches. Your skin tore a little when your baby was born. The doctor will do them, and check you and your son over.'

'I haven't heard him cry. He's all right, isn't he?'

'You'll hear him in a minute. We just want to clean him up before we give him to you.'

It was as the midwife said and Eliza was thrilled as she heard her son cry for the first time, and when he was placed in her arms, tears of joy ran down her cheeks. She wiped them away so she could gaze into his face. His eyes were blue, and he had a perfect little nose and a lovely shaped mouth with a full lower lip.

'Don't worry about your memory coming back right now,' said the midwife. 'You've more important things to think about. Your son needs you.' She paused. 'Let's put him to the breast. The first milk is especially good for him.'

Eliza was glad of their help and soon was feeding her son, and it was so pleasurable because she could see him enjoy the nourishment: she was giving him what would enable him to grow. He was in her arms and that was so much better than her imaginings of being a mother. He was her own dear son, and they could have fun together. She loved him so much that she would protect him with her own life if necessary. She gazed in wonder at the tiny hand resting starlike on her breast.

'Have you and your husband chosen a name for a boy?' asked the nurse.

'I wanted Alfred, after my dad, Alfie for short.'

'That's nice. Strong, and the name of a king,' said the nurse. 'So, we'll put Alfred down for his first name. Your husband can always choose a second name for him.'

Eliza agreed, thinking she had done all the work and besides, her husband wasn't there and she did not want to go on just calling her son 'the baby' for possibly months on end.

'It's a pity that you didn't have a chance to bring a suitcase with the baby's clothes,' said one of the nurses. 'Fortunately, we do keep baby clothes for such occasions.' In no time at all she had seen to the matter, not just returning with baby clothes but with nappies and a shawl as well.

Once the baby had been fed, and was dressed in a nightie and a nappy and wrapped in the shawl, he was placed in a cot and Eliza was given a cup of tea and a slice of bread and butter. After she had eaten and drunk, she was given her handbag. Delighted, she rummaged inside it and brought out her identity card, her ration book, her post office saving book and an envelope which held a wedding certificate. She perused it and found it difficult to believe that she had agreed to be married in a registry office and not at her local church, which she had attended regularly in the past, but not since she had met Bryn in the Blue Anchor pub near Aintree Racecourse. She was relieved that she could remember their meeting.

She was interrupted by the arrival of the doctor, who asked how she was feeling and then did her stitches, before checking the baby. After declaring him healthy, he turned his attention to Eliza again and spoke to her about her injuries sustained during the bombing and suggested her having an X-ray. She had no desire to leave Alfie, but the doctor insisted, and her baby was put in the care of the nursery nurse.

Once back in the ward, Eliza resumed writing her letter to Olive, a friend from the ammunition works who had been with her when she met Bryn. Olive's brother, Pete, was in the navy and involved with the Battle of the Atlantic, like many a Liverpudlian seafarer. A scrap had arisen between him and soldier Bryn, who had approached the two girls while Pete had been at the bar ordering what drinks were available in this period of shortages. She shook her head. Men! As if they didn't have a real enemy to fight. Even so, they had been ordered out of the pub and the girls had followed them after finishing their drinks. 'Waste not, want not!' Olive had said, annoyed with her brother for causing trouble, as if she couldn't look after herself! Pete had gone off in a huff when the girls had accepted Bryn and his soldier mate's invitation to a fish and chips supper. The last of the big spenders, Eliza thought, and resumed reading her marriage certificate, wondering what other memories she could recall. She found names interesting and read her father's name, Alfred Griffiths, feeling sad that her son would never know his granddad, who also had Welsh blood. He had always loved her visiting his parents in Anglesey. She still missed her grandparents and digging in the sand on the beach and baking with her grandmother. It was good for a child to have a grandparent. She thought of Bryn's mother, and imagined her a plump and jolly woman who she hoped could get down to a child's level and enjoy baking with her grandson.

She glanced at her son in the cot beside her bed and her thoughts shifted again. After agreeing to marry Bryn after only three weeks, he had taken charge of all the arrangements, saying they didn't have time for a church wedding. Olive would have had something to say about that if she hadn't gone away for a month to look after her spinster aunt who was ill, and so would Milly, a friend Eliza knew from church, who was married with ten-year-old twins. She realised now she had made a mistake, dropping her friend when she believed herself in love and agreeing to marry Bryn in a rush.

Eliza sighed, thinking that if she'd had her wedding all over again it would have been different – still, she wouldn't have her handsome son now, so she was thankful for being a wife and mother. So, she should have no regrets about the lack of guests, not even Bryn's army mate and his half-brother, Glyn, who had been unable to get leave, as Bryn had explained. Her own parents were dead, and Bryn's father was deceased. His mother was living in Colwyn Bay, but Bryn had told Eliza that she wasn't in good health and so couldn't attend the wedding. He had added that, with there being a war on, loads of couples were marrying without family and all the trimmings. She had agreed and now she thought of the two witnesses and recalled that one of them had come in off the street, while the other had been a cleaner, a woman who had just finished her stint in the office and had been roped in. The man who had come in from the street was named Jack Molyneux; she had barely spoken to him, beyond thanking him, before he had a few words with the registrar and left. He had shaken Eliza's hand and wished her happiness in an expressionless voice, but she had been aware of the look in his hazel eyes – a look which seemed to say that he didn't think she would be happy. Suddenly, she was aware of discomfort underneath, so she shifted into a more comfortable position and continued to think back.

Had it been even that early in her marriage when she had begun to question whether she should have rushed into it? Bryn had swept her off her feet with his charm and looks that reminded her of the handsome swashbuckling film star Douglas Fairbanks Jr, whom she had seen in *The Prisoner of Zenda* and *Gunga Din* before war broke out. That was, she remembered, shortly after she had left the Seamen's Orphanage and got herself a job in Barker and Dobson's sweet factory, and she had found digs in Norwood Grove.

She had continued living in Norwood Grove even after her wedding, as it seemed pointless to move when Bryn was away fighting, but she was now going to have to find herself and her son somewhere else to live, which wasn't going to be easy. What with so many homes being destroyed in the Blitz or not fit to live in.

She replaced the contents of her handbag and gazed at her son, and her heart swelled with love and she counted her blessings. She had survived a terrible night and so had her baby. Now she should relax, as she would most likely be in hospital with her darling son for at least ten days, if not more, as she had no home to go to. She even wrote to Bryn's mother with the news that she had a grandson and asked a nurse to post the letter.

That evening the bombers returned over Merseyside so Eliza, just like many others, was terrified for her safety and that of her son, unable to relax for the sound of aeroplanes, bombs exploding, guns firing, screams and shouting. She prayed fervently not only for herself and Alfie, but also for Liverpool's survival. The hospital was closer to the docks, so there was more chance of them being bombed. Every night one could smell burning, which caused her fear to increase, and she refused to leave Alfie in his cot and instead nursed him, singing lullabies to him.

The following day she decided she really must inform Bryn that she had given birth to a son, explaining that they were in Oxford Street Maternity Hospital and that she had been bombed out of her apartment. She would send the letter to his training barracks and hopefully it would reach him soon. She would also finish writing the letter to Olive and send it to her mother's address, hoping it would be sent on to Olive.

The rest of the week there was to be no let-up in the enemy's attempts to destroy the docks and shipyards, factories, and the morale of the people of Merseyside. Eliza longed to get away with Alfie after hearing about how those towards the north end of the city left in the afternoons with their children and walked to the countryside in Lancashire, sleeping in the fields. She would have given anything to get out of the city, to find safety for her and her son.

A couple of days later she was handed a letter postmarked Colwyn Bay and in it her mother-in-law expressed her pleasure at the birth of her grandson. She also suggested that Eliza bring the baby to see her and stay for a while. Eliza thought it over, and went as far as enquiring about the price of a train ticket, and decided to withdraw some money from her post office saving account. She did not buy a ticket straightaway, as there was the matter of speaking to the doctor and getting his say-so that she and Alfie were well enough to make such a journey. He agreed, but suggested she have a friend to travel with her.

As it was, the morning she bought her ticket, the bombing suddenly stopped and the mammoth task of rebuilding the docks and shipyards that had been damaged on both sides of the Mersey continued, as well as thoroughfares being cleared. The mending of gas pipes, water pipes, and electric and telephone wires continued apace, as help flooded in from other towns and cities and villages. Even soldiers at camps in Lancashire and Cheshire arrived to help. She sometimes thought about those who had rescued her and whether they had survived that terrible night after they saved her and Alfie's lives.

CHAPTER TWO

A week after the bombing had ended, a nurse entered the ward and came towards Eliza with the news that her husband was there. She felt confused, puzzled that he had been able to get there so swiftly. Not for the first time, she wished she had thought of having a photographer at their wedding. She could scarcely believe it was him – tanned with the burning sun of the Middle East. His fair hair surprisingly looked darker, rather than bleached by the sun, but his voice held that lovely Welsh lilt. He came close to the bed and she held her arms up to him, and he hesitated before kissing her gently, as if worried about hurting her.

'Bryn,' she whispered. 'I didn't expect to see you so soon.'

'I had to come,' he said after several moments. 'I could scarcely believe you'd had a son when I read your letter.'

'You look well,' she said.

'We're fed well because we need to be healthy and fit to fight.'

She nodded. 'So, what do you think of your son?'

He told her what a clever wife she was, and she frowned, annoyed at being spoken to in such a way. He had brought flowers for her and a fluffy blue dog toy for Alfie, which softened her mood slightly. He commiserated with her having been bombed out of her home. She said that they would need to find a house when he returned for good.

'How long will your leave be?' she asked as he clasped her hand gently.

'Twenty-four hours, that's all,' he replied in a tight voice. 'Can't do much in that time, especially with you stuck in hospital. I'll try and come and see you tomorrow before I leave. I had considered going to visit my mother if the train was running.'

'What do you mean if?'

'The bombing has damaged some of the tracks, as well as the trains.' He squeezed her hand and then rose to his feet. 'You're looking tired. I'd best go.' He kissed her again and glanced down at Alfie. 'He's a handsome little lad.'

She nodded. 'Have a safe journey.' It was on the tip of her tongue to mention her visiting his mother, but something held her back and she simply blew him a kiss.

After he had gone, she wondered how he had managed to visit her so soon, but perhaps military information was hush-hush. Eliza was now able to get up and go to the lavatory instead of using a bedpan, much to her relief, and to have a proper bath. She had had her stitches out but still felt sore underneath. She was also still suffering from concussion, and cuts and bruises, although the latter were now fading.

Alfie was now sleeping in the nursery during the night to make sure she could get enough sleep. She missed him being within reaching distance, but most babies were kept in the nursery a few days after the birth and fed from a bottle during the night by a nurse.

But despite this, she got little sleep, as she was uncertain what to do about travelling to Bryn's mother, even though she had written to tell her that she would be visiting her as soon as possible.

Then, horror of horrors, within a week of Bryn's visit, she was roused by a staff nurse and informed that Alfie was missing.

Eliza had managed to fall asleep towards dawn and was caught up in a nightmare, so when she was shaken awake by the nurse, bleary-eyed, she didn't recognise her and, reaching up a hand, she shoved her in the face. 'You're lying. You're not really a nurse but a German spy in disguise.'

'That's not true!' The staff nurse seized Eliza's wrist gently but firmly. 'I'm really sorry to have to tell you that Alfie is missing, believed to have been taken by a mother who had lost her baby.'

Eliza shook her head. 'I don't believe it. I was told he'd be safe and cared for by experienced and reliable nurses.' Her voice rose to a high pitch, and she flung back the bedcovers. She coughed and said hoarsely, 'Take me to the nursery. I want to talk to the nurse in charge.'

'That's not possible, Eliza,' said the staff nurse in a carefully controlled voice. 'The nurse has finished her shift and has gone home.'

'How dare she go home when my son is missing,' said Eliza in a seething voice. 'I will find him if I must tear this hospital apart. He trusted…' Her voice broke. 'I swore I'd protect him with my life.' Bare-footed and with her nightgown fluttering about her ankles, she marched down the ward as if to war. The sister rushed after her.

Eliza pushed a door open and went out into a corridor. She glanced left and right. Her head felt fit to burst and she could not decide which way to go, and then the sister seized her arm. Eliza tried to shake her off, but she held on to her.

'We'll go together but you must calm down or you'll scare the babies,' said the sister.

Eliza blinked and gazed along the corridor. She realised she was awake, but the sister's mention of babies reminded her that she was living in a nightmare. Alfie was missing, but perhaps the nurse had placed him in the wrong cot. 'We have to make a search,' she said, and hurried along the corridor, dragging the sister with her. They came to the nursery and went inside. Ignoring the nurse who came forward, she went over to the nearest cot and gazed down at the baby. 'No,' she uttered on a sob and continued to go from cot to cot, disturbing some babies when she turned them over and setting them wailing.

Eliza heard one of the nurses whisper, 'She needs a sedative.'

'Matron's already been in touch with her doctor and phoned the police,' said the sister.

Eliza thought, no way will they sedate me! I must stay alert to find Alfie. She left the nursery and entered the nearest ward, and like a whirlwind she began searching it, waking up the mothers. She had not got far when she was seized and escorted to a private room and, despite her struggles, was put to bed, but she was not to be left alone. A nurse stayed with her, while another brought her a warm milky drink, which Eliza refused to drink, believing it might be drugged. Shortly after, the doctor arrived and spoke to her soothingly and with sense, telling her that if she did not calm down and rest, she would be in no fit state to care for Alfie when he was found. The police had been notified and sooner or later would speak to her. Firstly, they were interviewing present staff and former staff who might remember patients who had suffered the loss of a baby.

For the rest of the day Eliza was almost out of her mind, especially when it came to feeding times. Despite the sedative, she worried whether Alfie was being fed and cared for properly. He would be missing her and really had to be found soon.

Later in the day a policeman came to see her and, to her astonishment, he told her that they had met before.

'We have?' she said, wondering if she should believe him, as she had never had anything to do with policemen. Then a thought occurred to her. 'Were you called out to stop a fight that had broken out at the Blue Anchor pub in Aintree last year?'

He shook his head.

She stared at him intently and he stared back, and she noticed that his eyes were hazel.

'What's your name?' she asked.

'Jack Molyneux,' he replied.

She gasped, reached for her handbag and took out her marriage certificate, although she really had no need to check the name because she remembered it. 'You're the witness who came in off the street to my wedding,' she said.

'Yes. I haven't forgotten your name and how apprehensive you looked. Big step to take, getting married in haste, so when I saw your case, I volunteered, telling my inspector I knew you.'

'But that's not quite true, is it?' she said, considering it strange that he should want to work on her case. 'We've met, but we don't know each other.'

'I know I want to find your baby for you,' he replied.

'Then find him,' she pleaded, stretching out a hand to him.

He took it and she was aware of the strength in his fingers. 'I will. We have a lead from a previous midwife about a mother who already has a daughter but who was desperate for a son. She had miscarried twice since the birth of her daughter but was told she couldn't have any more children. A search has already been made of the neighbourhood known as Little Wales down by the docks before we had this information, and another search is being made today. Hopefully, we'll discover more about this woman and her whereabouts, as the area was damaged during the recent bombing.'

'I understand,' Eliza said, relieved that the police had a lead and the woman had another child, meaning that Alfie would be cared for – still, what she had done was sinful. 'The search will take longer if she is one of them who has moved away.'

He nodded and freed her hand. 'We'll find her and him if she is the guilty party. Something the policeman forgot to ask when he interviewed the nurse was whether your son has any distinguishing marks.'

'Yes, he has a birthmark on his lower back,' she said excitedly.

He smiled. 'Noted. See you soon.'

As he left, she called after him, 'I'm praying for you.' She could not help but look forward to seeing him again, feeling she could depend on him to find Alfie.

He raised a hand in acknowledgement and as he exited the ward, she saw Olive's tall slender figure enter. Eliza would rather not have had her friend turn up at that moment. She needed to rest and decide what to do about visiting her mother-in-law. She wished she could see the vicar. She had missed going to church, having got out of the habit after meeting Bryn. Now she felt in need of his prayers and advice. Maybe Olive would visit him after she left here and ask him to come and visit her in hospital as soon as possible.

'You got my letter then?' said Eliza.

Olive sat on the chair beside the bed. 'I wouldn't be here if I hadn't, softie,' she said. 'So, where's the baby?'

'He's been kidnapped,' replied Eliza, her voice wobbling. 'The police have been called in.'

Olive paled and reached out to cover Eliza's hand that lay on the coverlet. 'That's wicked. But why would anybody steal your baby?'

Eliza told her what the staff and police thought, and what was being done, as well as about Bryn's visit. She paused, realising she had not mentioned Bryn's visit to Jack Molyneux. 'I also want to see the vicar at St Margaret's. I need his help.'

'You can stay at ours,' said Olive. 'You could come with me now.'

'Thanks,' Eliza said, having half-expected her friend to offer her a roof over her head. 'But I doubt they'll let me out right now. Besides, I need to be here for news of Alfie. It's been awful not knowing where he is. He could be crying his eyes out and she might smack him.' She choked on the words and her eyes shone with tears. 'But you can do something else for me.'

'Anything!' said Olive, patting her shoulder.

'I'm going to need some new clothes.'

'I'd offer you some of mine,' said Olive. 'But we're a different size.'

'You'll have to lend me some money until I can get to the post office. Although I probably have enough to enable you to take a taxi from the vicarage home to Aintree. I know it's out of your way.'

'Thanks, I'd have had to change trams several times and I haven't enough change with me. I can walk to TJ Hughes from here and then there's several trams I can catch from near there to get me to St Margaret's vicarage.'

That settled, Eliza reached for her handbag on the bedside cabinet cupboard and handed Olive half the money she had. She then decided to change the subject and ask Olive about work and her family. Afterwards, she told her about her promise to take

Alfie to see her mother-in-law in Colwyn Bay and she fought back tears again. Then visiting time was over so they said their byes, and Eliza lay back and dozed. It was about half an hour later that she realised she had not told Olive what items of clothing and sizes to buy or handed over any clothing coupons or told her how much to spend. She just had to trust her to use her common sense. Eliza knew that she would also need to buy Alfie clothes, as well as nappies and other items. She had to think positively and trust that PC Jack Molyneux would find Alfie safe and well. Thinking back, she should have asked Bryn for some money, as she had not received any from him for ages. She supposed he must be on his way back to his unit in the Middle East by now.

CHAPTER THREE

Bryn's half-brother, Glyn Owens, rested his arms on the side of the ship as it approached the coast of Egypt, thinking of Eliza and how she was proof of more of his brother's duplicity, but he mustn't think ill of the dead, he told himself. He still hadn't got over the shock of reading Eliza's letter when it had been passed to him at the training barracks and he thought about Ada, who had been Glyn's first love and whom his brother had married just as secretly once Glyn was out of the way, having volunteered to fight after war was declared. He had thought his heart would break when he had discovered the truth. Ada had worked herself up into one of her rages when he had volunteered, despite him having told her that, as a member of the Territorial Army, he would have been one of the first to be called up. They had gone all the way on the odd occasion, and he would have married her, but she had refused him and married his brother, who was a charmer, better looking and financially better off, despite being the younger one, as he had inherited his father's shares in the Jones slate business. Bryn had been desperate to have a son, as only a male could inherit shares in the firm when he died. Ada had failed Bryn there. Was that the reason Bryn had married Eliza before going out to the British occupied territories in the Middle East granted to them after the Great War as part of the peace-keeping forces?

He could imagine Ada's rage if she discovered the truth about Eliza and her having given birth to Bryn's son. Had Ada had any suspicion that Bryn had been carrying on with another woman? He had felt compelled suddenly to visit Eliza in hospital when he read her letter to his half-brother. She needed to know the truth about Bryn: he had a wife already and he had been killed by a sniper's bullet. It was not going to be easy, but he could offer her help – after all, Bryn's son was his nephew. He had wanted to visit his mother but there was no time and, besides, he didn't really want to see her expression when she heard that her favourite son had been killed.

Yet when he had seen Eliza and the baby, and the nurse had mistaken him for Bryn, he had chickened out, not wanting to spoil a happy occasion for her. Also, there had been no time to explain matters because he had received orders to go to Palestine immediately. There were others, after all, who could continue with the training of new intakes at the barracks.

–

The morning after her visit from Olive, and out of visiting hours, Eliza had a visit from the vicar, who was in his late thirties, tall and slender and with a ready smile.

'It's a pleasure to see you again, Eliza. I only wish it was in happier circumstances. Your friend Olive filled us in on what happened and explained why she had not been able to fulfil her errand for you, so Rachel went through the jumble that was piled up in the vicarage waiting for the sale in aid of the war effort and found a few items that might do you until you are able to go shopping for yourself and the little one.'

Eliza took the bag from him and removed the items inside, taking from the pile a white cotton blouse, a floral green-and-red flared skirt and a forest-green cardigan, but there was no underwear or stockings. She asked him to thank Rachel, his wife, and then explained why she wanted to see him, saying how sorry she was for not being in church for so long. She then spoke to him about Bryn, their hasty wedding in a registry office and him leaving the next day. 'I would have much preferred a church wedding, but it's done and I have a handsome son whom I love the bones of and am terrified for him, and want yours and the congregation's prayers for his safe return.'

'You will have them. Is there anything else?'

'Your advice.' She told him about Bryn's mother and the proposed visit to take Alfie for her to see him.

'I presume the police are searching for Alfie,' he said, clasping his hands as if in prayer.

She nodded and told him about Jack Molyneux.

He smiled. 'He's a good policeman.'

'You know him, too?' She could not conceal her astonishment.

'He's our local bobby on the beat and his heart is in his job. He cares about people. Milly at church knows him, as does Kyle at the Seamen's Orphanage.'

She wondered why she hadn't known Jack Molyneux, but after all she had only been young when she had lived at the orphanage opposite Newsham Park, where the boating lake was situated.

'As it happens, Milly and the children are in Colwyn Bay right now. You know, her mother-in-law has been living there since she left New Brighton, after the bombing over there last December.'

'Of course,' said Eliza. 'She works in a tearoom, doesn't she?'

He nodded. 'The sea air will do them good. Although I think they've been happy up in Lancashire since Jimmy went to pieces as a civilian defence volunteer. It would properly do your husband's mother good to have a visit from you alone, what with her sons being away in the army fighting. I presume she doesn't know that Alfie is missing.'

'No, I'd have to make up some excuse if he wasn't with me, and the doctor advised me to take a friend if I make up my mind to go. I've already bought my rail ticket but was told there had been damage to some of the rail tracks.'

'There's more than one way to reach Wales than through the Mersey tunnel and the Wirral,' he said.

She waited for him to tell her, but she was thinking back to when the last king had declared the tunnel open in the mid-1930s. It popped into her head unexpectedly. 'The Runcorn Bridge that crosses the Mersey at a narrow point from Widnes on this side,' she said, puzzled as to how her mind could remember that information when it couldn't remember the evening when the Luftwaffe had set the house alight, and she and her baby could have died.

He glanced at his watch. 'Time I was going, Eliza. I've a sermon to finish. Would you like me to say a prayer?'

'Please, I'd also like you to baptise Alfie after he is found,' she said, closing her eyes on her tears and putting her hands together.

She realised after the vicar had gone that despite the sense of loss and terror that she felt, the feeling of hope had increased and she decided to go to Colwyn Bay just for a day. When PC Jack Molyneux arrived, she told him of the vicar's visit and her decision to visit Colwyn Bay with a friend to see her mother-in-law, who must miss her two sons away in the army. 'I'm trusting you, PC Molyneux, to recover Alfie for me while I'm away.'

'I can tell you that one of our men was told by a woman in Little Wales that there is a Mrs Ada Jones who has a small daughter and who lived in a house whose yard backed on to hers. It was damaged in the raid early in May and she seems to have been coming and going for days on and off, since then. Apparently, she noticed this morning from the back window that the little girl had left a doll's pram in the backyard, which her granny had given her last Christmas, and her aunt had given her a doll that cried.'

'You consider that suspicious?' said Eliza hopefully.

'Worth looking into,' said Jack cautiously. 'But don't change your plans. If it comes to something, we'll phone through to Colwyn Bay police station and let them know. They work closely with Conway, so you visit the station if you work yourself into a state, worrying about Alfie being taken completely out of our reach. There is a policewoman whose parents have been a neighbour of our suspect's mother for years.' He paused. 'You just take care, and if you need help go to the station and ask to see the inspector.'

She nodded. 'Will do.'

'Take care and I hope when you return there'll be good news for you.'

CHAPTER FOUR

Olive gazed across at Eliza. 'Shouldn't be long now before we're there.'

'No, Dad and I used to make this journey often during school holidays, when we visited my grandparents in Anglesey. I wish they were still alive to see Alfie.'

'Which way do you think is the quickest to Wales?'

'I've never thought about it. Sometimes Dad and I would go by ferry to Birkenhead and then by bus to Chester and take the train from there through Wales and then to Anglesey.'

'It's been a lovely journey so far,' said Olive. 'The countryside is so green. It'll soon be summer. I'm glad you asked me to come with you.'

'I'm glad to have your company. I wonder if Alfie will enjoy the train journey when he's a bit older,' she murmured, wiping her eyes with a handkerchief that had been in her jacket pocket when she entered the hospital.

'He's bound to – most of the male sex are mad about trains.'

'He'll like the beach and making sand pies,' she said on a sob. 'I'd been dreaming of taking him to my favourite beach on Anglesey.'

Olive leaned across the carriage and patted her hand. 'Don't upset yourself. I thought you had faith in your policeman, and you don't have to go all the way to Anglesey for a beach – there's Formby and New Brighton.'

'I know that, and I'd take him to those as well: one to see the squirrels in the woods and the other to ride on the ferry.'

'That's better,' said Olive, getting up and crossing to sit beside Eliza so she could place an arm about her shoulders. 'Everything is going to be fine.'

Eliza rested her head against her arm and determined to put on a brave face when she saw Alfie's grandmother. She had to think up some excuse for why he wasn't with her. Perhaps she could say that the umbilical cord had not fallen off. She could give that, too, as the reason why she could not stay overnight. It would be less upsetting than saying he had been stolen.

Olive was quiet now and slowly removed her arm from about Eliza's shoulders. They both gazed out at the cows in the fields and Eliza thought of National milk powder, wondering if it was as good as breast milk. She told herself not to worry about that, as lots of babies were given it in a bottle, after it was made up with water, and survived. There had been a girl in the hospital whose milk had not come in and she'd had to bottle-feed her baby almost immediately, although the nurses had persuaded her to try and breastfeed, as it would be good for her and her baby daughter.

Eliza yearned to have her son in her arms, holding him close and feeding him. She found herself praying that Jack Molyneux and the other policemen, who were probably in Little Wales right now, would find Alfie.

The train chugged along, and Eliza began to feel slightly apprehensive as it neared their destination. Would her mother-in-law be cross with her for not inviting her to the wedding?

'Stop looking so nervous,' said Olive. 'She can't eat you.'

'I wasn't worrying about her eating me.' Eliza rose to her feet, ready to leave the train. 'I was thinking she might blame me for not inviting her to the wedding.'

'You could tell her the truth: no one was invited, and Bryn made all the arrangements because there had been so little time before he had to leave.'

'Of course, but will she believe me?'

The subject was dropped as the train had come to a halt.

They made for the main street, and it was then that Eliza remembered that Milly's mother-in-law had moved to Colwyn Bay after her apartment in New Brighton had been damaged during the Blitz last year. She remembered Milly telling her that she was a waitress in a tearoom on the main street. 'I'd like a cup of tea before finding where Bryn's mother's house is,' she said, thinking she could also ask for directions.

'I'm all for that,' Olive said.

Fortunately, Eliza remembered the name of the tearoom and had met Milly's mother-in-law with Milly when out shopping on West Derby Road, back in Liverpool. It did not take them long to find the tearoom, and they went inside and sat down at a table. They weren't kept waiting long before a waitress came to take their order and she recognised Eliza almost immediately. They chattered and Eliza was told that Milly – together with her husband Jimmy and their twins – had returned to Liverpool but would be coming to visit Colwyn Bay in August. Eliza told Cathy, who was wearing a name badge, that she had come to visit a Mrs Gladys Jones, and named the street where she lived and asked if she could have directions. Cathy drew a little map on a page of her order pad, ripped the paper out and handed it to Eliza.

'I didn't know she took in paying guests,' she said. 'But maybe she's needing to increase her income now that both her sons are away in the army.'

Eliza made no comment, only thanking her for her help and ordering two teas and two toasted teacakes. She was hungry. Once they had finished their refreshments, Eliza and Olive left in search of Bryn's mother's home. They found the three-storey Edwardian house without too much trouble but received no answer to Eliza's knock. A neighbour was sweeping her step and suggested they tried round the back, as she had seen her earlier and she was slightly deaf.

They went round the back and into a backyard. They knocked on the back kitchen door and tried to open it, but there was no response and when Eliza thought she could smell gas, she suggested to Olive to look through the kitchen window, as she was the tallest. She did so, and then gasped.

'There's someone on the floor in front of the cooker!'

Eliza said, 'D'you think she switched it on and then forgot to light it?'

Olive did not reply but took off a shoe and threw it at the window, which shattered, and the smell of gas grew stronger. Olive reached up and, with her gloved hands, began to remove the glass that was still stuck in the window frame. 'I'll carry on here while you get help,' she said.

Eliza hesitated, not wanting to leave Olive to cope on her own, but then she hurried out of the yard. The neighbour was gone, and her front door was closed. Suddenly, Eliza remembered passing a corner shop, which most likely had a telephone. She wasted no time rushing the short distance away and burst inside. The man behind the counter stared at her. 'You in a hurry, missus?' he said.

'Emergency! I need to dial 999.'

He did not bother her with questions but led her to the telephone and then went back to where he was slicing bacon, glancing at her every now and again.

Eliza dialled 999, asked for an ambulance and the police, and relayed the address of the house and what was wrong in a few short sentences. Then she replaced the receiver, thanked the shop-keeper and hastened outside, running back to the house where she found Olive standing on a bucket. She had hoisted herself into a kneeling position on the windowsill and was attempting to unlock the sash lock, which would enable her to lift the lower sash and climb inside. Eliza was lost in admiration and could only stand on another bucket, with both hands placed beneath Olive's bottom to help hold her in place. It was a struggle, due to her being short, but she could see inside now, and the woman's head was in the oven. She was stunned, unable to understand why that was so. She almost cheered when she heard a siren and the clanging bell of an ambulance.

It seemed an eternity before the police entered the yard, but it was only a few minutes and they soon had the back kitchen door open, allowing medical help to enter the building. A policeman helped Olive down, having moved Eliza aside so he could get to her friend, who was coughing and whose eyes were watering. She was helped to the ambulance; the woman presumed to be Glady Jones was carried outside on a stretcher and placed in the ambulance.

'Will she be all right?' asked Eliza, who was being held back by a policeman.

'She's still alive,' answered one of the bearers.

'Can I go in the ambulance with her and my friend?' she asked, struggling in the policeman's grasp. She watched as another policeman climbed in the back of the ambulance before she could, and it left.

'You can see them later,' said the policeman holding her firmly. 'Right now, I need to ask you some questions. Best do that down at the station.'

She could see the sense in that and stopped struggling. Another policeman came out of the house, waving a sheet of paper. He locked the back door and pocketed the key. She wondered suddenly if the paper was a suicide note, but why should her mother-in-law want to kill herself?

The two policemen did not speak but walked with Eliza to the police car and indicated she should get in the back, before they climbed in themselves. Another policeman had stayed behind. She thought that if anyone wanted to get inside the house, they could climb through the window, so it made sense for someone to stay on guard. No doubt the house would be made secure after the gas had cleared.

Nobody exchanged a word until they arrived at the police station. Once inside, Eliza was taken to an interview room and brought a cup of tea. 'Now, miss, if you could give me your name and address, and the reason why you were at Mrs Gladys Jones's house?' asked one of the policemen, while a PCW sat beside Eliza with a pad and pencil.

Eliza took a gulp of tea and swallowed before answering. 'I'm Mrs Eliza Jones, the wife of Bryn Jones, her younger son. I sent her a letter a few days ago telling her that I had given birth to a boy, a grandson for her, in a hospital in Liverpool, so I can't possibly see why she should commit suicide.'

'I can understand why you should think she had attempted suicide,' said the policeman, who held a sheet of paper. 'Her head was in the gas oven. And there's what appears to be a suicide note.' He sighed. 'It contains information that you seem unaware of, Mrs Jones. Tell me about your husband. When did you last hear from him?'

She frowned, wondering why he'd asked her such a question. Could something have happened to Bryn?

'Well, Mrs Jones?'

She stared across at the policeman and reached for the cup of tea, as her mouth felt dry again. 'He visited me in hospital a short while ago. I'd written to him about the baby and having been bombed out of my home. My son has since been kidnapped from the hospital, but neither my husband nor his mother was aware of this. The Liverpool police are searching for Alfie and the woman who took him. I can give you the number of the local police station so you can verify my story.' She was suddenly aware that she had been pleating part of her new skirt as she had been talking, and her fingers stilled for a moment as she told him the phone number.

The policeman stood and left the room. The woman beside Eliza patted her arm and said, 'He'll have gone to speak to the inspector, who'll phone the number you gave, and then be back with any news.'

'I'd like to know how my friend Olive and my mother-in-law, who are at the hospital here, are getting on,' said Eliza.

The policewoman went to the door, opened it and called a name, and the person must have come, because Eliza could hear whispering. Then the door closed, and the policewoman returned to her seat. A few minutes later the door opened, and a fresh cup of tea and a plate with a slice of bara-brith was put on the table in front of Eliza. Instantly, she reached for the cake and thoughts of her grandmother filled her mind, comforting her. No sooner had she eaten the cake and drunk the fresh tea than the door opened again, and a head popped in. 'You've to escort her to the inspector's office.'

Eliza shot up off the seat and went with the policewoman to see the inspector. He rose from the chair as she entered, and she observed that he was a well-built man of about forty, with keen grey eyes and dark hair greying slightly. He greeted her and shook her hand, before resuming his seat behind a large, uncluttered desk. He bid her sit down with a wave of a hand. 'I have spoken to my counterpart in Liverpool, Mrs Jones, and it appears we have a mystery on our hands. But first I have some good news for you. Your son has been found and is being cared for back home, after having been checked out over at the hospital.'

'Oh, thank God,' Eliza cried, relief racing through her. She felt lightheaded and put her hands to the table. 'Is he OK? Where was he?'

'I'll leave that for the Liverpool constabulary to explain. A police car is being sent here to take you and your friend back to Liverpool. Your friend is fit to travel, and your mother-in-law is making a good recovery, but she is not well enough to talk yet.'

'You will keep me informed of her condition?' said Eliza. She was desperate to get back to her son; she couldn't wait to hold him in her arms again.

'Naturally,' he said. 'We will phone through information to your local police station.'

'Thank you,' she said. 'You mentioned a mystery. I must admit that it puzzles me why my mother-in-law should attempt suicide after I sent her such good news.'

He clasped his hands and rested them on the desk. 'I agree with you, although she mentions no grandchild, only that her heart is broken by the news that her son Bryn was killed by a sniper in the Middle East.'

She gasped and clutched the desk in front of her, feeling dizzy. 'When did this happen? I've had no news of it.' Her voice shook.

He apologised for being the first to break such bad news but had no idea that she had not been told. Tears welled in her eyes. 'I can't believe it. He came to see me and the baby in the hospital not so long ago.' Her mind was racing – was it possible that he could have made it back to the Middle East already? How long would the boat journey have taken? Surely there hadn't been time for him to be...

He looked taken aback. 'I don't know enough of the conversation that took place between your inspector and the commanding officer at the training barracks in Liverpool. He'll be able to tell you more than I can. In the meantime, while you wait for your lift home, would you perhaps like a cup of tea or coffee and a bite to eat?'

'I'd like a coffee, please, but nothing to eat,' she said.

'Certainly.' He turned to the policeman who had brought her to the station and issued an order.

She left the office, supported by his hand beneath her elbow, and he took her to a waiting room where Olive was sitting. She stood up and they hugged each other. Then they sat and Olive placed an arm about her shoulders. 'What did he say? You look terrible.'

'Shock,' said Eliza in a voice muffled by a handkerchief.

'The baby?' cried Olive.

Eliza shook her head and her expression changed. 'No, thank God. He's been found. It's Bryn. He said that Bryn has been shot by a sniper and is dead. I know it's always been possible that he could be killed but I can't believe it after seeing him so recently.'

Olive hugged her closely and kept her mouth shut. Platitudes wouldn't help.

The coffee arrived and they drank it slowly, as it was hot. 'I'm hungry,' said Olive.

'I turned down the offer of food. I just felt too sick to the stomach to eat.'

The door opened and Jack Molyneux entered, escorted by a policeman they recognised from earlier.

Eliza stood up and stared at Jack in astonishment. 'I'm glad it's you,' she said, crossing over to him, and taking one of his hands and shaking it. 'Thank you so much. I can't wait to hear what's happened, and having you here is much better than travelling with a stranger.'

'I'm glad you feel like that but sorry you've had further trouble,' he responded. 'The sooner we get back and you and Alfie are reunited, the better you'll feel.'

She agreed but followed him out of the station silently, arm in arm with him and Olive, after introducing them. He helped them into the back seat after they had thanked and said ta-ra to the other policeman. Jack started the engine and drove off. It seemed no time at all before they had left Colwyn Bay behind and although Eliza was bursting to question Jack, she decided it was more sensible not to pester him while he was driving. She just wanted to get back to Alfie as quickly as possible.

CHAPTER FIVE

Once they were through the bottleneck that Queensferry could be during a weekend in the warmer months – it was June next week – Jack spoke, reassuring Eliza that Alfie had come to no harm, and was being cared for by his mother and sister.

She was taken aback. 'I can understand you not leaving him at the hospital, but I thought he'd be at the police station. What about the person who took him?' asked Eliza.

'You're going to find this hard to believe,' he said, 'but we found him in Little Wales in a doll's pram.'

'You're joking,' cried Olive.

'I believe him,' said Eliza, remembering that the woman suspected of having kidnapped Alfie had a daughter. 'What about the woman?' she asked.

'I can tell you that one of our men was told that she'd been going on about moving out ever since her house walls were weakened when one of the neighbouring terraces had been blown to bits in May,' Jack reminded Eliza. 'Apparently, she noticed this morning through the back window that the little girl had left a doll's pram in the backyard, her granny had given her last Christmas, and her aunt had given her a doll that cried.'

'I wonder why she didn't take him with her,' said Olive.

'I can only be glad that she didn't,' Eliza said loudly.

'Me too,' said Jack. 'Otherwise, God only knows how long it would have taken us to find him.'

'She could have left Liverpool,' said Olive.

Jack agreed. 'But she could still be there, and there isn't a woman at the police station to care for him. Anyway, I'm going back to the house tomorrow to look for any clues that could have been missed. The place is a mess.'

'It's Sunday tomorrow,' said Eliza. 'I was thinking of going to church. I'd also like to go with you to see where Alfie was found.'

'Where are you staying tonight?' asked Olive. 'I'm going to have to go home. Mam will be getting worried. Are you coming with me and bringing the baby? Mam would love to see him.'

'I'll run you home,' said Jack. 'But we need to go to my house first. As I've already said, I decided Alfie would be safer with my mother and sister at our home. He needed a nappy change and a change of clothes, and they were purchased by my mother in the shop on the corner of Breckfield Road North.'

'What about coupons?' asked Olive.

'My mother is known, and they trusted her to return later with the coupons, knowing mothers get extra coupons for new babies. She also purchased a couple of feeding bottles and a tin of baby milk from another shop.'

Eliza could only thank him, despite never having met his mother or sister. 'In the meantime, what about Bryn?' asked Eliza uncertainly. 'The inspector in Colwyn Bay told me he had been killed by a sniper. I'd like to know when it happened and how his mother got to know about it before I did.'

'Hopefully, she'll be able to tell us when she's up to talking,' said Jack. 'But...' He paused. 'But we do know that it was before he supposedly visited you in hospital.'

Eliza was filled with confusion. How could that be? Was that not Bryn she had seen after she'd given birth? And if it wasn't him, how did he know which hospital she was in? She remembered how she had not recognised him – the tan, the weight gain, the colour of his hair... and it had been so long since she had seen him.

'I don't understand,' she said.

'Maybe we should wait until we reach our destination before continuing with this conversation,' he said. 'It's Saturday and the traffic is going to be worse when we reach Birkenhead and the tunnel, and it will worsen in Liverpool,' he added.

'So, we're going through the tunnel?' said Olive. 'How exciting.'

'We'll need some change,' he said. 'I've some but could do with a couple of shillings.'

Eliza checked her pocket, withdrew a florin and held it in her hand, ready to give to him when he asked for it. She did not want to distract him while he was driving. She told him that she had it and would hand it over when they neared the tunnel. He thanked her and fell silent. Now she knew that she would be seeing Alfie soon, she closed her eyes and told herself to relax and not worry. She contained her impatience as best she could, not wanting them to have an accident that would leave Alfie an orphan if she started asking Jack questions again.

It was seven o'clock by the time they reached Rydal Street, where Jack lived with his mother and sister. It was not far from Breck Road. A woman was standing in the doorway with a baby in her arms. The car had barely stopped when Eliza opened the car door and almost fell out on the pavement. She straightened up and rushed up the step, and without hesitation the woman handed Alfie over to her, saying, 'You have to be Eliza.'

Eliza murmured indistinctly but all her attention was on her son: she hugged him to her, murmured words of love and kissed his petal-soft cheek. Tears of joy wet her face and as he held up a hand and touched her lips, she drew his fingers into her mouth and sucked them, marvelling at their size. He gurgled and she wanted to laugh out loud.

'Oh, he's lovely,' said Olive. 'Can I hold him?'

'Not yet,' murmured Eliza, having removed Alfie's hand from her mouth. 'I've only just got him back. I feel like never letting him go. I'd also like to breastfeed him and I think he needs another nappy change.'

'Come inside,' said Jack's mother. 'Our Jean will have the kettle on in no time and I bet you're ready for a cup of tea.'

'But I need to get home,' said Olive wearily.

'Come in and have a cup of tea,' coaxed Eliza. 'I'm parched and you must be, too.'

'For five minutes,' said Olive.

'It'll take me more than five minutes to feed Alfie,' said Eliza.

'You could finish feeding him in the car,' said Olive.

Eliza was exhausted and did not fancy getting back in the car and feeding Alfie there. She preferred sitting down with him and spending some time alone with him, but didn't know how to say that to Olive, who could feel hurt. As it was, Jack took the decision out of her hands.

'It's probably best if Eliza and Alfie stay here, if she wants to go to church and later to the house in Little Wales. I could take you home now and then tomorrow evening, if that's all right with you and your mother, I could give her and Alfie a lift to yours.'

'That sounds sensible,' said his mother.

Eliza knew it made sense, but she didn't like having the decision made for her. 'Thank you, Jack, we'll do that,' she said, not looking at him. 'We do need to talk, and my original plan was to take up Olive's invitation to stay at hers until I find somewhere for Alfie and me to live.'

Olive smiled. 'I won't bother with a cup of tea then. Mam will have the kettle on.'

Eliza went to the front door to wave her off and thank her for her company, adding that she would see her tomorrow. She waved until the car was out of sight and then went back indoors, looking forward to that cup of tea.

CHAPTER SIX

'Perhaps you'd like to be alone to breastfeed your baby,' suggested Jack's mother as soon as Eliza entered the kitchen living room. 'You could have your cuppa in the parlour, with some toast.'

'That would be lovely,' said Eliza, 'and if I can have the bag of stuff you purchased for him?'

'Of course,' said the older woman, going over to the sideboard and removing an oilcloth shopping bag.

'I need to give you some coupons – and how much money do I owe you?' said Eliza.

'You don't owe me anything,' she replied. 'Jack gave me the money.'

'I see. I'll need to go to the post office on Monday.' Eliza sipped her tea. 'I suppose he told you all that has happened.' She gazed down into Alfie's face, not able to get enough of the sight and feel of him. He was lying on her lap with his kicking feet towards her. He was still wearing the nightgown that Jack's mother had purchased for him, which was slightly damp. She really would have to change him.

'I'll show you into the parlour,' said Jean, taking hold of the shopping bag and Eliza's cup of tea, so she had both hands free to carry Alfie.

Eliza sat in a brown leatherette armchair, which had broad, flat arms perfect for feeding Alfie in comfort. She rested him on her lap while she unfastened her blouse and her bra, which fastened at the front, and put her son to the breast. It was delightful and she took her time, enjoying reinforcing the bond between them. Afterwards, when he had finished suckling and fallen asleep, she realised that she should have changed him first, but now she would be best leaving him sleeping for a while before doing so. She leaned back, resting her head against the back of the chair, and held her son close and closed her eyes. She heard a car draw up at the kerb and then footsteps, and the front door opening and the murmur of voices. It must be Jack back, she thought and hastily shifted Alfie to one side so she could fasten her bra and blouse in case he came in the parlour to speak to her. She closed her eyes and hummed, 'Rock-a-bye baby on the treetops, when the wind blows the cradle will rock.'

A few minutes passed and then there was a soft knock on the door. 'Can I come in, Eliza, or are you too tired to talk?' asked Jack.

'I would have thought you'd be tired after all the driving you've done,' she said sleepily. 'Let's talk tomorrow when I'm more alert.'

'Good idea, because we're going to have to be up early, as we have an appointment at the police station at ten o'clock.'

'Why? If I'm at the police station for any length of time, I could miss the church service,' she said, opening her eyes wide.

'I'm sure God will understand, and you can speak to the vicar later.'

'Didn't the inspector give you a clue as to why he wants to see me?' She moved to get Alfie in a more comfortable position and he whimpered.

'I'll leave you alone,' he said. 'I didn't intend to disturb Alfie.'

'You didn't answer my question,' she said.

'Don't want to keep you awake all night thinking about it,' he whispered.

'Saying that is stupid,' she retorted. 'I'm bound to wonder what it is now.'

'It was a message from Colwyn Bay. Your mother-in-law's awake and had several interesting things to say. And before you ask me again, he wouldn't tell me but thinks you should be the first to hear what she said, so you'd best get some sleep and we'll be up early tomorrow.'

She stamped her foot with annoyance and waited just a few minutes before picking up the shopping bag and leaving the parlour with Alfie. It was Jean who took her upstairs to the spare room, which had obviously been a box room, because there were still cardboard boxes piled up in a corner, as well as a broken chair beside a made-up single bed and a baby's cot. Happily, there was also a washstand and someone had thoughtfully placed water in the bowl, which steamed gently.

'The cot was mine,' said Jean. 'It's not that old. There's quite a gap between me and Jack. His father was a policeman, too, and he was killed when the boat he was in was sunk in the Irish Sea during the First World War. Mam remarried and I was born. I'm fifteen.'

'Are you still at school?' asked Eliza.

'In my last year. I leave at the end of summer term and will need to find a job.'

'Me too,' said Eliza. 'I've some savings but they won't last for ever. Anyway, I'd best get Alfie and myself to bed. I've had my orders from Jack that I've got to be up early. We've a busy day tomorrow.'

Eliza had expected to be awakened in the night by Alfie wanting a night feed but he did not rouse her with a wail until six in the morning and, as it was June, it was already light outside, so she changed him and then took him into bed with her and fed him. He dozed off afterwards and she stayed awake, rejoicing in those precious moments, so that when there came a knock on the bedroom door, she was able to climb out of bed with Alfie in her arms, go over to the door and say in a low voice that she was awake.

Jack replied that it was seven o'clock and he was preparing breakfast for them. He would expect her downstairs within half an hour. She made no reply but washed sketchily and dressed swiftly, before washing and changing Alfie again. She dressed him in items that had been in the shopping bag: a romper suit, matinee jacket, bootees and hat, all in blue.

'Now, don't you look a treat,' she said, kissing his cheek. He made what sounded to her like a chuckling noise, and she kissed him again and carried him downstairs, breathing in the smell of frying bacon.

When she entered the kitchen, she saw that the table was covered with a tablecloth and there were two place settings, and in the middle was a hand-knitted tea cosy, which must be keeping the teapot warm, and a plate of sliced unbuttered crusty bread.

Jack smiled and said, 'It's the only morning we have such a treat. I was going to suggest you pour the tea while I dish out the bacon and eggs but, seeing as you've got your hands full, I'll pour it out later.'

'Whose ration am I eating?' she asked.

'Part of mine, but I'm prepared to share with you. Mam said you need to have a good breakfast inside you, with you feeding Alfie and having a busy day ahead.'

'That's generous of you but just an egg would have done me,' she said.

He frowned at her across the table. 'Don't throw my sacrifice back in my face.'

He left the table and went into the back kitchen. He brought in two plates of bacon and egg, and placed one in front of her and one in his place. 'Now eat up.'

'You are bossy, aren't you?' she said, shifting Alfie into the crook of her left arm and then reaching for a slice of bread, which she dipped into the yolk of her perfectly fried egg that she guessed had been cooked in the fat from the bacon. The first taste had her closing her eyes in ecstasy.

'That good, hey?' he said.

She nodded. 'Thank you for your generosity.'

He flushed. 'Would you like me to cut your bacon for you?'

'Just in half… and if you could cut off the rind?'

'Why? The rind is tasty.'

'Then you can have it in exchange for you pouring me out a cup of tea.'

He smiled. 'Agreed. Can you manage to drink and eat with Alfie on your knee? I can take him while you do.'

'But how will you manage? I must get used to it because when I get my own place, I won't have help.'

He cut her bacon and poured her tea. 'Milk and sugar?' he asked.

'Milk and just half a teaspoon of sugar,' she replied.

'I presume you don't want to stay long at Olive's parents' house?'

'No, it's not fair on them. They have a son in the navy who can get home regularly, and I think I'll be having his room and he'll be sleeping on the sofa.'

'I see what you mean.' He looked thoughtful as he placed half a slice of bacon in a slice of bread and handed it to her. Then, he made himself a bacon and egg sarnie and bit into it with relish.

When they had finished eating and drinking, he stood and reached for his police helmet on the sideboard. 'What are you going to do with Alfie now? I'll take him up to Mam to look after if you want?'

She shook her head. 'I'm taking him with me. I'm not ready to be parted from him yet.'

'You can trust Mam,' he replied, frowning.

'I haven't said I can't, but right now I need to have him close,' she said.

'How are you going to manage to go to the lavatory, which is down the yard, by the way?'

'I admit to that being a problem, but hopefully in the future, if I can find myself a flat that has an indoor lavatory in the building, I'll manage somehow.'

'Can you trust me to hold him while you go to the lavatory now?'

'Only if you promise not to take him up to your mother as soon as I'm out of sight.'

He looked disbelieving. 'I'm only trying to help you.'

'I'm sure you are but you're not me, and I tell you I won't go with you to the police station unless you promise.' She paused.

'In fact I'll go a step further: you can come down the yard with Alfie and make a noise so I know you're still there with him.'

'You're crazy,' he said.

'You could go a little crazy if someone you loved and who was precious to you went missing,' she said earnestly.

He pulled a face. 'All right, you've made your point. I promise.'

'Thank you,' she said, handing Alfie over to him, opening the door and rushing down to the lavatory. She stopped outside and gazed up the yard, and she saw him approaching with Alfie held against his shoulder. She waved and went inside 'the little house', as her grandmother used to call it. As she sat there, she could hear him singing Brahms' 'Lullaby' and her heart lifted. She waited until he had finished, before pulling up her drawers and yanking the chain.

'That was lovely,' she said, closing the door behind her. She washed her hands at the sink in the back kitchen, put on her jacket and hat that hung on a hook in the lobby, took Alfie from him and then they left.

CHAPTER SEVEN

Eliza was aware of mixed emotions of curiosity, nervousness, and anger as she entered the police station in Tuebrook with Alfie in her arms and Jack leading the way. She told herself nothing could be worse than the last few days, other than losing Alfie again.

They were told to go straight into the inspector's office and so they did, after the desk sergeant had made a fuss of Alfie, who had woken up. The inspector welcomed Eliza with a grave smile and a handshake.

'Good to see you and this young man here, Mrs Jones, but we have a real mystery on our hands, or at least the Colwyn Bay police do.'

She said, 'So what is it that my mother-in-law had to say when she was feeling up to explaining how she ended up with her head in the gas oven?'

'Apparently, a woman visited her the evening before, claiming to be her son Bryn's widow. Shocked, Mrs Jones refused to believe her and told her to get out of her house. The woman refused, telling her to calm down, and produced a telegram that said Bryn had been killed during an uprising.'

'When did this woman receive this telegram?' Eliza asked, confused.

'More than a week ago. She said that she could not accept the news at first and went to see her mother to leave her daughter with her. Then she came back to Liverpool to visit the army training barracks where Bryn first trained, when he decided to enlist and fight for his country, like his half-brother.'

Eliza gasped. 'Perhaps that is part of the answer to the mystery. But continue, Inspector.'

'Apparently, she decided she wanted to see Bryn's mother and ask if she'd heard anything about it from Glyn, and to make herself known to her mother-in-law, so she returned to Wales. The old woman still didn't believe her – and why? Because she had a Welsh accent, instead of a Liverpool accent – she had received your letter about having married Bryn in Liverpool. She thought the woman was playing a cruel trick on her.' He paused. 'The woman demanded to see the letter. At first, Bryn's mother refused, but the woman had so frightened her that she went and fetched it. The woman exploded when she read it but when Mrs Jones told her to calm down or leave her house, she quietened down. She asked if she could make them a cup of tea. The old woman agreed because she was in a state herself and could do with a cuppa. She never suspected that the woman would put something in her tea that sent her to sleep or that she would attempt to murder her and make it appear like suicide. Fortunately, she never thought of checking the gas meter, which needed more money in it, so the gas ran out before it could kill her.'

There was a pause.

'Well, Mrs Jones, what were you going to say?'

'I sent my letter to Bryn, care of the training barracks, asking that they send it on to him. Perhaps she saw Glyn there and he confirmed that Bryn had been killed – and he might have also read my letter to Bryn and told her what it said. But that doesn't explain how Bryn could visit me when he was supposedly already dead or why she should pretend to be Bryn's widow.' She took a deep breath and rested her cheek on Alfie's cheek.

'Unless he pretended to be Bryn, having a faint idea you mightn't remember what Bryn looked like,' suggested Jack.

'And when he saw me and Alfie, maybe he felt sorry for me and couldn't bring himself to tell me that Bryn had been killed,' she said.

'I suppose that's a possibility,' said Jack. 'I suppose it's also a possibility that that woman is – or was – Bryn's wife at one time.'

'He never mentioned her,' said Eliza, staring at Jack.

'I suggest you drop the subject for now,' said the inspector. 'Just be glad that you have Alfie back and get on with your life.'

Eliza thanked him and left the room, followed a few minutes later by Jack.

'So, what do you want to do next?' asked Jack.

'Go to the house in Little Wales,' she said. 'Look for clues, as we still haven't got the woman who kidnapped Alfie and all I suggested was guesswork.'

'It fitted, if your guesswork was true,' said Jack.

'But that would mean...' She stopped.

'Yeah,' he said. 'But let's go sleuthing and see what we might find.'

CHAPTER EIGHT

'Do we go by police car?' she asked once they were outside.

He looked thoughtful. 'I'd rather not turn up there in a police car on a Sunday, and there's also the fuel. I used enough yesterday.'

'So, it's the tram,' she said.

'Two trams, and some walking there and back,' he said. 'I could carry Alfie some of the way if you want?'

'Thanks for the offer,' she said brightly, despite still being in shock. 'But the feel of Alfie in my arms comforts me and helps me to cope with this whole crazy situation.'

'You do realise that Glyn must know her if what we think is true,' he murmured.

'Of course! But why not be honest with me? If he was party to the kidnapping, he's as wicked as she is, although why should he be?'

'As well as that, he mightn't have been at the barracks, and perhaps she didn't know about you and Alfie until she visited Bryn's mother,' said Jack. 'A soldier at the barracks who knew the brothers might have known her and spoken to her.'

'I can't get my head around this,' said Eliza, shaking.

They had reached the tram stop in Rocky Lane: the tram would go past St Margaret's and then along West Derby Road and into town. Jack said kindly, 'Why don't you get off the tram at the stop nearest St Margaret's and I'll go to the house on my own?'

She shook her head and sniffed back her tears. 'I couldn't face them there, the way I feel. I might break down. Besides, I want to see where Alfie was found.' Her voice had gained strength. 'Here's the tram.'

He didn't argue with her but helped her onto the tram, followed her to the nearest seat and took some coppers out of his pocket. They sat down and he paid the conductor when he came to collect their fares.

They were silent on the journey, and it was not until Jack rose at the stop nearest TJ Hughes on London Road that she spoke. 'Why are we getting off here?'

'It's the shortest walk,' he answered, helping her up.

Alfie stirred and she hushed him as she followed Jack. He assisted her down from the tram, drew her free arm through his and helped her along. Alfie wriggled and she said, 'I can manage, Jack.'

'If you say so.' He freed her arm from his and slowed his pace to match hers.

Alfie let out a wail and Eliza rocked him, and he turned his head against her. Instantly, she realised that he was hungry and for a moment she was at a loss what to do. Then she glanced about and saw that the street they were walking along was empty so decided to risk it: she concealed him inside her jacket, undid a few of her buttons and freed a breast from her bra, sure he would know what to do. He suckled and she allowed herself to relax, until she realised that he was suckling noisily. Naturally not wanting Jack's attention to be drawn to what was going on, she began to hum a hymn and fall behind him.

He called over his shoulder, 'You should have gone to church.'

'I gave you my reasons. Is it much further?' They had come to a main road, and she realised they were going to cross it and there were several people about. She controlled her panic and caught up with Jack, walking as close to his back as she could without bumping into him. She reckoned Alfie had drunk enough to keep him going for a while and drew him carefully off her breast, before covering herself and rocking him again as he wailed. Just in time, because Jack halted, and she crashed into him. He turned his head and looked down at her. 'What are you doing there?'

'I could feel a cool breeze and wanted to keep Alfie warm, so I thought staying close behind you would help,' she said, crossing her fingers.

'Sensible,' he said, 'but I've a woolly scarf in an inside pocket that you could borrow to wrap him in.'

He took it out and handed it to her. She thanked him and wrapped it round Alfie, thinking she should have wrapped him in his shawl before leaving the house. Still, Jack had believed her, thus saving her embarrassment.

They crossed the road and went along another street, came to another road and close by she could see the Anglican Cathedral looming, but they passed it and eventually turned in the direction of the Mersey. She did not know this part of Liverpool well, so could only trust that he knew where he was going. Eventually, they turned into an area of small terraced houses and he slowed his pace, glancing up at the street names, and she realised that they must be in Little Wales.

'Is it true then that it's illegal to play football in the street?'

Jack nodded. 'Windows can get broken, as well as people getting hurt.'

'But kids play other ball games, such as rounders,' she said.

'I don't make the rules,' he said. 'Anyway, we're here.' He led the way up the step, pushed open the front door cautiously and went inside. She followed him just as carefully and noticed a large crack in a wall. 'I shouldn't have let you come with me,' he said. 'This building is dangerous.'

'We're here now. Let's go into the backyard where you said the doll's pram was found.'

'It's not there now. It was taken away to be tested for finger-prints,' he said.

Not for the first time, she wondered aloud, 'Why didn't she take him with her?'

'She probably realised that the police were on to her,' said Jack.

Eliza guessed that was a real possibility if a neighbour had gossiped about the police when she was within earshot.

Whatever, it was up to the police to find her and, more importantly, she had Alfie back. Even so, she followed Jack's example and began to search amongst the rubbish on the ground in the yard, kicking it about. Suddenly, she spotted what looked like a train ticket and would have bent down and picked it up if she hadn't had Alfie in her arms. Instead, she drew Jack's attention to it, and he picked it up, brushed specks of dirt from it and let her have a close look at it.

'You're right. It's a return train ticket from here to Colwyn Bay,' he said, his face alight. 'You've good eyesight.' He took a small bag from a pocket and placed the ticket inside.

'Can we leave now? I don't think it's healthy here for Alfie.'

'Of course! Besides, you might just reach the church before the service is over,' he said.

'I don't like walking in late,' she said. 'But I'd like a talk with the vicar, so there's no rush. What I would like is a walk through Newsham Park.'

'We could do that,' said Jack. 'How do you feel about walking to the Pierhead first and getting a tram from there to Rocky Lane and through onto Newsham Drive? Check how things are there and then go into the park.'

'Sounds fine and then it won't take me long to visit the vicarage,' she said. 'Do you have to go back to the police station?'

'I could nip up there and drop the ticket off while you see the vicar. Then I'll knock on the way back and we can go back to my home and pick up my car, and I can take you to Olive's parents' house in Aintree. Does that suit you?'

'Yeah, but why do you have to check out Newsham Drive?'

'It's part of my beat and there've been complaints about a bag-snatcher on the prowl there.'

She shivered. 'Are they snatching bags in the park, too?'

'It wouldn't surprise me, but I've only been ordered to call on a widow living on the drive. She's a Mrs Jones and an authoress.'

'I was an orphan at the Seamen's Orphanage years back,' she said. 'I always admired the houses on Newsham Drive. I really liked the yellow bricks they were made of but my flat when I left the orphanage was in Norwood Grove and that, you'll know, was made of ordinary red bricks, sooty with the smoke from chimneys. But that house has gone now, and I must find another flat.' She paused. 'There's so many Joneses, but not so many authoresses,' said Eliza. 'Is she Welsh?'

'No, I think she told me that she was from Shropshire.'

'Which borders part of Wales,' said Eliza, repositioning Alfie up higher. He was feeling heavier and slipping down.

'Would you like me to carry him for a while?' asked Jack.

Eliza gave in and held her son out to him, thinking it wouldn't be for long, as she could see the Liver Birds. The tram terminals were almost opposite the Liver Building but when they arrived, there wasn't much of a queue for the trams they could take and soon they were on their way.

CHAPTER NINE

After a walk in Newsham Park and a rest on a bench for a while, watching some children playing rounders, they walked on towards Newsham Drive and crossed the road to where one of the houses was painted pink and cream.

'Am I right in thinking this is your authoress's house?' asked Eliza.

'Yes,' replied Jack. 'I thought you might like to meet her, as there's a possibility of digs here.'

'What's she like?'

'It's up to you to make up your own mind,' he said. 'But it will do her good to have someone else living in the house.'

'But can I afford it and does she like babies?'

'She's childless and she will probably offer you a job.' He opened the gate and held it open. Eliza hesitated. 'Come on,' he said, 'what are you waiting for?' She did not move, thinking he really was high-handed. He shut the gate, went up the path and banged on the door with his fist, shouting his name through the letter box.

Eliza opened the gate and scooted up the path as a curtain twitched in a side window. There came the pad of footsteps and then the sound of bolts being drawn, and the door opened to reveal a middle-aged woman wearing glasses, who was clad in navy-blue slacks and a Fair Isle twin set; her brown hair was permed, and sparkly earrings dangled on the curves of pale pink cheeks in her oval face.

'Constable Molyneux, how lovely to see you,' she said in a pleased tone. 'And who is this you've brought with you?'

'May we come in?' he asked. 'This is Mrs Eliza Jones, and we have a lot to say.'

'Another Mrs Jones,' she said. 'Do come in, my dear, and you of course, Constable.'

They crossed the threshold and followed her past a door on the right that she said was her writing room and a staircase to the left, and along a passage and into a lounge on the right, overlooking a garden. The kitchen and a small morning room were to the left at the rear, she later told Eliza. But first she and Jack spoke about what had been happening to Eliza since she had been rescued from her home that terrible week in May, and how she had come round in the maternity hospital, having gone into labour, and given birth to a son called Alfie.

Amelia was wide-eyed and listened without interruption, although she gasped when she heard that Alfie had been kidnapped. When Jack told her that he had brought Eliza because she needed an apartment for herself and Alfie, and was looking for employment, Eliza wanted to put a gag on him and say that she could speak for herself, Constable!

But the authoress was speaking. 'But of course you must come and live here. There's a couple of rooms upstairs that will do you fine. I'll show you after we've had a cup of coffee and some buns from Sayers.'

Eliza thanked her and offered to make the coffee, as well as toasting and buttering the buns. Amelia accepted the offer, so Eliza went and found the kitchen, made coffee, and toasted and buttered the buns and brought them in on a tray. It seemed it was Amelia's turn to talk and this she did, explaining how she had recently lost the help she'd had in the house and with her writing work. The girl had joined the ATS.

Eliza asked Amelia about her books and in what way did she need help with her writing.

'It's not just research for my writing, my dear, it's that I want to discover more about my husband's family tree. I am in touch with one of his nephews, Theo, who is in Intelligence but, as you can imagine, he is far too busy right now and as for his cousin, she is caring for her mother, who is ill. They have promised to pay me a visit as soon as possible, as they weren't able to attend the funeral of my darling husband Thomas.' She paused. 'And, of course, there is Thomas's cousin, Rosie, who lives here in Liverpool and seems to have gone a little doolally since she lost her husband.'

'That's all very sad. I'm sorry to hear of it. What about your books? I'm sorry but I haven't had much time for reading for a while, so I don't recognise your name,' said Eliza, feeling slightly embarrassed.

'I write what I believe some people call love taps under my maiden name Amelia Truelove, would you believe, but it is an old name dating back to medieval times. Much better than Jones for a romantic novelist. It was my husband's idea. My books are very popular in the libraries and have red covers. I've been told they are good escapism, much the same as Westerns and Crime, would you believe?' She smiled. 'But they bring me in a very useful income since my husband died, although that would increase if the campaign by authors to be paid a small remuneration by the government when their books are borrowed from libraries was implemented.'

'That seems only fair,' said Eliza, who still had her library card. She decided she really must start reading again if she could find time, not just the odd magazine that one could skip through.

'So, how about it?' asked Amelia. 'I could take you up to see the rooms as soon as we finish our coffee.'

'I'd like that,' Eliza replied. Then she threw a glance at Jack. 'Have you time to wait for me or is it time you were leaving for the police station?'

He replied, 'While you're here, I'll get on with my beat and return in an hour for you.'

'That's settled then,' said Amelia. 'You can see yourself out, Constable?'

He nodded and drained his coffee cup. 'Don't forget to lock up before you go upstairs.'

She raised her hand in acknowledgement and soon after Eliza bolted the front door and then she followed Amelia upstairs.

They paused on the first floor and Amelia indicated her own room and the rooms that Theo and his cousin would have and the guest bathroom. Then they climbed another flight of stairs to the second-floor landing and Amelia walked along a short distance and opened a door. Eliza followed her inside and gasped in delight.

The front room was a good size and contained enough furniture for her needs. She crossed to the window and looked out over the road, to the park, where there were several children playing and a game of football was taking place and groups of grown-ups were watching. Then she was shown a smaller room, which contained only a wardrobe, and realised she was going to have to buy a bed, bedding and a cot. She must visit the post office and withdraw some of her savings in the morning. She moved over to the window that overlooked the back garden, at the bottom of which was a wall with a door in it.

'The top floor isn't used often, mostly just for things kept in case they might be useful,' said Amelia. 'You can check them out and help yourself to anything that will be useful. I'm sorry there is no bed.'

'You're too kind,' said Eliza. 'I knew it was likely that I would need to buy a bed.'

They returned to the ground floor and Amelia told her more about what was involved in tracing Thomas's ancestry and how they had met at the cheese counter in Chester market.

'Thomas had been born in Chester, although his parents were from Mid Wales, not far from the border with Shropshire. His father had been a farm labourer who had travelled the country for seasonal work with his wife, and that's how Thomas came to be born in Chester. There they had met Thomas's father's brother, who was a stonemason, doing renovation work to St Asaph Cathedral, known as the marble church, which is situated in Denbighshire on the main road to Colwyn Bay from Queensferry. He was father to Rosie, whom I met for the first time here in Liverpool, which is where her father moved to after finishing the work in St Asaph, because there was plenty of building work in Liverpool at that time.' Amelia paused for breath. 'Thomas didn't want to be in farming, but he had the wanderlust when he was young and worked in a village bakery for a while, before moving on to Chester, where I was on a day trip. We married after he moved to Liverpool. I learned to type at the Mabel Fletcher College here in Liverpool and worked in an office until I married. Thomas enjoyed cooking and prepared all the meals when I started writing and had some success quite quickly.'

Eliza asked, 'Did you want to be a writer before you worked in an office? Is that why you learned to type?'

'Oh yes, but my parents thought I was being fanciful and told me I must get a proper job and earn a wage to help with household expenses,' said Amelia. 'My father was a foreman in a factory and my mother was a seamstress who worked from home.' She paused. 'Now, tell me about your parents?'

Eliza proceeded to tell her story. 'My father was a sailor and died in a storm at sea, and then my mother was killed in a cycling accident when I was ten, and I was taken in by the Seamen's Orphanage. I worked for a while in Barker and Dobson's and then after the war broke out, I went into Ammunitions, where I met my friend Olive and was able to stay on after I was married for a few months, before leaving when I was four months pregnant. I didn't like the thought of what the chemicals might do to the baby, but I needed the money, despite my husband sending me some once a month.'

It was at that point in her story that there was a banging at the front door and so she went to see if it was Jack. He stood on the step, smiling. 'Are you ready?'

'Nearly, I just need to know when I start and can move in. Perhaps you should come in and wait,' she said.

'I'll wait here,' he said. 'We'll get away quicker.'

'All right,' she said, turning and hurrying back to the lounge where she told Amelia it was Jack and he seemed in a hurry.

'Then I won't keep you,' said Amelia. 'Could you move in and start work on Monday?'

'I'd like that,' she replied. 'Thank you!'

CHAPTER TEN

'So, are you sorted out?' asked Jack, opening the front gate for Eliza to pass through.

'Yeah, I move in on Monday,' she replied. 'We had a good talk and I'm sure we'll rub along all right. Tomorrow I'll need to visit the post office, and buy a bed and a cot and a pushchair and bedding.'

'I'm sure Mam will let you have the cot,' said Jack, striding along.

'Could you please slow down?' she asked. 'My legs are shorter than yours and I'm tired.'

'Sorry,' he said. 'I could go on ahead home and return with my car and pick you up at the vicarage.'

'You do that,' she said. 'I don't know why we couldn't have gone in your car earlier.'

'I had to return the police car,' he said, slowing to a snail's pace.

'Sorry,' she said, hiding a smile. 'But if you're going home for the car, you'd best get a move on, slowcoach.'

He blew her a kiss and tore off. She dawdled in his wake as far as West Derby Road, waiting for a gap in the traffic before crossing and walking the short distance to the vicarage.

The front door was opened by the vicar's son, Paul, whom she had taught in Sunday School a few years ago. He stared at her in astonishment. 'Miss Griffiths!' he exclaimed.

'I know, long time no see,' she said. 'Is your father in? I won't keep him long.'

Even as she spoke, the vicar appeared at the back of the hall. 'Eliza, I wondered when you'd turn up, and I presume this is Alfie.'

He beamed at them both and invited her in. He told his son that Miss Griffiths was now Mrs Jones, and he took her and Alfie into his study, but not before asking his son to ask his mother to bring two teas. That done, he pulled out a chair and bid her be seated.

'I'm so pleased that I will be christening Alfie when you're ready. What a fine healthy baby he is.'

She nodded. 'I wanted to come and show you that our prayers have been answered. The woman responsible escaped, though.'

'And your mother-in-law? Did you manage to see her?'

'No, but I will take Alfie to see her in the not-too-distant future,' she replied. 'It would be nice if she could come to Alfie's baptism, but I need to sort that out first. I do have some other good news to tell you, though. I have a new apartment and employment. I don't know if you know of Mrs Amelia Jones, the authoress who lives in Newsham Drive. Jack Molyneux, her local bobby, introduced us. The girl whom she had employed left to join the ATS, so I am to live in her house and help her in a variety of ways, and I can have Alfie with me most of the time.'

Before the vicar could respond, there was a knock on the door and he called, 'Come in, my dear.'

Rachel, the vicar's wife, entered, bearing a tray. 'I've brought you two buttered scones as well as tea,' she said. 'But I have to remind you, love, that you'll have to be leaving soon for Evensong.'

'I wish I could attend,' said Eliza, 'but Jack Molyneux will be picking me up soon to take me to my friend Olive's home, where I've been invited to stay the night.'

'Then drink your tea and eat your scone,' said Rachel, 'and hopefully he'll be here by then.' She smiled at Alfie and said what a lovely baby he was. Then she left the study.

A short while later Eliza left, saying she hoped to be in church next Sunday morning. Once outside, she spotted a car parked at the kerb and as she walked down the path, Jack got out and opened the rear door for her. She climbed in and sat down with Alfie on her knee.

'I thought it would be safer for Alfie if you sat in the back with him on your knee,' said Jack, 'although it's more difficult to have a conversation.'

She agreed, thinking he could be thoughtful. Then she said, 'Have you something to tell me?'

'Yeah, but it can wait.'

'No, I'll only be guessing what it might be,' she said.

'Colwyn Bay phoned up. Alfie's grandmother asked who it was who found her and when she was told it was you and your friend, tears ran down her cheeks. She said she would like to see you and Alfie as soon as possible. And that you must stay for a week or more.'

'That will have to wait,' said Eliza. 'I can't take time off when I've just started work and there's the train fare. I do feel sorry for her, though, all alone and frightened.'

'But she's not all alone,' said Jack.

'Why? Who's with her? Is it Glyn?'

'No, it's not him.'

'You sound very definite,' she said.

'That's because he's in the Middle East. I don't want to upset you, but he's there because...' he hesitated, 'of Bryn's funeral. Sorry, but that's why he had to leave so quickly. They thought he'd want to be there when Bryn was buried.'

She was stunned because she had given no thought to a funeral. Perhaps because she had not been completely convinced he was dead. 'How long has Glyn been there?'

'Long enough not to be involved in the kidnapping. The inspector has been in touch with the officer in charge at the training barracks and he said they'd had a visit from a Mrs Bryn Jones, asking questions.'

'But didn't they consider that odd after receiving my letter addressed to Bryn?'

'Apparently, one of the soldiers recognised her. He'd been a mate of Glyn from Territorial Amy days and he told her what Glyn had told him about his half-brother remarrying and his wife giving birth to a son during the Blitz in early May.'

'So, there's our answer,' said Eliza.

'Not the whole answer,' Jack said.

'So, who is staying with my mother-in-law?' she asked.

'A policewoman, I hear,' replied Jack, starting up the engine.

Eliza sat back, hugging Alfie close and trying not to think too much, but her head was spinning with questions. When had Bryn been first married? Why hadn't he told her that he had been married before? Why had they broken up? When did they get divorced? One thing was for sure: he hadn't been honest with her. What about children? There were more questions she wanted answers to, but she wanted to stop thinking and go to sleep. However, she was going to have to make decisions about Alfie's christening, such as when and who to have for godparents. And where to have the party afterwards.

Alfie wriggled and let out a cry, and instantly she thought, what a lousy mother I am! He hasn't had a full feed, or his nappy changed since breakfast time, he must be really uncomfortable. Should she ask Jack to stop at his mother's so she could do both those things or was it better to carry on straight to Olive's so she wouldn't be too late? Of course, she would have to ask for somewhere she could do both those things almost as soon as she stepped over the threshold. She was so glad that after this night she would have her own flat.

'Is Alfie all right?' asked Jack, throwing the words over his shoulder.

'He's hungry and most likely needs his nappy changing,' she said in a muffled voice.

'Can you manage in the back? My eyes will be on the road. Or d'you want me to stop at Mam's?'

'That would make me late for tea at Olive's.'

'I'm sure they'll understand,' he said. 'Besides, you'll need the cot.'

'I don't know. I think she's already hurt because I didn't invite her to the wedding and then I had your mam look after Alfie... And now I'll be moving into our local authoress's house.'

'Ask her to be his godmother. I'm sure she'll forgive you then,' he said. 'In the meantime, Alfie's needs come first,' he said.

So, they stopped off at Jack's and only then did Eliza remember that she would need to take some of her and Alfie's few belongings, but there was little time and she decided just to feed him and change his nappy, and change her own clothes, as they were dirty after her visit to the kidnapper's deserted house.

CHAPTER ELEVEN

'I'll just drop you off,' said Jack when they arrived at Olive's parents' house. 'Olive and her mother will want to chat with you and fuss over Alfie.'

'You're probably right and I'll most likely see you around when you're on your beat, trying to catch the bag-snatcher or if you have any news for me. Thanks for putting up with me.'

'It's a pleasure,' he said. 'Mam would like it if you dropped in again with Alfie. She likes babies.'

'I'll do my best to make time. No doubt I'm going to be busy this coming week.'

When they arrived at their destination, Olive was standing in the doorway. Eliza did not wait for Jack to get out and open the door for her, but said, 'See yer,' and slid out of the car and waved to Olive.

'Sorry I'm late, but I dropped in at the vicarage, and was persuaded to have a cup of tea and a home-made scone.'

'I hope you're still hungry because Mam's saved some cake and sandwiches for you.'

Eliza beamed. 'I'm still hungry and I wouldn't turn down a slice of your mam's cake for all the tea in China.'

Once Eliza was over the threshold, Olive said, 'Can I have a hold of Alfie now, while you take your jacket off?'

'Of course!' Eliza handed her precious son over to Olive and said at the same time, 'I mentioned getting him christened to the vicar, but I don't know when that'll be.' She followed Olive up the lobby. 'But I'd like it if you'll be one of the godparents.'

'I'd love to,' said Olive.

'It mightn't be for a while, because I'd like Alfie's grandmother to be there, but that will take some arranging.' Eliza opened the kitchen living room door and held it open, so Olive could go first with Alfie.

'You're here at last,' said Olive's mother, getting to her feet and hobbling over to them. 'Let me have a hold of him.'

'I've only just got him, Mam,' said Olive. 'You'll have to wait.'

'I'm always waiting,' said the older woman. 'It's time you found yourself a husband and gave me a grandchild.'

'Don't go on, Mam,' said Olive. 'I'm only in my twenties.'

'I was eighteen when I got married,' she said. 'There's a war on and there'll be a shortage of men when it's over.'

'Oh Mam, don't be depressing,' said Olive. 'I've heard all about the last war and about all the women who never experienced the joy of motherhood and how there would have been no Suffragette movement if they'd had husbands.'

'That's most likely partly true,' said Eliza. 'But not completely, because the fight for women's rights began in other countries before the Great War and if I'm not mistaken, New Zealand was the first country where women achieved their aim.'

'I wouldn't know about that,' said Olive's mother. 'But let's drop the subject. Olive, go and put the kettle on and make the tea, and I'll take the baby.'

Eliza hid a smile, as Olive obeyed her mother. Her father was absent, and Eliza could only presume he was in the parlour, having a bit of peace to read his newspaper. Unless he'd gone down the backyard to have a smoke, as he was not allowed to enjoy a cigarette indoors. His wife nagged him about the smoke penetrating the fabric covering the furniture and the curtains if she caught him, or so Olive had told Eliza.

She watched the older woman make herself comfortable in an armchair and tickle Alfie's tummy. 'Please, don't do that,' she asked. 'He hasn't long had a feed.'

'But he likes it,' said the older woman. 'He's giggling.'

'Well, I'd rather he wasn't sick over his new clothes.'

'You've been shopping?'

'No, I was given them for him,' replied Eliza. 'I'm going shopping soon. Not only for clothes but for a few bits of furniture.' She paused and wondered if this was the right time. Nevertheless, she was going to have to tell them sooner or later and they should be pleased for her. 'I've been offered rooms and a job in one of the houses on Newsham Drive. I move in tomorrow and start work.'

'We thought you and Alfie would be staying with us for at least a month,' said Olive.

'That would mean your son having to sleep on the sofa. Anyway, this offer was too good to turn down,' said Eliza. 'I thought you'd be pleased for me.'

'I am,' said Olive. 'I thought I'd see more of you.'

'You can come and visit. We can take Alfie for walks in the park.'

'But you're going to be a live-in servant by the sound of it,' said Olive's mother. 'What does your employer think of you having Alfie with you?'

'She's a childless widow and she thinks he'll liven the place up. She's an authoress and I'm going to be her researcher, as well as helping her in the house.'

'An authoress! You mean she writes books?' asked Olive's mother.

Eliza nodded. 'She's a romantic novelist and you can find her books in the library.'

'How old is she?' asked Olive's mother.

'I didn't ask her,' replied Eliza, wishing she hadn't started this conversation.

'Guess,' said Olive's mother, moving Alfie to the crook of her arm and sighing.

'Fifty, maybe.'

'I see. Could you ask her for a signed copy of one of her books for me. I could give it to my sister for a birthday present.'

'I couldn't. It would be a cheek. I only start work tomorrow.'

'But it's my sister's birthday on Friday,' she wailed.

'Then she'll have to do without. Maybe next birthday,' said Eliza. 'Now where's me cup of tea and cake, Olive?'

'Coming,' called Olive.

She placed an occasional table in front of Eliza, with a place mat, and set down a cup of tea and a plate with a slice of carrot cake on it. 'Thank you,' said Eliza, taking a sip of tea and then a bite of cake. 'The cake is delicious as usual. Could I have the recipe?'

'I'll write it down for you before you leave,' she said.

'Anyway, changing the subject,' continued Olive. 'Have you had any more news about your mother-in-law?'

Eliza nodded. 'She had a woman visitor the evening before we arrived, who claimed to be Bryn's widow.'

Olive and her mother gasped. 'What did she say about that?' asked the older woman.

'She didn't believe her because she didn't have a Liverpudlian accent but a Welsh one.'

'You're joking,' said Olive.

'No, anyway, the woman said she'd received a telegram saying Bryn had been killed by a sniper's bullet in an uprising.'

'Goodness me! The poor woman, poor you,' said Olive's mother.

Eliza swallowed the sudden lump in her throat. 'To cut a long story short,' she said huskily, 'my mother-in-law told the woman that she was a liar and to get out of her house, and the woman lost her temper and became violent. Then the woman calmed down and my mother-in-law showed her the letter I'd sent her about Alfie and my being in the hospital and coming to visit her. The woman offered to make a cup of tea and drugged it. Then she wrote a false suicide note, stuck my mother-in-law's head in the oven and turned on the gas.'

'My goodness, how terrible,' said the older woman. 'You both have been through it. Have the police any idea who this woman is?'

'I'm thinking she must have known the brothers years ago, even up to when they joined the army, because she went and visited the army training barracks and asked questions about them. A soldier who knew Glyn from when they were in the Territorial Army together recognised her and told her about the letter from me addressed to Bryn. Glyn has been ordered to the Middle East, as they are going to bury Bryn.' Eliza sniffed.

'It sounds fishy to me,' said Olive's mother. 'Some very strange things go on during wartime.'

'I've had my thoughts,' said Eliza. 'But I don't want to talk about them yet.'

'What are you going to do about your mother-in-law?' asked Olive.

'She wants me to go and visit her as soon as possible, but it's going to have to wait. Besides, she's not alone but has a PCW staying with her. I'll discuss it with my employer and the police,' said Eliza. 'I'm in no mood for travelling for several days.'

'Your romantic novelist could give you the whole weekend off if you tell her the whole story. She might put you in a book.'

'We'll see,' said Eliza. 'Anyway, tell me what you two have been up to? Seen any good films lately?'

'We saw a Will Hay film which made me laugh,' said Olive's mother.

'It was about a ghost at a school,' said Olive.

'What about work?' asked Eliza. 'No accidents, I hope.'

'No, thank goodness,' said Olive. 'Anyway, I'll show you which room you're sleeping in, and we've brought down my old cot from the loft for Alfie.'

'Thanks,' said Eliza, stifling a yawn. 'It's been a real busy day.'

It wasn't until they were in the bedroom, with football posters on the wall as well as pin-up Betty Grable – whose legs were said to be insured for thousands of dollars – that Olive told her that Alan Murray in work had his eye on her and had asked her out.

'What did you say?' asked Eliza, remembering he was a bit of a flirt, but extremely good looking.

'I told him I'd think about it,' said Olive.

'And have you thought about it?'

'I'm still thinking but I'll probably say no. I don't think Dad will like him.'

'Your mam will. He'll flatter her and she'll love it.'

'There's a new bloke just started, and he's shy. I feel sorry for him.'

'I suppose the other fellas tease him?'

Olive nodded. 'Led by Alan. His name's George and they sing: "Georgie Porgie, pudding and pie, kissed the girls and made them cry." He has ears that stick out.'

'Mean.'

Olive nodded. 'I think he likes one of the new girls, but he doesn't have a chance. She's a young Mary Pickford and there's several fellas already hanging around her like bees around a rose.'

'You must tell me how things go on,' said Eliza, drawing back the covers and tucking Alfie in the cot. She undressed and put on her nightie.

'I think I'll go to bed,' said Olive. 'If you're going. I hate getting up early on Monday morning.'

'I'm looking forward to this one,' said Eliza, kissing Alfie's soft cheek before getting into bed.

'Will you be seeing your policeman tomorrow?' asked Olive.

'Maybe, Newsham Drive is part of his beat, so I just might catch sight of him,' said Eliza. After a restless night, Eliza was woken by Alfie crying, so she rose immediately, not wanting him to disturb the household. She changed and breastfed him and then, with him cuddled to her, she dozed until a ray of sunshine through a gap in the curtains shone in her face and woke her. It was still only six o'clock, but she decided to get up and go downstairs, and to the lavatory down the backyard, and afterwards make a cup of tea. She almost bumped into Olive's dad at the foot of the stairs.

He bid her a good morning and added how nice it was to see her and her little boy, and wished her well. She responded with a good morning and wondered just what his wife might have told him in bed last night about her situation. She thanked him for his hospitality and asked what time he had to be in work.

He said, 'Eight o'clock and I have my carry-out to get ready.'

She passed him and went through to the backyard, leaving Alfie surrounded by cushions so he couldn't roll off the sofa in the kitchen. Olive's father was there, opening a tin of Spam while seated at the dining table on which there was also a crusty loaf. She was not away long and when she entered the kitchen, she was told that he had made a pot of tea and to pour herself a cup.

It was an hour later when Olive came into the room and told her that she could have the cot for Alfie as a gift. 'I've asked a neighbour if you can borrow his handcart to get it to Newsham Drive.'

Eliza could only thank her and, shortly after, the neighbour appeared with the handcart and said he would come to pick it up that evening or Tuesday evening. She thanked him and handed him a slip of paper with the address written on it; she made a mental note to give him two bottles of Walker's beer as payment for his kindness to a stranger. She said her goodbyes to Olive and her mother, and invited them to a meal at her flat. 'I'll let you know when. Thank you for having me and for the cot for Alfie.'

She had to walk, pushing the cart all the way to Newsham Drive, which was quite a way, so she was tired out by the time she arrived at the house. She parked the handcart at the kerb and lifted Alfie out, and then she opened the gate and walked slowly up the path and knocked on the door, but it was obvious that Amelia had been watching out for her because the door opened almost immediately.

'I'm so glad you're here,' she said. 'Come on in and we'll have a cup of tea.'

'Thank you,' replied Eliza. 'But I have a handcart with a cot for Alfie, which is a gift from my friend's mother.'

'A handcart!' exclaimed Amelia. 'You've pushed a handcart all the way here from Aintree?'

Eliza nodded. 'One of their neighbours lent me it. He's coming to pick it up this evening or tomorrow, so can I park it on the path, please?'

'Certainly, but let's hope he arrives sooner rather than later?'

Eliza nodded. 'I'd better go and see to it, and bring the cot in.'

'You'd best give me Alfie then, while you do so,' suggested Amelia.

Eliza handed Alfie over, thanking her, and then hurried to bring the handcart through the gate and onto the path. She parked it to one side, as much out of the way as she could, and removed the dismantled cot, part by part, and carried it inside and up the stairs to her rooms – along with the bedding and the shopping bag that contained nappies and other necessities.

Then she went into the sitting room where Amelia was seated in an armchair with Alfie on her lap. She had a rattle and was shaking it, and he was gazing up at it.

'Did you buy that for him?' Eliza could not help asking. 'How kind of you.'

'I'm going to tell you something that few people know about,' said Amelia. 'Sit down, Eliza.'

'You don't want me to make a pot of tea first?' asked Eliza.

'Perhaps that would be best,' said Amelia. 'You must be thirsty, and I could get parched. Use the best Assam tea in the caddy, the one with an elephant painted on it.'

Eliza made a pot of tea and carried it – with cups and saucers, milk and sugar – into the sitting room on a tray, set it on an occasional table and poured out two cups. She handed the first to her employer, after taking Alfie from her, and sat down and reached for her own cup of tea.

'I had a baby,' said Amelia after a large gulp of tea. 'But she was premature and stillborn. Thomas had wanted a son, hence the blue rattle, but he felt the loss of our daughter as much as I did. It was late November and we were planning our first Christmas as parents, so we bought toys and decorations for a tree, and they're still up in the attic, as we couldn't bear getting rid of them or decorating a tree either. I never became pregnant again and my books are my babies.'

Eliza felt sad and was unable to speak; she could only reach out and place her hand over Amelia's. At last, she found her voice. 'I'm sure your books have made a lot of women happy.'

'I've never looked at them like that,' said Amelia. 'Thank you, and I'm sure Thomas would be pleased to know there is a baby boy with the surname of Jones.'

She took a sip of tea and then continued, 'To business.'

Eliza waited and then said, 'Any ideas what you'd like for dinner this evening? I do need to go shopping in Breck Road and order a bed. I could buy food while I'm out.'

'Thomas had a fondness for pigs' trotters. He'd buy them already cooked from Lister's, the cooked-meat shop on Breck Road. I got a taste for them myself.'

'I know it,' said Eliza, thinking she could make a sauce to have with them and mashed potatoes. Apple pie and custard for pudding. 'Is there any research work you want me to do?' she asked.

'Yes, you can do that tomorrow. It means going into town to the street where the ruined church is, on the corner. Not Leece Street, the other one.'

'Berry Street,' said Eliza.

'That's it. There's a second-hand bookshop and I want you to ask the owner if he has a copy of *Mrs Beeton's Book of Household Management*, printed in Victorian times but not a first copy. I don't expect that, but I don't want a copy printed this century. Also, a book of costume through the ages, including men's costume, not just women's. Ask him to put them on my account.'

'Will do,' said Eliza, thinking she could also go into Pollard's, the baby shop that was on Renshaw Street. She finished her cup of tea, washed the crockery and put on a hat and jacket, after changing Alfie's nappy and feeding him. She then told Amelia that she was going, and was given a pound note and some change, as well as ration books.

Eliza remembered she needed to go to the post office while she was out if she was going to go into Pollard's. She went there first, as it was around the corner from the furniture shop where she ordered a single bed to be delivered that afternoon, but they were not able to deliver it until the next day. She was told she was in luck they were able to deliver it so early. Then she went to Lister's and bought the pigs' trotters. There was already a queue and, after that, she went to the greengrocer's for vegetables, baking apples and a bunch of dried herbs. Finally, she went to Irwin's for groceries, where she had to queue up again, and then to Sturla's for bedding. She realised it was a good job that she wasn't going to town until tomorrow, as all the queuing up had left her very little time. She also went into Sayer's and bought a fresh Vienna loaf and a couple of meat pies for lunch. Fortunately, bread was not rationed.

She ate her lunch and fed Alfie in the kitchen, where she also unpacked the shopping. Later that day Amelia set the dining table for two. 'I don't like eating alone, and I hope we can regard each other as friends, not landlady and tenant.'

'Thank you,' said Eliza. 'I won't take advantage of your kindness.'

She concocted a sauce from the top of the milk, chopped spring onion and finely shredded cabbage, added dried parsley, and served this with the trotters and mashed potato after she made the apple pie and baked that in the oven. Then she made custard from a packet of Bird's custard powder and milk.

'That was delicious,' said Amelia. 'I did the right thing hiring you.'

'Thank you,' said Eliza. 'Now do you want coffee or tea?'

'The Assam tea, please,' she replied.

Eliza thought, no Brook Bond for her employer, but Twinings, which was dearer, and the leaves were darker. She asked herself whether Amelia needed more coupons for it – and had it come all the way from India or had she stocked up on it when war was rumoured?

Eliza brought in a tray and after pouring out the tea, she sat down with Alfie on her lap. She told her mistress about her invitation for a meal to Olive and her mother. 'I'd like them to come here for lunch, which hopefully would not inconvenience you. We could have it in the kitchen or upstairs.'

'I'll be going to London Wednesday week to an event being held by my publisher. I won't be back until evening, so they could come then,' Amelia told her.

'Thank you,' said Eliza. She then also mentioned her mother-in-law's wish to have her visit her with Alfie in Colwyn Bay.

Amelia leaned across the table and said, 'You can have this weekend off, but only Sunday the following weekend. A full weekend off once a month,' she added.

'Thank you,' Eliza said. 'So, tomorrow you want me to go to the second-hand bookshop on the street where the bombed church is on the corner and ask if they have a copy of *Mrs Beeton's Book of Household Management*. One that was printed during the Victorian era. You don't need a first edition, though, as that would be too much to expect.' She paused, trying to remember her tasks for the week ahead. 'Then I am to go to Lime Street railway station and purchase you a ticket for a reserved first-class seat on the nine-twenty train to London. You might stay overnight, so you will buy your return ticket at Euston.' She added, 'Will you phone and let me know if you are going to stay in London?'

'Of course, and you mustn't forget to bolt the doors and lock the windows,' said Amelia.

Eliza nodded, thinking that was a task she already did, so she was unlikely to forget. She rose from the table with Alfie in her arms and passed him over to Amelia, who liked to have a little cuddle. Then Eliza cleared the table, took the crockery and cutlery to the kitchen, and washed up and dried and put everything away. She wiped all the surfaces down before going to the lounge. She took Alfie from Amelia, who went into her writing room and, after a short silence, the tap-tap of her typewriter could be heard.

As it was still light and the weather fine, Eliza decided to go for a walk in the park. She slipped a note under the writing-room door, saying where she was going and, with her door key in her pocket, left the house. Despite Alfie being only a baby, she took him to see the ducks from the bridge over the boating lake. She wished she had brought some bread to feed them, thinking again how at least bread was one of the few things to eat that wasn't rationed. She stayed for a while, watching the ducks' antics, before setting out back home by a different route.

She tried not to think of Bryn being killed, and their dream of having a house and settling down as a family after the war, as it made her sad – not only for herself and Bryn, but also for Alfie, who would grow up never having known his father. It also made her sad to think she would never see him again and that she didn't even have a photo of him. His image was fading and that was why Glyn had been able to trick her into believing he was Bryn. Maybe it hadn't been a trick. Perhaps he really had intended to tell her that Bryn was dead, but when he saw how much she had been through, he decided not to upset her further. But then she thought about him kissing her and decided that she could not offer him the benefit of the doubt. She slowed her pace as she turned on the path that went round the other side of the lake, which ran almost parallel with Orphan Drive for a while, and she roused herself from her reverie and became aware of footsteps. She then was almost knocked off her feet by a thrusting shoulder. A few minutes later she felt hands on her upper arms steadying her and she was able to hoist Alfie higher. She heard a familiar voice asking her if she was all right and it was only then that she realised it was Jack and that he must be in pursuit of the man who had almost knocked her over. Jack had stopped and was staring into her face. 'What are you doing here alone?'

'Never mind me,' she said. 'Go and catch him.'

He hesitated and then moved off, limping slightly. She could only presume the man was the suspected bag-snatcher he had mentioned the other day. She decided not to hang around, as if he caught up with the man, Jack would most likely take him to the police station. She wasted no time hurrying back to the house that she now called home.

She waited up for a while, not sure what to do with herself, and then decided to put Alfie down in his cot and, after locking up, she said goodnight to Amelia. She said her prayers and added in one for Jack, praying that he caught the bag-snatcher and had not been hurt in doing so – the man had felt strong when he almost knocked her over.

It had been a busy day and she fell asleep on the sofa almost immediately. She was going to the bookshop in town in the morning, so would have to give herself plenty of time to get ready and cook breakfast for herself and Alfie, as well as her mistress if she was awake.

–

Eliza went into Pollard's, and bought a pushchair and enjoyed looking around. There were also toys in the shop, but she decided to buy one or two another time, as she came across a sling for carrying a baby and she thought that would be handy. She also enjoyed her visit to the bookshop, where she put the sling to good use, as she wandered around the bookshelves and was fortunate enough to purchase the book that Amelia wanted. She had mentioned her name to the owner of the shop, and he produced the Mrs Beeton volume immediately and asked whether Amelia was planning on writing a different kind of book. 'I don't know,' she paused. 'What I can say is that she wants me to trace her husband's family tree.'

'That will be a job and a half,' he said. 'I hope she has his birth certificate, as that will be a help.'

'She knows he was born in Chester and his family hailed from further south in Wales, close to the border with Shropshire.'

'Well, good luck to you, lass. I wonder if she's ever read *Her Benny*?'

Eliza said, 'I've read it. I borrowed it from the library.'

He looked thoughtful. 'I might have a copy here. It could be in the back. I'll have a look while you have a browse in here.'

'The pushchair's not in the way, is it?'

'No,' he said. 'There is a children's section with newer copies of books.'

'He's only a baby,' she said.

'But you can read to him and show him the pictures, and he'll grow,' he said.

'I'll have a look,' she said.

He left her alone and she set off, aware that Alfie was making noises, as if he was trying to speak. A book caught her eye and she read its title: *When We Were Very Young* by A. A. Milne. She had heard that name and opened the book, and then she remembered he was the author of the Winnie the Pooh books. She decided to buy it, thinking she would enjoy reading it. She still had some money from what she had withdrawn from the post office and it was second-hand, so she wasn't having to pay the cost of a new hardback book.

The bookseller appeared in front of her with two books. 'Here we are,' he said, 'and what have you got there?'

She handed the book to him, and he glanced at the price in pencil inside and said, 'You can have it for tuppence. For our writer friend, I will wrap her Mrs Beeton and *Her Benny* up and put them on her account. Give her a reminder that she needs to pay it. Writers are inclined to forget things once they're buried in their imaginary world.'

Eliza thanked him and then, with the books wrapped in brown paper and string in her shopping bag, and the children's book in her capacious handbag, she was about to leave the shop when she remembered about the book on fashion through the ages that her employer had wanted. So she went back to the shopkeeper and spoke to him, not forgetting to mention men's fashions. That purchased, she left the shop and walked to St John's Market, where she bought minced beef, cheese, freshly baked bread rolls, boiled ham and custard tarts; then she caught the tram to Rocky Lane and went into Amelia's house via the back gate into the garden, thinking the beds needed weeding, as there were dandelion clocks and groundsel growing everywhere. Then she noticed what looked like lettuces in a patch and herbs, and said to herself, 'I'll come back and check them out later. Right now, I need to see to Alfie and unpack the shopping.'

No sooner had she stepped into the kitchen than Amelia appeared. 'I've good news. Constable Molyneux called to tell me that he caught the bag-snatcher, and he made me a cup of tea when I told him you'd gone into town to the bookshop on Berry Street. He also suggested moving the handcart round to the side of the house after I mentioned you having a bed delivered.'

'Has it been delivered?'

'Yes, and they took it upstairs and set it up.'

Eliza was thankful about the handcart being moved as she had almost forgotten the bed being delivered, so she was pleased about the men taking it upstairs. She would have to drop into the shop and thank them. As she unpacked the shopping, she wondered what else Jack and Amelia had talked about, but first she handed the brown-paper wrapped parcel to her employer. Amelia stared at it and hastened to unwrap it, carefully conserving the paper and string to be reused at some other time. She stared at the three books and picked up *Her Benny*. 'What is this?'

'We thought you might find it interesting. It's set in Liverpool during Victorian times. It wasn't written by a native of Liverpool and it's not a social history as such, but fiction, much as Jane Austen's books are.'

'You've read Jane?'

'Me gran introduced me to her. I haven't read all her books, as she borrowed them from the library in Holyhead.'

'I see,' said Amelia. 'I will read it with interest.' She had picked up the other books now and was turning the pages. She sighed. 'If only there wasn't rationing, you could try some of these recipes, Eliza. Of course, in smaller measures.'

'What if I make a pot of tea and put some lovely, boiled ham on buttered crusty cobs? I noticed what looked like lettuce growing in the back garden. I was thinking of taking a few leaves to put on the cobs.'

'Why not? One of my neighbours gave me a packet of seeds and put them in a patch she cleared for me. I watered them, but sometimes forgot and left the watering to the Almighty. She also gave me some herbs, which were already plants.'

'They're still there,' said Eliza. 'I'd like to meet this lady.'

'She's a Scot and has a son who's in the Royal Navy. I can't remember her name right now, but the house is four doors up, and is painted maroon and cream, I think.' Amelia added, 'Do I owe you any money, Eliza?'

'No, he put the cost of your books on your account,' she said.

A wail from the pushchair drew Eliza's attention to Alfie and instantly she went over to him. Amelia left the kitchen and went to her writing room, carrying her books.

Eliza went outside and plucked some lettuce leaves, considering doing some gardening later if her employer agreed. She would bring Alfie out in his pushchair, where he could see her, and get some fresh air and sun, but first she must see to her employer's needs.

As she gave Amelia her lunch, she told her that the bookseller had mentioned she needed to pay her account. 'He also asked whether you had your husband's birth certificate. I mentioned you wanted me to research his family tree and he said that would be of help.'

'I see. What else did he say?'

'He thought you were showing interest in the Victorian era.'

'I am interested and that's most likely because so much happened of historical interest, and Thomas and I were born during that era. I haven't yet gone through all his papers, which is remiss of me, but I do know some are with our solicitor. I shall get in touch with him and see if his birth certificate is amongst them.'

Solicitors, thought Eliza. Had Bryn and his mother made wills? Was this something she should investigate for Alfie's sake? She tried to remember whether her father had made a will, but she had been too young at the time to be aware of it. Surely servicemen would have to make wills, as they could be killed at any time. Where should she start? Liverpool, or Colwyn Bay on Saturday?

CHAPTER TWELVE

Saturday morning and Eliza was struggling to get the pushchair with Alfie in it onto the train.

'Want a hand, Eliza?'

She glanced in Jack's direction and said, 'She told you, didn't she?'

'She's the cat's mother.' He smiled. 'If you mean Mrs Amelia Jones told me you were planning to go to Colwyn Bay today then, yes, she did. She didn't like the thought of you going all that way with Alfie without...' He paused.

'A bodyguard?' she said.

Before he could reply, a voice said, 'Are you getting on this train or not?'

'Sorry, mate,' said Jack, proceeding to grip the foot of the pushchair and lift it, so Eliza could back into the carriage, glad to have some of the strain removed from her arms and shoulders.

'Thank you,' she said.

Jack followed her and sat opposite, with the pushchair between them. 'I thought you could fold it up,' he said.

'It does fold up but it's not easy when your child is asleep, and you only have one pair of hands.'

'That's why I'm here,' he said. 'I'm the extra pair of hands.'

'You're not in your police uniform,' she said.

'I'm off duty,' he responded. 'It's my day off, so when I heard you were going to Colwyn Bay, I decided a day at the seaside was just the thing to set me up.'

'You could have taken the ferry to New Brighton or the train to Southport.'

'We could do that another time,' he said, cocking an eyebrow.

'We?' she said, sounding outraged despite being unable to prevent a smile dawning in her grey eyes. 'We hardly know each other.'

'I thought I could show Alfie how to build a sandcastle.'

'He's too young to build a sandcastle.'

'He can see how it's done. We could also visit Conway Castle, so he can see the real thing.'

'You're being ridiculous. Why don't you admit you're a plain-clothes policeman wanting to catch the person responsible for kidnapping Alfie?'

'I'm hurt,' he said, placing a hand in the region of his heart. 'You had it right the first time: I'm your bodyguard, and Alfie's, but I do want to show him how to build a sandcastle. It takes time and practice to get it right. I also want to find the person who tried to murder a weak, sad woman.'

Eliza started. 'So, you do think the two are linked?'

He nodded. 'This case is about more than a bereaved mother pinching a newly born baby boy. I consider it no coincidence that Alfie was taken after his father was killed in the Middle East.'

'So, you believe Glyn tried to murder his mother?'

'No, I believe it was a woman who did that.'

She blinked. 'The kidnapper.'

He nodded. 'Oh, what a tangled web we weave when we practise to deceive,' he quoted.

She frowned and said, 'Shakespeare.'

He shook his head. 'No, Sir Walter Scott, I believe.'

'Oh, my mistake. Where will I find it?'

He pulled a face. 'Now you're asking. I believe it can be found in a book called *Marmion*, which has a connection with the Battle of Flodden.'

She sighed. 'A sad time for Scotland.'

He agreed and added, 'Let's change the subject. This is a complicated case because I believe you've been deceived from the beginning,' he said.

'What do you mean?'

'Our local authoress told me she has asked you to trace her husband's ancestry, which means you'll most likely not only be looking up Joneses in the births, marriages and death records.'

She agreed. 'Amelia's husband was born in Chester, but his parents were from further south in Wales, close to the Shropshire border. Are you saying that he could be related to Bryn?'

'I don't know. You should talk to Rambling Rosie.'

'Who's she?'

'Never mind now.' He glanced out of the window. 'We'll be coming out of the tunnel soon.'

She had not even been aware that they had passed Birkenhead underground station, and there were several stations on the Wirral before they arrived in Chester, where they needed to change trains for their destination in Wales.

'Just look up your Bryn Jones in the marriages in Liverpool.'

She stared at him. 'Can't you tell me what you found?'

He shook his head. 'You mightn't believe me.'

She was silent and thinking deeply as the train came out into the daylight. Then she remembered something she had read in the *Echo* about servicemen committing bigamy, some even marrying three times without divorcing their previous wives during the Great War. The same thing could be happening in the present war. She lifted her head and gazed at Jack. 'Are you telling me that I'm not Bryn's real wife? That he was already married when he married me?'

'You can check it out yourself,' he said. 'You don't have to take my word for it.'

'No, I don't,' she said. 'I can scarcely believe it. I believed we were in love.'

'There's a difference between being in love and loving someone,' he said.

'You're splitting hairs,' she said.

'No, although, I'll admit one can be both.'

'I'm confused,' she said, trying to stay calm, even though she felt sick. 'Why should Bryn do that?'

'We'll find out sooner or later,' he said. 'In the meantime, you've got to be on your guard and have a close eye kept on Alfie.'

She gulped, wondering why her son had been targeted. 'You're not joking!'

'Of course I'm not. I don't find this situation the least bit funny. I feel very protective towards Alfie, much as I've always felt towards my younger sister.'

'Jean. I like her.'

'I'm glad. She's fifteen and animal mad. I have a cat and a dog. She takes my dog for walks when I'm working. Otherwise, Mam looks after both.'

'I didn't see them.'

He nodded. 'Mam doesn't like hairs on the furniture, so she shooed them out.'

'I've just realised I'm not a widow if Bryn was already married when he married me,' she said, disbelievingly.

'Neither are you a Mrs Jones,' said Jack.

'I'm an unmarried mother! Miss Eliza Griffiths.' She wondered how this was going to affect her and Alfie's future. She would have to find a better paid job to support the two of them, unless she found herself another husband. Of course, there was the possibility of staying in her present position if she didn't remarry and her employer kept her on.

She was about to ask Jack if he'd ever thought of joining the army, but decided that would be tactless and instead said, 'I've never been to the Lake District. Mam used to go there with the cycling club, and Dad and me would go and stay with his parents on Anglesey. He could only stay a week and then had to go back to work, while I stayed on for the whole of the summer holidays.'

'I've been to the Lakes,' he said. 'I love walking in the mountains.'

'Maybe I'll be able to take Alfie there one day,' she said. 'If I can afford it.' She groaned. 'I've just realised I won't get a widow's war pension if I was never Bryn's legal wife.'

'Alfie could take you when he grows up and has a job.'

'He could have a girl by then and not want my company,' she murmured.

'He's only a baby – make the most of his company now. There's a war on, remember. Once it's over, who knows what might happen. One thing is that the Blackpool lights will be switched on again. It'll look fantastic after the gloom of the blackout.'

'It'll still cost money.' She sighed. 'I remember our street getting a charabanc to go to see the lights. The parents would give so much money a week to pay for it.'

'Our street did the same in between the wars,' he said.

'Maybe I should start saving now,' she said.

'Can you afford to save?' he asked.

'Pennies can add up,' she said. 'I don't pay rent and I'm paid a wage, although not as much as when I worked in Ammunitions, naturally, but this job is better for Alfie and me.'

'Of course, perhaps you should get in touch with a solicitor to see where you stand for financial help with Alfie.'

'Thank you for that suggestion,' she said. 'As it is, I'd already considered seeing if Bryn made a will. It's something I'm planning to ask his mother today.'

'It's worth checking,' said Jack. 'I'll see you to the door and return in an hour and a half to pick you both up, so we can take Alfie to the beach. I'll just have a mosey around, as our American friends say. Have you met some of them over here? They were out with vans in Liverpool to help feed those made homeless – like yourself – during the Blitz, along with the WVS.'

'No, but apparently you have,' she said, wondering why he had mentioned the Americans while she was thinking about Bryn's mother having a policewoman companion staying with her. Her nerves were in a state, perhaps believing there was the possibility of the woman watching the house, thinking that Eliza might turn up with Bryn's son.

They both fell silent. Alfie had woken up and she lifted him onto her lap, so he could look out of the window. Jack folded up the pushchair, so they could have more leg room, and to make it easier when they had to leave the train at Chester and catch the mainline one to Colwyn Bay. Once they left Chester behind and had crossed the border into Wales, it was not long before they could see Snowdonia in the distance.

'Now there's mountains you could climb, Jack,' said Eliza, bouncing Alfie on her knees.

'Been there and climbed Snowdon itself,' he said. 'If you want to get to the top and don't fancy the walk, there is a train.'

'I'll make do with climbing the Great Orme overlooking Llandudno,' she said. 'Kill two birds with one stone: Llandudno has a beach as well as a decent-sized hill to climb.'

'Good idea, although you won't get a fabulous view.'

'It's good enough for me, closer to the sea and Anglesey,' she said. 'And the path will be better underfoot.'

'We could push Alfie up there in his pushchair in autumn, when it's not so busy,' he suggested.

'We?' she said, wondering if she and Alfie weren't just a case to him. Maybe his mother had put the idea in his head that it was time he was married and giving her some grandchildren? Did he see the two of them living happily in his house, with his mother and sister? Surely, he would consider it was a bit too soon after Bryn being killed. She wished she knew what was going on in his mind and whether he'd ever had a girlfriend.

'We could go in my car,' he said.

'What about petrol? I haven't forgotten it's rationed.'

'I'll save my coupons. It's only a suggestion. We don't have to go if you don't want to. I thought it would be a treat for you and Alfie. I could even run you across to Anglesey if you wanted.'

'I'll think about it, but only if you allow me to pay towards the petrol,' she said, her heart yearning to see the place where she had spent so many happy holidays with her grandparents.

'Deal, weather permitting,' he said.

'Scared of a bit of rain?' she taunted.

'No, wind that can blow you into the sea,' he said seriously.

She had felt those winds and dropped the subject, not believing for a moment that he feared them. She closed her eyes and could see the headland of the bay in her mind's eye. Then she felt Alfie's hand clawing at her cheek, so she opened her eyes and rubbed noses with him. She gazed out of the window and watched the fields with cattle tearing the rich green grass flashing past and she knew it wouldn't be long before they arrived in Colwyn Bay. Her stomach seemed to do a somersault and she wondered just how much to tell Alfie's grandmother.

CHAPTER THIRTEEN

Eliza took a deep breath as she raised her fist and knocked on the door. She heard footsteps, so she turned and waved to Jack, who was standing on the pavement, watching her and Alfie. The door opened to reveal a young woman of sturdy build and homely features. Her eyes were blue and piercing: they took in Eliza and the pushchair with Alfie strapped in it and she said, 'I'm Mairi Lloyd and, no, I'm not a singer on the stage. My mother was just an admirer of hers.' She paused. 'Constable Molyneux phoned the station and told us to expect you.'

Eliza wondered why Jack had not told her that he had phoned ahead, and she held out a hand. 'I'm pleased to meet you. I'm Eliza. I'd appreciate your help to lift the pushchair in.'

That done, Mairi led the way along the lobby to a room to the rear, where a woman whom Eliza had last seen looking half-dead was sitting in an armchair, her feet resting on a pouffe.

'I'm glad to see you looking so much better,' said Eliza.

'Thanks to you and your friend, lovey,' Bryn's mother replied. 'Please, bring my grandson closer, so I can see him better. My eyes aren't what they used to be.'

Eliza was relieved that she was friendly and seemed so happy to have a grandson, as after having two sons, she could have wanted a granddaughter. She lifted Alfie from the pushchair and crossed the room. She placed her precious son in his grandmother's arms but kept a hand beneath for safety, gazing down at the two as the older woman peered through small metal-rimmed spectacles at Alfie. 'The Almighty has brought joy back into this house,' she cried in a wavering voice. 'He has the look of his father as a baby.

There are pictures on the dresser over there,' she added, indicating a far wall.

Mairi went over to it and brought several framed photographs to Eliza, who presumed they could all be of Bryn, not just as a baby, but at various stages in his life. She stroked the photograph of Bryn as a young man, thinking that if Jack was right, he had changed from this person who looked as if butter wouldn't melt in his mouth into one who had deceived and betrayed her. She felt sad as well as angry. There were several pictures of two boys, whom she took to be Bryn and Glyn, dressed alike in rugby kit and there was one of Glyn wearing a uniform that was like a soldier's, when he was probably in his late teens. Then she remembered he had joined the Territorial Army. They were all studio photographs, and Eliza decided that she really should have one taken of Alfie and have two prints done. One for his grandmother, who would appreciate the thought.

As if she had read her mind, Alfie's grandmother suggested it and said that she would pay for it to be done. Eliza thanked her and said that she would see to it. Then she asked if there were any photos of Bryn's father. Immediately, Gladys asked Mairi to go up to her bedroom and bring down the photograph on the bedside table. In a short time Mairi was back with it and Eliza was gazing down at the image of a man who, although he must have been in his late thirties, was very like his son. He was dressed in a pinstriped suit and wore a dicky bow and had a flower in his buttonhole. He wore a bowler hat on his fair hair. He was a handsome man and there was an air of confidence about him, as he posed against what appeared to be a marble pillar, but was most likely constructed of strong cardboard.

'It was taken on our wedding day,' said his widow. 'We had to wait a long time before we married. My father had someone else in mind for me and eventually I was forced into marrying David Glyn, who was a solicitor's clerk, the son of a friend of my father's.'

'Were you very unhappy?'

'I was desperately unhappy, but I pretended to be content with my lot and then when Glyn was born, matters improved: my husband was so proud when I produced a son for him. Sadly, for him, his pleasure didn't last long. He was kicked in the head by a horse when he was crossing the road and not looking where he was going. Very unlike him not to take care. Glyn was only five years old. Anyway, he left this house to me with the proviso that it would go to Glyn, but I could live here until I passed away.'

'Did he ever suspect you would marry again?' asked Eliza.

'It was possible he knew of my feelings for Daffyd Bryn Jones, who worked in the slate industry, but if he had been absolutely sure, he would have made a proviso about my not marrying again if I was to live in the house until I passed away.'

'I see what you mean,' said Eliza.

'As it was, my father was wrong about Daffyd, as he inherited shares in the slate business from his father. My son Bryn inherited them from his father and this little man here…' She bounced Alfie on her knee. 'He will inherit them from his father.' She sniffed back tears. 'The Jones slate business is owned by one family that has come down from the original founder, who had three sons. Since then, the first-born son of each of the descendants of those three sons inherits his father's share in the business.'

'What if the first-born is a daughter?' asked Eliza.

'She would not inherit any shares, although I'm sure that the daughters' fathers or brothers would see to it that the girls in the family were not left penniless.'

'What about the widows of the sons who inherited?' Eliza asked.

'Life insurance was taken out on the husband's life when the marriage took place. When a husband dies, and his son has not reached twenty-one, his mother becomes a trustee, along with the family solicitor. You should go and see Mr Davies. He's an honest and nice man.'

Eliza hesitated before asking quietly, 'You are aware that Bryn has been killed?'

She nodded, trying not to cry but there was a sob in her voice. 'The woman who drugged and then attempted to gas me told me the night before you found me. She made a mistake in using gas as a method, as the meter needed money in it and eventually ran out.'

'Jack, a Liverpool policeman, told me about this woman,' said Eliza.

'It's all very confusing. Why would she want me dead? It's not as if she would gain by it.' She hugged Alfie close to her. 'Thank the Almighty for this little man.'

Eliza considered what Jack had said about the possibility of Bryn being a bigamist. She supposed a lot depended on what he had written in his latest will: who would collect his life insurance, and Alfie was bound to inherit the shares in the slate company. She kept her thoughts to herself, thinking Bryn's mother was suffering enough while grieving over Bryn's death and recovering from her ordeal. To tell her that her favourite son had most likely been a bigamist would only cause her more suffering. She was roused from her reverie by Mairi bringing in a tea tray that not only held cups and saucers, a teapot, milk jug and a sugar basin, but also a plate of buttered Welsh cakes. Eliza took Alfie from his grandmother and placed him in the pushchair, before removing a feeding bottle in which she had expressed some breast milk, which she gave to him while they drank their tea and ate the Welsh cakes. They tasted good, although not as good as she remembered her grandmother's tasting.

She checked the clock on the sideboard when she had finished feeding Alfie and saw that she could stay another half hour, so she handed him back to his grandmother for another cuddle before they would have to leave. When she said that, the older woman suggested that they stay the night.

'I can't,' replied Eliza. 'My boss and landlady is expecting us back, as I have a special job to do tomorrow.'

'You could always come and live here rent-free,' said Alfie's grandmother.

'I can't,' said Eliza. 'But we could come and stay with you for a while in August.'

'That would be nice.' She paused. 'What about Christmas?'

'What about you coming to stay with us in Liverpool?'

She looked thoughtful. 'What about the bombing?'

'Hitler seems to have turned his attention to Russia. Liverpool has seen nothing of the Luftwaffe since May. Although a lot of the shops in the city centre have closed, there are still plenty doing business, and you'll be able to see what the city looks like after the bombing. Several visitors come in to look at it from parts of Lancashire, Wales and Cheshire.'

'I'll give it some thought,' she said. 'Perhaps the war will be over by then.'

Eliza could only smile, remembering her mother telling her that was what lots of people said in the Great War, and it had gone on for over four years. She thanked her for the solicitor's address and telephone number, as well as the photo of Bryn and Glyn in the chapel choir. She kissed the older woman on the cheek before she and Alfie left, and said she would be in touch. She wanted Alfie to have a happy relationship with his grandmother, as she'd had with her paternal grandmother, and that meant spending time with her. She liked Bryn's mother and wanted her to have some happiness in her later years, after the sadness of her life so far.

CHAPTER FOURTEEN

Jack was waiting across the road, and she was glad to see him, even though he was too much of a policeman sometimes, acting as if he knew what was best for her and Alfie. He crossed as soon as she closed the gate behind her. He took hold of one side of the handle of the pushchair and turned it left. 'This is the quickest way to the beach where there's an incline so we can wheel Alfie down.'

'All right, I can manage myself,' she said, edging his hand from the handle. 'I'm not a weakling.' She noticed he had a carrier bag with him. 'What have you bought?'

'A bucket and spade for Alfie. It's a present.'

'Nice thought but he's a bit young, don't you think?'

'They'll keep,' he said. 'How did you get on? You sound edgy.'

'Very well. I have the family solicitor's name, address and phone number. She suggested I get in touch with him.'

'Good. Did she give you a reason?'

She nodded. 'Bryn inherited shares in the slate business from his father, who was a first-born son of Bryn's grandfather, who was the first-born son of—'

He held up a hand. 'I get it.'

She continued, 'Originally, the first owner of the slate business had three sons and each of them were left shares in the business when they married and had a son, and each first-born son inherited his father's shares.'

'I suppose daughters and other sons went without,' said Jack.

'According to her, they were helped financially in other ways. Bryn's shares will go to Alfie but are held in a trust until he's twenty-one. The solicitor and she were trustees until Bryn reached twenty-one. Presumably, I'll be a trustee now Bryn is dead and until Alfie is twenty-one.' She paused.

'It's a good job that the papers say the trustee is his mother and not Mrs Bryn Jones, his wife,' said Jack.

'Yes. You're still convinced Bryn was a bigamist?' she said.

He nodded. 'Did you mention it to her?'

'No, I thought she had enough to cope with. I'm going into town again on Monday and will be visiting the Central Library to look up the birth records for my employer, so I'll see if I can check out Bryn's details at the same time. It's not that I don't trust you. I just want to see it in writing for myself.' She stopped and gazed in a shop window. 'Bryn's mother wanted me to stay the night, but I told her I couldn't. I did say Alfie and I would visit in August.'

'That's when Milly is coming with the twins. I dropped into the teashop and spoke to her mother-in-law. Jimmy was there. They hadn't seen each other for two years. He told me that Milly had thought it would be nice for him and his mother to have some time alone, just the two of them.'

'I must drop by and see Milly and the twins when I get back to Liverpool. Although, if I manage to get to church tomorrow, most likely I'll see them there.' She paused. 'How is it you know Jimmy and Milly?'

'I know Milly through Kyle, one of the guardians at the orphanage. He and his wife and children have a house on Newsham Drive, part of my beat. He talks to me about the lads in the orphanage. He worries about how they'll cope after leaving the orphanage.'

'He's a caring person. I know Kyle Anderson from when he was a volunteer there, when I was a lot younger, after my mother died.'

He said, 'So your father was a sailor.'

'Yeah,' she said.

Jack changed the subject. 'As for Bryn being a bigamist... Mention it as a possibility to the solicitor and the vicar. Hopefully, they'll be able to give you some advice.'

She nodded, thinking he's telling me what to do again. Still, it shouldn't do her and Alfie any harm to take his advice. 'So, are we going down to the beach now?' She had the sea in her sight and quickened her pace.

They arrived at the front and Jack took her to where there was a slope that led down onto the sands. He found them a spot where the beach was flat and not crowded. Then from his haversack, he removed a couple of gaily coloured beach towels and spread them on the sand.

Wordlessly, she unbuckled Alfie and sat down with him on one of the towels. Jack put the metal bucket and spade on the sand and then, having removed his rucksack and placed it where Eliza could use it as a back rest, he sat down himself and removed his shoes and socks, and turned up the bottom of his trouser legs several times.

'Are you going for a paddle?' she asked.

'I'll need to fetch some water for the moat,' he said. 'Besides, I like the feel of sand between my toes.'

She could not prevent a smile, because she liked going bare-footed when she could, but she was not about to remove her stockings in front of him. But she did remove her shoes, and Alfie's shoes and socks, so he could feel the sand between his toes and possibly have a paddle while being held upright. She realised that Jack would have to be trusted for the paddle. Suddenly, she thought of Bryn as a little boy in one of the photos. He had most likely paddled here, and she felt sad, despite her suspicions of him being a bigamist. Why had he married her? He had been the one to rush the wedding. Could it really have been for love or did he have another reason for leaving his wife?

She turned to Jack and said, 'Why do you think Bryn married me if he already had a wife?'

He stared at her. 'You're not bad looking, you know? In fact, you're quite attractive.'

She felt awkward and couldn't meet his gaze. 'Are you saying he only married me for my looks?'

He didn't answer. She sighed. Would she ever understand what had been going through Bryn's mind? Everywhere she turned there were more questions, and no answers.

She watched Jack for a moment, while he pulled faces at Alfie, and suddenly found herself wondering if she was perhaps seeing Jack too often.

And then she told herself that her son needed a man in his life. Besides, Jack had not made any amorous advances to her. He seemed genuinely fond of Alfie.

'You look deep in thought,' said Jack. 'I should have bought two spades so you could help dig.'

'I can do that with my hands,' she said, thinking Jack wanted to build a castle. Did men ever grow up?

'No, you have the spade and I'll use my hands, they're bigger than yours.' He took one of her hands and placed its palm against his. She felt warmth spread up her arm and she pulled her hand away. Why was his touch making her feel hot and bothered?

'All right,' she said breathlessly, picking up the spade he had dropped. 'Let's get on with it.' Suddenly, she remembered building a sandcastle with her grandfather on the beach in Anglesey.

They proceeded to dig, and then Jack called a halt and began to form the pile of sand into a castle with a moat. She suggested he fetch some water and she some pebbles to prevent the water sinking into the sand. She decided to remove her stockings, so she could feel the sand between her toes. Alfie had fallen asleep on the towel, so she placed him in the pushchair, not chancing leaving him alone. She pushed him along the beach, pausing only to pick up shells and pebbles, some of which were lovely: purest white, speckled cream and brown, black, sandstone. She wondered if the latter had been washed from the Wirral coastline, or even Liverpool and its environs, by the Mersey and Dee into the Irish Sea; so many buildings were built using the local sandstone. She was having fun, something she had not had in ages.

Back at the sandcastle, and having placed the pebbles along the bottom of the moat, she watched as Jack poured in the water, but more was needed. Eliza picked up the bucket and said she would fetch more water while Jack kept his eye on Alfie. She was revelling in paddling in the sea, but then she heard Jack calling so she filled the bucket and walked carefully, so as not to spill it. Alfie was crying and Jack had him in his arms, trying to calm him. 'He's hungry,' she said, and suggested they go and have a cup of tea and a snack at the tearoom. Jack agreed, despite the sandcastle not being finished; the tide was coming in and soon their castle would be washed away. 'Do you want to keep any of these shells or pebbles, Eliza?' he asked.

'Why not?' she said. 'In years to come I can show them to Alfie and tell him about this day. The day he met his grandmother.' She placed the pebbles and shells in the biscuit tin that she had used to bring some nibbles in, which were now in her shopping bag, and placed it behind Alfie's pillow.

Cathy was delighted to see them and she gave Alfie a cuddle. 'He's a sweetie,' she said. 'Milly and the twins will love him. Jimmy's gone fishing and will be sorry to have missed you.'

Eliza thought it would be fun having the twins and Milly to spend time with her in August. She hoped that if she was in church tomorrow, she wouldn't be cross with her for walking out with Bryn and spending less time with her.

As for now, she asked Cathy if there was somewhere she could give Alfie a feed and change him. She showed her to a small back room and Eliza almost nodded off as she fed her son. Once she had changed his nappy and drunk a cup of tea, she was relieved when Jack said that they would have to leave straightaway. She was tired out and, on the train, dozed off with Alfie on her knee, only waking up when they reached Chester and Jack took Alfie from her and fastened him in the pushchair as they had to change trains. But after Alfie woke up in Liverpool and they left the train, he began to grizzle when they were on the tram and didn't stop. She was at her wits' end, as she couldn't think what the matter with him was. She had fed and changed him, and he really wasn't due a feed yet. Once back home, she took him upstairs while Jack talked to Amelia downstairs. She changed him again and sat on the sofa, eyes closed, wishing she could stay there and doze off, but she had to go downstairs and make omelettes for supper. She could hear a noise and opened her eyes and saw that Alfie was sucking his thumb. Suddenly, she remembered a discussion going on in the hospital between a couple of experienced mothers about dummies and whether it was right to use them or not. She remembered something being said about it affecting the upper jaw and the front teeth when they came through. One of the mothers had said they were rightly called comforters in America. Was it for situations like now that dummies could give both babies and mothers comfort and rest?

Eliza glanced at her watch and saw that the corner shop would still be open, and it possibly sold dummies. She placed Alfie in his cot, covered him up snugly and slipped the toy that Glyn had given him next to him and hurried downstairs.

'I've put Alfie to bed. He's still a bit grizzly but I need to go to the corner shop. I won't be long, and I'll make the omelettes when I get back.'

'Is there anything I could do to help?' asked Jack. 'You must be tired out.'

'All that fresh sea air and the journey there and back,' said Amelia.

'Tired out…' murmured Eliza. 'Could that be what's wrong with him?'

'He could be overtired,' said Jack. 'It can happen to us if we do too much, and are out of our routine and can't relax.'

'That makes sense,' said Eliza. 'I'll skip going to the shop and see how he gets on this evening, through the night.'

She smiled and went into the kitchen. Jack and Amelia followed her and offered help.

Eliza was about to refuse and then decided that would be stupid when she was so tired. She gave Jack a couple of large potatoes to peel and dice. Amelia shredded cabbage and an onion thinly,

94

and she mixed dried egg powder with milk and grated cheese. A teaspoon of mixed herbs and two slices of chopped bacon, all mixed together and then split into three.

Eliza trusted Jack to cook the first one while Amelia set the table and she went upstairs to stand outside the bedroom door and listen. She could just hear a slurping murmur and, puzzled, she opened the door and went inside. As she was doing her best to stay out of Alfie's vision, it was difficult to see what he was doing. Then she saw that he was sucking the toy animal's ear. For a moment she was torn about what to do, suspecting that if she drew the toy away from his mouth, he would yell the place down, but how hygienic was it to leave him sucking a fluffy ear? The desire to eat her supper and have a drink of tea in peace won the day and she left the room, knowing she would soon be back because she was ready to collapse into bed.

'He's nursing a toy and will be asleep within half an hour, I think,' she said, sitting at the table and eyeing the plate in front of her. The omelette was slightly brown and crisp around the edges, but it was tasty, and she complimented the chef.

'I enjoy cooking,' he said. 'I take my turn at home when I'm on early shift.'

Afterwards they had a cup of coffee with a slice of bara-brith in front of the newly lit fire in the lounge, and talked over their day, and then Jack said, 'I'll have to go.'

Eliza saw him out and thanked him for his company.

'It was fun,' he said. 'See you soon.'

He waved from the gate, and she stayed in the doorway until he was out of sight. Then she went inside and straight to the kitchen. She washed up and tidied, and then made mugs of cocoa and took them into the lounge. She asked Amelia how far she had got with the book she was working on.

'Not far enough. I had two phone calls, one from Tom's nephew Theo, asking if it would be all right if his girlfriend came with him, as well as his cousin Dilys. What could I say but yes. I felt sure you could cope with an extra one. The girls will have to double up, but I doubt they'll complain. Dilys, who is Tom's niece, is an easy-going girl.'

'When will they be coming?'

'Towards the end of summer,' Amelia replied.

Eliza could only hope it wasn't the week in August when Milly planned on being in Colwyn Bay. Recalling that she had not mentioned this to Amelia, she did so, and it was agreed that she could have one week's paid holiday – and her wages were settled at five pounds a week, and her flat would be rent-free. This was very generous, and Eliza thanked her profusely, and decided to mention about her mother-in-law possibly coming to Liverpool for Christmas. 'I'll need to book her into a B&B in plenty of time,' she added.

'She can come here,' said Amelia. 'The poor woman has been through a lot, and Theo and company will have left by then, so there'll be room. We Jones widows must stick together.'

Eliza felt a moment of unease and wondered if this was the time to tell her that she might just not be a Jones widow but decided to leave well alone for now. She needed to see the records for herself. She thanked her again and thought that Alfie's first Christmas was going to be very special, although it was a good way off yet.

CHAPTER FIFTEEN

Eliza would have overslept the following morning if Amelia had not roused her, having heard Alfie wailing. She thanked her and then saw to Alfie's needs and dressed him in his best blue-and-white romper suit, little white socks and blue strapped shoes. She had little choice about what she could wear and wished she had been sensible and not paddled in the sea. She was going to have to wear her best clothes after ironing them dry at the bottom, as she couldn't wear the ones from the jumble sale. Tomorrow she would have to spend some of her precious savings and use the few clothing coupons she still possessed to buy some new clothes. It wasn't until she was dressed that she came across the maternity skirt and top she had worn the night she had gone into labour. They were clean so must have been washed in the hospital. There was plenty of material in them so there was nothing stopping her taking them in and using them for everyday wear; that meant she would only need to buy one new skirt and a couple of blouses tomorrow. Feeling less miserable, she went downstairs and made a cup of tea and a couple of slices of toast. She was sparing with the butter and checked the pantry and the cool box for what she needed to buy tomorrow. She was roasting a breast of lamb stuffed and rolled for their main meal today and there would be dripping left from that, which could be used to spread on toast for breakfast tomorrow; the butter left could be used to make a pie or jam tarts with the little damson jam that was left in the jar in the pantry. That decision made, she went and spoke to Amelia about what she planned for that day's meal and told her that she was off to St Margaret's.

'I'll see you later, dear,' Amelia said. 'I'm going to listen to the service on the radio. It's coming from Shrewsbury Cathedral, which was not far from where I was brought up. It's very old, unlike Liverpool's which, I believe, is still not finished.'

'It has a wonderful sense of space inside, though, and a great view outside, built as it is on St James Mount,' Eliza could not resist saying. Then, having strapped Alfie in his pushchair, she left the house.

The sun was shining but there was a cool breeze sending the white clouds scurrying across the patches of blue sky. Eliza hummed 'All Things Bright and Beautiful' as she walked in the direction of St Margaret's. Alfie gazed up at her with his blue eyes and the blanket covering his legs lifted slightly as he kicked his feet. 'I wonder what you'll be when you grow up,' she said, thinking that it was going to be so much more difficult for him to find decent employment with no father or close male relatives to help him out. Of course, he had an uncle – or was that a half-uncle? Glyn was Bryn's half-brother, but he might make the army his career and, besides, could she trust him? There were other men who might be prepared to take an interest in their plight, besides Jack: there was the vicar, and perhaps Jimmy and Kyle, although those three had children of their own and jobs that were demanding. Then she remembered what Alfie's grandmother had said about the shares in the slate company. She supposed he could find employment there. Although, at least, he should be getting an income from his shares – but how much would that be? Even so, that did not answer the need for having a man in his life: someone who was there for him, who shared some of his interests and would listen to him; one who was also fun to be with and didn't talk down to him. One whom she could get along with and respect, and have fun with and rely on. She smiled as her thoughts went to the name of the man at the top of her list. There were questions she'd like to ask him, but she hesitated because he might resent them. She sighed and clamped down on her thoughts because they had reached the main road, and she could see Milly and the twins on the other side, outside St

Margaret's. She remembered the first time she had seen Milly and the twins, Mary and her brother – was his name John or George? She could never remember. It had been in church, at the family service, and the twins were toddlers, and despite their age, Mary was attempting to keep her brother under control. Milly had given up and was ignoring them. Later Eliza was to discover that Mary was the elder by twenty minutes and, unlike her brother, had appeared to know how to behave in company from birth. Yet it was him who was the favourite with his Irish relatives. In particular Milly's aunts, all but one, seemed to like the opposite sex to have a bit of the devil in them. Unlike Milly and her mother, who had married an English protestant sailor of whom they saw little. The day had come when the marriage was annulled and Milly went to live with her English grandmother in Liverpool, whereas her mother had married a Dubliner and settled in Dublin, far from the family farm.

By the time she had crossed the road, Milly and the twins had vanished inside the church. Eliza had planned on sitting at the end of a pew furthest away from the main aisle, not wanting to be the focus of the eyes of all those entering the church. She wanted to be able to say a prayer and settle down before being besieged by people who would recognise her. Some would be wanting to ask questions about the baby and his father. But she should have realised that Jimmy or his mother would have telephoned and told Milly that Eliza and her baby had been, with Jack Molyneux, in the tearoom. They would have some idea why they had been there: no doubt it was in connection with the incident that had happened a week or so ago in Colwyn Bay. Milly would be agog to know the whole story.

'Hello, stranger!' hailed Milly, as Eliza entered the church. 'I hear you've been busy while we haven't seen sight or sound of you.' She gazed down at the baby.

'Yeah, this is Alfie.' Eliza smiled at her son. 'I married a soldier, who has since been killed in the Middle East,' she said. Her voice trembled and there were tears in her eyes. 'I gave birth during the May Blitz and the flat where I lived was set alight, so I was also homeless. But I was fortunate in meeting someone who introduced me to a widow, who took me on as a lodger and gave me a job.'

'We were up in Lancashire, helping Kyle and his wife Jane and some others with the orphans who were evacuated.' She paused. 'I'm so sorry to hear about your husband, Eliza. What awful luck. I'm glad to hear you've found somewhere to live, as well as a job. I presume the widow likes children.'

'Yeah, she's really nice.' Eliza paused. 'Are you back from Lancashire for good now? And what about Kyle and the orphans?'

'They'll be returning when the war's over. He drops in at the orphanage now and again because it's being used by the homeless for now, and new homes will have to be provided for them.'

'I see,' Eliza said.

'Where are you living now?'

'I'm living in Newsham Drive. I'll tell you the rest of the story another time.'

'You can come and sit with us,' said Milly.

Eliza shook her head. 'I want to be alone to pray this first time back.'

'OK! See you soon,' said Milly.

Eliza watched her and the twins walk down the aisle for a moment and then headed to the place she had decided on earlier, where she would be partly concealed by a pillar. She kneeled and bowed her head and started with the Lord's Prayer, before saying her personal prayers. She did not sit up until she heard the vicar welcome the congregation and then announce the first hymn, which was 'The King of Love My Shepherd Is'. The choir started them off and she began to sing, rocking the pushchair, as the congregation joined in and the singing swelled. Her heart lifted and she was aware of the smell of incense. She enjoyed the sermon and planned on telling the vicar so, thinking she would wait where she was until most of the congregation had left. She wanted to speak to him about Alfie's christening and, if she felt calm enough, she resolved to ask him about bigamy, though she didn't let her mind dwell on that for now.

Twenty minutes later her chance came to talk to him alone, despite one of the churchwardens and a sidesman being around, still putting books away and tidying up in general. The vicar suggested they went into his vestry to talk.

'I don't want to keep you long,' she said as soon as they were in the vestry.

'Is this about this handsome young fellow's christening?'

'Partly,' she said, sitting on the chair he offered and placing her hands on her knees, which were trembling. 'Some of my questions are complicated. Am I right in presuming that even though I wasn't married in church Alfie can still be baptised into the Church of England?'

'Yes.' He gave her a close look. 'But I have a feeling that there is something deeper behind your question than just you not marrying in church. A registry office wedding is legal in law and this church accepts that. The law is there to protect your rights to what is due to you as a wife. Is it that you want to talk about inheritance, your husband's life insurance and what pension you could be entitled to as his widow?'

She was dumbstruck for several moments and then she took a deep breath. 'Not exactly. What if my husband had been married before and not divorced?' she said in a tight voice, removing her hands from her knees and twisting them together.

'You mean what if he was a bigamist?' he said gently.

'Horrible thought. I feel betrayed.' She looked away, not quite able to meet his gaze. 'It's what Jack Molyneux thinks.'

The vicar straightened up from where he had been leaning against a cupboard. 'Does he have proof?'

'I mentioned to him that my employer wants me to trace her husband's ancestry and that's when he mentioned the records for births, marriages and deaths and I remembered that they are said to be kept in Somerset House, which is in London.'

'Did he mention having been to London?'

She shook her head. 'And I didn't mention Somerset House.'

'Neither of you would need to visit Somerset House,' said the vicar. 'There would be records either in the church where they married or in a registry office.'

'Of course,' said Eliza. 'What about divorce?'

'They'd be in the court records I should think,' he said. 'Although, if he'd married and then divorced, I can't see why he couldn't have told you. He could still marry you if he produced evidence of the divorce, not doing so if he had been married before would make your marriage illegal.'

'I presumed that Jack knew exactly where to look, him being a policeman,' she said. 'Where does it leave me if Bryn married me bigamously?'

He looked sympathetic. 'Then his first wife gets everything, unless he made a later will naming you as the mother of his son Alfie. You really need to see a solicitor.'

'I already have the details of his family solicitor. I must phone him,' she said unhappily. 'I don't doubt his first wife has been receiving money from the army and that means they must have her address. I can't understand him doing such a thing. He was so eager to marry me before going overseas. I believed he really loved me.' She put her hands to her face, attempting to conceal her tears and fury. 'Did he have any thought to how things would turn out if he survived the war? Would his first wife have given him up so easily?' She bit down on her lip. 'I wish I knew their story, as I think I'd feel a little less confused. Does she hate me? Does she blame me? Does she want me to suffer? Does she still love him?'

'Don't torture yourself,' he said. 'It'll do you no good.'

'What if she tries to kidnap Alfie again and, this time, she leaves the country with him?'

'You'll be on your guard?' he said.

'Of course, and so will Jack,' she said, the thought of him making her feel calmer.

'Well, I pray it all gets sorted out. Alfie can be christened here in church, anyway,' he said.

She brightened, glad to have something to look forward to. 'Can I have four godparents for him?'

'If that is what you want, and they are willing to make the important vows and keep them.'

'Thank you,' she said, thinking she should be able to keep Olive and Milly happy, and she'd like Jack and Kyle to be Alfie's godfathers if they agreed. Most likely Olive and Milly would begin to think about what to wear, and what they had suitable in their wardrobes to doll up for a special occasion. They could buy some lace, shorten a dress, and use the scrap material to make a frill. She began to feel excited, thinking she would need to buy Alfie a christening gown and something new for herself, as she still had clothing coupons. She hadn't bought any new clothes during her pregnancy, as she had only made herself a smock or two and worn old skirts with elasticated waists. She realised the vicar was speaking and that time was going on. 'Thank you for listening to me. I'm not really a hysterical woman.'

'No, but you've been through a lot. Let's say a prayer now.' He placed a hand on her head. 'Dear Lord, bless Eliza and help her to keep calm, and provide her with what she needs now and over the next few weeks, bodily, spiritually and mentally, in the name of Our Saviour Jesus Christ. Amen.'

She said the 'Amen'. Then she thanked him and shook his hand. 'I'll have to speak to my friends before I can suggest a date for the christening,' she added. 'I'd best be going now.' She was thinking she had to rush to get the meat in the oven.

Outside she found Milly, waiting for her, who said, 'I've sent the twins on ahead, so we can talk.'

'I haven't much time,' said Eliza, 'but do you want to walk with me and then come back to go home?' Milly fell into step beside her. Eliza proceeded to tell Milly about her hasty wedding, Bryn's departure, her discovery that she was pregnant and her delight, then the bombing, her injury, being taken to hospital after having gone into early labour, how she regained consciousness and was handed Alfie for the very first time. Then she told her of the visit from a man pretending to be Bryn, how Alfie had been kidnapped... and on and on.

Milly most likely already knew through the grapevine what had happened in Colwyn Bay with her mother-in-law, so she skipped over that part. Then she paused. 'I was speaking to the vicar about having Alfie christened and asking about godparents. I'd like you to be one of his godmothers – what do you say?'

Milly smiled. 'All right, yes, I'd love to.'

'Olive will be the other and I'm going to ask Jack and Kyle to be his godfathers. I need to ask them first, before arranging a date.'

'If there's anything I can help you with, in the meantime, let me know,' said Milly.

Eliza jumped at the offer. 'I must go into town tomorrow to visit the Central Library. It's work, so could you possibly look after Alfie for me?' She felt certain she could trust Milly.

'It'll be a pleasure,' said Milly, and smiled down at Alfie.

'I'll bring him to your house,' said Eliza.

That agreed, they parted and went to their separate homes.

CHAPTER SIXTEEN

Eliza had asked Amelia for permission to use the phone to ring the solicitor and now she was speaking to Mr Davies, who told her that Mrs Jones Senior had informed him of Eliza's visit with her grandson Alfie. He paused. 'What can I do for you, Mrs Jones?'

'That's my problem,' she replied. She took a deep breath. 'It could be that I'm not legally Mrs Bryn Jones.'

There was a long silence before he asked, 'What do you mean?'

She told him her story and heard him tut-tutting. When she finished, he exclaimed, 'Quite extraordinary. Although I have read in the newspapers of cases of servicemen committing bigamy. I must speak to Constable Molyneux. I presume you haven't mentioned the subject of bigamy to Bryn's mother?'

'No. I thought she'd been through enough for the moment.'

He agreed. 'She is delighted to have a grandson,' he said.

'Yes,' said Eliza. 'What I want to know is will Alfie still inherit Bryn's shares in the slate business?'

'If enough evidence is produced to prove that you married him in good faith, when and where, and that he is truly Alfie's father.'

'I can have my wedding certificate copied and produce evidence of where we spent our wedding night before he left to join his regiment. As well as Alfie's birth certificate,' she said.

'Excellent,' he said. 'And if you could let me have Constable Molyneux's address?'

'Of course, but I'll drop into the police station and give him your phone number. That way you can tell him what you want.'

Mr Davies agreed and, after bidding each other good morning, she ended the call, feeling better after having spoken to him and knowing what to do next. She went and readied herself to call in at the police station, before catching a tram into town to visit the Central Library and seeing what help she could get there for her research. Amelia had still not found her husband Thomas Jones's birth certificate, but she did have their marriage certificate, which provided his father's name, place of residence and occupation. What she really needed were copies of his father's birth and marriage certificates. He was another Thomas Jones but at least he had a middle name, David, just like Bryn's father.

Eliza expressed some breast milk into a feeding bottle, and placed that and a couple of nappies in a bag, strapped Alfie in his pushchair and set off to Milly's. In her handbag she also put a notebook and pencil, as well as her purse, ration books and clothing coupons. When she needed to cross West Derby Road, she spotted Jack on the other side, waiting to cross to her side. She waited until there was a space in the traffic and then approached him.

'Hello, Jack, I need to have a few words with you,' she said.

'Well, hurry up. I'm on duty.'

'I'm in a hurry, too,' she said, unclasping her handbag and handing him the sheet of paper with Mr Davies's name, address and phone number. She explained quickly about her conversation with him that morning.

He pocketed the paper. 'OK, I'll deal with it.'

'I've something else to ask you but you're working and I'm off into town to do some research, but first I need to take Alfie to Milly's.'

'If it's about your employer's husband, you should talk to Rambling Rosie. She's his cousin and could help you. She's probably out now, but you're bound to catch her in sometime. I'll give you her address if you decide to call on her. I'll let her know about you if I see her on her travels.'

They parted, only for Eliza to call after him that he hadn't told her Rosie's address. Besides, she wanted to know why he called her Rambling Rosie. Could it be that she was getting senile and had started wandering? She realised she wasn't going to get her answer now. He could not have heard her, because he continued walking. She decided to leave it for now, crossed the road and went up Lombard Street to Milly's house. She was on her own, the twins having gone to school. She had found some of their old toys and placed them on the sofa. She sat there and, hesitantly, Eliza placed Alfie on her lap, and produced his bottle and left the nappies in a bag on a chair. Then she kissed her son and thanked Milly and, reluctant to leave, she lingered in the doorway.

'Go!' whispered Milly. 'Trust me. He'll be fine.'

Eliza left and felt anxious again, as she heard him wail when she opened the front door. She would have gone back to him but didn't want to give the impression that she didn't trust Milly, a mother of twins, so she whispered a quick prayer and left.

The library had a little bomb damage, but the museum a short distance away was badly damaged. She was aware that most of the exhibits had been transferred to underground caves or mines in the mountains of Wales. She went into the library and when she asked for the Archives, she was directed upstairs. Once there, she was told there was little they could do to help her, as she did not have enough information. The birth records for Liverpool would be of little help to her, as she already knew that Thomas Jones had been born in Chester; also, with a name like Jones, she would have real difficulties.

Eliza decided that Thomas's cousin Rosie was her only hope, so she headed in the direction of TJ Hughes in London Road to go shopping for a new skirt, a couple of blouses and a jacket for the christening. She eventually bought a floral skirt in red and green, and a cream cotton blouse with a frill just above the bust and long sleeves; the other blouse was grass-green rayon with short sleeves and buttoned all down the front. She couldn't find a jacket she liked that she could afford, so she did not buy one but caught a tram to Breck Road, where she bought sausages and bread, and then went past St John's Church. She walked along Richmond Terrace, which came out onto Whitefield Road, almost opposite Norwood Grove, where she had once lived, and tears pricked her eyes as she remembered those who had died. She blinked them back and hurried on to where Milly lived, and in no time she was there, knocking on the door with her fist.

She heard hurrying footsteps and the door opened to reveal Milly with Alfie in her arms, a wooden train engine pressed between them. 'You're back earlier than I thought you'd be. I've had lunch. I'll go and get the pushchair if you take Alfie.'

Eliza reached out for her son eagerly, and he came to her, the train slipping to the floor.

Milly returned with the pushchair and picked up the train. 'John said he could keep the train. You've missed the kids. They would have stayed longer playing with Alfie but would have been late for afternoon school. Mary would like to take him for a walk in his pushchair sometime, if that was all right with you.'

Eliza was reminded of being told that Alfie had been found in a doll's pram when he was only a week or so old. The girl who owned the pram must have been the daughter of Bryn and her mum his other wife – no, his legal wife. She felt a sinking feeling in her stomach and her heartbeat quickened.

'What's wrong?' asked Milly. 'Don't you trust Mary?'

Eliza put a hand to her head, not able to think things through right now. 'Of course, I trust her. I'm very fond of Mary. If it was a weekday, it would have to be about half past four and she'd have to bring him home by half-five.'

'The summer holidays will be here soon,' said Milly.

'And you'll be going to Colwyn Bay in August, and so will me and Alfie,' Eliza said.

'Me and the kids are staying the whole of August, and Jimmy will pick us up,' said Milly. 'I'd like to offer you and Alfie a lift one way or the other, but the car's not big enough.'

'I understand,' said Eliza. 'But we'll see each other there.'

Milly nodded. 'Have you spoken to Kyle and Jack yet about Alfie's christening?'

'No, can you give me Kyle's address up North?'

'Of course, he's been back several times when the call for help for Liverpool went out. I'm sure he'll be willing to come for a christening. He's fond of kids, as you know.'

Eliza knew that from her time in the orphanage. 'What's his wife like? I've never met her.'

'I think you'll like her. She used to live in Ormskirk. Her daughter Lily is only a baby, but her son is three or four, I can't remember exactly.'

'Anyway, I'd best be going,' said Eliza, only to pause on the pavement. 'Do you know a woman called Rambling Rosie?'

Milly chuckled. 'I know of her. She's quite a character. I suppose Jack told you about her. She's a childless widow but lives in a house bigger than this one, more the size of some of those in Norwood Grove, where you had your flat.'

Eliza nodded. 'Do you know where she lives?'

'I don't know the number, but you're bound to see her sooner or later. She's not called Rambling Rosie for nothing, but be on your guard. Jack arrested her once. She pushes a small handcart and pinches stuff. Overall, people feel sorry for her but there was a woman who complained to the police.' Milly waved, went inside and closed the door.

As Eliza walked home, she wondered how she would recognise Rambling Rosie if she were to see her. She was tempted to ask Amelia more about her, but then recalled that her employer had not seemed to approve of her husband's cousin. She thought again about the little toy pram and the fact that Bryn must have had a daughter with his first wife. Only wife. What did that mean for her and Alfie?

CHAPTER SEVENTEEN

Eliza was still wondering about Rambling Rosie at the end of July, when Jack finally called to talk to her about his conversation with the solicitor, Mr Davies. She had not seen him for ages and said as much when she invited him upstairs to her sitting room, where she had strapped Alfie into his feeding chair. She was now giving him some Farley's Rusks mashed up in milk in a bowl as she had felt something sharp when she was breastfeeding him and discovered he had a tooth. She did not intend to put him on solids because he wasn't quite three months old, but it could be that he needed more than milk to satisfy his hunger. She had been advised by a couple of experienced young mothers to add crushed rusks to his bottle if he still appeared hungry. It could be that her diet or theirs was lacking the necessary nutrients due to shortages and rationing.

'I've been away on a course,' Jack said. 'You could have asked at the station for me, and they'd have told you where I was.'

'What for? Are you getting promoted?' she asked. 'You deserve to, after all the work you've put in on Alfie's case. I even wondered if you'd been moved on to another case. I've missed you. I had something important to ask you. And it wasn't only that I've been wondering how you got on with the solicitor. I haven't heard a word from him. I'd like you to be one of Alfie's godfathers.'

'I'd like that,' he said, smiling. 'When will the christening be?'

'I'm not sure yet. I'll let you know, though, in plenty of time.'

'Good.' He rubbed his hands together. 'Thanks for asking me. But you're right, I have come to see you about the solicitor,' he said, placing his helmet on the floor next to a chair and going over to Alfie. 'You've really grown, milad.'

'He'll be three months old on the fifth of August.'

'How time flies,' he said.

'More reason for this matter to be sorted out before any more time passes.'

'Anyway, Mr Davies wants me to visit him and take the copies of the marriage certificates with me. I had the impression that he didn't believe me and that I could just want to blacken Bryn's name. We had a bit of an argument, and I told him I needed to consult you first and show you the certificates.'

Eliza took a deep breath and despite having felt the same as the solicitor at one time, she said, 'The nerve of the man.'

'I also told him that I couldn't visit him at the drop of a hat, nor would I post them. I couldn't risk them going missing in the post. He told me that your affairs would be held up. Anyway, before I go and visit him in Colwyn Bay for my yearly holiday with Mam and my sister, I decided to not delay, but bring them to show you.'

'You're going to Colwyn Bay?' she said. 'When? Me and Alfie will be going the second week in August to stay with Alfie's grandmother.'

'Were you wanting a lift?' he asked. 'We could probably fit you and Alfie in the car with a squeeze.'

Her spirits rose despite being about to see proof of Bryn's duplicity. 'Thank you. I'd enjoy spending time with you, Jean, and your mother. What about your pets?'

'A neighbour will look after the cat, but we're taking my dog with us. The B&B we always go to allows dogs, if they don't go on the beds.' He paused and took a deep breath. 'Little as you want to read the wedding certificate of his first marriage and their daughter's birth certificate, here they are.' He took a brown envelope from his pocket and removed two certificates, leaving her wedding certificate in the envelope and handed the certificates to her with a sympathetic expression.

She gulped and hesitated before unfolding them. The words seemed to blur as she read the wedding certificate and she felt sick and furious. The ceremony had taken place in the Welsh Congregational Church in Kensington, Liverpool, on 30 August 1936 between Bryn Jones, aged twenty-two, and Ada Meredith, aged twenty-four. Eliza's gaze slid down to the bottom, to the name of the witnesses: Roger Jones and Mrs Megan Jones.

'Were the witnesses married, do you think?' she asked, placing a trembling finger on the last two names.

'What does it matter?' he said harshly. 'The question is: are they related to Bryn and the rest of the Joneses?' he replied. 'Notice, though, that Bryn's brother is not one of the witnesses and that makes me wonder if he was even at the wedding – or away with the Territorials training. Many of those in positions of power believed there would be war with Germany sooner or later, so he mightn't have known about the wedding until much later. I think we can be sure that his mother wasn't there. The wedding took place in Liverpool, and it looks like Ada was living in Kensington then. It gives her address. Maybe she was staying with a friend to be near Bryn. The church is no longer in use. It was damaged during the Blitz, so no church records. Fortunately, there was another record of the marriage, but I couldn't find anything about a divorce.'

She put the marriage certificate down and picked up the birth certificate, which stated that Ada Jones had given birth to a daughter, Gwendoline Ada Jones, on 31 March 1937, and the address given this time was in Little Wales. Father was named as Bryn Jones.

'The baby was premature,' said Eliza.

'Or they had jumped the gun,' Jack said quietly.

She glanced at him. 'Bryn must have been terribly disappointed it wasn't a boy.'

He nodded. 'They had been married four years when he asked you to marry him. Four years… They could have had another child in that time.'

'She miscarried. It's not unknown for that to happen to some women more than once. Poor woman!'

'You feel sorry for her. Yet she's probably the one who put you through agony when Alfie was kidnapped, and she tried to murder your mother-in-law,' said Jack. 'I'd still like to find her.'

'I wonder if she hates me.'

'I would have thought she'd hate Bryn, but then she could hate you both.'

'How must she feel now that Bryn's dead?'

'She would have been informed by the army, as next of kin,' said Jack. 'Now, when did Glyn get to know of Bryn's first marriage? He must have only known about you after he read your letter to Bryn and had received news that his brother was dead. If he knew by then about Bryn's marriage to Ada, it would mean he was aware that Bryn had two wives.'

'There's possibly another way he could have got to know that,' she said tersely.

'I think I know what you're going to say.' Jack's lips set in a straight line.

'The army paymaster must have sent her an allowance out of Bryn's pay since they married and that's why Bryn used to send a postal order once a month to me,' she said. 'It must have left him short, so there was some good in him.' Her voice shook.

'Don't be fooling yourself. He'd realised he was in a fix and would have to sort it out sooner rather than later if he had received your news that you had given birth to a son.' Jack sounded disbelieving and angry.

Eliza gasped. 'None of us are perfect!' She felt sad about Bryn dying not knowing he had a son. She also thought of something else. 'He would have been receiving an income from his shares in the slate company,' she said, 'so, he wouldn't be that hard up. If Glyn had known about him and Ada having married by then, and he visited her before visiting me in hospital,' said Eliza, 'he might have told her about me and Alfie.'

'We can only surmise,' he said. 'For all we know, he might have visited you first and then Ada.'

'We have to find them both,' she said.

'Glyn's back in the Middle East,' said Jack. 'He was involved in a crash after he landed in Egypt, and his commanding officer didn't know about it for a couple of days and didn't think of informing us. He's now on sick leave and his mother has been informed.'

'You're not going to tell me that he's going to convalesce at his mother's house while me and Alfie are there?' She shivered, thinking she would cancel staying there if so.

Jack placed an arm around her and hugged her. 'Don't be worrying. I'm going to be in Colwyn Bay at the same time, remember? Besides, you're forgetting his mother's bodyguard.'

She sagged against Jack, feeling safe with his arm around her, despite them not always seeing eye to eye. 'Why hasn't Glyn been arrested?'

'Because an arrest is up to the Colwyn Bay police, and they don't believe he tried to kill his mother. And hopefully, he'll lead us to Ada, if he has been in touch with her,' said Jack. 'Besides, she's just lost a son. It would be cruel to take the other one.'

'I agree,' said Eliza. 'But she doesn't love him the way she loved Bryn.'

'A lot of parents have favourites,' he said.

'And some have a child that gets picked on and blamed for anything that goes wrong,' she said.

Jack agreed but he had to go. He told her that he would be in touch about arranging what time they would pick her up to go to Colwyn Bay. 'It would be early,' he said, 'so be packed and ready to go.'

She saw him out, feeling a mixture of happiness and apprehension. She tucked Alfie up in his cot and read one of the poems from *When We Were Very Young*. She sang him a Sunday School chorus, 'This Little Light of Mine', and kissed his forehead and, leaving a small lamp on the chest of drawers on low, she left the room but kept the door ajar.

–

The following week Eliza had Olive and her mother over for lunch in the garden. She also told them about her getting a lift with Jack, his mother and sister in his car to Colwyn Bay.

'That will save you money,' said Olive's mother.

'I'm going to offer him money to pay towards the petrol,' Eliza said.

'Or you could pay the toll for the Mersey tunnel,' suggested Olive. 'Although, I doubt he'll take it. He fancies you,' she added in a teasing voice.

'You think so?' said Eliza, blushing, pleased at the thought but wondering why he had not given any sign of it. Or could it be that he thought it too early in the circumstances? 'I'm just a victim to him and when he went away on a course recently, he didn't let me know.'

'Men aren't like us women,' said Olive's mother, reaching for a jam tart, which was a real treat for her. Her husband loved jam, which was rationed because of its sugar content, so he claimed more than his fair share of it, as he was the breadwinner. 'They're secretive.'

Eliza decided to keep the news that Bryn had been a bigamist to herself. She asked Olive if she had found the perfect fella for her. She had seemed uncertain last time they had spoken.

'There is someone…' Olive said. 'But what man is perfect? I've been to the flicks with him twice and I enjoyed the films he chose. Next week we're going to Southport, but it'll be Saturday afternoon. The fair might be open then, although some of the rides and booths won't be because several of the men will have joined up or are working for the war effort in other ways. My Alan is an auxiliary fireman.'

'That's a dangerous job,' said Eliza.

'I worry about him, but now the bombing seems to be over for good here, I don't worry the same,' Olive said. 'He told me that he worries about me working in Ammunitions. I told him we've all got to do our bit.'

Eliza changed the subject, offering Olive a sausage butty, before giving a feeding bottle of National milk containing a crushed Farley's Rusk to Alfie. In a month or two he could start teething in earnest, and so he needed weaning off the breast and starting on solids. She remembered her mother telling her that Eliza's first teeth had come through early, at four months. Besides, it would be more convenient on the journey and while staying in Colwyn Bay. At the end of a lovely long lunch in the garden, Eliza thought she should remind her employer that she was making the journey to Colwyn Bay with Jack, his mother and sister the second week in August.

Amelia looked surprised. 'I remember us discussing you going to stay with your mother-in-law, but I don't recall you saying that you were going with Jack and his mother and sister. I'll miss you and Alfie, but I'll also miss Jack dropping in to see how we are on his beat. But then it's not long now until Theo, Dilys and his girlfriend come to stay.'

'We'll be well back by then,' said Eliza.

CHAPTER EIGHTEEN

Eliza heard Jean let out a sigh of pleasure. She was sitting beside her on the back seat. They had just driven past the signpost saying 'Welcome to Colwyn Bay' in English and Welsh. Alfie had taken to the girl who was giving him a bottle. His fingers spread starlike on the back of Jean's hand. Fortunately, Jack had changed his mind about taking his dog with them and a police mate had offered to look after him until Jack's return.

'Soon be there,' said Jack. 'Eliza, shall I drop you off first?'

'Thank you,' she replied. 'Then shall we meet up at the beach where we went down last time we were here?' she added.

'About two o'clock?' he suggested. 'Give us time to unpack and put our cossies on under our clothes.'

'Well, you can go,' said his mother. 'I'm going to have a wander around the shops and stretch me legs.'

'Whatever pleases you, Mam,' he said. 'Don't get lost.'

'As if I would,' she snorted.

No more was said until Jack pulled up at the kerb outside Alfie's grandmother's house. Jack opened the rear door and took Alfie from Eliza, while she stepped out. He handed Alfie back to her while he removed her luggage from the boot and the pushchair from the roof-rack. He placed both on the pavement and then unfolded the pushchair, so Eliza could strap him in, and he picked up her luggage and followed her to the front door. Eliza knocked and a few minutes later Mairi stood in the doorway. She looked past Eliza and Alfie to Jack.

'We weren't expecting you,' she said.

'I've only given Eliza a lift here, with my sister and mother,' he said, placing the luggage in the lobby.

'Is it them, Mairi?' called a man's voice.

'It is, indeed, sir,' she said.

Eliza caught sight of a man clinging to the open door of the sitting room. It was Glyn, and she wasn't sure what to say to him. Was he going to admit to what happened at the hospital? She was aware of Jack gazing over her shoulder. Jack pushed past her with an, 'Excuse me,' walked a little forward and placed the luggage beside the staircase. 'Will you be needing help taking these upstairs, sir? Word's going round that you've had an accident.' Jack had adopted a Welsh accent and Eliza realised he was trying to appear undercover.

'The girl will manage,' said Glyn, surprised. 'Your help is not needed.'

Jack turned and winked at Eliza as he passed her, and she joined in his subterfuge by pressing a coin into his hand, as if tipping him. 'Thank you, Taffy.'

'It's a pleasure, missus. Anytime.'

Jack left the house. Mairi closed the door after him and followed Eliza, pausing to pick up a Gladstone bag and carrying it upstairs. Eliza lifted the other bag and would have followed her, but that would have meant leaving Alfie behind, so she hung the bag from her arm and wheeled the pushchair into the sitting room in Glyn's wake. It was then that she noticed that his right arm was in a sling and, when he stepped aside for her to approach his mother, she saw that there were healing cuts, scratches and fading bruises on his face. She felt awkward around him, wondering how she could bring up the questions she wanted to ask and whether he would give her straight answers.

'You have been in the wars, Glyn,' she said.

'Is that meant to be a joke?' he asked with a twisted smile. 'And how do you know who I am?'

Eliza sensed he was scared but was trying to put on a brave face. 'To your first question, my parents used to say that to me if I came in with scraped knees or hands. I was a bit of a tomboy when I was young. To your second question… I recognise you, although

I thought at the time you had a look of Bryn.' She noticed his face had paled. 'I've been here before and saw the photographs of you and him. I begged your mother for one of them and she was kind enough to give it to me. In return I have brought her one of Alfie, her grandson.' Glad that she had remembered to bring it, having had it done when she had passed a photographer's shop on Breck Road, Eliza removed a brown paper parcel from her bag. She went over and gave it to Alfie's grandmother, who was dressed in black and was sitting in an armchair in front of the window. Eliza also wheeled Alfie over and placed the pushchair next to her armchair.

'Thank you, Eliza, for remembering,' she said, unwrapping the parcel and taking out a framed photo of Alfie dressed in his best romper suit, lying on a blanket draped over a chair. He was smiling and attempting to reach out to the toy dog that she was dangling a short distance from him. His grandmother kissed the glass of the photograph, before turning and smiling at Alfie. Eliza unstrapped him, lifted him out and placed him in his grandmother's arms. 'My goodness, he has grown,' said the older woman, 'and is the spitting image of his father.' Her voice broke on the last two words. Then she reached out and twisted a strand of Alfie's fair hair into a curl around her finger.

'You have brought light into my darkness, Eliza,' she said.

'May I hold my nephew?' asked Glyn, having joined the small group by the window.

'As long as you're gentle with him,' said his mother harshly, before Eliza could speak, 'and can manage to do so with one arm.'

Eliza felt an unexpected wave of sympathy for Glyn, thinking their grief for Bryn should have united them. She took Alfie from his grandmother, who tried to cling on to him, and Eliza hesitated before settling him comfortably in the crook of his uncle's left arm. Then Glyn smiled at Eliza and rocked his nephew gently. In that moment she saw an expression in his brown eyes that made her realise that he wanted to be friends and play a role in his nephew's life. She understood that there was a lot about him she did not know, but she would like to know, and that she mustn't judge him by Bryn's actions. She only left Alfie in his arms for a short while and then she took her son back.

Mairi came into the room with a tray and placed it on an occasional table. Eliza was glad of her company and, without being told, she sat in a chair and shifted Alfie on her left side and then accepted a cup of tea and a toasted teacake from Mairi with thanks. Glyn moved a dining chair and placed it next to Eliza. 'So, what are your plans now you're here? Maybe we could have an outing to Conway Castle.'

She tried a smile. 'Thanks, but let me think about it. I have friends here on holiday and will need to consult them.'

His mother said, 'That'll be Cathy's son's wife and twins you're talking about. She works at the tearoom.'

'Yeah,' answered Eliza, thinking that it was just as well Glyn and his mother thought that and were unaware that she had come here with a different family. 'Scousers love Wales. In fact, Liverpool has been known to be called the capital of Wales.'

'I didn't know,' said the older woman.

'It's because there's so many Welsh people living there,' Eliza said. 'We even have a neighbourhood called Little Wales. Isn't that true, Glyn? You've visited Liverpool, haven't you?'

He stared at Eliza with a hint of suspicion. 'Of course, you know I have. I'm in the Liverpool King's Regiment, and Bryn decided to join as well.'

'If you'd joined a Welsh regiment, he could have still been alive,' said his mother, tears in her voice.

'Perhaps, but then soldiers are at risk wherever they are sent,' he said. 'Don't you agree, Eliza?'

Her mouth was full of toasted teacake, so she did not answer immediately. Eventually, she said, 'Not only soldiers are at risk these days, but civilians as well. I was nearly killed during the May Blitz. There's evil in the world, and we must accept that and do what we can to eradicate it.'

'Someone tried to murder me,' said Alfie's grandmother in a heavy voice. 'And it was no German bomb, but a Welsh woman.

The police are no closer to catching her… I wish I hadn't started this conversation. I feel even more depressed.'

'You need to get out,' said Glyn. 'When did you last go to chapel?'

'I haven't been in the mood. God's let me down,' she said tightly. 'Some of my so-called friends visited me off and on for a while and then stopped.'

'They're probably overworked now,' Glyn said. 'It's high season.'

'Also, they mightn't know what to say,' said Eliza, thinking that feeling sorry for yourself did no good. 'When my mother was killed in an accident a few years after my dad was killed, people were at a loss how to talk to me and then I was put in the orphanage because my grandparents had died the year before.'

'Enough, Eliza,' said Mairi. 'You'll have us all crying next.'

'I cried, but not for long. After a while it upsets people and what's the point of that?'

'You were only a child and had your life all before you,' said Alfie's grandmother. 'I'm old and have lost those I cared for.'

Eliza was tempted to say that she had Glyn and now Alfie to watch grow up. Instead, she just said, 'I was told I must pull myself together, and I must do so more than ever now. And now you must get out and about, and take an interest in other people – it will enrich your life, and they'll take an interest in you.'

'Besides, how can you say that, Mrs Jones Senior?' said Mairi. 'You've still got a son and a grandson.'

Glyn had paled but now some of the colour returned to his face. 'Mairi is right. When Dad died, you told me to pull myself together, and in no time at all you married again and had Bryn who became the apple of your eye. I would have been pushed right out of the family if Bryn's father hadn't been a kind and sympathetic man. I was sorry when he died because I liked and respected him, and his death allowed you to spoil Bryn. I would have been a complete outsider if my father had not left me the house, allowing you to live here until you join him.' He ran out of breath at this point and his voice tailed off.

'Well, I never in all my born days heard such nonsense,' said his mother, placing a hand to her heart.

'You know it's true,' said Glyn quietly. 'I must apologise to Eliza and Mairi for the scene they've just witnessed. It must have been embarrassing for them.'

'I'd say enlightening,' Mairi said.

'Shall we have another cup of tea?' said Eliza. 'I'd like one and I'll make a pot if anyone else wants one.'

'I'll have one,' Glyn said. 'I'll make it. I know my way around the kitchen.'

'I want my doctor,' said his mother.

'I'll phone him,' said Glyn.

But his mother seized the phone, as she was closer to it, so he followed Eliza into the kitchen. 'I'd like us to be friends, Eliza. But first I have an apology to make to you.'

'You mean your pretending to be Bryn when you visited me in the maternity hospital?' she said.

He nodded. 'When I saw you and my nephew, I just couldn't bring myself to tell you that Bryn had been killed.'

'But you went too far when you kissed me.'

He reached up for the tea caddy. 'I thought it was what Bryn would have done and you'd think it was suspicious if I didn't kiss you.' He added, 'I enjoyed the kiss.'

She blushed. 'When I discovered that Bryn had been killed, I did wonder if you had pretended to be him for that reason, but you took a risk.'

'I know, but I had been told of your amnesia.'

'So, did you tell anyone else about me and Alfie?' She poured hot water into the teapot to warm it.

He scratched his head. 'I can't remember. I had so little time and didn't even get to see Mother.'

'Oh! What's your mother's Christian name, by the way? I've forgotten it.'

'Gladys! I haven't heard anyone call her that for ages.'

At that moment Mairi entered the kitchen. 'She told me to skedaddle, as she's talking to the receptionist at the surgery.'

'She's going to lay it on with a trowel,' he said. 'I think I'll go for a walk. Unless you ladies think that's cowardly of me?'

'I think we should all speak to the doctor,' said Mairi.

'I agree,' said Eliza. 'You should stay, Glyn. After all, you are on sick leave and the doctor should check your blood pressure and the like, and see how you're getting on.'

'It'll cost money,' he murmured, 'and soldiers don't get paid a lot.'

'He might not charge you a fee,' said Mairi. 'He's coming to see your mother and could be interested enough in your accident to check you out. Your mother's not short of money.'

'No, Dad left her everything, except the house, which is mine,' he repeated. 'He thought I'd marry one day and have a family.'

'You've still got time,' said Mairi.

'I did have a girl, but she went and married someone else after I joined the army and was away a lot.' His voice was carefully controlled.

Eliza could sense the hurt and anger in him. 'Couldn't you have married her before you left?'

'I suggested that, but she told me she'd only marry me if I didn't go,' he said. 'She's another one who likes her own way. I couldn't do that. I'd already signed up and she knew it. Besides, she was besotted with this other bloke. It was only later that I discovered she had her own agenda in marrying him.' He paused. 'I've said too much. You should have stopped me. I don't know what's wrong with me. I've never spoken to anyone about my blighted love life.' He sounded horrified.

Eliza would have liked to have known more but knew she couldn't push it, so she changed the subject. Besides, she could hear the kettle boiling. 'Tea,' she said. 'We need a cup of tea.'

'I'd like a cup of real coffee,' he said. 'But Mother only has Camp, which is made with chicory.'

'She has a secret store of real coffee,' said Mairi. 'I'll make four cups.'

'Won't she realise what you've done?' Eliza said.

'So what? I work my fingers to the bone looking after her and besides, you're a guest. Guests should be given the best.'

Eliza waited and then offered to carry the tray in, but Glyn took it and added the jug of cream with a cover over it, which he had spotted in the pantry on the cold slab. Eliza half-expected Mairi to say something but she remained silent. Eliza felt they were joined together in a conspiracy.

When they entered the sitting room, Gladys smiled at them. 'The doctor will be here within the hour. I expect you all to make yourselves invisible.'

'Impossible,' said Glyn. 'A fine lot he'll think us if we left you alone when you're not feeling well.'

'Besides, Glyn's on sick leave and the doctor might see it as his duty to check him out while he's here,' said Eliza.

Glyn smiled at his mother and leaned over and kissed her cheek. 'Buck up, Mother. You've a lot to look forward to… such as seeing Alfie growing up. And maybe one day, I could get married and give you a granddaughter or two and another grandson. We'd live here and you'd never be lonely again, and Alfie would have cousins to make friends with.'

'It's all right you saying that, but what if you were to get killed?' she mumbled.

'Trust you to look on the bright side,' he joked. 'Perhaps I should find someone before I return to my regiment, and my wife could live here and wait for me. I have every intention of staying alive and making that future come true.'

Eliza was thinking of their earlier conversation, and what he had said about enjoying kissing her, and felt uneasy. He must be mad if he was thinking she would even consider him as husband material, especially after the stunt at the hospital.

She found herself thinking of Jack, and she remembered she was meeting him and his mother and sister soon. She checked the clock and saw that she would not have time to wait for the doctor to arrive.

'I'm going to have to go,' she said. 'I'm meeting my friends in a quarter of an hour.'

'You could leave Alfie with me,' said Gladys. 'I've spent hardly any time with him.'

'We'll be back,' Eliza said, preparing to leave with Alfie strapped in his pushchair.

'Ask the doctor to give you his special tonic. My grandmother had great faith in tonics.'

She left the room and almost ran down the lobby. Both Mairi and Glyn saw her out.

'Enjoy yourself,' said Mairi.

'Don't forget to come back,' shouted Glyn.

Eliza waved without looking back, wondering what had been in Glyn's mind when he had kissed his mother. How could he be fond of her the way she treated him unless he was just desperate for her love.

CHAPTER NINETEEN

Jack was standing on the other side of the road and her spirits lifted. He took hold of the front of the pushchair and lifted it up onto the pavement. He smiled down at Alfie, who gurgled and reached up a hand to him. 'He knows me,' said Jack.

'That wouldn't be surprising,' she said. 'He sees enough of you.'

'I hope you don't mean that you see too much of me, Eliza?'

'No, one can't have too much of a good thing. I mean his memory must be developing if he not only recognises me and my employer, but you as well...' She paused. 'What are you doing here, Jack? We arranged to meet at the beach.'

'I wanted to ask how you got on in private,' he said.

'Ever the policeman,' she said. 'You mean how did I get on with Glyn?'

'Yes, but I also wanted to make sure you weren't prevented from coming or were followed.'

She gazed up into his hazel eyes and realised he meant it. 'We got on fine. He apologised for pretending to be Bryn at the hospital and it was as I thought – he didn't want to upset me by telling me Bryn had been killed.'

Jack said, 'Now does that mean he's a decent bloke or does he want to get in with you and closer to Alfie?'

She stopped in the middle of the pavement, which meant he had to stop. 'What are you doing?' he asked. 'We're blocking the way.'

'Do you really think he's only being nice as part of some plot to get close to Alfie? He is, after all, Alfie's uncle.'

'There are such beings as wicked uncles,' said Jack.

'True,' she said, walking on.

'I care about you and Alfie's safety,' he said, catching up with her.

'I know you do, and I love the feeling that Alfie and I are safe with you,' she said softly. 'But it would be a feather in your cap if you caught the woman who kidnapped Alfie and attempted to murder his grandmother. You could be promoted.'

His eyes flashed. 'I could. I'd get a rise and that would make a tremendous difference to my future. I'd like to get married and have kids, and I need a higher income to ask a woman to marry me. Besides, I don't want to walk a beat for ever. I like detective work and I want to bring to justice the woman who kidnapped Alfie and worried you sick, and I suspect Glyn knows who she is.'

'He told me that he hadn't mentioned to anyone that he had seen me and Alfie in the maternity hospital.'

'And you believed him?' snapped Jack.

'Calm down! You're upsetting Alfie.'

It was true: Alfie had started to whimper. 'It takes two to argue,' said Jack under his breath.

'Then let's not argue,' she said. 'Let us agree to differ or you could always ask to be taken off the case.'

He took a deep breath. 'Is that what you want?'

'Of course not. I gave you an option. Let's agree to differ and stay friends.' She took a breath. 'Anyway, I wouldn't have asked you to be one of Alfie's godfathers if I wasn't fond of you.'

He smiled broadly. 'Who's the other godfather?'

'I want to ask Kyle. If he's not available, I'll have to ask someone else.'

'Rightio! Now let's get a move on or Mam and Jean will be wondering what's happened to us.'

She bit back the words she was about to say and quickened her pace to keep up with him. She was relieved when they arrived at the place where his mother and Jean were waiting.

'Sorry to be so long,' said Eliza. 'I had difficulty in getting away, Alfie's grandmother wanted me to leave Alfie with her, but of course I wanted to get out of the house and take him to play on the beach. Besides, she had phoned the doctor because she wasn't feeling well.'

'Nothing catching I hope,' said Jack's mother.

'No, her son Glyn thinks she doesn't get out enough and, of course, she's grieving for Bryn. He was her favourite. She's also recovering from almost being gassed to death.'

'Surely, she's glad to have her other son visiting her? Jack was telling us he'd been in an accident.'

While they were talking, they were walking down the slope onto the beach. Eliza said, 'His arm is broken, and his face is scratched and bruised.'

'I bet you felt sorry for him,' said Jack.

'I did, a little, and so did Mairi. His mother wasn't. She only lamented and said, not in so many words, that she had nobody left whom she cared for. Then she and Glyn had a horrible conversation about the past, and Mairi and I could only wish we were elsewhere. But Mairi said something about it explaining a lot. She was obviously on Glyn's side.' She paused because the pushchair had begun to shake, as Alfie was wriggling and making noises in what she could only imagine was excitement. Of course, he might already want another feed, despite Jean having given him a bottle in the car.

Jack said, 'He wants to get out of the pushchair. Where's his bucket and spade?'

'Behind the pillow, with a towel,' she replied. 'Although, I do believe he's still not old enough to help build sandcastles.'

'He'll learn by example,' said Jean. 'Let's find a place to sit down. I want to put my cossie on and go for a swim.'

'The water will be cold, however warm the sun is,' said her mother. 'I'm going to make the most of the sun and bask in it on a blanket and towel and use my bag for a cushion.' She did exactly that, while Eliza and Jean held up towels for each other as they changed into their bathing suits. Jack had his trunks on beneath his clothing, and Eliza could only admire the width of his chest and his biceps. One of his legs, though, looked odd. His mother must have noticed her staring and said in a low voice, 'Jack's never told you he had polio as a child? He volunteered for the army, but they turned him down on medical grounds.'

'He never said,' murmured Eliza, thinking how he walked the beat and that she had noticed a limp when she'd seen him chasing a bag-snatcher.

'It's the marching,' said his mother in an undertone. 'He couldn't keep that up for hours or climb cliffs or crawl over rough ground. Of course, I was glad when they turned him down and he realised during the bombing that he was doing his bit for his country.'

Shortly after this exchange, Eliza became aware of just how many children on the beach had Liverpool accents. It was Jean who told her that they were evacuees. 'Our landlady told us – apparently, even before war was declared – they started arriving; some of the large hotels and B&Bs and Rydal Boys College were requisitioned by the Government and lots of office worker types from London moved here. She said it was considered safe from bombing or invasion here.'

Eliza could see that. Colwyn Bay was just a seaside town with no important factories like those in the Midlands, such as Birmingham and Coventry, or vital ports like Liverpool, London, Bristol, Belfast, Glasgow, and those along the coasts facing Europe. She shuddered, remembering how close to death she and Alfie had come during the May Blitz. 'Where did the boys go?' she asked.

'The other side of Conway to Oakwood Park in the Sychnant Pass. The Duke of Devonshire offered his home, Chatsworth House in Derbyshire, for the girls from Penrhos College. Keep all this information to yourself, though,' she added.

'Goodness me, who'd believe it,' said Eliza, wondering if Mairi and Jack knew about this. Of course, being police officers, they could have been sworn to secrecy. Although if Jean's landlady knew of it, no doubt most of the town knew and had guessed it was to do with the war effort. She wondered what kind of work it was and thought of asking Jack. Then she decided that Mairi would know more about it, as she lived in Colwyn Bay. She pushed it to the back of her mind and looked to where Jack was already building a sandcastle with Jean. They hadn't got far when Milly and the twins, Mary and John, arrived on the scene, spades in hand.

'Can we help?' asked Mary. She was the eldest by twenty minutes, but her brother was taller than her.

'The more the merrier,' said Jack. 'Just be careful of Alfie and don't fling sand about.'

Eliza watched Mary, who was careful where she placed her spade. But John set about digging with gusto. She remembered Milly telling her that it galled him to be the younger twin and although he was fond of his sister, he was always trying to go one better.

Then came a voice that slowed him down. 'Go easy, son. You don't want to bury Alfie. He's only little and is watching from his pushchair.' Eliza had propped him up with a folded towel each side and his pillow behind him so he could see what was happening.

John glanced up at his mother, who had been ruling their household since his father had been injured while digging out those whose houses had collapsed during the Blitz.

'Who's for a paddle?' asked Milly.

'You could take a couple of buckets with you, Milly, and fetch back some water,' suggested Jack. 'We'll be making a moat.'

'I'll come with you,' said Eliza. 'I can carry Alfie into the water, and he can watch the waves.'

A reluctant Alfie was dragged away from the castle builders and yelled with rage until Eliza stepped into the water, but then he watched the sunlight dancing on the waves as if fascinated. She sighed with relief that he had quietened down, as people had been watching them.

'How are things?' asked Milly. 'I see you've made friends with Jack's family.'

Eliza nodded. 'Jack told me they were coming here and offered me a lift. We all get on fine.'

'Are you staying at the same B&B?' Milly's tone was casual.

'No, I told you that I'd be staying with Bryn's mother.'

'I thought she had someone living with her to take care of her.'

'She does and, as well as Mairi, her son Glyn is staying. He's on sick leave.'

They were silent until Milly said, 'There are the buckets to fill.'

Eliza sat in the sand at the water's edge with Alfie between her thighs, so he could kick the incoming wavelets. Milly lowered herself onto the sand and began to scoop water into her bucket, and then she took Alfie's bucket and filled that with water, too.

'So, what did the pair of you have to say to each other?' asked Milly.

'Do you mean Glyn?' Milly nodded. 'He apologised for pretending to be Bryn when he visited me in hospital,' said Eliza. 'He wants us to be friends.'

'And what did you say to that? After all, not so long ago you thought he might have attempted to kill his mother.'

'Jack doesn't believe that now, but he believes Glyn knows who did. His mother said it was a woman who came to see her the evening before. So, I was prepared for us to be on speaking terms. He is, after all, Alfie's uncle.'

'Maybe you should ask him to be one of Alfie's godfathers.'

'I've already asked Jack,' said Eliza.

'Have you asked Kyle yet?'

'No, because I'm not sure if he'd be able to make it.'

'Then ask Alfie's uncle. I bet he'll be made up at being asked.'

'I don't doubt it but I'm not making any hasty decisions,' said Eliza thoughtfully, convinced Jack wouldn't like the idea. Even so, she couldn't help remembering Glyn's expression when his mother had spoken of losing those she loved most. He had been hurt, and his mother had behaved as if she didn't really care about him having been injured. 'I'll think about it.'

'If you want him and his mother there then you need to speak to the vicar as soon as possible.' Milly paused. 'Can we get up now? Not only is my cossie wet, but my bum is numb.'

'There's no pleasing you,' teased Eliza, and with difficulty managed to get to her feet, clutching Alfie against her chest. Millie had hold of the two buckets of water. Carefully, they trudged through the sand to the castle builders, who had done sterling work and were ready to fill the moat.

Mary had collected what shells and pebbles she could find to line the bottom of the moat, so while Jack carefully poured some water in, the twins and Jean went for more water. They did not return immediately, as they messed about in the sea until Jack called them back. The twins responded instantly but Jean was talking to a young man and passed her bucket to John to take back. She carried on talking until Jack strolled casually to the water's edge and had a few words with her. Eliza could not hear what was said and could only watch as the young man turned away. Eliza heard Jean call after him, and he looked back at her over his shoulder and smiled forlornly, then he hurried away.

Jean glared at her brother and then raced up the beach ahead of him, towards the three women watching her and the children whose attention was on pouring water into the moat. As she reached them, words burst from her, 'Mam, will you tell our Jack to stop bossing me about? I'm not a kid anymore. I'll be sixteen soon and will be looking for a job.'

'He was only looking out for you,' said her mother. 'Who was that young man you were talking to?'

'I can't pronounce his surname, but his Christian name is George in English. He's a Polish soldier who was wounded in the fighting and was brought here to recover. Apparently, there's a place in Colwyn Bay for wounded European soldiers to receive treatment. He's only seventeen and is hoping to learn English while he's here.'

'He must be doing well if he told you all that,' said Eliza.

'He's picking up words from the nurses,' Jean said. 'His mother and two sisters are still in Poland. He wants to get fit again so he can fight the Nazis.'

'Then, it's best you don't get too fond of him,' said Jack behind her.

'Shut up, you,' she said rudely. 'Get on with your castle building.'

'Enough, Jean,' rebuked her mother. 'Have some respect for your elders.'

The girl fell quiet and went over to a shopping bag. She removed a packet, opened it, took out a sandwich and took a large bite, before passing it to her mother who took one, too, and then passed the packet around. The twins took one sandwich each and thanked her, but Milly refused, saying she was going to see her mother-in-law at the tearoom and would have something there. Jack said that he'd go with her.

'I want to go and see Granny. They have dee-li-cious cakes,' said John, stuffing the rest of the sandwich in his mouth.

'Greedy guts,' said Mary.

'What about the sandcastle?' asked Eliza. 'Alfie and I can't finish it on our own and we need more water for the moat.' She held out the twins' buckets to them.

'I wasn't planning on going straightaway,' said Milly. 'I'm sure Jimmy's mam would love to see how Alfie's grown.'

'We'll finish the castle first,' said Jack.

'You don't have to put yourself out,' Eliza said. 'The tide's coming in, anyway, and will soon wash it away.'

'You are a grump,' said Milly.

'I want to stay and watch the sea wash it away,' John said, prancing around the castle and whooping.

'That will teach us a lesson,' said Jack. 'Only build sandcastles when the tide is going out. It'll be easier, too, because the sand will be damp and stick together better.'

'Reminds me of the parable in the Bible,' said Mary. 'The wise man built his house upon the rock and the foolish man built his house upon the sand.'

'And the rain came down and the floods came up,' said John.

'The house on the rock stood firm and the house on the sand fell flat,' sang Milly. 'I learned the chorus when my English grandmother took me to church when I was only little.'

The twins clapped their hands loudly.

'My Welsh grandma taught me it,' said Eliza.

'I never knew my grandmothers,' said Jack mournfully. 'I think I missed out.'

'My mother died of consumption when she was only thirty-two and I was only a toddler,' said his mother. 'You're all fortunate to have known your mothers.'

Eliza said, 'I got on better with my father and was only a girl when he died. There are lots of children of my generation who grew up either grieving for their father or never having known them... and it's going to be the same for some children of today's generation.'

She glanced at Jack and their eyes met, and she wondered what he was thinking. 'You and me both,' he said. 'Pity the wives who had to be both mother and father to their children.'

'John and I are lucky,' said Mary, who had been listening intently. 'We have a mam and dad, two grannies, a granddad and a step-granddad.'

'You are fortunate,' said Jack's mother. 'Now shall we decide whether we're going to split up or stay together? I'd be happy to go to the tearoom right now. I'm all for a hot cuppa and a dee-li-cious cake.'

'Then let's go,' said Eliza. 'I'm getting a numb bum.'

They gathered their possessions together and left the beach. The twins were leading the way, with Jean wheeling the pushchair with her mother beside her, and Jack, Eliza and Milly bringing up the rear. Carrying most of the possessions, they made their way to the tearoom where Cathy, Milly's mother-in-law, worked.

Fortunately, the lunchtime rush was over and there were only a few people in there. John rushed over to his grandmother, who was talking to a lone man at a far table. Milly called him back, but he was already tugging at the ties on Cathy's apron. She turned round and told him to stop it and then she spotted the group over by the door. She signalled for them to come over and set about tidying the next table. It was only then that Eliza realised that the lone man was Glyn.

CHAPTER TWENTY

Eliza hesitated only a short time before curiosity sent her hurrying across to him.

'What are you doing here? Is your mother all right?'

'Yeah, it wasn't her heart but her nerves. The doctor gave her a sedative and left a tonic because she asked for one.'

'Did he check you over?'

He nodded. 'Said I could return to active duty, but I was to take things easy.'

'I thought you were on sick leave,' she said.

'I won't be doing any marching or patrolling, but I had a telegram saying that Bryn's burial must go ahead. Also, they need a soldier to replace him, because the unit must go to Egypt to help guard the Suez Canal.'

'Goodness me! Have you told your mother?'

'No, I thought it best not to, and instead just say I'd been called back.'

'I was hoping you could attend Alfie's christening. I haven't set a date yet. It will be in Liverpool.'

'Mother will want to be there,' he said. 'I don't know if I'll be able to make it. It's a long journey and if the christening is soon, I wouldn't be able to get leave.'

'She's supposed to be coming to stay for Christmas,' said Eliza, aware that the rest of her party had turned up at the next table. 'It's quite a long time to wait for Alfie to be baptised but if you could get leave in December, I could try to arrange it for then.'

'I'll mention it to my commanding officer,' he said, picking up the rucksack on the floor next to the leg of his chair. He held out a hand. 'See you when I see you.' They shook hands, and he kissed her cheek, turned away, gave a little wave in the direction of the next table, and left. She felt a mixture of relief, sadness and regret as she watched him go. What he needed, she thought, was a good woman to care for him – but it would not be her.

Eliza took a deep breath and then went over to Alfie and asked Cathy if she could use the little back room again to change and feed him. Cathy waited until Eliza took a bag from behind the pillow in the pushchair and then led the way to a door to the rear of the room, which she opened before signalling that Eliza could enter.

She washed Alfie and changed his nappy, and then put him to the breast, needing that closeness with him once again, certain that he would benefit from it, too. She needed some time alone with him to gather her thoughts, before she was going to have to tell those waiting for her to return what Glyn had wanted and where he was going.

Once Alfie was back in his pushchair and had fallen asleep, she drew a chair up at the next table. 'That was Glyn, Alfie's uncle. He's had a telegram from his commanding officer about Bryn's burial. They can't put it off any longer, so Glyn's leaving right away.'

'Generally, they bury people straightaway in those hot countries,' said Jean.

Her mother shushed her.

Milly said, 'Did you ask him?'

Before Eliza could open her mouth, Jack said, 'Ask him what?'

'To be one of Alfie's godfathers,' said Milly. 'It was my suggestion. I thought it would make him feel better. He's been through a rough time.'

Jack faced Eliza. 'And did you ask him?'

She shook her head. 'I invited him to the christening, and he was pleased, but whether he'll be able to come or not, I don't know. His mother will want to be there, and she is supposed to be coming to stay for Christmas, so I will ask the vicar if we could have it in December.'

'It's a bit of a way off,' said Milly. 'And Glyn mightn't be given leave.'

'If that's the case,' said Jack, 'he could always have someone to stand proxy for him.'

'Jimmy could do it,' said Milly.

'Let's see what the vicar has to say,' Eliza said. 'Anyway, I'm for a cup of tea.' Jean picked up the teapot and poured tea into a cup and passed it to her. 'You can add your own milk and sugar.' Eliza thanked her and then said, 'Where are we going after we leave here?'

'What about Conway Castle?' suggested Jean.

The twins were immediately in favour, but Milly said that she had planned on taking them there another day.

'I'd rather wait until Alfie's old enough to enjoy it and I don't need the pushchair,' said Eliza.

'Makes sense,' Jack said.

'What'll we do instead?' asked John.

'I'll treat you and Mary to fishing nets and we can see what we can net in a rock pool,' said Jack.

'That's kind of you, Jack,' said Milly. 'I'd like to go round the shops.'

Jean's mother said, 'I'll come with you, if you don't mind.'

Jack frowned at her. 'That would leave our Jean on her own.'

'Not if we took Alfie with us in his pushchair,' Milly said. 'Then Eliza could go with her and enjoy the castle unhampered by Alfie.'

'That's fine by me,' said Jean.

Eliza could only agree.

So, they split up and went their separate ways.

Eliza liked wandering around the castle, enjoying the view from the battlements. She was so absorbed in imagining what it must have been like in the thirteenth century, after Edward I had it built, that she forgot about Jean and did not notice she was nowhere in sight, until she headed for the nearest tower to go down the staircase. On her way down she heard Jean's voice, but could not see who she was talking to because of a bend in the spiral staircase. However, she heard an accented male voice replying to her question. Eliza began to wonder if Jack's sister had planned on meeting... what was his name? George... She could think of no way of avoiding them and then realised that the only thing she could do was turn and go back up to the battlements, pretending she was still absorbed in the view and had not noticed Jean had gone missing. Young love! She didn't want to think what Jack would say if he knew his sister was loitering with a foreign soldier, and Eliza had no intention of telling him about it. She would keep her eye on the girl, though, when Jack or her mother were not around to do so.

But later, as they neared the tearoom, Eliza began to have second thoughts. What if the soldier took advantage of Jean's innocence and got her into trouble? Eliza could not always be there to keep an eye on her when Jean was left to her own devices. Or what if Jean was not as innocent as Eliza thought and she led him on? Eliza decided to mention her concern to Jean's mother – after all, she was her responsibility. And Jean had sneaked away behind Eliza's back to meet George. Having come to a decision that she was happier with, and praying that Jean's mother would not tell Jack about it, she hurried forward to collect her son and thank his minders, as well as drawing Jean's mother aside to tell her about her daughter's behaviour at the castle. She was not going to hang around until Jack arrived with the twins. She needed to get back and see how Mairi and Glyn's mother were taking the news of Glyn being ordered to return to the Middle East.

She was sorry to upset Jean's mother, but she had not seemed that surprised and thanked Eliza for letting her know. Eliza also asked for the name of the B&B, so she could always get in touch if necessary.

She did not linger but only exchanged a few words and left, saying she needed to get back and see how Alfie's grandmother was doing. 'See you soon,' she said.

'We'll be in touch,' they said, re-entering the tearoom.

It took Eliza no time at all to reach her destination and the door was opened by Mairi, who helped her in with the pushchair and asked if she had seen Glyn.

Eliza nodded. 'His news came as a bit of a shock.'

'She's going to miss him, despite her not appreciating him and thinking the sun shone out of your husband—' Mairi paused. 'Sorry, I shouldn't have said that.'

'No, but we both know it's true about Bryn. I presume you grew up here.'

Mairi shook her head. 'Conway.'

'It's not far away. The castle's marvellous.'

'The best in the country,' said Mairi.

'Great views,' Eliza said. 'I always wanted to see it, but Dad always said my grandparents, who lived on Anglesey, would take me to see Beaumaris Castle.'

'Attractive, but small,' said Mairi. 'The ones on the mainland were built by Edward I to keep us warring Welsh from the mountains under control.'

'I can see that,' said Eliza. 'Castles aside, did you ever come across Bryn and Glyn when you were younger?'

She nodded. 'There was a girl called Ada that we thought Glyn would marry. She even followed him to Liverpool, but we heard later that he had been called up because he was in the Territorial Army, so I don't know what happened to her, but she wasn't a nice person, even when we were at school. She bullied the smaller girls and stole their sweets. Then she made the mistake of picking on a smaller girl who had brothers and they had taught her how to stick up for herself. There was a right barney, and they were both expelled.' She paused. 'My mam has told me that there's a rumour going round that she was spotted going into her mother's house a few weeks ago.'

Eliza had stiffened at the name Ada and thought that Glyn must be aware that Bryn had married Ada, but how had it come about that she had married Bryn instead of Glyn? She needed to speak to Jack. She decided not to tell Mairi what she knew, as it was obvious that Jack had kept the information to himself. Could it be true, what she had accused him of, wanting to solve this case, so he could be promoted? And what was wrong with that? It showed he was a responsible person. Was it that she was jealous of this woman he wanted to marry? Who was this woman he had in mind to marry? It surely couldn't be Mairi, because he had only met her recently and, the way she stood up for him against his mother made Eliza sense that she had feelings for Glyn. She must speak to Jack of what Mairi had told her about Ada as soon as possible. Perhaps she should visit the B&B where he was staying after she put Alfie down that evening. She could ask Mairi to listen out for him if he were to wake up. She could surely trust Mairi to care for him.

CHAPTER TWENTY-ONE

Eliza was shown into the smoking room where Jack sat reading a newspaper. He lowered the pages and gazed at her through the smoke of his cigarette, which he removed before saying, 'Changed your mind, have you?' His voice held a thread of anger.

She thought his mother must have told him about Jean and the young Polish soldier. 'I don't know what you mean.'

'Fibber!'

'I beg your pardon!' Her tone was haughty. 'I came to bring you some information about the case but, if you can't keep a civil tongue in your head, I'll keep it to myself.'

His expression altered and he stubbed out his cigarette in an ashtray. 'Sorry. Let's go for a walk and sort matters out.'

She folded her arms across her breasts and said, 'I don't want to go for a walk with you in the mood you're in. I know from your actions earlier on the beach that you have a temper. How do I know that you won't push me in the sea?'

'Don't be ridiculous,' he retorted quietly.

She calmed down because, after all, he was right. 'I know I am being ridiculous. I don't know what's got into me.'

'You've been through a lot and maybe for the first time you've given thought to Bryn being buried and you not being there as his wife to pay your last respects.'

'You're right in one way. I hadn't thought until today about a funeral. But I'm not his wife, Ada is, and it's her I've come to talk to you about.'

Jack's eyebrows rose and he took her arm. 'Let's go for that walk. I promise I won't push you in the sea. I was thinking of going in the opposite direction.'

'You'll push me off a mountain,' she said in a jokey voice.

'If that was my intention, I'd wait until you gave me your information.'

'Naturally, you're not a stupid man,' she said. 'You just don't know much about teenage girls with romantic souls.'

His lips twitched. 'Were you a teenage girl with a romantic soul?'

'I fancied derring-do film stars like Douglas Fairbank Jr and Errol Flynn.'

'Robin Hood and Captain Blood – some would class them as thieves,' he pointed out.

'They robbed the rich and helped the poor.'

'Of course, they robbed the rich, they were the ones with the money,' he said. 'But did these so-called heroes really exist?' He paused. 'As for the very real Richard the Lionheart, he wasn't much of a king. He spent more time abroad than in England ruling the country and supporting the poor.'

'The people loved him.'

'Only because they hated his brother John,' said Jack, adding swiftly. 'Anyway, we've strayed from the subject. What's this information you have?'

She hesitated. 'Mairi knew Ada when they were younger and there was a time when Ada was walking out with Glyn. Then he went to Liverpool and was called up and joined the Liverpool King's Regiment. Ada went to Liverpool, and nothing was heard of her again. But we know now that she didn't marry Glyn, but Bryn. Mairi also said that a rumour was going round that a few weeks ago Ada had been seen in the vicinity of her mother's house in Conway.'

Jack swore under his breath as the road they were walking along left the town behind and came to open country. 'I can't believe she kept that to herself.'

'Most probably because she doesn't know what we do, and that Ada married Bryn while she was in Liverpool.'

'That's most likely it,' said Jack. 'But why marry Bryn?'

'I don't know the woman, but I guess there were two reasons. Glyn had left her to join the army and Bryn was going to inherit shares in the slate quarry, whereas Glyn only had that big, dark, old-fashioned house coming to him after his mother died.' She paused. 'And then she didn't give birth to the son Bryn wanted so, after she miscarried twice, he left her and their daughter, joined the Liverpool King's, met me, took a fancy to me and believed we were in love, and he married me. He clearly hoped to get me pregnant before going abroad with the army, so the family tradition of the shares being passed on to the eldest son could carry on.' Her voice trailed off.

'No wonder she went a bit crazy and kidnapped Alfie,' said Jack.

'We know that she knew about Bryn being killed, but how did she discover about my being in the hospital after giving birth to Bryn's son?'

Jack said, 'Perhaps Glyn did tell her.'

'You're probably right.' She felt angry and disappointed. 'There's also another way. A muddle in army records, with there being two Mrs Bryn Joneses living in Liverpool.'

'But why kidnap Alfie?' said Jack.

'Spite! Hurt! Anger! To get back at Bryn and hurt me as well for having what she didn't have. We can only guess,' said Eliza.

'You could be right,' said Jack. 'But if it was her who attempted to kill Bryn and Glyn's mother, for what reason?'

Eliza shrugged. 'Me head's beginning to ache. Let's drop the subject for now and just enjoy the countryside.'

'All right,' said Jack. 'We could come across a pub with a beer garden and a marvellous view.'

'I'd enjoy a glass of iced lager and lime,' said Eliza as the road began to twist and climb.

Jack said. 'I'd like a pint of cold beer. That's if they have any lager or beer, what with rationing.'

Their shoulders brushed, and Jack took her hand and swung her arm. 'So, will you get in touch with the vicar as soon as you get back to Liverpool and try and arrange the christening for December?'

'Yeah, it won't be easy, but it's worth a try. If Glyn can manage it. I suppose I should try and book a room in a B&B. Amelia has invited his mother to stay, but I think it's too much to expect her to invite Glyn as well.'

'You're still considering having him there?'

'He mightn't be able to make it,' she said. 'I have been wondering whether to invite Mairi. She'd probably enjoy a change of scene.'

'And she could look after the old lady on the journey,' said Jack.

They turned a corner and a few yards away was a picturesque inn, and a view of a valley and the mountains of Snowdonia that almost took their breath away.

He increased his pace, pulling her by the arm into the beer garden and an empty table with benches facing each other. A few minutes later a waiter approached them, and Jack ordered a pint of the local brew and a chilled shandy for the lady, presuming they had both available.

The waiter said, 'I can let you have one pint of beer, but no lager. But I've just had some cider delivered today from Herefordshire, if the lady would like a glass of that.'

'Yes, please,' she said eagerly, smiling.

The waiter asked if they would like freshly baked sausage rolls to have with their drinks. Jack raised an eyebrow at Eliza, who nodded. She found herself relaxing in a way she had not for what seemed ages and told herself that there was no need to worry about Alfie. He was safe with Mairi, and having some time away was doing her good. The evening was turning out much better than she had thought it would.

'Have you thought of anyone else you want at the christening?'

She nodded. 'It's a long way off yet,' she said. 'But I won't be asking many people, what with it being Christmas and wartime.'

'We've passed the longest day and, before you know it, harvest festival will be here, and the days will be shorter.'

'Then Bonfire Night,' said Eliza, but corrected herself. 'No, no bonfires or fireworks because the blackout will still be in place.' She sighed with disappointment. 'Although hopefully, we've seen the last of the Luftwaffe.'

'We can still roast chestnuts and have bob apple,' Jack said.

'You're thinking of Halloween,' she said. 'Then Christmas. I wonder if there'll be anything in the shops to buy. Unless the war's over by then.'

'I can't see the Battle of the Atlantic being over,' said Jack. 'And victory on land to defeat the German army still has some way to go.'

'But the Luftwaffe seem to be leaving Liverpool alone now,' said Eliza, taking a gulp of her drink.

He nodded and changed the subject. 'The sun is sinking. We'll have to make a move soon. I don't fancy walking down the road in the dark, with its twists and turns.'

'We'd be all right if there was a full moon,' she said.

'I'd enjoy seeing the stars clearly here, out in the countryside,' he said.

Having long finished the sausage rolls, which had been very tasty, they drained their glasses, said goodnight to the waiter, left a tip and headed off down the hill to the town.

They walked hand in hand, and she felt happy and hopeful that their relationship was heading in the right direction. She waited for him to say something but then, to her surprise, Jack broke into song.

'Why are you singing?' she asked. 'You'll wake the birds.'

'I'd like to hear a nightingale,' he said.

'You might here,' she said. 'But do you think they sing in Berkeley Square in London?' she said.

'Like in the song?' he said. 'I've never been to London, but they have trees, so maybe they did have nightingales before London was blitzed.'

'The song is making out a nightingale is a love bird,' she said, resting her head against his arm.

He stopped. 'How right you are.'

She felt his fingers lift her chin and she glimpsed the stars far up beyond his shoulder. Her heartbeat quickened as his lips covered hers. She was caught up in the moment, aware of his arm pressing her against his body, sending a thrill through her. His kiss deepened and she wanted it to go on for ever. Could this be real love? Or were they just reacting to the moon and the stars, and the scent of honeysuckle and the singing of a lone bird? She told herself to stop thinking and then his mouth lifted, and she let out a moan. She would have drawn his head down, but his lips were tracing kisses around the curve of her chin and down the side of her neck in a way that felt wonderful. She whispered, 'What's happening to us?'

He sighed against the material that covered her breast, and then raised his head and gazed into her face. 'I'm doing what I've been wanting to do ever since I first set eyes on you.'

'But I was marrying Bryn,' she said in an undertone.

'I should have swept you in my arms and run off with you. I would have if I'd known what we know now.'

She giggled. 'It would have been more dramatic in a church. Having said that, I didn't know you then, and besides, I wouldn't have Alfie.'

'Some good can come out of the worst of things.' He paused. 'I suppose we have to make a move and get back to our lodgings.'

She agreed. 'Mairi will be wondering what's happened to me, and Alfie could have woken up and be crying for me.'

'Same with my family, although I doubt they'll be crying.'

She laughed, in no mood to discuss Jean. They carried on walking arm in arm down the road, taking extra care at bends. Jack escorted her to the house through the darkened streets. He kissed her good night and said, 'Shall we keep our feelings for each other to ourselves for now?' She nodded.

CHAPTER TWENTY-TWO

Eliza woke the next morning feeling bright and breezy, looking forward to seeing Jack again. She relived those moments when he had kissed her and held her tight. She could almost feel his lips on hers, and then Alfie woke up and started wriggling in his cot. She went over and lifted him out and kissed him, happy that Jack was fond of him. How would she feel towards him if he was one of those men who didn't like children, especially other men's children?

She danced around the room with Alfie, humming 'A Nightingale Sang in Berkeley Square'. Then she stopped and returned him to his cot and went to the bathroom. When she returned to her bedroom, she washed Alfie, and put on a fresh nappy and romper suit and the matinee jacket she had knitted in eggshell blue. Then she removed her pinny and went downstairs to the kitchen to make Alfie a bottle. She found Mairi preparing a breakfast tray for the old woman upstairs in bed.

'I've just made a pot of tea,' she said. 'Help yourself to one.'

'Thanks, I will once I've made Alfie his bottle and fed him,' said Eliza.

'What are your plans for today?' asked Mairi.

'I really should go and see the solicitor,' she replied, wondering if Jack had made an appointment to do so.

'I see,' said Mairi. 'Mrs Jones has got it into her head that she'd like to go around the shops with you and wheel Alfie in his pushchair.'

'What!' Eliza almost screeched but managed to control her voice.

'I think she wants to show him off,' said Mairi.

'I suppose that's natural for a grandmother with her first grandchild,' said Eliza. 'What time was she thinking of going?'

'About a quarter to ten.'

Eliza agreed to the plan, adding, 'I'll need to phone Jack.'

'Do you have the phone number?' Mairi placed a small dish of marmalade on the tray.

'No, do you have a telephone book?'

'Somewhere!' Mairi picked up the tray and left the kitchen.

Eliza finished making Alfie's bottle, poured herself a cup of tea and sat down at the table with Alfie on her knee and popped the teat in his mouth. He started to suckle, and she reached for her cup. It was peaceful in the kitchen, and she might have dozed off if it was not for a knocking on the front door. She attempted to rise with Alfie held against her, but then she heard footsteps on the stairs and relaxed back in the chair. She heard the murmur of voices and the door closing, and then Mairi entered the kitchen, waving an envelope.

'For you,' said Mairi. 'It's been forwarded from Liverpool, and I had to sign for it.'

Eliza stared at her. 'I wonder who it's from?'

'Do you want me to take over and feed Alfie while you open it?' suggested Mairi.

Eliza hesitated and then lifted Alfie up, while he was still sucking the teat, and handed him over to Mairi and reached for the envelope that had been placed on the table. She slit it open with a finger and removed the sheets of paper inside. She began to read; it was the last thing she would have expected. A letter from the chairman of the board of Jones slate business shareholders inviting her and Alfie to a meeting in Newtown. The date was in two days' time, but the letter had been written a week ago. What was she to do? She really should attend. She must speak to Jack. She ate a slice of toast and drained her cup of tea, and then donned her coat and hat and left Alfie with Mairi. She left the house and hurried to the B&B, where she found Jack and his mother and sister just having breakfast. She explained the situation to them, including how Alfie's grandmother wanted to go around the shops with her and Alfie at about a quarter to ten.

'You do that,' said Jack. 'I have an appointment with the solicitor.'

'Doesn't he want to see me as well?' she asked.

He shook his head. 'I found it strange, too.'

'But you have to go to find out what's going on.'

Jack agreed. 'I won't stay longer than an hour, and I'll pick up you and Alfie at the house afterwards and we'll go straight to Newtown.'

'What about fuel?' she asked.

'Don't you worry about that, leave it to me.'

She said no more, and he saw her out. He kissed her lingeringly and watched her until she was out of sight, and then went inside and finished his breakfast.

Gladys Jones was disappointed when she was told that she would only have an hour to go around the shops with Alfie and Eliza, but she could see that Eliza was not going to change her mind or tell her where she and Alfie were going. Still, she found enjoyment in meeting those who knew her and admired Alfie and congratulated her, making no mention of Bryn's loss to her. Cards of sympathy had already been sent.

Eliza felt less guilty about cutting short the outing, when it came to leaving with Alfie. Newtown was further south, in Mid Wales, not far from the border with England. As she made herself comfortable with Alfie on the rear seat, Jack said, 'It'll take about two hours through some nice scenery. We'll stop and have a picnic lunch about two o'clock.'

She was desperate to know how he'd got on with the solicitor but thought he would tell her when the time was right. She guessed that would be when they stopped for lunch so instead, she asked, 'Did they make that for you at the B&B?'

He nodded. 'And I only asked this morning. Excellent service.'

They didn't talk much on the journey, as it would have meant shouting and, besides, Eliza felt that Jack needed to concentrate on his driving.

They stopped for lunch by the River Severn. As he unwrapped their food, and Eliza unscrewed the top off the thermos flask, Jack said, 'I wonder why they're meeting in Newtown. According to the landlady, it used to be a centre for the Welsh textile industry, nothing to do with slate. Apparently, there's a Dolforwyn Castle nearby, built by the Welsh Prince of Gwynedd in Medieval times, but later taken by the English.'

'Good place for a break. Perhaps they like to meet somewhere different every year and make a holiday of it,' suggested Eliza. 'I'll ask if I get the opportunity. Now tell me, what did the solicitor have to say?'

Jack frowned. 'I found him a bit backward in coming forward and he seemed a bit annoyed when I told him about you considering asking Glyn to be one of Alfie's godparents. I told him that I was the other godfather, and it was really none of his business, as the role did not need legal representation. He almost burst and he said more than he meant to, in my opinion.' Jack smiled.

'What did he say?' asked Eliza, placing the thermos and cups on a nearby rock after she had poured out tea. Her attention strayed a moment to the car, a couple of feet away, where she had left Alfie asleep on the back seat with the window half-open.

'Go and check him if you're anxious,' said Jack.

She smiled apologetically, and went over to the car and looked in. 'Still asleep,' she said. She returned to her spot by the rock and handed a cup to Jack and picked up the other cup. They both took a mouthful of the hot tea, and gasped and spluttered and swallowed, before biting into a sausage roll.

'So, what did he say?' she asked a few minutes later.

'That Ada Jones had visited him. She asked him about the will he had made when she and Bryn were still living together. He told her that her husband had made another will, with another legal representative, while in the army and he had gone through a form of marriage with you and included any children you and him might have – and that will cancelled any earlier will.'

'Poor Ada and her daughter,' said Eliza. 'I'm not interested in any money Bryn might have left. I just want Alfie to inherit the shares in the slate business that are due to him.'

'Which means the other solicitor would deal with that, not Mr Davies,' said Jack. 'No doubt the new man will be in touch with you soon.'

'I'd like Bryn's daughter to have the money.'

Jack said, 'I understand your motive but while she's a child, no doubt her mother will get her hands on it if she can. But hopefully we'll find them, and Ada will be arrested and most likely go to prison for a long time.'

'Poor little girl,' said Eliza. 'I wonder if she understands anything that's going on.'

There was a pause and then Jack started speaking again. 'There's something else,' said Jack. 'Ada wants to get in touch with Glyn. I told the solicitor he'd returned to the Middle East, and I did not know where to get in touch with him.'

'Maybe she thinks she can worm her way into Glyn's good books again,' said Eliza.

'Surely, he's not so stupid as to trust her,' murmured Jack. 'Besides, I thought he was interested in someone else now.'

'We'll just have to wait and see,' said Eliza. 'In the meantime, there's the meeting in Newtown.'

There came a wail from the car, so she rose and climbed into the back seat, and set about feeding and then changing Alfie's damp nappy. Jack gathered everything together from the picnic site and placed it in the boot, before climbing into the driving seat, starting the engine and setting off.

They were soon in the county of Powys, over the border of Montgomery, where there was another castle called Montgomery, which, Jack informed her, had been built by the English.

'Did you like history when you were at school?' asked Eliza.

He nodded. 'We had a good teacher who brought it alive. He was writing a book on castles. Did you know Liverpool had a castle once upon a time?'

'If I thought about it, yes, because there's a North and South Castle Street not far from the Pierhead. It's a pity it's not still there. It would attract more visitors.'

'Or been blown up by the Luftwaffe while trying to destroy the docks.'

'Chester still has a castle.'

'But it doesn't have a port as busy and large as ours,' said Jack.

'True, but let's change the subject. How much further to Newtown?' she asked, settling Alfie comfortably against her shoulder and handing him a teething ring attached to a stuffed toy cat by a blue ribbon.

'Can't be far now,' he replied.

'We need to find somewhere to stay the night.'

'I'm sure they'll have booked you in somewhere,' said Jack.

'But what about you?'

'I'll find somewhere.'

'There could be somewhere at the hotel where I'm to meet Jones the chairman,' she said.

'Too expensive and it's most likely booked up.'

'How d'you know?'

'It's August, prime holiday time.'

'Oh no! I shouldn't have put you to all this trouble,' she said.

'Stop worrying. I can always drop in at the police station and sleep in a cell,' said Jack.

'You are joking,' she said.

He laughed. 'I'll ask if they can recommend a place.'

As it was, the chairman was able to help him out. 'My grand-mother will squeeze you in and, as it happens, she has Cousin Rosie from Liverpool staying with her.'

Eliza and Jack exchanged looks.

'Do you know her?' asked David Jones.

'I think I might do,' said Jack.

'I haven't had the pleasure,' said Eliza. 'I was planning on looking her up back home. My employer, Mrs Amelia Jones, wants me to trace her husband's ancestry.'

'Amelia, the writer,' he said. 'She's not a true Jones.'

'Neither am I,' said Eliza. 'Although, my son Alfie is, and I have Welsh blood. My father was a Griffiths from Anglesey.'

'How did he end up in Liverpool?'

'Like many Welsh men and women in Victorian times, work took him there. But he and my mother and grandparents have passed away now,' she said. 'So, it's good that Alfie has relatives on his father's side.'

'We'll help you the best we can and, of course, you and Bryn's son will have the income from the shares in the business.'

'I'm sure he'll appreciate that as he gets older,' she said. 'In the meantime, why am I here?'

'They wanted to look you over and get some idea of your attitude to Alfie,' said Jack.

'You mean they wanted to see if I was a good and loving mother?' she said, looking the chairman in the eye.

'Reasonable, don't you think?' said David Jones.

She nodded. 'What do you think of Mr Davies, the solicitor who is one of Alfie's trustees?'

'He was Bryn's mother's choice for her son. I don't trust him, and we don't have to keep him in that position. We have a company solicitor and a separate treasurer we'd prefer you to use.'

'Do I have any say in the matter?' she asked.

'You can express your opinion, but you won't be on the committee or have a casting vote. However, much you mightn't like it, our company does not like women being in power in a business such as ours.'

'You mean men do all the hard graft, so your women are under your thumbs?' said Jack.

Davy stared at him. 'Mr Molyneux, whatever your relationship to Eliza and Alfie may be in the future, you'll have no say in matters.'

Jack nodded. 'As long as you and your male shareholders are fair to Eliza and Alfie. My relationship with them is ongoing. I'm a policeman, and my aims are to keep them safe and see that justice is done to those who would harm them.'

'Understood. We look after our women, too, Molyneux. But we don't approve of the actions and claims of the suffragettes since before the Great War, taking men's jobs and wanting equal pay to men.'

'But it was women who worked in factories and trams and swept the streets while their men were away fighting. This war isn't much different, except those on the home front are in danger of losing their lives,' said Eliza.

'But what about those who had children? They need to care for the children,' said the chairman.

'Of course, they do,' she said. 'As I must care for Alfie, but I'm fortunate enough to have a job that means I can have him with me sometimes and support myself and him. I will have to carry on doing so, the same as thousands of women whose husbands won't be coming home.'

'And what of the single women whose hopes of their own home, husband and children are gone because those men they could have married have been killed in the war?' said Jack.

'Whether you like it or not, more women will need to work outside the home, and their contribution to the country's economic recovery after this war is over is vital,' said Eliza.

'Enough said,' muttered the chairman. 'We've gone way off the original subject.'

'I agree,' said Eliza. 'But you must understand that attitudes towards women must change. The government must alter the law and give women equal rights with men, and if they have children or a sick husband to care for, then the government must give them welfare benefits to provide for their needs.' She paused. 'I could say more but I won't.'

'Then I'll bid you good evening, Eliza, and see you and Alfie tomorrow,' said David, shaking her hand. Then he turned to Jack and bid him good evening, too.

Jack and Eliza left with Alfie.

'It was a waste of time coming,' she said. 'Male chauvinist pigs.'

'We were right to come… and where did you learn words like MCP?'

'From plays on the radio,' she muttered.

'He's only saying what a lot of people who believe both men and women have fixed roles would say. It doesn't say they're right or wrong. There are still men in the force who don't agree with having policewomen,' said Jack.

'But you accept women in the force?'

'I agree that they have a role to play, especially when dealing with women and girls. I've heard many a copper saying they don't understand women.'

'Do you think the chairman has a male or female secretary?' she asked.

'You could probably find out tomorrow,' he said. 'Anyway, let's change the subject.'

'Where are you going to stay?' she asked.

'I haven't decided yet,' he replied. 'Right now, a police cell seems more welcoming than our chairman's grandmother's house.'

'What about Rambling Rosie? Won't she be expecting to see you?'

Jack drew Eliza's arm through his and said, 'I'm not so sure. I arrested her once.'

Eliza halted and stared at him. 'Milly told me. You wouldn't mention it, though.'

'Of course not, but she might. She relishes having a reputation for being a bit naughty in her neighbourhood.'

'Aren't you curious to see how she is with family? I know Amelia doesn't approve of her.'

'I'd rather spend time with you,' he said. 'Let's find a chippy and buy some fish and chips and a bottle of Tizer, if they have any, and find a bench in the nearest park and relax.'

'Sounds good to me,' she said, handing Alfie over to him, as her arms were aching.

They met a bobby on his beat and asked him where the nearest fish and chip shop was, and he pointed them in the right direction. Eliza left the two men discussing petty crime and went on ahead to the chippy, having been told there would likely be a queue. Jack joined her shortly after and by then she had reached the counter and given her order. Then they went to the park that the bobby had told Jack about and settled on a bench.

'So, what did you talk about?' she asked, putting down the newspaper-wrapped parcel of fish and chips on the bench and taking Alfie from him.

'He asked whether Alfie was mine.'

'And what did you reply?'

'That I was hoping to be a father to him. That I worked in Liverpool and had met you when Alfie had been kidnapped.' He paused. 'I do want the three of us to be a family.'

She swallowed the sudden lump in her throat. 'I'd like that, too,' she said huskily. 'But it's early days yet.' She changed the subject. 'So how did the bobby react to Alfie being kidnapped?'

'He was shocked, told me that they'd never had a case of kidnapping and asked what it was like working in a tough port like Liverpool,' said Jack.

'Did you tell him that it was tough?' She chuckled and almost choked on a chip.

'Funny,' he said. 'No wonder there are so many comedians from Liverpool on the radio.'

'What else did you tell him?'

'I told him about the Irish priest who smuggled in a bottle of whisky in a welly in a rucksack.'

'Now it's you who are the joker,' she said.

'No, cross my heart and hope to die, I was told it by a mate who's a customs officer. The priest swore it was for his granddad, who's a cocky watchman but was a fire watcher during the bombing.'

'Was he believed?' she asked, offering a chip to Alfie to suck.

'He was given the benefit of the doubt, as my mate's mother was Irish.'

'But Southern Ireland are on the Jerries' side,' she said.

'It's neutral,' he replied. 'You talk to Milly. Her mother is Irish and lives in Dublin, and has relatives who farm and others who live in Belfast, which has been bombed by the Luftwaffe.'

Eliza sighed. 'I wish the war would hurry up and be over.'

'Don't we all,' he said, placing an arm around her shoulders. 'Any chips left?'

She took one and placed it between his lips. 'Are you looking forward to getting back to Liverpool?'

'As long as you'll be there,' he said.

'I thought Alfie and I would be returning with you,' she said.

'Of course, but Mam and Jean are talking about staying on as long as Milly and the twins.'

'Whatever for?' asked Eliza.

'I'm sure you can guess,' he said.

'The Polish soldier?'

'Jean introduced him to Mam and, apparently, he'll soon be moving to London. He hasn't told her why, but it must be something to do with the war effort and Jean has it fixed in her head that he'll get killed and she'll never see him again.'

'The—'

'Don't say it,' Jack said. 'I knew you'd be sorry for them, but she'll get over him.'

'Girls feel deeply at that age. She could hate you if you prevented her from staying on in Colwyn Bay a bit longer.'

'What if she gets herself into trouble and follows him to London?' He sighed.

'Your mother will be watching her. Have some trust in them.' She paused. 'Anyway, where are you staying tonight?'

'I want to keep my eye on Rosie. I think there are two sides to her. Why is she here? And where did she get the money for the journey? Back in Liverpool she's viewed with a certain amount of sympathy and most think she's a real character who's looking out for herself when she steals stuff.'

'So, you're going to stay at David Jones's grandmother's house?' She frowned. 'Is that wise?'

Jack's eyes twinkled. 'Don't let your imagination run away with you. She's not going to stick a knife in me. However much she hates the police.'

Eliza believed him. Yet she lay awake that night, worrying about him, but finally fell asleep after convincing herself that Rosie was most likely just visiting her female relative in the hope of cadging money from her.

–

The following day she met the other shareholders, including one of the younger men, Theo Jones, who told her that they would meet again in Liverpool at his aunt Amelia's house. It was then that she remembered he was the guest that her employer was expecting. She asked about his cousin, who was also to be a guest, and he told her that he was picking her up in Ludlow, where she lived with her parents. They parted just before the AGM started and Theo said he looked forward to meeting again in Liverpool.

Eliza and Jack had arranged to meet in the park where they'd had the fish and chips. He was already there when she arrived with Alfie and a picnic lunch provided by the hotel. They settled down on the same bench. Alfie had dozed off in his pushchair, after having been fed and changed at the hotel.

Eliza told Jack about her meeting with Theo, whose full name was Theophilus, which had been his great-grandfather's name. 'I didn't say anything at the time, but I think Bryn told me that was a family name and it was from the Bible, and that the great-grandfather had originally been a farmer.'

In turn, Jack told her that he had asked the chairman's grandmother if he could go straight up to his bedroom, as he was tired after the journey. He thanked her for offering to put him up and added that he would not need any supper, as he had already had something to eat that evening. 'That way I avoided seeing Rosie, although I did hear her having an overloud whispered conversation on the landing.'

'Did you manage to catch what was said?' asked Eliza.

'Some of it. They seemed dissatisfied with their menfolk's attitude to the females in the family and mentioned not only that the suffragettes had it right, but that Ada Jones did the right thing in having joined them recently. Apparently, she had been force-fed in Walton gaol. Bryn had treated her, and her daughter, disgracefully. Although, I got the impression that they believed she tricked Bryn into marrying her by telling him that she was pregnant with his baby when it was someone else's. It was Rosie who said that. She and Ada meet up in Liverpool sometimes.'

'Stop right there,' said Eliza, holding up a hand. 'You should, as a policeman, know that sort of thing no longer happens. After the Great War the suffragettes succeeded in some of their aims and there is no longer force-feeding. You've misheard. What I want to know is: did they mention me in connection with Ada?'

'There's nothing wrong with my hearing. I think they'd forgotten I was there and, as for you, they've never met you and, as you are now a widow, I think they most likely dismissed you as not being important.'

'But they're widows,' cried Eliza indignantly.

'From a different era,' said Jack earnestly. 'You're young and have the opportunity for a different life altogether. You'll have choices that they never had.'

'I doubt it'll happen that quickly,' she said. 'The men will want their jobs back and their women in the home, doing housework, caring for any children, and satisfying the men's appetites. I bet the divorce rate will increase.'

'A lot of women have tasted freedom, but divorces cost a lot of money,' he said.

'They'll make do then with separations,' she said.

'They'll still need legal grounds,' he said.

'Which will be weighed on the men's side because we're still not considered equal with men, who make the rules,' she said.

'That's too much of a sweeping statement,' said Jack, biting into a ham sandwich. 'Lots of men consider women their equal, and there are women who believe men to be their superior and like them to make the decisions, and men consider it their job to protect and cherish them. Lots of women are content with that, and to be a wife and mother.'

'I wouldn't argue with that but there are those who can't have children and those who will never marry, simply because they aren't cut out for that life,' she said.

'And there will be women who will want it both ways: marriage and children, and a satisfying well-paid job outside the home,' he said.

Eliza thought of Amelia working from home and then of the past, when women spun, weaved, sewed, and knitted at home to add to the family budget. Some probably still did in different parts of the country, as well as others who took in washing and still did, but at least their tasks were easier now there were washhouses, where one could also do the ironing.

'The suffragettes weren't only fighting for equal rights and votes for women,' she said. 'There were men who didn't have the vote and a decent wage for the job they did,' she murmured.

'I never realised you were political,' he said.

'I just want fair play for all and that means the poor, which includes men, as well as women.'

'Fair do's,' he said. 'You're not a suffragette, though?'

'No, besides, I don't agree with everything they did, such as giving white feathers to men who weren't in uniform during the last war. So many were doing their bit for their country in other ways. There were pacifists who worked down the mines or as medical orderlies on the battlefield.'

'Enough, please,' said Jack. 'I'm on your side. I'm not a pacifist but there's always criminals in wartime, as well as peacetime.'

'Your mother told me you tried to join up, but you were turned down as unfit,' she said.

'I thought she might, so shall we change the subject? Do you think we can go back to Colwyn Bay today?'

'I want to go there or home. I've had enough of being treated as a second-class citizen.'

'Then let's leave within the hour. I left a note and some money and thanked Mrs Wyn Jones, saying I had to return to work.'

'I'll leave a note at reception and wish the committee well and remind them that I would appreciate a newsletter of their deliberations.' She reached for a smoked salmon sandwich. 'But first let's finish eating.'

They did so and were soon on their way, and despite the rain, they arrived back in Colwyn Bay for afternoon tea at the tearoom where Cathy worked. She showed them to a table for two, and brought them delicious-looking cakes and buttered fruit scones, as well as fingers of toast with smoked mackerel pâté, Welsh cheese sandwiches and a big pot of tea.

As she served them, she told them that her son Jimmy had arrived, taking them by surprise. He had brought news that his friend and Milly's, Ben, whom Jimmy had worked with and who was now in the army, had moved from the camp in Wales to the south coast of England. He was on coast-watching with a gun placement ready to shoot down any of the enemy who still thought they had a chance of taking the Brits by surprise and invading.

Eliza was only half-listening, but she felt that she had heard the name Ben before. Of course, it was another Biblical name, like Theophilus, but more well known, because Benjamin was the youngest brother of Joseph, of the coat of many colours fame, who dreamed dreams with meaning. It was one of her favourite Old Testament stories. The next moment she was roused from her reverie by Jack nudging her and saying it was time to go. They'd be able to see Jimmy tomorrow.

CHAPTER TWENTY-THREE

They were to have other matters on their mind the following day. Jean had not returned to the B&B when Jack arrived there after dropping Eliza at Alfie's grandmother's house, lingering to talk and have a cup of good coffee with Mairi and Gladys. He had drawn Mairi aside to speak to her about Ada, while Eliza talked to Gladys about the trip to Newtown and gave her some time to cuddle Alfie, before feeding and changing him.

Eliza went for a walk around the shops with Gladys and Alfie to make up for cutting short their outing a few days ago. They called into the tearoom for a cup of tea and a cake but were told by Cathy that the family had gone to the beach, hoping the rain of yesterday had passed. She mentioned that Jack had called in first thing that morning asking if she had seen Jean, as her bed had not been slept in.

'I told him that she had called in during the afternoon for me to make up a picnic lunch for two. He thanked me and left in a hurry,' said Cathy. 'I was surprised, because it had looked like rain yesterday, and it did pour down, and I think we can expect more.'

'Perhaps they were caught out in the rain and had to find shelter,' mused Eliza, but then she remembered that George would be having to leave for London soon. Had Jack remembered that?

She told the two women that she had to go and find Jack but would be back to escort Gladys and Alfie back to the house. Then she hurried to the B&B, where she found Jack at reception, on the telephone. She waited until he had finished his call before going up to him and asking him if he had remembered that George was leaving for London sooner and maybe he had gone yesterday?

He nodded grimly. 'I've just phoned the convalescent place and he left but never arrived in London. I feel mad with her, worrying Mam and me like this. She's thoughtless and selfish.'

'So, you're thinking that he's gone off somewhere else with Jean?'

'What do you think... and where's Alfie?' he sounded vexed.

'I left him with his grandmother and Cathy in the tearoom,' she replied.

'You what?' he thundered. 'One will be busy serving and the other is too weak to run after anyone who attempted to take him away.'

'I had other things on my mind, and I believed he was safe with them.' Eliza's voice trembled and she had gone pale. 'I'll have to go back. I only came because Cathy told me that Jean was missing,' She left him and fled the building. He had put the wind up her and she was annoyed with herself for leaving Alfie behind at the tearoom. Ada could have been there, and she wouldn't have recognised her. Her chest felt tight with fear, and she could not breathe properly. She slowed down, leaned against a wall, and prayed that God would keep Alfie and Jean safe. She told herself to stop panicking, otherwise she would have a heart attack. She began to walk again, telling herself that Jack had been right to speak to her the way he did. She was getting careless and too trusting. Yet surely Alfie's grandmother would kick up a fuss if anyone tried to take Alfie? And Cathy would come running to see what was going on. As for George and Jean, he could be wrong about them. Love might make you do foolish things occasionally, but it didn't drive you completely crackers. Jean had a good head on her shoulders and knew that if she went off to London to be with George, Jack would get in touch with the Metropolitan police force and ask for a search for the couple. She thought deeply. Was Gretna Green a possibility? No! Jack might think of that. He did have a romantic streak, for all his toughness. An idea struck her. Was it possible Jean persuaded George to take the ferry to Southern Ireland with her and for them to stay there until the war was over? It was a neutral country, after all. She decided to keep quiet about her thoughts and concentrate on Alfie and keeping him safe. She hurried around a corner and within a few minutes she was pushing open the door of the tearoom. Gladys was still sitting at the same table as before, but she was talking to a woman who was bouncing Alfie on her knee. Eliza's heart felt as if it was being squeezed and she hurried over to them; as she drew closer, she realised it was Mairi.

Eliza smiled. 'What are you doing here?'

'There was a telephone call for you, and I thought I'd find you here.'

Eliza reached for Alfie. 'I'd better go back to the house.'

'Where's Jack?' asked Mairi, handing Alfie over reluctantly.

'At the B&B, his sister has disappeared.'

'That's worrying for him and his mother.'

'He thinks she's run away with the Polish soldier she's taken to,' said Eliza.

'I suppose finding them will be his main aim now,' said Mairi, making to follow Eliza and Alfie, only to be called back by Gladys.

'What about me?' asked the older woman.

'I thought you wanted to stay here,' said Mairi.

'Not now Eliza and Alfie are returning to the house,' said Gladys, accepting Cathy's helping arm to rise from the chair.

Eliza broke into the conversation, 'Who was it who phoned me?'

'Glyn,' said Mairi.

'All the way from the Middle East? You're joking!' said Eliza.

'He's received a threatening letter from Ada and wanted to warn you to be on your guard.'

'How did she know where to get in touch with him?' asked Eliza, terrified.

'I don't know,' replied Mairi. 'Can we go now?'

'Maybe the training barracks,' murmured Eliza.

They went, seen out by Cathy.

Eliza had strapped Alfie into his pushchair and was annoyed with herself because her first instinct was to head for the B&B

and seek Jack's protection. But why do that when she had a policewoman, Mairi? Surely, she would contact her inspector and inform him of the phone call from Glyn? And surely it was a possibility that either the inspector or Mairi would get in touch with Jack? Although, that might not be easy if he was out and about in search of Jean. In the meantime, what was she to do? She longed to go home, and in that moment, she wondered if that was where Jean had gone. Eliza decided that she would return to Liverpool without delay. She would telephone the railway station and ask the time of the next train to Chester, and then change there for Liverpool.

She was told there would be one in an hour and she wasted no time packing, much to the annoyance of Gladys. Mairi said that she would accompany her to the railway station. So, within an hour, Eliza and Alfie were on the train to Chester. They arrived in Liverpool by eight thirty and were on the doorstep of Amelia's house at a quarter past nine.

Eliza had her door key, but even so, she knocked on the door before entering the house. She heard voices, and then a woman came out of the lounge and stared at her. Eliza stared back at the stranger. 'Who are you?' they asked in unison.

'I'm Eliza,' she said, turning away to lift the pushchair up over the threshold.

The girl moved forward to help her. 'I'm Dilys and I am here with my cousin Theo to stay with Aunt Amelia.'

'I thought you weren't coming for another fortnight,' said Eliza.

'And Aunt Amelia thought you wouldn't be back until the weekend,' said Dilys, laughing.

'I had a longing for home,' said Eliza. 'And besides, it started raining.'

'Weather!' exclaimed Dilys. 'At least a change is as good as a rest, and Aunt Amelia is glad to see us and I'm glad to be here. We've heard that there haven't been any bombs dropped here since May.'

'Leaving a mess behind them,' said Eliza, pushing the pushchair in the direction of the kitchen. 'Have you had supper?' she asked.

'I was about to make a jug of cocoa,' said Dilys.

'I'll do it,' said Eliza.

'Aunt Rosie is here as well,' said Dilys, brushing back a strand of blonde hair. 'When Theo told her that he was picking me up and we were coming here, she asked for a lift. Then when we reached here, she said that she'd come in, as her larder was empty.'

'I bet that was a shock to your Aunt Amelia,' said Eliza, putting on the kettle and reaching up for a large jug from a shelf, only for a large hand to seize it before her. She turned and saw Theo.

'Aunt Amelia asked me to come and see who Dilys was talking to,' he said.

'I was homesick, so caught a train and here I am,' Eliza said brightly.

'What of your friend Jack?' he asked, going over to Alfie, who had woken up, and tickling him under the chin.

'He's stayed behind with his mother. His sister has wandered off and they're waiting for her to turn up. They think she has found herself a fella.' Eliza wondered how she could think up such words so quickly, although they were near enough to the truth.

'A holiday romance,' said Dilys with a sigh, as she placed mugs on a tray.

Eliza checked a cupboard for a packet of Rowntree's cocoa and a dark blue bag of sugar. Dilys took a bottle of milk from the cold slab in the pantry. Eliza made the cocoa in the jug, adding milk and the rationed sugar sparingly. And while Theo wheeled in Alfie, Dilys carried the tray of mugs and teaspoons, and Eliza carried the jug. Their entrance into the lounge was greeted with astonished smiles.

'You're back early,' said Amelia.

'It started raining.' She shrugged. 'I thought it would be better for Alfie here, where his toys and the park are so close, and I can carry on with my research into Thomas Jones's family tree.'

Theo said, 'I presume you mean Uncle Tom's ancestry?'

'Yeah, history is so fascinating, isn't it?' said Eliza. 'I might even have a go at mine if I ever have time.'

'I could help you with Tom's,' said the middle-aged woman wearing a dress in the style of the 1920s, who was sitting in an armchair close to the window, overlooking the road and the park. She had light brown, short, curling hair and faded blue eyes, chubby cheeks and a plump body. 'We were cousins, you know. Our fathers were brothers.'

'If I didn't have to return to the war office in London in a fortnight,' said Theo, 'I could have helped you.'

'I presume your father was the eldest,' said Eliza.

Theo nodded. 'Tom was the middle one.'

'And I was the third child,' said Rosie.

'And my father was the fourth and youngest,' said Dilys.

'So, you are all descendants of one of the three brothers who were the sons of the founder of Jones slate company,' said Eliza. 'And Bryn must have descended from one of the other two brothers, so Bryn was your second or third or fourth cousin? And Alfie is his only son, so he inherits his share.' She paused. 'What would have happened to Bryn's shares if he hadn't had a son? Or what if you have no sons, Theo? Only daughters.'

'It must never have occurred in the past,' said Theo.

'Did the founder have any daughters?' asked Eliza.

'I've no idea. It's never come up at a committee meeting,' he said. 'I can't understand why you're so interested. Alfie's not losing out.'

'He would have if he'd been a girl,' she said. 'It's unfair.'

'I've always thought it unfair,' said Amelia. 'Thomas and I did have a daughter but she was stillborn, so we didn't talk about it. I was heartbroken but Thomas seemed to accept it as fate. I never became pregnant again. If my daughter had lived, we'd have managed fine within a few years of my starting writing and being published, so I didn't worry about money after Thomas died, but I was fortunate. So many widows weren't. No wonder so many women joined the suffragette movement years ago.'

'How do you feel about it, Dilys?' asked Rosie.

'I figure in my father's will,' she said. 'And so do my younger brothers, but my oldest brother inherits just the shares. What if things were to go wrong with the company and it eventually had to close?'

'Fascinating as all this is,' said Rosie, 'I could never get interested in slate and the company, so I was allowed to go my own way, but I got along with the women in the family who, like me, did not get shares. I had a good dad, though, and I married a man I loved and who treated me well. I said as much to a young woman, Ada, who had set her heart on marrying a man who would inherit safe money and keep her in the style in which she'd like to live. A lot of good that did her. I told her a woman had to look out for herself one way or another. Instead of being dependent on a man.' She paused. 'I have great hopes for the next generation of women.'

'Pour the cocoa, Eliza?' said Amelia. 'And tell us about the parts of your holiday that you enjoyed. It's getting late, and Rosie will have to be going home. Theo, you'll escort her, and don't forget to take a torch to light your way there and back.'

'I can find my own way,' said Rosie gruffly.

'I wouldn't mind a walk,' said Eliza. 'I'll come with you.'

'What about your little laddie?' asked Rosie.

'I'm sure Amelia and Dilys will keep him safe,' she said, believing in all honesty that Alfie was safe with them.

Eliza and Rosie set out. Theo followed then a short distance behind.

'So, tell me about your friend Ada?' asked Eliza.

'Why are you so interested?' said Rosie gruffly.

'Because equal rights for working-class women is a cause close to my heart. But surely, the suffragettes pretty well achieved their aims and, while this war continues, women are proving they can do most men's jobs.'

'The men who return will want their jobs back and so where will that leave the women who've got accustomed to earning their own money and making their own decisions? I was a suffragette and spent time in Walton prison being force-fed. All our aims need to be met by changes in the law, and that means Parliament.'

'I agree,' said Eliza. 'It'll come, and maybe sooner than we think. We need to get this war won as soon as possible.' She paused. 'Where did you meet your young friend Ada, by the way?'

Rosie blinked at her through the darkness. 'At a Labour Party rally. She was with her sister, who was on leave. They're identical twins, but as different as chalk and cheese. Ada is a hothead and doesn't look before she leaps, whereas Glenys thinks things through.'

Rosie sniffed. 'Ada was named after their grandmother on her father's side.' Eliza said, 'Is the grandmother still alive?'

'Alas, no, but the girls' mother is and lives in Conway. She's looking after Gwennie, Ada's daughter, for a few days. Anyway, enough of them for now. I'm home.' Rosie pushed open the gate of a house at the bottom of Richmond Terrace, next to a doctor's surgery, on the corner with Whitefield Road. Eliza was surprised, because she had forgotten what Milly had told her and had expected Rosie to live in a small terrace, but it was a large house. 'Do you lodge here?' she asked.

'No,' replied Rosie. 'My husband's grandfather was in the building trade during the last century and built this house. He then rented it from his boss, before finally buying it and passing it down to my husband, as his father had been killed in an accident at the docks.'

'You could turn it into apartments and make money that way,' said Eliza.

Rosie shook her head. 'I have the occasional paying guest stay and that's enough company for me.' She held out a hand. 'Come and visit me sometime and bring that wee lad of yours.'

Eliza took Rosie's hand and shook it, thinking, not on your nellie if you have Ada to visit! Instead, she said, 'I will when I can, but I have a job to do first.' She waited until Rosie was inside before going down to the gate, where Theo was waiting. He offered her his arm and, shining the torchlight onto the ground, they walked carefully back to Amelia's through the darkened streets and across the main road.

As soon as they arrived back, Eliza took the sleepy Alfie from Dilys's arms with a word of thanks and then brought him upstairs to his cot. Amelia had already retired for the night. In the morning they would discuss the work she wanted Eliza to do, and the meals to be prepared and served, so Eliza would need to go shopping and, hopefully, be able to drop by at the house in Rydal Street to see if Jean was at home.

CHAPTER TWENTY-FOUR

The following morning, after talking to Amelia about what they had learned about Thomas's family tree, it was decided that Eliza should concentrate on feeding the guests during their stay. Amelia had reminded her that they could be having another guest, a woman friend of Theo's from Intelligence. Eliza would have liked a list of their likes and dislikes before going shopping but as it was, due to rationing, they would have to make do with what was available. At least Theo and Dilys had handed over their ration books.

She set off with Alfie in the pushchair, after having firmly strapped him in, as he was becoming a real wriggler. She carried on up the drive and crossed the main road at the traffic lights towards St Margaret's Church, thinking she might drop in at the vicarage on the way back, if she had time. She carried on along Belmont Road and then turned left onto Breck Road. The weather was fine, and she enjoyed the walk. She left buying the flowers until last. She wondered about taking Alfie out of the pushchair so she could put the shopping in. But as she tried to get the bags around the handle, the pushchair began to move towards the kerb: the brake had stopped working. She reached for the pushchair, but someone knocked her off balance and she missed. With horror, she watched the pushchair reach the kerb and wobble, as it collided with a scrawny black cat, which yelped, leaped in the air and clawed at the hood of the pram, only to fall back onto the road and disappear amongst the traffic. She threw herself forward and managed to grab the handle of the pushchair, which had tipped up towards her, not looking at the traffic, but only keeping her attention on her son, whose eyes were fixed on her. His bottom lip was trembling. She could hear horns and shouts. She managed to lift the pushchair onto the pavement before it could topple onto the road. A cyclist jammed on his brakes a few inches from the pushchair, after managing not to go over the handlebars, and he yelled, 'You bloody stupid woman!' He attempted to drag his bicycle onto the pavement, out of the path of a coal cart drawn by a horse.

'Sorry!' she shouted, too anxious about Alfie to spare the cyclist much of a glance – even so, that brief look caused her nerves to clamp up her throat, so she could hardly breathe, never mind move. The horse was rearing between the shafts of the coal cart.

The traffic on both sides of the road had slowed down and Eliza fought back tears. She unstrapped a crying Alfie and lifted him into her arms.

Then, unexpectedly, a bobby appeared, with a cat stuffed down the front of his tunic. He managed to seize the horse's bridle and bring it to a standstill. She recognised him immediately, and wished herself and Alfie back in her employer's house. Then she felt strength flow into her, as he glanced her way, replacing her shame and embarrassment. 'Sorry, everybody,' she called in a quivering voice. 'The brake wouldn't work, and the pram ran away before I could stop it.' She could no longer control her emotions. 'Alfie could have been killed,' she wailed, tears rolling down her face.

She felt strong arms go round her and Alfie, and heard Jack say, 'You're both safe, sweetheart, and I'll see to that brake getting fixed today. I need to see to the traffic now, though.'

'I shouldn't have left Colwyn Bay the way I did. I should have waited for you,' she said, glancing up at him. 'I do love you.'

'I love you, too. I must sort the traffic out now, love.'

'Of course,' she said, aware that Alfie was getting squashed between them and was wriggling to get free. As was the cat. 'Has Jean turned up?'

'She's been in touch. I'm sorry about yesterday.'

'Me too. I'm feeling a lot calmer now.'

'I'm glad to hear it.' A smile tugged at the corner of his mouth. 'Can we talk later? I really need to sort this mess out.'

They separated and she realised that the cat had managed to get a leg free and his claws were caught in her cardigan. Without another word, she gave Jack a look and he removed the cat from inside his tunic.

'Could you?' he asked.

She nodded. 'See you later.'

Her heartbeat had begun to slow down, but it accelerated again when she approached the pram and saw that her shopping had gone. She gazed wildly left and right along the pavement, and then asked those standing nearby whether they had seen anyone remove the shopping bags from the pushchair. An elderly man with a thatch of grey hair shook his head and said that he had only just got there, but a boy of about ten said that he thought he had caught sight of a woman with tatty hair and a weird hat, and wearing a fur coat, grab the bags and turn up the street where the church was, on the corner.

'How long ago was that?' asked Eliza, annoyed beyond measure.

He shrugged. 'Five minutes ago, maybe.'

She wondered if there was any chance of catching up with the woman, burdened as she was with Alfie and the cat. But then she thought she could place Alfie in the pushchair and the cat inside her buttoned-up cardigan. She asked the boy to tell the policeman what had happened, and where she was headed. Then, without more ado, she set off at a jog, pushing the pushchair. Eventually, she reached St John's Church and turned into Richmond Terrace, where she was able to pick up some speed. She stopped only once to ask two women, leaning on their sweeping brushes and talking, whether a woman wearing a mangy fur coat and carrying two shopping bags had passed them.

They both nodded. One said, 'It sounds like Rosie.'

Eliza thanked them, scarcely able to believe it, and carried on, determined to get her shopping back and give Rosie a piece of her mind. She had almost reached the house, when she heard running footsteps and, glancing behind her, she saw Jack. She waited until he caught up with her. 'I presume the boy told you what happened,' she said.

'Yeah!' he replied, slightly breathless. 'And I recognised the description. Rosie. She walks the streets, seeing what she can find.'

'And obviously thinks nothing of stealing someone else's property,' said Eliza.

'I think she does it to draw attention to herself.'

'Well, she's certainly done that,' murmured Eliza.

'It isn't that she's completely skint. Her husband was killed rescuing a cat from a bombed building that was unsafe. She's sad and lonely.'

'Are we talking about the same Rosie?'

'I can't think of another.'

'What does Rosie do with the stuff she finds or steals?'

'She eats any food.'

'Well, I don't want her eating my shopping. Food for dinner for the household, including two guests.'

'Well, let's go in and ask Rosie to return your stuff,' said Jack. 'Then I'll escort you home.'

'At least it's not far. So where is Jean?' she asked.

'On her way home. They went for a walk in the hills and were caught in the rain so took shelter in an inn, waiting for the rain to stop – only it didn't. He told her to stay there while he went back to catch his train to London. She wanted him to stay but he wouldn't. His mother and sisters are still in Poland, and he wanted to fight the Germans and free his country. He said he'd write to her.'

'Couldn't she have phoned you from the inn to pick her up?'

'I wasn't there at the time, remember?'

'Of course, I'd forgotten.' They had reached the house and paused a moment. 'I feel a complete fool and a bad mother. Alfie could have been killed.'

'He wasn't, so don't dwell on the worst scenario,' said Jack. 'It's what I did yesterday about Jean.' He opened the gate. 'Now, are you ready for this? She'll put up a defence for her actions.'

'I can believe that. We've met. She was there with Theo and his cousin when I arrived last night. She had cadged a lift from him when she learned he was coming to Liverpool. She had a lot to say about her young friend Ada.'

Jack's eyes narrowed as he gazed down at Eliza. 'It seems you were meant to come home to Liverpool when you did.' He hammered on the front door. 'We'll talk later.'

The front door eventually opened to reveal a figure that Eliza could scarcely recognise, in a mangy fur coat and weird hat atop a head of tangled hair. 'What are you doing here, Constable?' she snapped and the eyes in her wrinkled face glared up at Jack.

'Why do you think I'm here, Rosie?' He shot a glance at Eliza and Alfie. 'You were seen taking shopping bags from this little lad's pushchair.'

'I wasn't stealing,' said Rosie. 'I thought they'd just been left.'

'I suppose you thought they were for the poor and needy?' said Eliza.

Rosie stared at her, and a tide of red flooded her face. 'Well, some people are shy.'

'I'll tell you what we'll do,' said Eliza. 'You return my shopping to me, and I won't bring charges against you because, after all, we're both widows and have to look out for ourselves.'

'Much appreciated, girl,' she said, removing her hat and the terrible fur coat. 'You wouldn't have any cast-offs, would you? I've baked in this rabbit-skin coat.'

'Why don't you give the Sally Army a visit?' Eliza said. 'They'd probably give you a good meal as well.'

'I'll bear it in mind,' said Rosie. 'Although, I can't abide all that hymn singing.' She left them standing on the step and closed the door in their faces.

Eliza and Jack exchanged looks. 'You're too soft,' he said.

'There's method in my madness,' she retorted.

The door opened and Rosie held out two bulging shopping bags. 'See you around.'

'Not if I see you first.' Eliza smiled.

Rosie's pencilled eyebrows shot up. 'That's not nice, girl.'

'Neither is stealing, so don't push your luck,' said Jack.

'You're prejudiced against me,' said Rosie.

'No, he's not,' said Eliza. 'He just thinks there's good deep inside you and you could use your time more wisely.'

'How do you know?' asked Rosie. 'Have you two been talking about me?'

'Would that be so surprising?' said Eliza. 'I know you care about the rights of women, and young women in particular, when life is tough for them, especially those who are struggling to survive with their husbands away or who are widows and have a child – ones like your friend Ada. She's lucky to have you.'

'She's a good girl and so is her daughter Gwennie. Visit me regularly, they do, once a week. Gwennie's a dab hand at housework. Strong as any lad. I tell Ada, a daughter's a daughter all your life, whereas a son's a son until he takes a wife.'

'Good on you, Rosie,' said Eliza. 'I hope she takes those words to heart.'

'We'd better be going,' Jack said. 'Keep your nose clean, Rosie. See you around.'

'You keep your eyes to yourself,' she muttered.

'Ta-ra,' said Eliza.

Alfie waved, and Rosie's expression softened. 'Hang on a mo!'

She disappeared but soon reappeared with a toy car in her hand. She gave it to Alfie, who smiled at her.

Eliza stopped herself from asking if the toy was stolen and instead thanked her. Then she turned and hurried away. Jack followed her, carrying the shopping, but did not speak until they were in Whitefield Road and had crossed to the other side.

'Well, that was a turn-up for the books,' he said. 'I presume she was unaware she was giving us information that would prove useful to the cases that me and the Colwyn Bay police are working on.'

'What I'm unsure about is whether she was pretending not to recognise me, or if she really didn't. I wonder if there's something wrong with her eyesight and she needs spectacles but can't afford them.'

'It's a possibility. She made no sign of recognising me in Newtown, not that I gave her the opportunity to see me close,' said Jack, coming to a halt. 'Have a look in your bags to see if anything is missing. If there is some food missing, it could be that she's expecting a visit from Ada and her daughter this evening or tomorrow... What do you make of all that?' he asked.

'She almost as good as admitted that her Ada is the one we're interested in.'

'What she said about a daughter was all waffle. She has a soft spot for little boys, hence the car.'

'I must admit I did wonder if it was stolen,' said Eliza with a gentle laugh.

'We can't prove anything, so don't let it worry you. Anyway, get checking your shopping.' He pulled a face. 'You might need to go shopping again.'

'You have a suspicious mind,' she said. 'But you could be right.'

'That's what happens when one becomes a policeman.'

'Can you hold the bags open then, please, so I can look?' she asked.

He did so and she rummaged through the bag that contained the meat and felt the items wrapped in paper, trying to remember what the butcher had offered her for the points that she had available. The sausages were there, and so was the liver, but the shoulder of mutton she had managed to get felt smaller. She removed it from the bag, unwrapped the joint and gazed at it. 'She's cut a piece off,' she said. 'The crafty so-and-so. I've a good mind to go back and give her a piece of my mind.'

'I know how you feel,' said Jack, 'but leave it be. We don't want her talking to Ada about it.'

'You mean what you said about her cutting it off to feed Ada and her daughter this evening or tomorrow?' Eliza wrapped the mutton up again. 'I was going to make scouse with the left-overs, but there won't be any now.'

He reached for her hand and squeezed it. 'You could make soup with the bone.'

'It's a thought,' she said. 'Thanks.'

He stopped. 'I'll leave you here and carry on with my beat. You're going to the vicarage, aren't you?'

'Thanks for reminding me,' she said. 'When will I see you again?'

'Could be this evening or tomorrow,' he replied. 'Depends.'

'Understood,' she said, standing on tiptoe and kissing his chin. Then she stepped back, but he brought her close and kissed her on the lips. 'I'll come and see you, even if nothing happens at Rosie's. We could go for an evening walk in the park.'

He chucked Alfie under the chin and crossed the road.

CHAPTER TWENTY-FIVE

Eliza paused outside the vicarage, unsure whether to try and speak to the vicar now or another time. The episode with Rosie had taken up time and she had work to do back at the house. Even so, she needed to sort out the arrangements for Alfie's christening. She decided to knock, as the vicar might not be available and, if so, then she would come back another time.

She knocked and the door was opened by the vicar, and she could tell by his expression that her timing wasn't right. 'You're busy,' she said. 'I'll come back another time. I was going to ask if it was possible to have Alfie's christening in December. I'll leave it with you.'

'I'll drop by at your apartment tomorrow about two and we can discuss it then. If that's convenient?' he said.

'Fine, thanks,' she said, turning away and crossing the road.

She was surprised to meet Milly coming along Newsham Drive. 'What are you doing here?' Eliza asked.

'Mam wants me to go and stay with her for a few days. She wants to see for herself that I'm all right. I've left the twins with Jimmy's mam.'

'You could have taken the ferry from Holyhead,' said Eliza.

'I know, but Jimmy and I thought it would be nice to have two nights on our own at home. Besides, I've something to tell you,' Milly said. 'Presuming you haven't already heard.'

Eliza had a sudden sense of foreboding. 'Is it to do with Alfie's grandmother?'

'How did you guess?'

'What else could it be? What's happened?'

'She's certainly had a shock.'

'Did Ada turn up while Mairi was seeing me to the station?' She paused. 'Nobody's dead, are they?'

'No one's dead. Mairi came in the back way, and Ada and Gladys were talking, but then she heard sounds that caused her to go into the room and to seize hold of Ada. She was strong and a dirty fighter, though, and managed to escape. Mairi put a call through to the police station and told them Ada's mother's address, but she wasn't there.'

'Maybe she's returned to Liverpool,' said Eliza, worried.

'The police are bound to consider that and will get in touch with the police here,' said Milly. 'So, what next? Have you seen anything of Jack since you've been back?'

'Briefly, by accident, but we're friends again. Jean was in touch and is back home in Liverpool.' Eliza gave the pushchair a shove. 'Anyway, I'll have to get a move on. I've work to do. The boss has guests staying, which makes more work, but I've also some research to do.' Her brain was in a whirl, wondering if Jack knew already about what she had just been told and whether Ada was in Liverpool right now. She decided not to let Alfie out of her sight.

As soon as Eliza arrived back at the house, she spoke to Amelia about the vicar coming tomorrow to see her about Alfie's christening.

'Have you fixed a date?' asked Amelia.

'I'm hoping for some time in December, because that will fit in with his grandmother's visit and, hopefully, his uncle Glyn might be able to get leave. If not, I'll have to have Milly's husband stand in as a proxy godfather. It also depends on what the vicar has to say, as it's a busy time.'

Theo and Dilys had gone into Liverpool centre, and it was not until later that day that they sat down to the roast shoulder of mutton dinner. Eliza gave in to temptation and told them how they nearly had to go without, as it had been stolen. 'Fortunately, I persuaded Rosie to return my shopping, although the mutton had had a chunk cut off it.'

'Her family must have been hungry,' said Dilys.

'She has no close family,' said Eliza. 'Jack and I decided that she could be having visitors. Probably the mutton was an answer to a prayer.'

'You said Rosie,' said Amelia. 'Are you talking about my husband's cousin Rosie, who was here last evening?'

Eliza nodded. 'Although, she didn't appear to recognise me. And she looked different, but for the eyebrow pencil. I left the shopping in the pushchair and went to talk to Jack. Sooty was his cat, which reminds me, I forgot to return the cat to him. It was nearly run over. The neighbour can't have been feeding him properly while Jack and the family were away, because it looked half-starved. Hopefully, he'll remember and come for it this evening.'

'I could put it in a book,' said Amelia in a dreamy voice.

'Which part of it?' asked Theo.

Dilys said, 'Aunt Amelia writes fictional romance, so it must be about the cat bringing the girl and the policeman together. This is their first meeting, and he must catch the thief.'

'Enough!' said Amelia. 'What about the thief?'

'You mean in your story you could make him a man or boy instead of a woman called Rosie?' said Dilys.

'No,' said Amelia. 'I want to know if the thief is Rosie, your aunt and my Thomas's relative.'

'How could you think that?' asked Dilys.

'She's well known for swiping stuff, as well as cadging lifts and meals. She's also a Labour supporter,' said Amelia. 'She could make an honest living by letting out rooms to those who lost their homes in the Blitz. She owns her house. Her husband inherited it and left it to her. I can't understand her and never will.'

There was a silence. Dilys and Theo exchanged looks, and Eliza wished she'd kept her mouth shut. There was a sigh of relief when they heard a bang on the front door. Eliza, Theo and Dilys shot to their feet, but Eliza reached the front door first and opened it. She stared at the figure standing there. 'It's not Jack!'

'No, I'm Theo's friend from Intelligence. I do have the right address, don't I?' said the woman.

Eliza was about to step aside to allow Theo to come forward, when a voice shouted, 'Eliza, hold the door there. I'm here and I want to come in.'

Eliza stepped outside, managing to squeeze past Theo's friend, and hurried down the path to Jack. He reached out a hand to her and drew her close. 'Who's that woman?' he asked in an undertone.

'A woman Theo knows from Intelligence,' she replied. 'How did you get on at Rosie's place?'

'The strangest thing,' he said, leading her onto the pavement.

'Eliza, we'll leave the door ajar for you and Jack?' called Dilys.

'Thanks,' shouted Eliza. 'What's so strange?' she added in a lower voice.

'I watched the woman I presumed was Ada go into the house with a girl. Then, ten minutes or so later, another woman came to the house. I didn't get a close look but her stance and the way she held her head reminded me of the first woman. Then the door opened, and she went inside. Nothing happened for a while but about an hour later a woman came out and I followed her here.'

'You mean the woman who's just gone in?'

'Yes, the woman you let in.'

'But I've just told you she's a friend of Theo's,' said Eliza. 'Ada's managed to give you the slip.'

'No, she's the woman I followed from Rosie's. Anyway, Rosie's house is still being watched, front and back, so I suggest we go in here and meet the woman who's just gone inside,' said Jack.

She agreed and had the strangest feeling that something they had been told by Rosie would explain the mystery. She held the door wide, so Jack could enter, and then she closed it behind her and led the way into the lounge. Dilys was sitting on the sofa beside Theo and on the other side of him was a woman and then Eliza suddenly remembered the missing piece of the jigsaw that had been tugging at the edge of her consciousness: 'I hear you're a twin,' she said.

'Yes, I have a twin sister,' she replied. 'I'm Glenys. Mam managed to get a letter to me about my sister Ada having got herself in a fix. She was worried about her mental state and the effect it could be having on her daughter, Gwen. She really needs to see a doctor again, but she doesn't trust them and believes they'll commit her to a mental institute.'

'I know a doctor who could help her, but he's a naval doctor and what with the war...' Jack's voice tailed off.

'I presume Ada's mental state is due to the miscarriages I heard she's suffered,' said Eliza, wondering what Glenys would have to say if she mentioned Bryn marrying her bigamously. Was Eliza having the son he so wanted the last straw for Ada?

Amelia spoke up, 'I had a stillborn baby and was distraught, but we accepted our loss, and I had the support of the local midwife, who knew a doctor who understood women's problems and prescribed a sedative that was able to help me.' She paused. 'Rumour has it that the son of one of my neighbours, a Scottish woman, is a naval doctor. His name is Angus and he is home because his ship is in dock being repaired again. He could be the man you mentioned, Jack. I think he helped your friend Milly's husband when he had a nervous collapse.'

'I'll go round and speak to them now,' said Eliza. 'By the way, Milly's off to Dublin tomorrow to see her mother.'

'We don't have to bother Milly; I know where the Scottish lady lives, and she has a mother and daughter lodging with her, and the daughter is a nurse. I'll come with you,' said Jack.

'Perhaps Glenys should come with us,' said Eliza. 'She knows her twin better than us.'

Glenys agreed, so the three of them set out to a house a few doors further up the drive. Jack knocked on the door and, a few minutes later, they heard the heavy tread of footsteps. The door was opened by a handsome man who looked to be in his thirties.

'Is that you, Jack?' he asked, with a hint of a Scottish accent.

'It is, Angus, and I'm hoping you won't mind me and these two ladies imposing on you. They have a problem that I thought you might be able to advise them about.'

Angus hesitated momentarily, before inviting them in and leading them into the parlour. 'Perhaps you'd like to go and talk with Mam while I talk to the ladies, unless it's a police matter.'

'I think Jack should stay,' said Eliza.

'And you are?' asked Angus.

'Eliza Griffiths Jones, I'm a friend of Milly and Jimmy,' she answered.

'And I'm Glenys, and it's my twin sister, Mrs Ada Jones, we've come to see you about for advice.'

Angus arrowed a swift glance at Jack, who led the way into the parlour, and they all sat down when bid by Angus. 'I won't be a moment. I just need to have a word with my mother.' He was back again in a few minutes and then they heard footsteps going upstairs.

Angus sat down with his hands on his thighs and gazed expectantly at the three of them sitting on the sofa. 'So, who's going to start?'

'It's a long story, so I'll start at the point when I was drawn into it,' said Jack. 'Last September I was asked to go into the registry office and be a witness at a wedding between a Mr Bryn Jones, a soldier, and a Miss Eliza Griffiths. Then just towards the tail-end of the May Blitz, I was asked to go to Oxford Street Maternity Hospital where the baby son of Mrs Bryn Jones had been abducted. I remembered the name and suspected that the mother was Eliza. I was proved right. After a few days we were able to trace Alfie, the baby, to an area known as Little Wales, where another Mrs Bryn Jones lived with her daughter, Gwen. They had both vanished and the baby was found in a doll's pram in the backyard of the house where they had lived. A clue to their possible whereabouts was found a few days later, which led us to believe she had visited the Conway–Colwyn Bay area. Eliza had written a letter to her husband to tell him that he was father to a son, c/o the Liverpool training barracks. She also wrote a letter to his mother in Colwyn Bay, informing her of the birth and saying she would visit her with the baby as soon as possible. Eliza then had a visit from a man claiming to be her husband, but he could only stay briefly. Due to a concussion, Eliza's memory was hazy at this point.' Jack paused to have a drink, before continuing, 'Then Eliza decided to visit Alfie's grandmother in Colwyn Bay to see if her husband had visited her, only to discover the old woman with her head in the gas oven, but still alive. An ambulance and the police were called, and they thought it was attempted suicide because there was a note, and she mentioned her son having been killed. Eliza did not believe she had committed suicide, because of the letter she had sent with the news of Alfie's birth. We got in touch with her husband's commanding officer through the training barracks, who confirmed that her husband had been killed by a sniper several days earlier, and his half-brother had been informed, and it was him who had visited Eliza in hospital.' He took a long drink of tea.

Eliza took up the tale. 'I need to add a couple of things before continuing where Jack left off. I was caught up in the May Blitz and lost my home. I had no family and had lost nearly everything. I had a head injury and had just given birth to a premature baby. So, it was easy for Glyn to trick me into thinking he was his half-brother. Much later, Glyn told me that when he saw me and Alfie in the hospital, he just couldn't bring himself to tell me that his half-brother was dead. I had even wondered if he had attempted to kill his mother.'

'But why would he do such a thing?' asked Angus.

'Bryn was her favourite and she had never shown Glyn any love,' Eliza replied. 'But that wasn't what happened. She recovered and said it was a woman who had visited her the night before and who had told her that Bryn was dead.'

'My sister went out with Glyn before she started walking out with Bryn,' intervened Glenys. 'When I asked her about it, she told me she was pregnant with Glyn's baby, but she had not told him because she did not want him to feel like she had tricked him into marriage.'

Eliza interjected, as things clicked into place. 'So that explains it: she tricked Bryn into marriage, perhaps because she resented

Glyn volunteering to fight. He had been in the Territorial Army for years so maybe she thought Bryn was a better bet, as she knew about the shares in the slate business.'

Glenys said, 'I told her at the time that Glyn would have been one of the first to be called up, with him having been in the Territorials. She wouldn't accept that and said he could have told her and married her before he left, but he didn't, so she married Bryn to spite Glyn.'

'That wasn't nice,' said Eliza.

'The baby was a girl, and she knew that Bryn had wanted a son to inherit the shares he had in the family slate business. So, she told him the truth about the baby most likely being Glyn's. She went on to get pregnant by Bryn twice, but miscarried each time – the first had been a boy – and then she was told not to get pregnant again, as it might kill her. Bryn was horrified and left her and never returned.'

'Wicked,' said Angus.

Eliza agreed. 'He fooled me, tricked me into believing he loved me, and married me. I did not know he had been married before and, of course, I had no idea that he was a bigamist.'

Glenys said, 'Ada only told me this evening that she wrote to Glyn after she discovered that Bryn had been killed, insisting he do the right thing by her and his daughter, or she wouldn't answer to what else she might do to make him regret his and his brother's behaviour towards her. She has a terrible temper and if she lost it and was angry with a person, she would hit out physically, as well as verbally.'

'Maybe he visited her,' said Jack.

'Definitely not the way to go about getting the man you want. I wonder if Glyn told her about my being in hospital after giving birth to Bryn's son,' said Eliza.

Glenys said, 'The times our mother rammed into us not to mess around with fellas and not to be sweet-talked into having sex with a man until we had a ring on the third finger of our left hand. Ada never listened, always believed she could get away with anything, but the brothers behaved badly.'

Angus said, 'So what is it you think I can do for her?'

'What she fears is being confined to a mental institution or prison,' said Glenys.

'She should have had more help from the medical professionals earlier on,' said Angus. 'I can't help her, but I know someone who might be able to.'

'Will it cost a lot?' asked Glenys.

'I wouldn't worry about that right now,' Angus reassured her. 'Professor Jenny Macintosh is someone who, in certain cases, gives her services for free. She's a gynaecologist who has been of great help to me on occasions with the wives of some of my male patients in the services before I joined the navy. I will speak to her and arrange an appointment for your sister. In the meantime, you must make certain she doesn't do anything to hurt anyone.'

'That won't be easy,' said Glenys. 'I have to report for duty in ten days' time in London.'

CHAPTER TWENTY-SIX

Eliza exchanged glances with Jack and guessed he was thinking the same as her, so she gave a slight nod.

Jack intervened: 'The safest place for your sister, Glenys, and those she might damage is police custody. It is true she deserves some sympathy, but we mustn't forget she kidnapped Eliza's baby son, causing her deep anguish, and she also attempted to gas Bryn and Glyn's mother, and make it appear like suicide. You've stated that your sister Ada is not one to listen to advice and that she always expects things to go well for her, so it's only right that she learns that she can't get away with doing wrong. Besides which, her behaviour is not a good example to her daughter.' He paused and Glenys made to speak, but he continued, 'So far, she has not killed anyone but if she is free to wreak revenge on those she resents, then she might go too far. My orders were to have a watch kept on Rosie's house, which we suspected she would be visiting soon. So, you will need to accept that she will most likely be taken into custody this evening for the serious crimes she has committed. I know that this is not what you want to hear, and I advise you to find her a good lawyer and involve Jennifer Macintosh in her defence, if she is willing.'

'What about Gwen?' asked Glenys fiercely.

'I suggest you take her under your wing until your mother or brother can come for her,' said Jack.

'My sister-in-law will not want her, and my mother is too old to care for her full-time,' said Glenys.

'We'll work something out,' Jack said. He paused. 'Eliza, are you all right to return home on your own?'

'She can wait here and talk to Mother while I speak to Jennifer and fill her in a bit more, then I'll walk Eliza back,' said Angus.

'Thanks,' said Jack, saluting them both and ignoring Eliza's vexed expression.

Angus and Eliza followed the other two out of the parlour. Angus saw them out and closed the door behind them, and then ushered Eliza into the rear room where his mother was knitting. Eliza's interest was immediately aroused, and she walked over to the older woman, introduced herself and asked what she was knitting.

'It's a school cardigan for Mary, such a pleasant girl. Milly told me about you. I'm so glad your baby was found, and you've settled in well with our local authoress. I hear from the librarian at the library in Lower Breck that her books are very popular. Good for her to have an interest and a means to earn money after her husband died. Angus was telling me that she has his niece and a nephew staying with her.'

'Yes, did he mention Glenys to you, as well?' asked Eliza.

'He's told me everything, as he wanted my advice.'

'He must think a lot of you,' she said.

'He's turned out well, considering my husband died when Angus was only a boy,' she said. 'The little girl, Gwen, how old is she?'

'I don't know exactly,' said Eliza.

'She'll be at school, though.'

'I really don't know.'

'Her father should be informed of the situation.'

'Angus told you that her real father, Glyn, was not told about her being his at the time?'

'Aye, her mother behaved very badly, but the threat of war and them not being married and him being called up and probably sent to France would have sent her into a spin.'

'I wish I could help the girl myself,' said Eliza. 'As it is, she's going to be in Glenys's care, and she has to return to London soon, which means Gwen staying here on Newsham Drive until another relative picks her up, but neither seems suitable.'

'That's why I say her father should be informed of the situation as soon as possible. Besides, if I understand the situation correctly, she is related to your son, as they share a grandmother who lives in Colwyn Bay.'

'Of course, she should be informed,' said Eliza, jumping to her feet. 'But firstly Glyn needs to know what's happening. I'll speak to Jack about it as soon as I see him.'

As it was, she did not have to wait long before everyone was back at Amelia's house, including Gwen. Eliza thought the little girl appeared ready to drop and the grown-ups looked shattered.

Dilys took the little girl by the hand. 'Shall we go and make some cocoa?'

Gwen nodded and went with her.

'Was it terrible?' Eliza asked, closing the door behind them.

'Awful!' said Glenys. 'Ada was raving. I didn't realise but she had already planned on leaving Gwen with Rosie and running away to Ireland with some Irishman, only he must have spotted one of the policemen on watch and skedaddled. She had been watching for him and saw him drive away. She blamed Rosie for the police being there and attacked her. Fortunately, Gwen had been put to bed, so she didn't see the worst of it, but she must have heard the screaming when one of the policemen entered the house by the back way and stopped Ada. Then we arrived and she would have gone for me if she hadn't been held back.'

Jack spoke up. 'She was read her rights and arrested there and then and taken to the station. I wanted to see you, love, and besides Rosie needed attention, so I went to the nearest phone box and phoned for an ambulance. They took her to the hospital.'

'Jack, you have to get in touch with Glyn and explain the situation to him.'

'I agree,' said Glenys. 'He is her father after all.'

Jack checked his watch. 'I must be going. I'll speak to my inspector about it as soon as possible. I'll let you all know what happens tomorrow.'

Eliza saw him out, and they hugged and kissed goodnight. She did not expect to sleep that night for all the thoughts going round in her head, but she was that exhausted, she fell asleep almost as soon as her head touched the pillow. She woke to find Dilys standing by her bedside with a tray.

'Tea and toast, and Jack's downstairs with Theo and Glenys,' said Dilys.

Eliza said, 'I'd best get up. Is Alfie awake?'

Dilys nodded. 'He and Jack are on the floor in the lounge, playing with the car Rosie gave him.'

'How's Gwen?'

'She's on the floor watching them. She seems composed, considering all she's been through.'

Eliza sipped the tea and then dressed swiftly. 'I'll have a wash later,' she said, brushing her hair. She reached for a slice of toast and left the bedroom. Dilys followed her with the tray. They could hear the tap–tap–tap of typewriter keys, and the murmur of voices, before they reached the bottom of the stairs.

'One wonders how she can carry on writing with all that's going on,' said Dilys.

'Discipline, and it's how she gets her income,' Eliza said. 'I need to speak to her, but I know better than to interrupt her when she's working.' She opened the door to the lounge and held it open for Dilys to enter with the tray. Then she apologised for keeping them waiting.

'No need to apologise,' said Jack, getting to his feet and hauling Alfie upright. 'He's had breakfast. Gwen was having Rice Krispies, so he wanted some.'

'That's a first,' said Eliza. 'I presume he managed to eat them all right?'

Gwen surprised them by saying, 'He reached out to take my spoon. He liked them and didn't choke at all.'

Dilys said, 'I was feeding him. I did change him and give him a quick wash beforehand.'

'He was a good boy,' said Gwen.

Alfie smiled at her, as if he could understand what she was saying.

'I'm grateful,' said Eliza and crunched into a slice of toast. 'So, what next? Has Glyn been told what's happened yet?'

Jack shook his head. 'He can't have leave now, as he's already applied for leave in December and it's been approved. We were told by the training barracks, who got in touch with his commanding officer by radio, that he's been sent with the unit to the Egyptian border, as the Jerries were getting too close and needed to be driven back, so he knows nothing about Gwen and Ada at the moment, due to enemy action.'

–

The trial of Ada Jones took place at the beginning of September in Liverpool's crown court. She was charged with three separate crimes: kidnapping a baby, Alfie Jones, from Oxford Street Maternity Hospital during the May Blitz, attempted murder of her husband's mother in Colwyn Bay in June and an attack on the same woman in mid-August, and late in August an attack on an old defenceless woman known as Rambling Rosie in Liverpool. Jack was called as a witness on several accounts; Eliza, Olive, Gladys Jones and Mairi were called as witnesses in the incidents in Colwyn Bay, as were several policemen; and Rosie and Glenys gave an account of the crimes in Liverpool.

The trial seemed to go on for ages and Eliza hated every minute of it, as parts of Ada's life were laid bare and her mother could be heard weeping as evidence was produced concerning her daughter's behaviour. Gynaecologist Professor Jennifer Macintosh was called upon to give her opinion of Mrs Ada Jones's mental health during the times she had been pregnant and the years after her last miscarriage.

'Mrs Jones was not a patient of mine at the time but I have gathered information about her then and in the years since she gave birth to her daughter: her husband was desperate to have a son and she suffered two miscarriages before she was told that she could die if she was to become pregnant again. I would therefore diagnose that she was in a serious nervous and depressed state of mind and should have received professional advice and support. She could have felt guilty, angry and shocked and, most of all, a deep grief and sense of loss. Her husband left her and married bigamously another woman who gave birth to a son. Imagine how she must have felt. What she did was wrong, but she believed that baby boy should have been hers. When she realised that the police were on her trail, she left the baby to be found in the backyard of the house she rented and left.'

At this point the judge asked her to step down and suggested they take a break.

Eliza could not get out of the courtroom quickly enough, despite knowing she would have to return and give more evidence, having been told the trial could go on for days. Tomorrow Olive would be with her, as well as Bryn and Glyn's mother, and Mairi, with other members of Colwyn Bay police force. She pitied Ada and her family, despite her appearing composed and defiant, and smartly dressed in a check costume and a chic navy-blue hat with a white ribbon tied in a bow at the side. Even though Eliza knew that she was Glenys's twin, it had come as a shock to see her standing in the dock, looking so like her sister.

Eliza left the building and walked round to the side, to the rear, and sat on a bench in St John's Gardens. Jack sat next to her a few moments later. 'You alright?' he asked, slipping an arm around her shoulders.

'I wish it could be all over with today,' she said, sighing. 'Ada doesn't look the sort to commit the crimes she has.'

'But she did and I'm sure the jury are aware of that, and I'm sure you created a good impression. The slight tremor in your voice when you spoke of Alfie and how terrified you were when you were told he had been kidnapped spoke volumes about how dastardly the crimes were.'

As it was, Eliza need not have worried about the coming days. Alfie's grandmother showed no sign of nerves the following day and spoke clearly and positively when cross-examined about the evening before she was found. She described Ada's visit, and what she had told her about her son Bryn having been killed and her being his widow, and she suggested that they comfort each other in their grief. She had made no mention of having a son and that was enough to make her suspicious, but she could never have imagined that she would have drugged her tea and wanted her dead. She had thought a lot since about why the woman should want her dead and could only think that she was mad, whatever the professor said about her not being insane. She had certainly not liked Gladys standing up to her and that was when she exploded and hit her, saying she was to blame for her sons' behaviour towards her.

Ada was cross-examined next and although she agreed with some of what the older woman had said, she added that Gladys had said that she did not want to carry on living. Olive was up next but was only questioned briefly and then Eliza was called to the stand and when asked about why she had not believed the eldest Mrs Jones had attempted suicide, she stated that she had written to tell her that she had given birth to Bryn's son. She explained that this had happened before his abduction, and she knew that she would be delighted, and it would give her something to live for. The police, who were next, said that they had found the letter and that later at the hospital when Mrs Gladys Jones had recovered, she had told them she had not written a note or attempted suicide. If she had wanted to do so, she would have put extra money in the gas meter to make sure it did not run out. A ripple of laughter went through the court.

Eliza decided she'd had enough and, besides, she was still feeling suspicious of Glyn having told Ada all the details about her having given birth to Bryn's son after learning of his having a close relationship with Ada. He had lied to her when she had tried to befriend him, and she was not going to ask him to be Alfie's godfather. As she was not needed further, she left with Olive and Gladys, and went for refreshments to Fuller's cafe on Ranelagh Street, before showing Gladys around the devastation caused by the Luftwaffe in the city centre and down by the river. She was stunned and admired the girls' courage to have stayed in

Liverpool, working in an ammunition factory. Then they caught a tram that stopped near St Margaret's Church and walked to Amelia's, where Dilys was looking after Alfie and Gwen.

The trial continued for three more days but Eliza decided not to attend, even for the judge's summing up and sentencing, when no doubt Ada's mother would have been in tears again.

PART TWO

DECEMBER 1941–SEPTEMBER 1943

CHAPTER TWENTY-SEVEN

Eliza gripped the handle of the pushchair holding her seven-month-old son Alfie and hurried past the theatre on Lime Street towards the railway station. She was going there to meet Alfie's paternal grandmother, Gladys Jones, and her lodger, twenty-six-year-old Mairi, who had come from Colwyn Bay for Alfie's christening the day after Boxing Day. Today was Tuesday and tomorrow would be Christmas Eve. Amelia's niece Dilys, nephew Theo and his fiancée Glenys, as well as her young niece Gwen, were coming on Boxing Day and bringing with them Alfie's uncle Glyn. They were picking him up from a military hospital on the south coast, where he had been sent from Egypt after being seriously wounded in an explosion during rioting on the streets of Jerusalem earlier in December.

She felt nervous and excited at the thought of the service and the party that had been in the planning since summer. The atmosphere in Liverpool itself was very different to last December, as then the Luftwaffe had bombed the city on three consecutive nights the week before Christmas. Eliza remembered it well because her husband Bryn had been abroad, fighting, and she was pregnant and still working in the ammunition factory. At the time she had not known any of those who would be arriving for the christening, not even Glyn or his mother. Although she had known her friends Milly and Olive, who were to be Alfie's godmothers, for a couple of years.

Gladys and Mairi were waiting outside the station. She waved at them, and they approached and greeted her and Alfie rapturously, almost banging heads when they bent over him. He reached up both hands and touched their cheeks.

'Oh, what a little love he is,' cried his grandmother. 'Is all well?'

'Everything is fine,' said Eliza.

'But you haven't gone and bought him a christening robe, have you?' said Gladys. 'Because, if you remember, I promised to bring his father's.'

'I remembered,' said Eliza.

'We've also brought some food,' said Mairi. 'Those who had met you and knew about Alfie and the christening, and Glyn having been badly wounded, were very generous with donations and points.'

'He'll look a treat in his daddy's christening gown,' said his grandmother. 'I only wish Bryn was here.'

'Naturally, but at least we have Alfie,' said Eliza. 'Which wouldn't have been so if it weren't for those men who rescued me at the risk of their own lives. I would have liked to thank them and show Alfie to them.' She paused. 'Anyway, Glyn will be here on Boxing Day. I felt upset when I heard of his injuries. I should imagine he'll be invalided out of the army. It's great he's being transferred to the military hospital in Colwyn Bay that's being used for wounded foreign soldiers, and it's near enough for him to see his daughter at her other grandmother's home.'

'He could come home,' said Mairi, 'once they let him out of the hospital.'

Eliza remembered it being said that Gwen's maternal grand-mother was not fit enough to care for the girl, and she was also thinking of the young Polish soldier whom Jean had cared for. She wondered where he was now. It had been a while since Jean had mentioned him.

Grandmother Gladys said, 'Poor child. Maybe we could have her stay now and again.'

'I'm sure Glyn will have something to say about the situation,' said Eliza. 'Anyway, we won't have long to wait.' She called a taxi and soon they arrived outside Amelia's house.

Mairi was to sleep on a camp bed in Eliza's lounge. Eliza was sleeping on the sofa and Gladys was to have her bedroom. When they arrived, Dilys and Glenys were to share a double bed in one of the furnished spare rooms, Gwen would have a camp bed in one of the spare bedrooms, and Theo and Glyn would share a room. These sleeping arrangements were agreed only once all the guests had arrived.

But on that Tuesday the women were more interested in food. Eliza thanked Mairi for the christening cake made by the tearoom where Cathy worked, and a pork loin, which was from a pig that her brother had reared, fattening it up in time for Christmas. Eliza had a feeling that was illegal but kept her mouth shut, thinking it would go down a treat in sandwiches at the christening party. There were also packets of jelly and several tins of salmon.

'How did you manage to carry all this?' asked Eliza, her eyes wide with delight.

'There's two of us,' said Gladys, who then produced with a flourish the satin christening gown, which was oohed over, trimmed as it was with seed pearls and blue ribbons. Amelia was charmed by it but felt sad, thinking of the child she had lost. She had bought a gold cross for her present for Alfie but was saving it for the occasion. She remembered her father saying that gold never lost its value and if one was hard up, it could always be pawned.

Eliza carried the food through to the kitchen with Mairi's help and placed the items in appropriate places for safekeeping, before heating up the savoury mincemeat pie she had made for the evening meal, while Mairi got on with peeling potatoes and carrots. Amelia and Gladys were in the lounge, drinking tea.

After their meal was over and Eliza was getting Alfie ready for his bath, his grandmother asked if she could help bathe him. They went upstairs together, and squeals and splashing and the odd complaint could be heard coming from the bathroom. Within half an hour, bath time was over and Alfie, clean and smelling deliciously of Johnson's baby shampoo and talcum powder, was soon dressed in a nappy, rubber waterproof pants, vest and a winceyette nightgown, and taken to his cot. His grandmother tucked him in before pulling up the side of his cot.

Eliza was taking no chances of her son rolling out of his cot and crawling across the floor, through the doorway and into her lounge where the fire had been lit a short time ago. She had put up a fireguard, but when she made to close the bedroom door, his grandmother asked her to leave it open so she could unpack her suitcase; she also wished to stay up there and rest, while keeping her eye on Alfie and maybe telling him a story or singing him to sleep. Eliza answered in the affirmative and promised to bring her up a mug of cocoa in half an hour. Then she went downstairs to talk with Mairi and Amelia about plans for Christmas Eve.

'I'd like to go into town and see if I can find a present for Glyn,' said Mairi. 'His mother doesn't want to go because she has something for him that was his father's, which she is sure will be useful to him. I'm quite happy to go on my own.'

'I want to make some paper chains,' said Eliza, 'as we haven't had time to put up decorations yet.'

'Balloons, we should have balloons,' said Mairi.

'It'll be a miracle if you find any in the shops this close to the big day,' said Amelia.

'I'll phone Jack and see if he can find a shop that has any or even if anyone he knows has bought a couple of packets and has some over,' said Eliza.

'I've ordered a Christmas tree,' said Amelia. Excitedly, she added, 'It should be delivered tomorrow.'

'What about tinsel and baubles and candles?' asked Mairi.

'There's a box in the attic,' Amelia answered. 'They've never been used. My husband bought them, having in mind our baby's first Christmas.' She sniffed back tears.

Eliza and Mairi were silent for several moments, and then Eliza said gently, 'Shall I fetch them down?'

'Yes, dear, you do that. I'm certain Alfie will enjoy them.'

'We'll all enjoy them,' said Mairi. 'Shall I make a pot of tea while Eliza fetches them?'

Amelia said, 'That would be nice. Thank you.'

Eliza popped into her apartment while she was upstairs and asked Gladys if she would like a cup of tea, as Mairi was making a pot, but she turned the offer down. 'I'll wait for my cocoa.' She was knitting a duck-egg-blue garment, which she held up. 'It won't be ready for his christening, but it should be finished for Easter. It's a long time since I knitted anything.'

'Maybe you could knit a pink cardigan for your granddaughter when you have time,' suggested Eliza.

'Pink would make a change. I'll think about it,' she said gruffly.

Eliza took a quick look at her son sleeping, and then left and went up to the attic, where it took her a little time before she found the box containing the tree decorations, and then hurried downstairs. She was halfway down the last flight when she heard the knock on the door and, thinking it might be Jack, she rushed even more, but Mairi got there before her and flung open the door. Jack stepped over the threshold, brushed past Mairi, and managed to catch Eliza before she landed on her knees and the box went flying.

'I do believe you really have fallen for me,' he said, lifting her up with only the box between them.

'Don't squash it,' she said breathlessly.

He removed the box and handed it to Mairi, who said, 'I'll give this to our hostess.'

Jack looked up. 'No mistletoe.' From his pocket he produced a sprig and kissed Eliza soundly.

When she had breath, she said, 'Just the man I wanted. Can you get me some balloons?'

He kissed the tip of her nose. 'That's what I call a romantic response.'

'You know I love you,' she said. 'But you have to get me some balloons.'

He fiddled in his pocket once more and produced several packets of balloons and handed her two packets. 'You're in luck. I bought the last lot in the shop. Mam and Jean wanted some for the kids to play a game at the mission hall party.'

'Will they have enough now you've given me these?' she asked, dangling the two packets under his nose.

'Of course,' he said. 'Now, how are things?'

'Everything is fine now you've brought the balloons. Tomorrow is all about decorating for Christmas.' She took his hand and led him into Amelia's lounge, just in time to see her employer place the box from the attic under her chair.

'Jack, how nice to see you,' she said. 'Just in time for a cup of tea.'

'Thanks,' he said, sitting on the sofa and pulling Eliza down beside him.

Eliza waved the two packets. 'Balloons! How's that for prompt service?'

'He's a mind reader,' said Amelia. 'Now, Jack, will you have time tomorrow to help us decorate here, not just for the festive season but the christening, too?'

He looked pensive. 'As long as I'm allowed to leave here as soon as I drink my tea now. I'll be here at three in the afternoon until six. I'm on earlies but I've been asked to put in an extra couple of hours, as Christmas Eve evenings are busy times for certain criminals.'

Thinking that Jack could not run as fast as some, Eliza asked if he would be working in pairs, when she saw him out. 'Of course,' he replied. 'Don't be worrying.'

CHAPTER TWENTY-EIGHT

Jack was late, thought Eliza, although it was stupid to worry when it was only afternoon. Even so, after an hour she phoned the police station and was told that he had been discharged from the hospital and should be with her in less than half an hour.

The other women watching her saw her pale. 'What's wrong?' asked Amelia.

'He'll be with us any minute now he's left the hospital,' she replied in an undertone.

'The hospital!' cried Amelia.

'They didn't tell me what was wrong,' said Eliza.

'But if they've let him out it can't be serious,' said Mairi.

A few minutes later there was a thunderous banging on the door. Eliza rushed to open it and experienced a rush of relief when she saw Jack on the step, leaning against the doorjamb. 'Sorry I'm late,' he said, 'but I can stay longer. I've been declared unfit for duty.'

'Let's get you inside,' she said, aware that Mairi was standing behind her. 'Then you can tell us all about it.'

Eliza and Mairi helped him into the house, despite his protests and wincing. He fell silent until he was lowered onto the sofa. 'There was an armed robbery at the post office.' He paused as they gasped. 'We gave chase, but I couldn't keep up because of this blasted leg of mine.' He grinned. 'The doctor at the hospital said my leg was a blessing because if I'd been any closer, they could have wounded me more seriously. As it is, they got me in my left upper arm, and I fell. An elderly couple were watching from a shop doorway: the husband went in and phoned for help, and the wife came to my aid like a mother with a son.'

'God bless them both,' said Eliza fervently and held a cup of tea to his lips.

He tasted it cautiously before taking a gulp and then several more. Then he said, 'I didn't want to let you down. I can still use my right arm.'

Eliza smiled. 'You never give up, do you, love?' Suddenly, she was aware of Alfie grasping the hem of her skirt, but he was sitting on Jack's foot. Reaching down, she lifted him up and placed him on her thigh, which was alongside Jack's. 'Here's a job for you, if you're willing. Keep your future godson out of mischief while we get on with a few things. If you both get fed up with watching us, you can read to him *When We Were Very Young* by A. A. Milne and show him the pictures. He'll turn the pages for you if you have difficulty.'

Jack raised his eyebrows. 'I'm sure we'll manage, but if you have any difficulty, do ask for help. I could blow up some balloons for you.' This was said as the Christmas tree was brought into the room. It was tall enough for Eliza to need help to attach a star or a fairy to the highest point, but she didn't say that she could use a chair to stand on. Instead, she went and found a large plant pot and some soil, and a couple of bricks to wedge it upright.

Then Amelia produced the box containing her precious Christmas tree decorations, and Mairi and Gladys the bags of tinsel and baubles. Alfie was not the only one who watched in fascination as Amelia brought out Dinky cars made at the Meccano factory in Liverpool, and beautifully carved farm animals, as well as ones that would have marched in Noah's ark two by two. There were also colouring books, crayons, and a sailing boat, a small stuffed teddy bear, a skipping rope and a rubber ball, a celluloid doll, and a fan.

'Goodness me, this Christmas tree is going to resemble Santa's Grotto in better times,' said Mairi.

Eliza was silent, pausing in her task of making paper chains, just watching and thinking of Amelia's child, who had been still-born, and of Gwen's mother in prison over the Christmas season, wondering if she was thinking of her daughter. And what of all those other families who had lost loved ones due to war? She thought of her parents and grandparents and wished they could have seen Alfie. At least Alfie had a grandmother.

'What are you thinking about?' asked Jack in a low voice.

'Of those dead and gone,' she whispered.

'A natural thing to do at this time of year,' he said. 'But don't dwell on them too long, sweetheart, be thankful for what you have and look to the future.'

'Hopefully, I'll be able to do that when the fighting has stopped completely.' She paused. 'I presume you know that the Japanese have taken Hong Kong.'

He nodded. 'They also made a surprise air strike on Pearl Harbour on the seventh of December.'

'Where's Pearl Harbour?' she asked.

'Hawaii. The Americans have bases there,' he replied. 'You can bet the Americans will enter the war now. Japan and Germany are allies and have declared war on us, so now that America has declared war on Japan, they'll join us in the fight against Germany, too. Churchill and Roosevelt have been talking about ways to help us. You must have heard about the Lend–Lease Agreement?'

She nodded. 'The Yanks send us what we need to fight the war and we don't have to pay for them straightaway,' she replied.

'You can bet we'll have the Yanks over here soon,' he said.

At that moment Alfie pulled on his sleeve and pressed a finger on the open pages of the book. 'I'd best get back to my job,' said Jack with a wry smile.

'And I'd best get on with mine,' she added. 'Before I forget, do your mam and Jean know what's happened to you?'

'No, but they know I was coming here, so they won't be worrying.'

'They will if they see an early edition of the *Echo* and the raid hits the headlines,' she said, 'which it probably will.'

He groaned. 'You're right, but surely, they'll report that I was only wounded?'

'That will still worry them,' she said. 'You could phone them from here.'

'Mam doesn't have a phone,' he said.

'I bet the corner shop does,' said Eliza.

'I could phone them and ask them to let Mam know I'm all right,' he said.

'Do you know the number?'

There was a comical arrested expression on his face and Alfie was tugging on his shirt sleeve. Eliza suppressed a giggle. 'You poor man. You should be resting instead of being harassed by Alfie and me. It'll be in the book.'

Eliza went over to where Amelia was holding a star in one hand and a fairy in the other.

'Which do you think for the top of the tree?' she asked.

Eliza took both objects and explained Jack's dilemma to her. Then, just as Amelia began to answer her, there came a knock at the door. Mairi went to see who it was and found Jean with a dog on a lead.

'He's here,' said Mairi, before Jean could speak. 'Come in.'

'What about the dog?' asked Jean.

'I'll ask,' said Mairi, and did so.

Amelia came out of the lounge and viewed the dog, who wagged his tail. 'He looks friendly enough,' she said, 'and you are Jack's sister.'

'Yeah, I'm Jean.'

'Nice to meet you.' Amelia stretched out a hand.

Jean shook the hand offered. 'Likewise, Mrs Jones,' she said. 'I wouldn't be disturbing you, only one of the neighbours was in Breck Road when the post office was being robbed, and she mentioned the police turning up and wondered if my brother was involved.'

While they were talking, the dog had been sniffing the air and, before Jean could prevent it, he had bounced into the lounge, and made straight for Jack. Alfie reached out and patted the dog's nose and made some incomprehensible noises. The animal made what

Eliza could only call waffling noises and wormed his head past Alfie and onto Jack's other thigh.

'All right, boy,' he said, fondling one of the dog's ears. 'Sit!' He spoke in a tone of voice that ensured instant obedience, causing Eliza to wonder if he ever used that tone on the criminals he managed to catch in the act.

'You are okay,' said Jean, with obvious relief. 'I'll have peace of mind now when I take your dog for a walk in Stanley Park, after I tell Mam you're okay.'

'You must have a drink of lemonade before you go, Jean,' said Amelia.

'You came in the nick of time,' said Jack. 'I was about to phone the corner shop and ask them to pass a message on.'

'You can walk home with me once I've drunk my lemonade,' Jean suggested.

He agreed and passed Alfie to Eliza. 'Sorry I wasn't much use, ladies,' he said.

'You entertained your future godson,' said Eliza, 'and, here, while you're at it, hold these out to him to choose which one to go at the top of the tree. One of us will have to stand on a chair to reach the top.'

'We'll see,' he said, taking Alfie from her and showing him the star and fairy. The boy reached for the star and held onto it with one hand and clasped Jack's sleeve with the other hand. Then he indicated for Jack to carry him over to the tree. Once there, he touched several items already attached and attempted to balance the star on a branch but looked disgusted when the star wouldn't stay put. He turned in Jack's arm and pressed the star against his chest.

Eliza moved closer to them and would have taken Alfie from Jack, but he held onto him and whispered, 'Let's both hold him and lift him up, and somehow, we'll tie the star to the very top.' She could never work out how they enabled Alfie to hold the star in place while she tied it there, but a cheer went up. Jack removed his arm and stepped back and sat down with a grimace of pain.

CHAPTER TWENTY-NINE

Eliza did not wake until it was light on Christmas Day, and all was quiet. But when she glanced at the clock, she realised she should be up making breakfast and preparing the goose to go in the oven. She was dressed and had just opened the door to go to the bathroom when she heard the bedroom door open and Gladys stealthily entered the room. She stopped when she saw that Eliza was up and dressed.

'I'm desperate for the lavatory,' said Gladys. 'I didn't want to disturb you, so I've been holding on.'

'I hope Alfie didn't disturb you,' Eliza enquired. 'Anyway, you go ahead.'

'Thank you,' said Gladys, bustling past her without answering her question.

Swiftly, Eliza went into the bedroom, where she found Alfie in the bed, lying on his back, hugging a stuffed doll dressed as a soldier and gazing up at the ceiling. Annoyance held her speechless for a moment, and then Alfie spotted her and attempted to roll over towards her, but he became tangled in the bedclothes. The doll had got squashed beneath him and one of its arms looked odd. 'Oh dear,' she muttered. She did not want Alfie to picture his father as a stuffed soldier doll. Childhood memories stood out in one's mind and for all Bryn's faults, she wanted his son to have a better image in his mind when he thought of the father he had never known.

'Dada,' cried Alfie, reaching for the doll.

'No!' said Eliza, almost speechless with shock. What was wrong with the woman? This was no way to solve a difficult problem. When Alfie was old enough, he would be told that his father had been a soldier and, like many other children's fathers, he had been killed fighting for his country. She was tempted to give his grandmother a piece of her mind, not only for this but also for taking Alfie into her bed. She could have turned over and squashed him, just like Alfie had squashed the toy.

Then, as she held her son close to her, Eliza heard church bells, and was reminded it was Christmas Day: goodwill and peace to all. If she could pity Bryn's legal wife after the pain she had caused them, surely, she could try to understand his mother, who was still coming to terms with his death and the attacks on her, and now waking in a strange place on Christmas morning. Eliza wondered again why Ada had attacked her and attempted murder. She had wondered about it several times and decided what Bryn's mother had said in the court had been the right answer. She would stay silent about the soldier doll and show Alfie the photograph of Bryn and Glyn when they were boys. She would mention it to Jack and see what he thought. Although she would not see him until this evening, as his mother wanted him to have Christmas dinner with them. His mother and Jean also wanted Eliza to take Alfie to their house for a light tea, which Eliza quite fancied. It would be a nice little break from the busyness here at Amelia's, and it would get busier tomorrow and the day after. Then life would settle down again after Grandma Gladys, Mairi, Glyn, Gwen, Glenys and, presumably, Theo left for Colwyn Bay.

When Gladys returned from the bathroom, Eliza was in the lounge and Alfie was sitting in his feeding chair, eating a mashed Farley's Rusk in National milk from a spoon.

Eliza smiled at her. 'Could you take over from me, please?' She paused. 'I need the bathroom and then I must follow Mairi to the kitchen and see to the goose, and make just tea and toast, as we won't want a heavy breakfast. Mairi's said she'll make her mother's special stuffing. Don't ask me what's special about it because, apparently, it's a family secret.'

She handed the spoon to Gladys, kissed her son's thickening light brown hair and left the room, singing, 'Away in a manger, no crib for a bed,' quite forgetting that Amelia might still be sleeping. As it was, when she reached the foot of the stairs, her employer called from her office, 'Stop that racket! I'm working on a short story, and I want to finish this first draft before dinner.'

'Have you had breakfast?' called Eliza.

'A cup of coffee. I'll save myself for the goose.'

'Rightio!' Eliza said, vanishing into the kitchen, where she put on the kettle and took down three cups and saucers from a shelf, as well as three small plates. 'I'm presuming you'd like another cup of tea and a slice of toast?' she asked the young woman washing her hands at the large white sink.

'Thanks,' said Mairi. 'I let my first one grow cold.'

'Have you finished making your mam's special stuffing?'

'Indeed, I have,' said Mairi. 'It's in the basin over there. Some to stuff the goose with and some to be cooked on its own to serve separately.'

'Rightio!' said Eliza. 'Could you cut three slices of bread and toast then, please?'

Mairi nodded and set about her task. 'Have you seen the stockings hanging from the mantelpiece in the lounge?'

Eliza glanced at her. 'No, I didn't hang any up.'

Mairi's eyes danced. 'Go and have a look now.'

Eliza did so and after a few minutes returned. 'They've names on them. It'll be Amelia. I thought presents were to be placed under the tree.'

'They were,' said Mairi. 'Have you noticed Alfie's is a man's stocking?'

'Yeah, and it's not even brand new,' Eliza said.

'I think Alfie's grandmother put it there and it's one of Bryn's that she found in a drawer back home in Colwyn Bay,' said Mairi. 'I wonder if she'll ever get over his death.'

'Surely she'll give Glyn a bit of loving when he gets here,' said Eliza. 'Having your son's foot blown off is heart-breaking.'

'You can say that again,' said Mairi, with a catch in her voice.

'No need.' Eliza made a grab for the toasting fork and managed to pull the bread away from the fire before it went up in flames.

'I'll have that piece,' said Mairi. 'I like burned toast.'

Eliza said in a low voice, 'I know how you're feeling. You love Glyn, don't you?'

Mairi nodded. 'I think before he last went away, he was trying to get around to asking me to marry him. He won't do so now. He'll think he's only half a man and no good to me.'

Eliza could see the tears glistening in her eyes. 'You're going to have to convince him he's wrong. He's not going to be the only man whose wife is going to have to support him – and their children, if there are any.'

'Easily said,' muttered Mairi. 'Anyway, he's sure to get a war pension.'

'Yes, but he'll need you. You must get his mother on your side and then there's Gwen, his daughter. The three of you are going to have to pull together to make him see that the four of you must become a strong supportive family unit now, and after the war, if you're all to survive and be as happy as possible.'

'And what about you and Jack and Alfie?' asked Mairi. 'Grandma won't be happy if you and Jack get married.'

'That's because she's probably thinking she'll see less of Alfie, but she's forgetting she's Alfie and Gwen's grandma, and that'll mean Jack and me and Alfie being part of her family, too.' She paused. 'I could go on and on... Linking Glenys to Theo if they wed and hence to Amelia, and I already know of the link between her and Theo and Rosie.'

'You're staying quiet about the link to Glenys's sister, who is also Gwen's mother.'

'I am aware of it,' said Eliza, 'but I've gone far enough today. Glenys might be his fiancée but Theo might not marry her. What with all this nastiness with her twin sister.' She paused. 'Anyway, enough of that. It's time I should have a cup of tea and deal with the goose.'

'I'll put some of the stuffing for the goose in a little bowl for you,' said Mairi. 'If you don't mind me asking... Do you and Jack have marriage in mind?'

'It's early days yet, because of it not being long since Bryn was killed, but I live in hope,' she answered with a quiver of excitement which lasted the rest of the morning and afternoon, while she waited for Jack to come. They watched Alfie emptying his stocking, as well as opening his presents under the tree – the givers hadn't discovered much to buy in the shops, but all gifts were given the same treatment: turned over, examined and then placed in a circle around him. Then, when finished, he picked up the stuffed brown bear and a blue cat with a bow around its neck and placed the cat on the bear's back. She told herself not to wish Alfie's first Christmas away. After that, she watched with delight as he picked up the little trolley containing bricks, emptied them out and then placed the bear and the cat in the trolley and attempted to put the bricks back in the trolley. Then Mairi sat on the floor beside him, opened the packet of crayons and picked up one of the colouring books. She gave him a crayon and showed him how to colour in, and after he tired of attempting that, she handed him the tractor that his grandmother had bought him, and he sat wheeling it backwards and forwards within arms' reach. By then Eliza was thinking Alfie had had enough attention and it was time for him to have a rest. She ignored his struggles and screams and placed him in his pushchair and left his grandmother wheeling him up and down while singing 'Silent Night'. In the meantime, Eliza took the goose out of the oven and left it to stand, while the potatoes were put in the oven to roast. Amelia poured them pre-dinner glasses of sherry. Eliza asked Mairi to set the table. Afterwards, they sat at the table and ate while Alfie slumbered; the goose was praised, as were the stuffing and the roast potatoes. Asked whether they wanted Christmas pudding, the response was a resounding 'not yet'.

They had a quiet, lazy afternoon listening to the radio that had been on constantly the whole of Christmas week, as there had been religious performances of *The Man Born to Be King* by Dorothy Sayers. 'The authoress of the Lord Peter Wimsey detective stories,' Amelia had informed them. On Christmas Day Eliza found it amusing listening to Old Mother Riley, a man playing a woman, along with Kitty McShane, who played his daughter. There was also a performance of the pantomime *Dick Whittington*. And, not forgetting the war and their new Allies, there was a programme of exchanges of messages between America and Britain.

Around three thirty, Eliza decided that it was time she changed into the blue jumper, tweed skirt and jacket that she had saved her clothing coupons and money to treat herself to for Christmas. Amelia had given her a Christmas bonus and she had purchased a blue hat trimmed with rabbit fur. She applied a dusting of face powder and a sweep of lipstick, both presents, and performed a twirl for the women, before leaving the house to walk to the Molyneux's home. She was pushing Alfie in his pushchair, and he was also dressed in blue, and covered by a cream wool blanket with a pattern of two large blue dogs. Then she remembered she would need a torch, so went upstairs and took her torch from a drawer. Then hurried downstairs, called, 'Ta-ra!' and left again.

The weather was cold but dry and there were couples walking in the park. Some girls were playing with skipping ropes and boys were playing football. There were even a couple of lads with roller skates, just one each. She presumed their parents could only afford one pair of skates for Christmas, so the boys were having to share. In Breck Road there were no lights at all in shop windows, not even dimmed ones, so she had to tread carefully as she crossed the road, for the air felt slightly frosty as darkness fell. Fortunately, there was scarcely any traffic on the road and, once across, it did not take her long to reach her destination.

She did not have to knock on the door because Jack was waiting outside, watching out for her. 'Have you had a good day?' she asked.

He nodded. 'Restful, but Mam insisted we went to church at St John's to thank God for my safe deliverance. It was a short service, mainly for children who had brought a present with them, and the talk was about Jesus being God the Father's gift to us.'

'I have to confess that not only was I too tired to go to the Watchnight service, but I was too busy in the morning,' she said.

'But I did listen to a service on the radio, and then we lazed after dinner at midday and continued to listen to the radio.'

He took her hand. 'I missed you.'

She said, 'I missed you, too.' He drew her close and kissed her.

It was a long, deep kiss, and they only drew apart when Alfie attracted their attention by bouncing in the pushchair. 'Sorry, mate,' said Jack, lowering himself to Alfie's level. 'You wanting to come out?'

He glanced at Eliza, who nodded, and he unbuckled the straps and Eliza helped him to lift Alfie. 'How's the arm?' she asked.

'Sore,' he replied.

They were leaning against each other, cradling Alfie together.

She asked, 'Has your doctor made an appointment with you to see him again to keep an eye on the wound?'

He nodded. 'The day after Boxing Day. I told him I couldn't make it, as I was being a godfather at a christening, so it'll be Monday.'

'Surely it should be checked before then in case it goes septic?'

'He told me to go to the hospital if I was worried about it.'

'You could always ask Angus about it,' she suggested. 'I'm sure he wouldn't mind.'

'I know, but let's not worry about it now.'

'Hadn't we better go in? Your mam will be wondering where I am.'

'She's been looking forward to you and Alfie coming all day.' He shoved the door open and ushered her in first. He followed closely, as they still carried Alfie between them, and went up the darkened lobby. Eliza thought it was as if they didn't want to be separated from each other. She could see a line of light from beneath the kitchen living room, and then the door was opened from the other side and Jean stood there.

'You've arrived. Mam was worried in case you were having too good a time at the local writer's house to leave.'

'You must be joking,' said Eliza. 'I saw to cooking the dinner, although Mairi made her mother's special stuffing. She wouldn't give away the contents. I suspect it had mead in it, instead of sherry or port.'

'It sounds different,' said Jean. 'I've never tasted mead.'

'You're too young to drink,' said her mother.

'Monks have been making it for centuries,' said Eliza. 'I went on retreat once to Northumberland and it was made on Lindisfarne, also known as Holy Island. Although there's more than one Holy Island in Great Britain. Anglesey has a Holy Island, but it's nothing to do with monks and making mead.'

'Mairi must have bought a bottle here in Liverpool,' said Jean. 'Unless she brought it all the way from Colwyn Bay.'

'Her mam lives in Conway but that's no distance away and she's a neighbour of Glenys's mother,' said Eliza.

Jean's mother interrupted them. 'Here, let me take Alfie and then you can sort yourselves out, and make a decision whether we should see if we can buy a bottle of mead at the off-licence on Breck Road.'

'You're forgetting, Mam, it's Christmas Day,' said Jack. 'Besides, I think we'd have to go into town to get it and I've an idea where. If I have time, I'll go tomorrow.'

'It's not that important,' said Eliza. 'Here, take Alfie,' she added.

The older woman took Alfie, and Eliza asked Jean to bring the pushchair in. Then she sat down on the sofa and patted the space next to her. Jack sat and watched as his mother went into the back kitchen. 'Don't look so worried, love,' she said.

'I've a lot to think about,' he said. His uninjured arm slipped round her shoulders.

'You're not worried about being a godfather, are you?' she asked.

'Naw, it's the job,' he answered. 'The inspector is taking me off the beat for good.'

'But isn't that a good thing?' she said. 'After all, you were promoted to sergeant after the robbery. He must have something better in mind for you.'

'Probably desk sergeant,' he said.

'You wouldn't like that?'

'I like being out and about, finding out things,' he said.

She said, 'You mean detective work.'

'Exactly,' he said, his eyes brightening.

'Why don't you mention that to him?' she suggested.

'I want it to come from him,' said Jack. 'I never went to college because I lost schooling due to the polio, so I left school with no qualifications.'

'But surely you had a letter from the headmaster stating your good points?'

'Yes, and I went to night school, which was hard on Mam because Dad died and money was tight, so I got myself a paper round, which helped to pay for the cost of the English and Maths courses.'

'Good on you,' said Eliza. 'That shows initiative.'

'So, what next?' asked Jack.

'It's Christmas evening, so what about presents?' she asked.

'I have something for you,' said Jack, 'but here and now doesn't seem the appropriate time. But I could give Alfie his.' He withdrew his arm from about her shoulders, went over to the small Christmas tree and lit the candles. Alfie, who had managed to escape the back kitchen and was chattering away to himself, went silent and pointed to the tree, his eyes as round as saucers. He made to go over to it, but Jack was there before him, and scooped him up with one arm and blew out a light. Alfie watched, transfixed, as another candle was extinguished, and then pursed his lips and blew. He had to make three attempts before the nearest candle went out.

'Good practice for when he has candles on his birthday cake,' said Jack, removing a parcel from the tree.

'He'll only be one,' said Eliza, smiling.

'He seems more advanced,' Jack said. 'He must have his mother's brains.'

'Flatterer,' she said, wondering what Jack had bought her. He'd sounded quite mysterious. But she wasn't going to pry, she liked surprises. Instead, she sat on the sofa and accepted a sherry from Jack's mother, who also placed an occasional table in front of her and a plate with a sandwich, slice of cake and a mince pie with cream on it. Eliza thanked her and offered Alfie a bitesize bit of her sandwich. He did not hesitate in taking it into his mouth and chomping on it.

'I think he'll have more teeth through soon,' said Eliza. She sounded so proud, as if she had performed this stage in her son's life herself. She took a feeding cup out of her bag and asked Jean if she could put some milky tea in it. Jean took the cup and went away with it.

Jack was sitting on the sofa now and helping Alfie undo the parcel to reveal two books. 'I bought them from that shop you mentioned in Berry Street,' he said. 'He has some interesting second-hand books as well as new.'

'Were you tempted to buy some for yourself?' she asked, glancing up from the two books he had bought Alfie: *Winnie the Pooh* and *The House at Pooh Corner*.

'No, I was spent up.'

His mother said, 'What are you having to drink, son?'

'If you've some Guinness, I'll have a bottle,' he said.

She brought him a glass and asked Eliza how her day had been. 'I spent a fair amount of time in the kitchen with the goose and Mairi,' Eliza replied.

'I hope you saved the fat,' she said.

'Of course, I remember my gran rubbing it on my chest when I was little,' replied Eliza. 'She swore that it got rid of coughs and colds, and even pneumonia, although that was never put to the test. After dinner we listened to the wireless while Alfie sat on the rug in front of the fireplace, playing with his presents.'

'What did he make of Father Christmas?'

'He wasn't mentioned. We all had a stocking that Amelia had hung up and filled, although Alfie's was put up by his grand-mother and it was one of his father's stockings. Then we had presents from beneath the tree, and he enjoyed opening them and placing them in a circle and sitting in the middle of them. He's too young to be wildly excited about Christmas.'

'I think the run-up to Christmas is more exciting than Christmas Day,' said Jean.

'The anticipation,' said Jack. 'More often than not it's dull and most people are glad to get back to normal from what I've gathered.'

'It'll be different once the war's over,' said Jean.

'Have you heard anything from George?' asked Eliza.

Jean sighed. 'He's hoping to be back in Britain before too long but won't be able to get up here. He couldn't write much because it's hush-hush. I'd like to go down there and meet up, but I can't just do what I please and Mam doesn't like the idea, says it's more dangerous down in London, much safer here.'

'Hitler's an idiot,' said Jack. 'Now the Americans have become our Allies he's going to have to think twice about whatever his plans are for a victory.'

'Let's not talk of the war,' said his mother. 'Although, you're right about the Americans' involvement. Let's have a game of Snakes and Ladders?'

'You must be joking, Mam,' said Jean. 'We're not kids anymore and none of us got a box for Christmas.'

'We have an old set from years ago,' said her mother. 'We could have a game of cards instead?'

'For money?' asked Jean.

'Who has any?' asked Jack.

'The only card game I know is Snap,' said Eliza.

'I'm bored,' said Jean. 'I'd go for a walk, only it's pitch-black outside and someone might jump out on me.'

'Take a nice sharp hatpin with you,' said Eliza, not bothered that nobody had taken up her idea of Snap. Just like Jean, she'd have liked to go for a walk, but with Jack – but they couldn't leave his mother all alone on Christmas night. Unexpectedly, Rosie came into her mind, and she wondered if she was alone for Christmas.

'Penny for your thoughts,' said Jack in an undertone.

'I was thinking of Rosie, wondering if she was all on her own.'

Jack said, 'I haven't seen her out and about for a while. Mind you, it is winter.'

'I think I might pop in and see her for a few minutes tomorrow,' said Eliza.

'Will you take Alfie with you?' he asked, glancing at the boy who was turning over the pages of *Winnie the Pooh*. He glanced at Jack, and scrambled to his feet and attempted to drag himself up onto his knee. Jack assisted him the last few inches and glanced at the open book.

'He wants you to read to him,' said Jean. 'I'll read to him if you like, and you and Eliza could spend some time alone.'

'I'd like that,' said Eliza. 'If you don't think it's rude of me?'

'Mam?' asked Jack, raising his eyebrows.

'No, I don't mind,' she said. 'I could pop in and see Sadie up the street. She could be on her own.' She rose to her feet.

Jack and Eliza were ahead of her and out of the house. She slipped her arm through his right one and looked up at the sky, and a few cold flakes fell on her face. 'Do you think it's going to snow?' she asked.

'No, it's too cold.'

'I've heard people say that before,' she said. 'But how can it be too cold?'

'It's not going to set anyway, not enough to have a snowball fight.'

'So, where are we going to walk to?' she asked.

'How about us popping in to see Rosie,' he suggested. 'You'll be too busy tomorrow.'

'Only if you tell me what my Christmas present is,' she said.

He was silent a moment. 'Have you got me something?'

'How can you ask? Of course, I have. I only hope you'll be pleased with it.'

'You first then,' he said.

'It's dark,' she said, fumbling in her jacket pocket. 'How are we going to see?'

'I've got my policeman's torch.' He brought out of a large inner pocket a torch and directed its beam on her clenched hand. She opened it to expose a box, which she opened. The light gleamed on gold, and he peered at the gold St Christopher medal on a gold chain.

'I saw it in a jeweller's and thought of you,' she said. 'Tell me you understand why I thought of you, and you'd better give me the right answer.'

'St Christopher helps those in need of rescuing.'

'Correct. It's something you do, and I want you to wear it and remember that and stop thinking less of yourself,' she said, handing her gift to him. 'Now it's your turn.' She watched hopefully as Jack reached into his breast pocket and withdrew a small box, which he opened. He took out a ring with a ruby and a diamond each side. 'I don't want to rush you into marriage, but could we get engaged?'

'I'd love to get engaged to you,' she cried excitedly. 'How could you have any doubt?' She flung her arms around him and kissed him repeatedly all over his face Then she held out her left hand. 'Now place it on my finger and kiss me as if you never want to let me go.'

He did so and she sighed, as his lips met hers. They stayed in a warm embrace until they needed to breathe, and Eliza became aware that her feet were feeling stone cold.

Besides, a woman's voice that they had not heard for a while said, 'Enough of that in the street! There's no mistletoe around for you to make excuses.'

'I don't believe it,' said Jack. 'It's you, Rosie. We've been thinking of you.'

'Where's your cart?' asked Eliza.

'Don't use it now. Don't have need,' said Rosie. 'I took your advice and called in at the Sally Army. They're a nice bunch and make a good cup of tea. Been there today, sang carols and had a smashing Christmas dinner.'

'Are you all right to get home on your own?' asked Jack.

'Or shall we walk with you?' said Eliza.

'I'd enjoy your company,' said Rosie. 'Long time, no see. You two getting on all right?'

'We're fine,' said Jack.

'A right pair of lovers, I'd say,' said Rosie. 'Let me know when the wedding is. I've never been a bridesmaid.' She laughed and they laughed with her, presuming it was one big joke to her. But she was silent the rest of the way and when they arrived at her house, she did not want Jack to go inside before her to check the house was safe.

'Who's going to rob me? I'm Rambling Rosie, who has nothing. Now I have the Sally Army and the Lord to help me. He's a forgiving God. Forgive and forget if we repent.'

'You're preaching to the converted,' said Eliza, nudging Jack. 'Rosie has had a long day and wants to get to bed.'

'You're right there, girl,' said Rosie and blew her a kiss.

They left and strolled back to Jack's mother's house to find Alfie asleep in the curve of Jean's arm. She still held the book she had been reading to him. 'I tried to keep him awake,' she said.

'Don't worry,' said Eliza. 'It's past his bedtime and I'd better head home.'

'I'll go with you,' said Jack. 'It's slippery out there now.'

'You could always stay here, Eliza,' said his mother.

'I'd like to,' said Eliza, 'but I've lots to do tomorrow. Guests arriving and preparations to make for the christening.'

'Another time,' said Jack, his voice quivering as he drew Eliza and Alfie close to him. 'We have got news for you, though. Eliza and I are engaged, but we'd like you to keep it to yourselves for now.'

Jean whooped and said, 'What did I tell you, Mam.'

'OK, smart alec! I've also been watching hopefully for the best Christmas present ever.'

'Keep quiet about it for now,' said Eliza.

'Why?' asked his mother excitedly. 'I'm so happy I want to tell everyone.'

'Just wait until the New Year,' said Eliza. 'I don't want it mentioned because I don't want Alfie's grandmother feeling hurt. Today has been a sad enough occasion because of Bryn not being there to share his son's first Christmas, as well as her never seeing him alive again, and Glyn being in an explosion and having to have a foot amputated.'

'I see what you mean,' said Jean. 'She must be really sad.'

'But Alfie must be helping her to cope,' said her mother.

'She'll be going home the next day and won't be seeing him for a while,' said Eliza.

'But she'll have Glyn,' said Jack.

'And Mairi and Gwen,' added Eliza. 'And Mairi will smooth the way for them all if she is allowed to.' And on that note, she took Alfie from Jean, placed him in his pushchair and said, 'Good night!'

CHAPTER THIRTY

Despite being late to bed, Eliza was up and about at seven the following morning. She had placed her engagement ring on a gold chain and safely hidden it inside her Bible, which was inside its own box that was kept normally on her bedside cabinet but, while sleeping on the sofa, she had placed it down the side of the sofa cushion. She put the chain around her neck, made sure it couldn't be seen and went to wash and get dressed in the bathroom. Of course, it would have been simpler to do what Jack had suggested and return it to him for safekeeping, but she did not want to part with it, and on New Year's Day she would wear it on the third finger of her left hand.

Once breakfast was over, she prepped lunch, and then dusted and swept and polished the spare bedrooms. She made up the beds with fresh bedding and brought down the camp beds from the attic and made them up as well. She had left the care of Alfie in Mairi's and his grandmother's hands, and at ten o'clock Eliza had a break and took in a cup of coffee and a mince pie to Amelia, who was rewriting her short story that was due for publication on St Valentine's Day.

'That's a while off,' said Eliza.

'Not that far off,' said Amelia. 'Publishers have to plan ahead, so I have to send off this story in plenty of time if it's to be considered for St Valentine's week edition.'

'So, you're writing a love story?'

Amelia nodded. 'As they say: "Love makes the world go round."'

'Can I read it?' asked Eliza.

'It's not ready. You can read it when it's published and the magazine is available,' said Amelia. 'Now go and leave me alone.'

Eliza went and gave the lounge a thorough clean while Mairi offered to sweep the lobby, stairs and landings upstairs. The bathroom was being left until later in the day, as she wanted a bath and to wash her hair before returning to the kitchen and cooking, using left-over goose, lardons of bacon and button mushrooms, all in a creamy sauce and baked in a pie to be served with mashed potatoes, roasted honey and butter parsnips, and sprouts.

She had timed the meal right and Theo, Dilys, Glyn and Gwen arrived at a quarter past one. 'Where's Glenys?' asked Mairi of a vexed-looking Theo.

'I don't know,' he replied. 'Although Gwen says she didn't want to travel in my car with Glyn.'

'I thought she might have gone straight to Nanna's, but why didn't she take me with her if that was her plan?' said Gwen.

'Not if she didn't want you with her,' said Dilys. 'She must have been meeting someone else.'

'But who?' said Glyn.

'Perhaps there's another man in her life,' said Dilys. 'Maybe she's fed up with her sister and wants out of anything to do with her, and that includes her daughter.'

'No!' exclaimed Gwen explosively, stamping her foot. 'You don't understand what them being identical twins meant to them. There was a special tie between them. Aunt Glenys would do anything for Mam, including looking after me.'

Eliza stared at the girl, thinking she had a look of her grandmother: the same oval-shaped face and hazel eyes that wore a bewildered expression. She was young to have had to cope with all that had happened and yet she must have sensed an underlying atmosphere, and sometimes children can be forgotten about, and they overhear conversations that they should not have done. Eliza remembered her mother and a neighbour talking about a girl in the street who was pregnant, and she had asked her mother about it and had received a clout on the head for listening to other people's conversation.

She recalled herself to the present and said, 'Can we forget about Glenys for now? Mairi can explain the sleeping arrangements and show you to your rooms. You probably want to use the bathroom and freshen up and change. Now Glenys isn't here, Gwen can sleep on the camp bed, but it can be put in Dilys's room, and Theo can have the room that would have been Glenys's and have a proper bed to sleep in. Glyn will have a room to himself, and the camp bed will be removed. Mairi, have you got all that?'

Mairi nodded, shocked still by her first sighting of Glyn and the binding where his left foot should have been. He was struggling with crutches. 'You'd be more comfortable in a wheelchair,' she whispered in his ear.

'I know, but I can't get upstairs in a wheelchair,' he said sharply.

She flinched, and he flushed and stared at his mother, whose mouth quivered.

Eliza wanted to hit him for speaking to Mairi in that tone. She, herself, had still not quite forgiven him for lying to her. She said, 'If Jack was here, he and Theo could probably carry you up between them—' She stopped abruptly. 'I'd forgotten he can't. He was shot in the arm when the post office was robbed.'

The two men looked disbelieving and Dilys shocked. 'He'll be here later,' added Eliza. 'You can talk to him then. I'll go and set the table and tell Amelia you've arrived. You'd think she'd have heard the fuss but when she's writing, she's lost in her own little world.'

When Eliza knocked on the door and opened it, Amelia lifted her head and stared at her as if in a daze. 'Theo, Dilys, Glyn and young Gwen are here. Lunch will be served in half an hour.' She closed the door gently and waited, sighing with relief when the clatter of typewriter keys did not resume. She moved away from the door before it opened and Amelia emerged and entered the dining room and began to set the table.

It was not until everyone was seated that Amelia asked, 'Where's Glenys?'

'She's not coming,' said Theo, picking up his knife and fork.

'Where's she gone?' asked his aunt.

'We don't know,' answered Theo.

'Perhaps she's gone to her mother for Christmas?' she suggested.

He shook his head. 'She would have mentioned it if that was what she wanted and taken Gwen with her and left her at her mother's.'

'Nan would have told her to take me to my uncle and his wife. Nan thinks the sun shines out of him, but his wife hates Nan and Mum. She's a real fussy faggot.'

'What did you say?' asked Glyn, an edge to his voice.

'That's what Mum and Aunt Glenys call her,' said Gwen. 'I know what fussy means but not faggot. She makes you take your shoes off as soon as you enter their house. I did that and trod on a straight pin. It didn't half hurt, and Mum played merry hell with her. We never went there again.'

'Your mother should have had her mouth washed out with soap,' said her grandmother.

'Leave her, Mother,' said Glyn. 'She'll grow out of the habit of repeating what her mother used to say soon enough, so don't be frightening her by such threats. I haven't forgotten what it felt like.'

'Did you use naughty words when you were a boy, Uncle Glyn?' asked Gwen.

'Enough of such talk,' said her grandmother. 'Little girls should be seen and not heard.'

'That's not fair. Boys should be treated the same,' said Gwen.

Eliza spoke up, 'I'm going upstairs to fetch Alfie and when we come down, I'll be expecting you all to be eating your lunch or I'll believe I'm a dreadful cook.'

She left the dining room, and no one spoke for a while, as everyone fell on the food on their plates. Gwen was first to finish and said, 'That was great. What's for pudding?'

Mairi laughed. 'I agree. As for pudding, you have a choice. Christmas pudding or trifle.'

By the time Eliza reached the foot of the stairs, she could hear the babble of voices and a knock on the front door. She reached it first and opened it, and Jack stepped over the threshold and kissed her. 'Happy Boxing Day!'

'You sound full of beans,' she said, helping him take off his overcoat.

'I'm happy if that's what you mean,' he said, rubbing noses with Alfie. 'Everybody's arrived by the sound of it.'

'All except Glenys,' she said.

'That's unexpected.'

'Theo's angry because she just didn't turn up and didn't even leave a note saying where she was going.'

'Is the little girl, Gwen, here?'

Eliza nodded. 'And she has plenty of spunk, which surprised me. She has a lot to say for herself and is going to have to learn when to keep her mouth shut. Anyway, we'd best go in. You've missed my special goose pie, but I've saved you a slice to take home, as I presume you've had lunch. We're at the pudding stage if you want some. I'll set you a place at the table. Right now, you can take Alfie while I get his feeding chair to the table.'

Jack took Alfie awkwardly, but the boy clung to his Fair Isle sweater, and she opened the door and they went inside. There was a chorus of welcomes and as soon as Eliza had been given a list of what people wanted for pudding, Mairi accompanied her to the kitchen.

Eliza spooned out the trifle, while Mairi saw to the Christmas pudding and poured over the cream. After serving, both sat down, and everybody ate their dessert.

Then all moved to the lounge, but for Eliza, Mairi and Dilys, who offered to help clear away and see to the dishes. Tea and coffee were served, and conversation broke out. The men sat near each other, and Gwen was taken under Dilys's and Mairi's wings, while Amelia and Gladys talked together. As Eliza passed round a box of cigarettes and a bowl of chocolates and sugared almonds, she caught snatches of conversation. As she expected, the men were talking about the fighting in the Far East and the treachery of the Japanese, who while talking peace had not only made surprise attacks on American bases in Pearl Harbour, but also attacked Malaya, invaded Thailand, attacked Hong Kong and dropped bombs on Singapore. British troops were defending the island as best they could, and the Royal Navy were sending more ships with troops and the Royal Air Force were sending planes.

While in Europe there was bitter fighting between the Russians and the Germans, but now they had blizzards to contend with and the Germans were making slow progress.

The younger women were talking about an article in the *Echo* which stated that British women would fight with their last hatpin to keep the Nazis off the streets of Britain. Dilys laughed at the idea but not about the rumour that 100,000 women would be called up to help Air Defence Forces. The two eldest women talked about rationing and what there was to be had in the shops; Amelia mentioned the Bon Marché having blankets for sale.

Eliza became aware of Gwen watching her feed Alfie and she beckoned her over. 'Do you like babies?' she asked.

Gwen nodded. 'Mum got me one but then she said I couldn't keep it and we went away without it. I cried but she said that she would find me another one. But that was a fib, and we never went back home for my dolly's pram, but her friend brought me a baby doll from across the water. Can I hold your baby?' she asked. 'I won't drop him.'

'He'll be too heavy for you,' said Eliza, wondering if her mother had allowed her to hold Alfie after she had kidnapped him.

Gwen's face fell.

Eliza felt the girl's disappointment and thought swiftly. 'I'll tell you what we'll do. Once I've finished feeding Alfie, you can wheel him in his pushchair, but you can't take him out of the house.'

'I can't anyway, because I wouldn't be able to open the door or get the pushchair down the steps.'

'You're a clever girl,' said Eliza. 'Your father will be proud of you.'

Gwen frowned. 'My father's dead and he didn't want me.'

'I mean Glyn. He's going to adopt you and so he'll be your daddy.'

'I'll like that because he's nice to me and he has a house in Colwyn Bay. I'll be able to visit Nan, but I don't know whether I'll like my new grandmother.'

'You must be kind to her,' said Eliza. 'She's had a lot of sadness in her life and now is sad because of Glyn being injured.'

All the time they had been talking, Mairi had been standing close by and now she said to Gwen, 'I'll be living in your daddy's house, too.'

'That'll be nice,' said Gwen. 'Will you be my new mother?'

Eliza intervened: 'You'll have to ask your new daddy about that.' She determined to speak to Jack about it and ask him to encourage Glyn to marry Mairi. And soon.

CHAPTER THIRTY-ONE

The day of the christening dawned bright and crisp, cold but with no snow. The house was a flurry of activity and the dining table had been pushed back against a wall, ready for the buffet to be set out, as well as plates and cutlery. Drinks would be served in the lounge and dining chairs had been carried through there to provide more seating. Once the food was prepared and set out and covered with tea towels, Eliza was able to have a few words with Jack about Gwen, Glyn and Mairi. Then she went upstairs to get changed and to dress Alfie in his father's christening gown and the white bonnet that Olive had knitted. Milly had bought him a white lacy shawl and he was wrapped snugly in that. The godmothers and Eliza were dressed in what in the future would be their Sunday best and all those invited set off to the church in good time. As for the godfathers, Eliza had changed her mind and asked Glyn to be a godfather once she saw him with Gwen and Mairi. She so wished that her parents and grandparents could have been there, but at least Alfie had one grandmother present.

The service went off without a hitch and Alfie did not cry, which was a fault in him according to his grandmother, who said something about letting the devil out. 'Old wives' tale,' said the vicar to her after the service.

Then everyone went back to Amelia's house and the occasion was declared a great success. The buffet was enjoyed by all and there were only a few crumbs and crusts left. Cathy from the tearoom was there and shed tears. It was not until most of the guests had departed that Eliza placed her engagement ring on the third finger of her left hand. It was not long before it was noticed, so instead of waiting until New Year's Day she and Jack announced their engagement. There was a round of applause and when that died down to a murmur, Mairi approached Eliza and told her that Glyn had suggested that he and she should get married. He said it was Gwen's idea, as she needed a new mother. Ada was in a women's prison asylum. He added that he also needed a capable wife to help him in the task he had taken on and, if they were married, there was little chance of her being called up, what with him having been badly injured. 'Not the most romantic of proposals,' said Mairi, 'but I've got what I want and the sooner we're married, the better.'

Eliza agreed.

Later, when only the members of the household and Jack were there, Theo said, 'Glenys didn't turn up.'

'I noticed,' said Amelia. 'Bad form.'

'Perhaps she's had an accident,' suggested Dilys.

'I don't believe it,' Eliza said. 'I think there's someone else. Gwen said something to me and...' She hesitated. 'No, I'm getting muddled up with the sisters.'

'Anyway, it was a lovely service,' said Amelia, 'and everyone seemed to have enjoyed themselves. The next thing to look forward to is New Year's Eve.'

'We won't be here,' said Glyn's mother.

'Unless we stay here longer,' said Gwen.

'We can't outstay our welcome,' Glyn said. 'Amelia needs peace and quiet to get on with her writing.'

'That's true,' said Amelia. 'As much as I have enjoyed your company, it's as Glyn says.'

'And there's something for you to look forward to,' said Glyn. 'Mairi and I are getting married, and you can be a bridesmaid.'

'That's wonderful,' said Amelia. 'Don't you agree, Gladys?'

'Of course, and this wedding will be in the Welsh chapel,' said Glyn's mother.

'Have you set a date?' asked Theo.

'Easter would be lovely,' said Glyn's mother.

'Yes,' said Dilys.

'I want it earlier,' said Glyn.

'Me too,' Mairi said.

'How soon?' asked Eliza.

'Next week,' Glyn said, meeting Mairi's eyes.

'But there'll be arrangements to make and invitation cards to send out,' said his mother.

'We don't want a big wedding, do we, Mairi?' said Glyn.

'No,' she agreed. 'Just a simple ceremony with a short aisle for us to make our way up.'

'Can Jack and I come?' asked Eliza.

'Best man and chief bridesmaid,' said Mairi.

That settled, Eliza went to the kitchen, followed by Mairi and Dilys, and made a jug of cocoa.

'You lucky ducks,' said Dilys. 'I wish I could find a man who would want to marry me.'

'He'll find you,' said Eliza convincingly.

Dilys was staying on in Liverpool and Theo said he'd return in time for New Year, but he had to drive Glyn, Mairi, Gwen and the elder Mrs Jones to Colwyn Bay. In that moment Mairi determined to learn to drive. She would discuss it with Glyn later that day.

They were waved off, with Jack and Eliza saying they would see them the following weekend, on 3 and 4 January 1942.

—

The last few days of 1941 passed swiftly. Amelia and Dilys went into town to see if there was anything worth buying in the shops, and Eliza took Alfie with her to Breck Road to buy food for the next couple of days. She also changed the sheets on Theo's bed, and swept and dusted his bedroom, ready for his return in time for New Year's Eve. She also folded the camp beds and took them back up to the attic. Then, on the evening before New Year's Eve, Jack and Eliza went to the cinema to see *The Maltese Falcon*, starring Humphrey Bogart, Mary Astor and Peter Lorre, a detective story which they both enjoyed and that helped them to forget the war for a while. As Jack walked Eliza home, they discussed when they should get married.

'June,' suggested Eliza. 'Where is a bit more difficult.'

'Why?' Jack asked.

'I'd like to be married in the ruined chapel on Love Island, which is joined to Newborough beach on Anglesey. It's dedicated to Wales's saint for lovers.'

Jack said, 'It sounds romantic but is the ruin consecrated and acceptable for a wedding? And it doesn't sound as if it would be easy for guests to get to.'

'It's not that difficult,' she protested. 'My grandparents took me there. I would feel like they were with me in spirit.'

'What's wrong with St Margaret's?' he asked.

'She's not the saint of lovers,' she said.

'I think it's too far to expect guests to go,' he said, 'and where would we have the reception?'

'There are hotels on Anglesey,' she retorted.

'I'd like to see the place first,' he said.

She hesitated.

'I don't consider that unreasonable,' he said.

'No, it's not,' she said, hesitating to add that she did not believe he would find it romantic.

'Then let's make a trip when we go to Colwyn Bay for Glyn and Mairi's wedding,' he said, slipping his uninjured arm about her waist.

'But it'll be cold. It's winter and the sea could be rough,' she said.

'It's then or it's off,' he said.

'All right,' she said. 'But wait until you see the view of Snowdonia from the island,' she added dreamily.

'I can see the mountains from Formby beach on a clear day,' he said.

'Oh, Jack, where's your romantic spirit?'

'I'll know when I see your Love Island,' he said. 'Now let's drop the subject.'

They walked the rest of the way in silence, and he refused to come in for a cocoa, but he did kiss her good night and say that he would see her tomorrow evening.

CHAPTER THIRTY-TWO

Eliza slept uneasily that night and woke wondering if she had been unreasonable about wanting a romantic site for their wedding, but after all her first wedding had been a farce. Anyway, the important thing was that they stayed together and did not fall out. She found herself thinking of Theo and Glenys, and wondering why she had gone off the way she did, when she could have had a lift to her mother's house. Eliza could not think where else she could have gone, unless... she recalled what Gwen had said about identical twins. The only twins she knew were Milly's, but they weren't identical. They weren't even the same sex.

She wished she knew more about twins but what she did know was that identical twins could have a special bond. She recalled the gynaecologist who had been consulted in Gwen's mother's trial. Surely, she would know something about identical twins, but she could not remember how they'd got in touch with her without Angus, and his ship could have sailed by now. Still, she had heard it said that twins could sense when something was wrong with each other, even when they weren't in touch in the normal way. Setting that aside, it was possible that Glenys had gone to see her twin sister and didn't want Theo to know. Eliza realised that she had wandered some way from thinking of her wedding. Best to put it all to the back of her mind for now and wait until tomorrow for Theo's return to hear any news of Glenys. And as for her wedding, that decision would have to wait until Glyn and Mairi's wedding was over.

236

Theo arrived back in time for afternoon tea at four; supper would be at ten, as they waited to see the new year in. It was not the big occasion that the Scots made of Hogmanay, but like the rest of the world at war, they were desperate to know if 1942 was going to be a year to welcome with glad hearts and if this would be the year when peace was declared.

But firstly, the household wanted to know if there was any news of Glenys.

'Her mother and brother haven't heard from her,' said Theo. 'Gwen spoke of her mother and is convinced that her auntie Glenys has gone to visit her.'

'Surely that's easy enough for you to check?' said Eliza. 'But before you answer that question, what did Glenys's mother say about Mairi and Glyn getting married, and adopting Gwen, when you told her?'

'I didn't tell her,' Theo replied. 'Gwen told her and made no bones about being pleased about it.'

Then he added, 'She told us to get out of her house and that Gwen was an ungrateful little brat. Gwen stuck her tongue out at her, so we beat a retreat. I did wonder if Glenys would turn up after we left.'

'The little madam,' said Amelia. 'I hope she isn't going to be too much to handle for Mairi and Glyn.'

'It's out of our hands now,' said Jack. 'It could be that you'll get some answers from Glenys when you return to London, Theo.'

'I'll let you all know,' he said.

Nothing more was said about Glenys that evening: the radio was switched on to hear the news and the men had a whisky. Amelia drank a sherry while she read to Alfie, and Eliza and Dilys went into the kitchen to prepare supper. Amelia handed Alfie over to Jack and went to her writing room to make some phone calls.

As they worked harmoniously together, Dilys said, 'Do you think we'll have any first-footers?'

'I honestly don't know. It's my first New Year in this house.'

'We could always go first-footing,' said Dilys.

Eliza smiled. 'We could go to the Scot lady's house. The one whose son is the doctor and whose ship was in dock for repairs.'

'That sounds good,' said Dilys. 'Do we tell the men and Aunt Amelia?'

'No, we won't disturb them. They could guess when they realise we're missing. We need to take a bit of coal, a slice of bread and some money.' Eliza found what was needed, and they left the house quietly and headed along the pavement in the dark to the house a few doors down.

To Eliza's surprise, the door was opened by a stranger. 'Who are you?' she asked.

'I'm a sailor and a friend of the Doc,' he said. 'Who are you?'

'I'm Eliza and this is Dilys, the niece of my landlady. We're from a few doors up, and we've come to first-foot and wish Angus and his mam a happy Hogmanay. If you're here, I presume Angus still is.'

He nodded. 'I hope you haven't come empty-handed,' he said.

'Cheeky,' said Dilys.

'You're not a Scouser or a Scot,' he said.

'No, I'm from Shropshire,' she said. 'Are you going to let us in?' She produced a florin.

He grinned. 'I'd have let you in for tuppence,' he said.

'Donny, who's at the door?' shouted a voice with a Scots accent.

'It's Eliza, Angus,' she shouted. 'We're freezing out here and Donny expects us to pay an entrance fee before we can come in.'

'You Scousers,' said Angus, approaching and cuffing Donny across the top of his head.

'That's a lie,' said Donny. 'I expected the usual gift. A lump of coal, a slice of bread and a couple of coppers.'

'Here you are then,' said Eliza, producing the items mentioned and handing them to Angus.

He and Donny stepped aside and ushered Eliza and Dilys inside. Eliza asked for a shandy and Dilys asked for a sherry. Eliza went and talked to Angus's mother, Alice, while Donny chattered to Dilys and after a while she asked him where in Liverpool he lived. His mouth drooped at the corners.

'It's a ruin now,' he replied. 'It was bombed during the May Blitz and my parents were killed.'

'I'm sorry to hear that,' she said, placing a hand over his.

'I still feel guilty about it. There's me out on the briny, trying to prevent the Jerries from hurting them, and here's me alive and kicking, and them dead and buried in their own home.'

'That's not your fault,' she said. 'Your life is at risk every time you set sail.'

'Mam worried about me all the time. "Those pesky U-boats," she used to say. "Sneaky, that's what they are." I didn't argue with her. I just said that's war, Mam. You just keep praying it'll be over soon.'

'So, when will you be returning to sea?' she asked.

'When the ship's seaworthy,' he replied. 'I'm staying here at the Doc's until then. He's a good bloke, nothing hoity-toity about him.'

'Perhaps I'll see you again,' she said.

'We could go to the flicks or for a walk in the park,' he suggested.

'That would be nice,' Dilys said. 'Angus knows where I'm staying.'

Eliza and Dilys only remained for another five minutes and then they returned to Amelia's house. Once there, Eliza took Alfie upstairs and put him in his cot.

–

A few days later, she and Jack set off to Colwyn Bay. Fortunately, by then, Jack could drive and the weather was milder. He had seen the doctor and been told his wound was on the mend. It was still a little sore and was bound up again. It was a fine day for the journey and Eliza could only pray that it would be fine in Colwyn Bay and Anglesey.

There wasn't a cloud in the sky when Eliza, with Gwen in charge, and Mairi, wearing a dress of cream satin that had been her mother's wedding dress altered to fit her, set out for the chapel with the bride's father. Eliza had noticed a curtain being lifted in a house nearby and a face at the window, and for a moment she had thought it was Glenys, but then it was gone.

The service was short but inspiring and the singing gorgeous. Jack was a stalwart best man to Glyn, who had left his crutches at home, having obeyed his bride's advice to conserve his strength for their honeymoon. The reception was held in Glyn's house in Colwyn Bay with just twenty-five guests and, as soon as the speeches and toasts were done with, the meal ended with a slice of wedding cake. Jack and Eliza excused themselves and set out for Anglesey, having left Alfie with Jack's mother and sister back in Liverpool – something she still felt apprehensive about, but if she couldn't trust them who could she trust?

The journey did not take them long and soon they were parked in Newborough Warren car park. Eliza watched Jack look about him doubtfully at the surrounding trees.

'So, where's this Love Island of yours?'

She took his hand and led him in the direction of the beach, which seemed to stretch for miles, and turned right and began to walk. After a while, he said, 'This isn't easy walking. Is it much further?'

She did not disagree with him but said, 'There's a path through the trees which is easier.' So they climbed through some sandhills and joined the footpath, and eventually went back onto the beach at a place where she was able to point out the island, which seemed to be joined on to the mainland, due to the tide being out. In no time at all they were climbing up a path after crossing the beach and, as they followed that path, the island stretched out before them. They eventually came to a ruined building, and she took a deep breath, 'It's centuries old, you know.'

'It looks it,' he said.

He followed her inside. 'Can't you feel the atmosphere?' she said.

'Show me the rest of the island. And is that a lighthouse I can see not far away?'

She nodded, knowing she had let her imagination run away with her. She reached out to him, and he took her hand and they walked on until they came to a simple huge cross with several steps up to it. The lighthouse was now only a short distance away, on a rise with a flight of steps running up to it. They wasted no time climbing up the steps, going round to the other side and looking out over the sea.

Jack took a deep breath of cold salty air, and it was a few minutes before he said, 'Thanks for bringing me here.' His gaze took in the mountains slightly to the left. 'I presume that's Snowdonia?'

She nodded. 'And somewhere below the mountains is where the Menai Strait meets the Irish Sea.'

'The chapel won't do for our wedding, sweetheart,' he said. 'But let's find a hotel on Anglesey and spend our honeymoon where we can explore the rest of the island. You can show me where you spent some of your youth and childhood.'

'I'd like that,' she said. 'When we get back to Liverpool, we should visit the vicar and arrange a date for our wedding at St Margaret's.'

They hugged and kissed. 'Now let's find a handy hotel and have a meal and a drink, and make a note of its name and phone number so we can reserve a room for our honeymoon in June,' said Jack.

She kissed him and then they had another look at the view, before leaving.

CHAPTER THIRTY-THREE

Eliza put on the kettle and spooned tea into the teapot, and sighed deeply, thinking of that day with Jack on Anglesey. It seemed an age ago now and the war far away. The date had been fixed for their wedding at St Margaret's Church on the weekend before Midsummer's Day, so they could watch the sun rise on Love Island. The thought of it helped lift her spirits – that and watching Alfie develop into a toddler. He was walking now, and she needed eyes like a hawk to see he didn't get into trouble. He had five teeth and could also say several words. His grandmother would be delighted when they visited her at Easter.

If only Britain and her allies could bring the war to an end with a victory, but at the beginning of this month, the Japanese had invaded Singapore, and British servicemen and civilians had been killed or captured and marched off to prisoner-of-war camps. Today was St Valentine's Day and Dilys's expression was like a wet weekend. Ever since she and Donny, a sailor on Angus's ship, had started walking out, her emotions had been up and down like a yo-yo, especially now that he and Angus were back at sea and in danger from German U-boats. Thank God they weren't alone in the fight, as the Americans had declared war on Germany, who was an ally of Japan. At least there were no bombers over Merseyside, as Hitler's main attention was on Russia, and the first American servicemen had arrived in Britain.

Not far away from Liverpool, near to the town of Warrington, was Burtonwood airbase for American airmen. When they had time off, some came into Liverpool and soon made friends with some of the women of the city. Milly had told her that her twins had seen some in Newsham Park and been given candy and chewing gum, as well as American comics with such heroes as Superman, who could fly and rescued people from the baddies.

While lots of folk were reassured by the Americans' presence, Dilys wasn't, for she was obsessed with something happening to Donny. Now his ship was seaworthy, it was employed, like numerous other British ships, in either taking troops to Asia to assist those fighting the Japanese or sailing the North Atlantic to take food and arms to help the Russian people in the German invasion.

Eliza was thankful that Jack was in a job that meant he was fighting for good in Liverpool. It never failed to shock her that there were people who considered the war an opportunity to make money out of their fellow citizens' misfortune. But she also believed that there were lots of people prepared to make sacrifices for others.

Angus's mother had taken in a mother and a daughter, who was a nurse, and her neighbours had let their house to the relatives of a friend of Milly's, who had been bombed out. Then there were those who organised events to raise money for the war effort, and those men and women, old and young, who enlisted in the forces. Olive had left the factory and answered the call for women to join the Women's Air Force to work on the ground at airfields, one of which was not far from the seaside resort of Southport.

There were shortages of coal, and what coal there was available was overpriced, and Eliza was glad when the days lengthened, and it was warmer. The fires did not need to be lit until evening and Easter was only a week away.

Amelia had finished her novel and parcelled up the manuscript and sent it off to her agent in London. She had considered taking it herself, catching a train to London and dropping in on Theo. He had telephoned Amelia to tell her that Glenys had not turned up and neither had she sent a letter to provide a reason why. Eliza recalled that face at the window the day of Glyn and Mairi's wedding. Should she tell Amelia so she could pass on the news to Theo? She did so and Amelia decided to go to London. Dilys was still at the house in Liverpool, despite her mother writing several times and asking her to come home. She decided to stay on there and mind the house while Amelia was in London, as Eliza and Alfie were staying in Colwyn Bay at Easter. Dilys lived in hope that Donny and Angus's ship would return safely, and she could spend time with Donny. She was feeling broody, since a letter had come telling them that Mairi was having a baby.

Eliza had wanted Jack to accompany her and Alfie to Colwyn Bay, but he could not have time off, especially now he was in the detective division, and he had booked time off for their wedding and honeymoon. She would never forget when he came to the house and lifted her off her feet and swung her around, his face alight with joy and satisfaction. 'I've been promoted,' he shouted. 'I'm now a fully-fledged detective.'

'I'm so glad,' she'd said. 'You're so clever and deserve it.'

'It could mean getting a police house after the war,' he said. 'A house of our own where we can raise a family. Two girls and a boy, that will be two of each and they'll all have a brother and a sister, including Alfie.' And they had kissed again and again, hugging tightly. Amelia rejoiced with them and produced a bottle of whisky and one of champagne from somewhere. And along with Dilys, Jack's mother and Jean, and Milly, they celebrated with a fish and chip supper from the local chippy, Garnet's, where Jack had got Sooty from after their cat had produced six kittens.

'You're going to be missed,' said Milly. 'I feel sorry for the bobby who replaces you on your beat.'

Jack shook his head. 'He's a retired policeman, who they might remember, and they will make him feel welcome.'

—

So, Jack saw Eliza and Alfie onto the train and kissed them both and told her to give his congratulations to Mairi and Glyn. She waved until she could see him no more. The journey would have dragged if her son had not pestered her to read the new book that Jack had bought for the journey: *The Tale of Peter Rabbit* by

Beatrix Potter. Alfie fell asleep when she had reached the end, so she read the latest edition of *Woman's Weekly* and then gazed out of the window at the passing scene.

When the train arrived at Colwyn Bay station, to her surprise Mairi was there to meet them. 'I thought you might need some help,' she said. 'I was going to bring the car, only I couldn't get petrol. I wanted to show my prowess in driving.'

'You passed your test?'

'Yes, and it's proving useful when I can put petrol in the tank. Otherwise, I walk.'

'Oh well done! How's Glyn and his mother? How have they taken the news of the baby?'

'Both delighted, and also looking forward to seeing you two and catching up on news.'

Eliza told her about Amelia finishing her book and going to London.

'I suppose London is safe now,' said Mairi.

'As far as I know,' said Eliza. 'I think Theo would have told us if it wasn't. Anyway, she was determined to go and, let's be honest, we don't know how long the war will last and we need to take calculated risks sometimes. Trains and cars may crash, and people can be killed crossing the road.'

'No news of Glenys?' asked Mairi, taking Eliza's bag while she strapped Alfie in his pushchair.

'No, although I told Theo how I thought I saw her peeping round the curtain on your wedding day.'

'I didn't know about that,' said Mairi.

'At the time I thought I'd imagined her. Anyway, if it was her, she'll have scarpered by now. She hasn't turned up at the Intelligence office in London and that means she's in trouble. Desertion.'

'Gwen says she's gone to visit Ada,' said Mairi.

'Has that been looked into?' asked Eliza, feeling the old fear of Alfie being kidnapped.

Mairi nodded. 'The only visitor she's had is her mother. Gwen doesn't believe her Nan would visit her in that place.' She paused. 'Nobody took any notice of what she thinks.'

'She's a bright kid,' said Eliza.

'Anyway, I wish we could have some good news about the war,' said Mairi. 'Glyn gets all worked up about it.'

'You can't mean he wishes to be back in the army, making a difference?'

'No, not now we're having a baby,' said Mairi. 'He's made up.'

'Congratulations again.' Eliza hugged her. 'You'll have to give police work up, though.'

Mairi nodded. 'We'll manage and at least we don't have rent or a mortgage to pay.' She paused. 'Although more income would be helpful. I told Gladys about the baby, and she astonished me. She said that she'd give Glyn all the rent she hasn't paid since his father died. I sensed he was going to turn her down, so I nudged him and whispered, "Think of our baby," so he thanked her.'

'That's marvellous, and she and Gwen will get a lot of pleasure out of having a baby in the house.'

'I know. She's started knitting and is teaching Gwen how to knit.'

'I hope you'll all still be able to come to mine and Jack's wedding in June,' said Eliza.

'You can bet we will. The baby's due in August, so all being well, we'll be there. If only the war will end before then! But Glyn believes we've some way to go yet.'

During that short Easter break Eliza would often stare across the water as she sat on the beach helping Alfie and Gwen build a sandcastle, agreeing with her son that it would be better if Jack was there, while daydreaming about their honeymoon on Anglesey. They had still not decided whether to take Alfie with them, as Jack's mother had offered to look after him and so had Dilys. Sooner rather than later, Eliza was going to have to come to a decision.

CHAPTER THIRTY-FOUR

Jack was waiting on the platform to help Eliza down with the pushchair. Then he kissed her and Alfie. 'I've missed you both.'

'We've missed you. I got the impression that you were preferred as a sandcastle builder to me, and I couldn't help thinking of all the sandy beaches on Anglesey,' she said.

'So, you've made up your mind?' he said.

'You have the final answer,' she replied.

'I enjoy building sandcastles,' he said.

'Oh, you are a love,' she responded, hugging him.

'We mustn't forget to go to Blackpool when the war's over,' he said. 'They not only have the lights, but also a great expanse of beach. Anyway, let's make a move. Amelia's back from London and Dilys is cooking.'

'You don't look pleased,' she said.

'She can't cook like you or me mam,' he said. 'Besides, I don't think she's been sensible while you and Amelia have been away.'

'What do you mean? Has she been spending too much money and borrowing from you?'

'No. Angus and Donny's ship has returned with some injured sailors they managed to rescue after their ship was hit and sank.'

'Was the ship one of ours?' she asked.

'One of ours, which is a blow, but some of the crews have been saved, as they did manage to damage the enemy ship,' said Jack. 'They had to pick up the dead bodies, too, so they could be identified.'

His words triggered a memory, and she recalled one of her rescuers shouting, 'Ben, there's one alive here. The other two are dead.' She gasped.

'I shouldn't have said that about dead bodies, should I?' said Jack.

'Yes, because it's triggered my memory of when I was rescued. One of the men shouted to another called Ben about there being two dead bodies and a live one.'

'So, it was probably Ben Evans and Milly's husband Jimmy who rescued you,' said Jack, hugging her tightly. 'We'll both thank them because I wouldn't have you and Alfie if they hadn't done so.'

'Angus must have been kept busy helping the injured. And Dilys and Angus's mother must be over the moon,' said Eliza. She was still thinking of Jimmy and Ben Evans.

He nodded. 'The trouble is that I've dropped in at Amelia's to see if things are all right with Dilys, and Donny's there every time.'

'So, did you play gooseberry?' she asked.

'I hung around for a while the first time and got him talking about what had happened at sea, but eventually, I had to leave because I was on duty and had only intended to drop in for a few minutes.'

'It's a bit of a temptation to have a house to yourselves,' said Eliza, concerned for Dilys and remembering the girl telling her that her mother had wanted her to go home. 'Well, there's nothing we can do now.'

He nodded. 'She won't be the first to get pregnant before marriage in wartime.'

'If she does, I bet her mother will blame Amelia,' said Eliza.

'Well, we'd best keep our thoughts to ourselves. After all, I could be doing them both an injustice. It's something I could imagine our Jean getting into trouble with, if her Polish young man wasn't miles away.'

'I thought he was in London,' she said.

'That was months ago,' said Jack. 'I've no idea where he is now.'

'I wonder if she knows.' Eliza sighed. 'I don't know how I'd cope if I didn't know where you were.'

'We make the most of our time together each day,' he said. 'I suppose Donny and Dilys could get married before he goes back to sea.'

'What if it was too soon and it didn't work out?' she said, thinking about her own hasty marriage. 'I question how life would have gone for me if Bryn hadn't been killed. I can't believe he would have been faithful.'

'If you had discovered he was a bigamist, you could have freed yourself.'

'But would he have let go of Alfie?'

'You're forgetting he broke the law. The courts would have given you custody of Alfie.'

'I don't know how I could doubt it,' she said.

'Because you haven't been able to rid yourself of the fear you felt when he was kidnapped.'

'I thought I had,' she said. 'Because I have you.'

'Then I got shot and you realised that, although the Blitz was over, there was still danger even here.'

She nodded. 'I'm selfish, I have so much more than so many other people and I should be counting my blessings and praying for those worse off and thinking of what I can do for them. I haven't even been to see how Rosie is.' She turned in his arms. 'Have you seen her around?'

'No, but I presumed she was still involved with the Sally Army.'

'Perhaps I should look in on her,' she said. 'I don't want her to think we've forgotten about her.'

'Leave her to me,' he said.

'But you have work,' she said.

'So do you,' he said.

'Not to the same extent. I'm more of a housekeeper than a researcher now Amelia has finished her book.'

'But she's bound to start another one,' he said. 'And what about her husband's family tree?'

'I think she knows all she wanted to know, and she prefers fiction. Over Christmas she was writing a short story for a magazine.' Eliza felt Alfie tug her skirt. 'We'd better make a move. He thinks we've forgotten about him.'

'And we did for a short while,' said Jack. 'Let's go. I've got a report to write this afternoon and you haven't told me how Mairi and Glyn are getting on.'

'They're pleased as Punch about the baby,' she said. 'It's due in August, so they're still coming to our wedding.'

'I'm pleased for them,' said Jack. 'And how are his mother and Gwen?'

'Grandmother is teaching Gwen how to knit.'

'That's a good sign,' he said, as they left the railway station.

When they arrived at Amelia's, Jack did not linger and so the two women had a good natter, interrupted now and again by Dilys bringing them coffee and barm cakes from the bakery on Whitefield Road. They were spread with the blackberry jam that she and Eliza had made from the fruit growing wild that they had picked last autumn in Croxteth Park.

Amelia told them about her stay with Theo and that there was still no news of Glenys, who had been declared having gone AWOL. It was suspected, though, that she might have visited her twin in the high-security asylum wing of a prison in Lancashire disguised as her mother and then changed places with Ada, who most likely had caught a train to Liverpool, where she had been lost in the crowds.

'It's all very odd that she should have vanished the way she has,' said Dilys. 'She could have caught a train to London or Conway.'

'That was considered,' said Amelia. 'Her mother's house has been under surveillance, but there's been no sighting of her, and a photo of her was shown to the attendants on the barrier to the London platform.'

Eliza had an idea but kept it to herself, saving it until she could put it to Jack. She changed and fed Alfie and let him play with his toys for a while, before putting him down for a nap. Then she unpacked and changed into a clean frock and checked with Dilys whether she would like her to prepare the evening meal. Dilys told her that she had presumed Eliza would take over as soon as she returned. So, having checked that Alfie was still sleeping and after asking Dilys to check up on him from time to time, Eliza went shopping, but not without a certain sense of doubt. Having collected ration books, she was hoping to be able to get a shoulder of mutton, which should do them for two days. She had also checked the store cupboard and so bought a quarter of tea, flour, margarine and sugar, as well as baking apples, potatoes and carrots. Then she hurried back home, not wanting to leave Alfie too long.

When she returned, she found Donny at the house, attempting to soothe Dilys. Eliza immediately guessed he'd received inform-ation that he would be sailing soon. It was to be in two days and so Dilys was having difficulty in pulling herself together. Eventually, Amelia came into the room and told her to stop making such a noise. She waited until Donny had left with Dilys to tell Eliza that she had received a letter from Dilys's father, saying that her mother needed her at home straightaway, as they'd had to take in a nephew and niece whose mother had died unexpectedly and whose father wasn't fit to care for them and had been taken into a nursing home.

'If she doesn't come immediately, he'll come and drag her home. How am I going to tell her that she must leave today?' asked Amelia.

'You have no choice,' said Eliza. 'And if she has any sympathy in her heart, she'll know that she has no choice but to do what her father asks of her.'

'I wonder where she is now,' fretted Amelia.

'She could be just a few doors away,' said Eliza. 'I'll go and see.' Wasting no time, she left the house and went to Angus's house and banged on the door.

A few minutes later she heard footsteps and then the door was opened by a young man she had never seen before.

'Hello, can I help you?' he asked.

'I'm Eliza and I live with Mrs Amelia Jones a few doors away. She's the local authoress. A letter has come from Dilys's father, and we wondered if she was here with Donny.'

His face lit up. 'You're Alfie's mam. Come in. We'll be glad for you to take her with you. I'm Simon Evans, and Barbara, the nurse who lives here, is my fiancée. She's told Dilys to pull herself together because she's upsetting Donny and making the situation worse for him, but she just carries on yowling and clinging to him. The trouble is, she needs something to do that'll take her mind off herself. It's a wonder she hasn't been called up. My dad has and he's in his late forties. He's been at a training camp in Wales.'

'Well, her father has the very thing, so if you could tell her she's needed and must get a move on…' She hesitated. 'Your father is called Ben, is he?'

He nodded and told her to wait a moment. Eliza was bursting to tell him that his father had helped save her and Alfie during the May Blitz. She did not have long to wait before he reappeared with Dilys and Barbara but realised this was not the time to tell him about his father and Jimmy saving her and Alfie.

'So, what is it?' asked Dilys sullenly, mopping her tear-stained face with a crumpled man's handkerchief.

'Your aunt will tell you, so you'd better come immediately,' said Eliza.

Dilys pulled a face. 'I don't like your tone.'

'I don't care, but your father will dislike yours if you don't do what he asks.'

'He's not here, so he can't do anything to me,' she said.

'I wouldn't be too sure about that,' said Eliza. 'You're lucky to have a father who cares about you. I lost mine when I was only a kid.'

'My heart bleeds for you,' said Dilys.

Barbara gasped and Simon exclaimed, 'If Donny heard you speak like that, he'd have nothing more to do with you!'

'And you'll tell him, I suppose,' she retorted.

'Enough!' snapped Eliza. 'Where are your manners, Dilys? Now we're leaving, so say goodbye and let's go.'

'I must speak to Donny first,' she said.

'Leave the poor lad alone,' said Barbara. 'You've got him in a right tizzy.'

'I love him, and he loves me,' Dilys said frantically, turning her back on Eliza, only to have Barbara block her way so she couldn't get to the rear of the house.

Eliza seized Dilys's arm and forced her out of the house. There was a struggle on the step and they both could have injured themselves if Simon hadn't sorted things out and escorted Eliza and Dilys to Amelia's house. She was standing in the doorway, talking to a middle-aged man with a mop of white-silver hair.

'Oh, here they are,' said Amelia in a high-pitched voice.

Dilys tried to free herself from Barbara's and Eliza's fingers on her wrists, but it was too difficult, so she smiled and said, 'Time to say goodbye, ladies.'

Barbara released her hold and said, 'Goodbye, Dilys.'

Eliza linked her arm through Dilys's and urged her through the open front gate. She smiled at the man making his way towards them. 'Mr Jones,' she said.

'Mrs Jones,' he said, inclining his head. 'I think we've met before.'

Eliza stretched forth a hand. 'We were introduced at the meeting in Newtown but never had a chance to talk.'

He smiled. 'But I did get to meet your son Alfie, a charming young man who no doubt will be a credit to the company when he comes of age.'

Eliza returned his smile, despite having taken a dislike to the man when she had first met him, and she felt a pang of sympathy for Dilys.

'Amelia was telling me that Theo returned to London just after Christmas, after paying a visit to Colwyn Bay, but that young lady of his didn't go with him. Oddly enough, I thought I caught sight of her in Lime Street railway station when I got off my train. I greeted her but she mustn't have remembered me because she looked straight through me.'

'How strange,' said Eliza. 'You're not that easy to forget.'

He beamed. 'My wife told me I'm distinguished looking.'

At that moment Dilys approached and said, 'So, what's the emergency, Daddy?'

'Your mother's niece and nephew have been sent to live with us. Her sister has died unexpectedly, and her husband is seriously ill and in a nursing home.'

'Poor kids,' said Dilys. 'But I don't know anything about children, Daddy,' she said.

'You'll soon pick it up,' he said bracingly, patting her shoulder. 'Now go and pack, I want to be home no later than six. I have a meeting to attend.'

'You're always at meetings. You work too hard, Daddy,' she said, moving away swiftly and running upstairs.

'Daughters,' he said with a laugh. 'Give me boys, anytime. Girls don't understand cricket.'

'My fiancé prefers watching rugby and football,' said Eliza.

'Is he still in the police force?' he asked.

'He's a detective sergeant,' she said proudly.

'Never thought of joining the armed forces?'

'Yeah, but he had polio as a boy and was declared unfit.'

'But he was shot a short while ago, when the post office was robbed and he gave chase,' said Amelia.

Eliza said, 'Would you like a cup of tea before you have to leave, Mr Jones?'

He shook his head. 'No thank you, my dear. If you could just run upstairs and hurry my daughter along?'

Dilys was in tears when Eliza entered the bedroom. 'Your father wants you to get a move on. I'm sorry you must go home but I can understand why your mother needs you.'

Dilys wiped her eyes. 'I'm sorry I was rude to you. But I'm so unhappy.'

'I understand but keep your pecker up and do what you can for your little cousins. They must be feeling miserable.'

Dilys nodded. 'Will you keep in touch, please? Aunt Amelia has my address.'

Eliza agreed, adding, 'And don't do anything stupid.'

As soon as father and daughter had departed, Eliza prepared dinner for that evening, before phoning the police station and asking to speak to Sergeant Molyneux. She did not have to wait long before she was put through to Jack and was telling him what Dily's father had said about seeing Glenys in Lime Street railway station earlier that day.

'It seems like she could have been in Liverpool for some time,' she added. 'I've been wondering if she could have been staying at Rosie's after she had visited her sister up in Lancashire.'

'Don't you go along to Rosie's,' he said. 'I'll go.'

Eliza reluctantly agreed and tried to put it out of her mind. She made an apple pie for dessert to go with the scouse, which she prepared using some of the mutton and was simmering on the stove. She thought of Simon saying his father was called Ben and hugged herself after putting the apple pie in the oven. Then she went to do some weeding in the front garden and heard police sirens not that far away. She could not help wondering if they had anything to do with what she had told Jack and would have rushed to Rosie's house if she didn't have the apple pie in the oven. She went into the kitchen and checked the pie, which needed a bit longer, and switched off the heat under the scouse. Then she climbed the stairs and looked in on Alfie in his cot. He was standing up, grasping the bars and rattling them. She told herself that she was going to have to be patient until Jack came and told her what was going on.

CHAPTER THIRTY-FIVE

Eventually, Eliza took the apple pie out of the oven and placed it on the windowsill to cool, and then she set the dining table for two and spooned out the scouse – she even gave Alfie some in his feeding dish once it was cool enough – and called Amelia.

'How nice it is to be just the three of us,' she said. 'Thomas never cared for his elder brother. I do hope Dilys will settle when she arrives home.'

'She's unhappy,' said Eliza, spooning pickled beetroot onto her scouse. 'She became too fond of Donny while we were away. Anyway, he and Angus's ship sails in a day or two. Although, I question whether she would make a good sailor's wife.'

'I understand what you mean,' said Amelia.

'You need to be strong in body and spirit, and able to think for yourself,' said Eliza, wondering when Jack would arrive. 'My mam was all those things.'

'This scouse is really tasty, Eliza,' said Amelia. 'Thank you.'

'My pleasure,' she said, adding, 'I wish Jack would come.'

'I sensed you were on pins. What's up?'

Eliza did not reply immediately but gave a spoon of scouse to Alfie, making certain the mutton was not too difficult for him to chew.

Then she told Amelia what she had been told about Glenys and that she had suspected that she might have been staying at Rosie's. She also explained they now believed her not to be Glenys but Ada, so Jack had gone there, and she had heard police sirens.

No sooner was the tale told than there came a banging on the front door. Eliza dropped her spoon, splashing juices over the tablecloth, and rushed out of the room.

Without being invited, Jack entered the house and followed Eliza into the dining room. She placed a plate on the table, spooned scouse into it and set a bottle of brown sauce next to his right hand. Then she made a pot of tea, filled three cups, and set a sugar basin and a milk jug in the middle of the table.

'Now talk,' she said.

'Give us a few minutes,' he said, upending some brown sauce onto his plate. 'This is going to upset you,' he said once his mouth was empty. 'Rosie's dead.'

They gasped.

'It was made to look like she had died in her sleep, but there were signs that she had been smothered. We suspect that she was drugged first and are just waiting for results to come back.'

'But why?' asked Amelia. 'I can't believe that Glenys would do such a thing.'

'Best person to ask is Theo,' said Eliza. 'They were both in Intelligence. Who's to say that they mightn't be trained killers and been dropped over France to work with the French resistance against the Germans?'

'But she's a woman,' said Amelia.

'There are French women in the resistance,' said Jack. 'A friend of Milly's is a journalist down south and he's been talking to the French who are over here having a rest from their dangerous work or have information they want to pass on. He's from Liverpool and used to work for the *Echo* when he was younger. His next-door neighbour is the sister of Milly's mother-in-law.'

'You mean Cathy, who works in the tearoom in Colwyn Bay?' said Eliza.

Jack nodded. 'It's a small world, isn't it?'

'This hasn't got us any closer to knowing for sure that Glenys killed Rosie,' said Amelia.

'You have to be patient, and this is secret,' said Jack. 'We're not certain she is Glenys. You keep what I've told you to yourselves. Careless talk can take lives.'

'Understood,' said Amelia. 'But one day, when the war is over, I'll put this in a book. Until then my lips are sealed.'

'You mustn't make any notes either,' said Jack and Eliza in unison.

'I'm not stupid and I have a good memory,' said Amelia. 'Now, how about a beer, Jack? What'll you have, Eliza?'

'A shandy,' she replied, although she was feeling fearful. Jack had hinted, but not confirmed, that it could have been Ada in Rosie's house, but what if he was just trying not to frighten her off?

Over their drinks, and some crackers and cheese, Eliza brought up the subject of Alfie's first birthday, which was only a few weeks away, to lighten the atmosphere. 'I'm wondering whether to have a party for him in the garden if the weather's fine.'

'Who would you invite?' asked Jack.

'And would you want a birthday cake?' said Amelia.

'I'm sure Milly's twins would like to come,' said Eliza, 'and Milly and Olive, his godmothers, which reminds me, I haven't seen Olive for a while.'

'I'd like to be there,' said Jack. 'It would also be fun to go to the beach.'

'Or bring the beach here,' suggested Amelia. 'How good are you at woodwork, Jack? I'm thinking of a sand tray about eight inches deep, four feet wide and eight feet long for a birthday gift from me.'

'It shouldn't be difficult to make,' he said. 'And there's still sandbags around from the Blitz.'

'We need more children,' said Eliza. 'I'm sure Gwen would like to come, and Mairi and Glyn, but they'll be needing petrol for the wedding, so if they came it would have to be by train and I'm worried that would be too much for Glyn and for Mairi, who is pregnant.'

'I bet Milly will have other friends who have kids and who'd enjoy a party with cake,' said Jack.

'I'll ask her,' said Eliza.

So it was that Milly, who had returned to Liverpool for a while with the twins, introduced her to Grace Evans, Simon's stepmother, who had a daughter, Irene, who was younger than the twins by several years, but older than Alfie by months and was delighted at the thought of going to a party with cake. She missed her daddy, who was away at an army training camp, but adored her stepbrother Simon, who asked if he could come to the party to help entertain the children, if he was free. He was training on Captain Johnny Walker's ship that set out from Liverpool daily, with a fleet of vessels under his command, intent on tracking down the U-boats that plagued shipping entering the Mersey or the Dee estuary, which was known as the larder or pantry of Britain.

Eliza often thought of Dilys but as Angus's mother had not received any bad news of Donny, she was not fearful. She hoped that Dilys's mind was occupied with helping her mother care for their young relatives, as she had not received a reply to the letter that she had sent to her.

The day after being told of Rosie's death, Jack called with the news that traces of drugs had been found in her innards. Eliza asked him a question that she had forgotten to ask before.

'What about fingerprints?'

He shrugged. 'None on the obvious places, like doorjambs, but everywhere appears to have been wiped clean.'

'The trouble is that most people know about fingerprints from watching films and reading crime novels,' she said.

'I had an idea and one of the team has gone back to check it out,' said Jack.

'What was it?' she asked.

'I'll tell you if I'm right.'

She pulled a face but knew she had to be satisfied with that and changed the subject. 'Have you made a start on the sand tray?'

'I haven't had time.' She thought he sounded harassed so dropped the subject.

He glanced at the clock and said, 'I'll have to go. Why don't you drop in on Mam this evening and I'll make a start on the sand tray?'

'All right, I'll see you then.' She saw him to the door, and they kissed.

She went back inside and knocked on Amelia's writing room door, as she could not hear the clatter of typewriter keys.

'Yes?' asked Amelia.

'Is there anything you want me to do? If not, I'll go shopping and take Alfie with me and then go to the park.'

'Can we have something light and cold for dinner this evening?'

'Of course,' said Eliza. 'I might be out some time. I'll take my key. Make sure the back door is bolted.'

'Don't fuss. I'll be fine.'

Eliza smiled, thinking she probably was fussing, letting her imagination run away with her. She took Alfie out of his feeding chair and fastened him in the pushchair, buttoned up her cardigan and picked up her handbag, which had her purse inside and ration books. She then remembered to bolt the door in the wall at the bottom of the back garden, plucking a couple of lettuces and spring onions as she walked past, before entering the kitchen, and bolting the back kitchen door. She left the house by the front door and crossed to the park, planning to shop in West Derby Road after they had fed the ducks and then call on Milly to tell her about the birthday party.

Eliza decided she would write a letter to Olive after preparing a ham salad with crusty rolls from the bakery and would post it on her way to Jack's mother's house.

She guessed she wouldn't be pleased about them taking Alfie on honeymoon with them, as she had been looking forward to having his company. Perhaps she should invite her to Alfie's birthday party. It would be an outing for her, and maybe she should also ask Olive's mother. She had been kind to her and Alfie when they'd had nowhere to go after leaving the hospital. Having made these decisions, she gave her attention to Alfie and throwing crusts to the ducks.

Eliza gazed about at the fresh green of spring and the flowering hawthorn, which her grandmother had called May blossom, and wished she was still alive to enjoy her great-grandson. But Eliza would always be grateful for being fortunate enough to have had a grandmother, as so many women had died young in Victorian times from childbirth or consumption. She recalled, too, the coconutty scent of yellow flowering gorse, beneath which rabbits would dig and hide. Not for the first time, she counted the days to her wedding and told herself not to let her thoughts wander to who could have murdered Rosie, even though two names kept coming to her. She shuddered and told herself that she was being daft – or was there really a murderer and a kidnapper in their midst?

She was glad to find Milly at home when she arrived at her house, and it came as no surprise to hear that she knew about Rosie's death. She believed, though, that she had died of pneumonia from walking the streets during the cold days. Eliza kept silent about the police's suspicions and told her instead about Alfie's birthday party, and her memory returning and how she believed it had been Jimmy and Ben Evans who had rescued her.

Milly smiled. 'I did wonder if that was a possibility but felt I couldn't ask Jimmy.' Then she said that she and the twins would hate to miss a party. 'I'll tell Jimmy that he'll have to bring us in the car, and suggest he goes on to see his mother in Colwyn Bay and then come back for us.'

'Rightio!' said Eliza. 'I met Simon Evans, and he said his stepsister Irene would enjoy coming to a party with cake. He and his stepmother are going to come as well.'

'I don't know, Eliza, I thought we were best friends and I'm only hearing about the party now.'

'I only thought about it the day Dilys's father came to take her home and she was in a state because Angus and Donny were going back to sea. They had been on a rescue mission and had some leave, but not much. She was having to leave, as her father turned up and took her home to help her mother. Then after Dilys left with her father, whom I didn't like one little bit, we got talking and Theo was mentioned, and Glenys, who has been declared AWOL. Eventually, that led to the mention of the French resistance and a Liverpool journalist who worked in London—'

'How did all this lead on to you thinking of having a birthday party for Alfie?' asked Milly abruptly. 'It's a puzzle to me.'

'Me, too,' said Eliza. 'Let me think…'

They were silent. Then Eliza said, 'I remember. Jack called with the news about Rosie.' Eliza realised she was going to have to be careful now about what she said. 'Jack and I had been talking about Rosie earlier, as we hadn't seen her or heard from her since December, so he decided to drop by and see if she was all right. When he came and told us she was dead, it upset us and, what with all the upset with Dilys, Jack suggested we think of something more cheerful. I suggested our wedding and honeymoon on Anglesey, and that reminded me that Alfie would be one in May, and then I thought how easily he and me could have been killed in the Blitz if those two men had not risked their lives rescuing me; I decided Alfie's birthday was worth celebrating.' She felt breathless when she had finished talking, but managed to add, 'I know now who they were… your Jimmy and a man called Ben.'

'Jimmy and Ben were rescuers, but Jimmy had a breakdown and never talks about the terrible things he saw,' said Milly, her eyes shining.

'What about his friend?' asked Eliza eagerly.

'He's away in the army and, truthfully, they were out so often I doubt if they'd remember every place they were sent to – and they weren't, or aren't, the type who want thanking. Like most of them doing such work, they saw it as their duty.'

Eliza sighed. 'I'll just give up wanting to thank Ben in person for now. I'll be grateful, and pray they survive the war and their wishes come true.'

Milly nodded. 'I'll tell Jimmy and you can mention it to Simon who is Ben's son.' She took a deep breath. 'In the meantime, is there anything you want me to make for the party?'

'You make the best cake,' said Eliza. 'I'll ask Jack's mother to make jelly creams.'

'What about Mairi?'

'I've mentioned the party to them, but I think it'll be too much. What with Mairi being pregnant, Glyn's disability, Gwen's and Grandma's ages, and the expense of train fares – or the cost of petrol if they were to come by car. As well as petrol coupons. They'll be coming here for the wedding in June after all.'

'Which is more of an occasion for adults,' said Milly.

'I'll make jam tarts and fairy cakes – they're easier to make than a big cake.'

'What about little sausages and meat paste, and sardine sandwiches?'

'We'll have to go with what we can get,' said Eliza.

'Is Olive coming?'

'I'm going to drop her a line this evening,' said Eliza. 'I've no idea what she's up to these days.'

Later, Eliza wrote to Olive and posted the letter in Breck Road, and then walked on with Alfie to the Molyneux's home. She was greeted warmly, and she could only think that Jack had not told his mother that they were taking Alfie with them to Anglesey but had told her about his birthday party. She asked if there was anything she could help with, and Eliza mentioned jelly creams, thinking that a lot of women kept packets of jelly in their store cupboards. While Jack measured, sawed, sanded, screwed, and glued, making the sand tray in the backyard, the women discussed clothes, hats and shoes for the wedding.

Jack had progressed well with the sand tray and Eliza did not doubt that it would be finished in time for Alfie's birthday. When Jack walked her home, she told him about hers and Milly's conversation.

'So, it was them as I thought,' said Jack. 'Can I take it that your memory of that time has come back?' He hugged her tightly.

'Yes!'

Something niggled at the back of her mind, but she decided to drop the subject for now. She had enough to deal with in the coming weeks and months. At least they did not need to worry about where they were going to live after they returned from honeymoon, for Amelia had said they could have Eliza's apartment, and an extra room, until they found their own place. After a while, as they walked down the street where Rosie had lived, Eliza remembered to ask Jack whether his idea had come to anything.

He hesitated.

'What is it?' she asked. 'Don't you trust me?'

'Of course, I trust you. It's just that the fingerprints under the wooden base of the bed don't prove the owner guilty of murder.'

'Do you mean they were Rosie's? Or someone from the Sally Army?'

'Neither,' he said. 'Think over what you know about Rosie and see if you can come up with an answer.'

'Right now? I'm not the detective.'

'No, but you're smart. Tell me tomorrow if you have come up with a name.'

CHAPTER THIRTY-SIX

Eliza could not sleep for pondering over what Jack had said and felt cross with him. Why couldn't he just have told her, without playing this guessing game? Was he just teasing her? She heard Alfie snuffle and was tempted to take him out of his cot and cuddle him, finding comfort in doing so. So, then she found herself remembering those terrible days and nights when he had been kidnapped, and how thankful she had been when he had been found and returned to her. When she had been told about the woman who had stolen him, and discovered she was Bryn's first wife, she had pitied Ada for a while. Then further events had revealed that Ada was a bitter, revengeful, and violent woman who, when she couldn't take her hurt and anger out on her husband because he was out of reach, acted against the women he cared about. She even lashed out at Glyn because he had once loved her but had found someone else. So, she had turned to an older woman whom she had met at a Labour Party rally and found a refuge in her home, but once she thought that Rosie had betrayed her by becoming friendly with a local policeman, Ada began to believe her friend talked too much and could give her away to the policeman. So, Ada felt she had to punish Rosie, especially after the police had turned up and frightened off her Irish lover, who was besotted with her and, according to what Gwen had told Eliza, with whom her mother was going to run away to safety. Of course, this was all conjecture.

Safety when the world was at war? Eliza thought and sat up in bed. The Irish Republic was neutral, though. But then the police had arrested her and that had led to a trial and the involvement of her identical twin sister Glenys, as well as a doctor who considered Ada mentally disturbed due to her not having received proper medical care after her miscarriages and being told she should not get pregnant again, as that could be fatal. This information at the trial had led to leniency and she had been sent to the asylum wing of a prison in Lancashire. Her *identical* twin sister had visited her there against the wishes of Theo. She had not turned up to a wedding she was supposed to attend or returned to London with Theo. Rosie, who had been attacked by Ada, had joined the Salvation Army and when Glenys... or was she *Ada*? Had the twins really exchanged identity? Eliza remembered Gwen saying that the sisters had a strong bond, and her mother believed her sister would do anything for her. As Rosie had become religious, she was prepared to forgive and help Ada. But Ada had tired of Rosie and her religion, fearing she might slip up and give her away by accident. Even so Ada had decided to give her a gentle death: she drugged and smothered her, hoping Rosie would not be found by her religious friends for days, but the policeman had been worried about Rosie. Ada had a narrow escape and, to confuse the police, had gone to Lime Street, hoping that if anyone recognised her, they would believe she was Glenys, there to catch the London train.

Eliza's head flopped onto her pillow. She was exhausted, but she had a good idea what Ada had done next. She would tell Jack when she saw him. The only problem was: would it be that easy for the twins to fool security? Surely by then Glenys would have told the guards who she was and that her sister had escaped, most likely because she wanted to see her daughter one last time.

That thought bothered Eliza for the rest of that day after she was woken by Alfie chanting, 'Duckie, duckie, duckie!' Her head felt fuzzy because she hadn't had enough proper sleep and, although it was light outside, it was only six o'clock, so she decided a walk in the park was needed. She got dressed, put Alfie's outdoors clothes on after changing his nappy and went down to the kitchen. They had a bowl of porridge and a drink of orange juice and, taking some crusts, they left the house.

The air was fresh, and she felt more awake. She did not take the pushchair, so Alfie could use his legs more and he had brought a ball with him, which he kicked down the grassy expanse where the bigger boys played football. As they approached the path that led to the bridge where they usually threw crusts to the ducks, Alfie held his arms up to her and she picked him up and they fed the ducks. The normality of the act soothed her, and she felt happier, thinking it was not long to the party and then the wedding and then Anglesey, with Jack and Alfie, and freedom from worry for a whole week. She and Alfie played ring-a-ring-a-roses on the way back, falling on the grass at the appropriate times. Eliza was out of breath by the time they reached the front door, as she had to carry him the last few yards.

Amelia emerged from her writing room as they entered the house. 'Where have you been? I've been worried about you since I looked everywhere and couldn't find you.'

Eliza waited until she got her breath back, before explaining they had been to the park and fed the ducks because the sun had woken them up early. 'Then we danced back.'

'Ring-a-ring-a-roses,' sang Alfie, who toddled over to Amelia and hugged her knees.

She lifted him up and kissed his cheek. 'You're both quite mad. But then it is the first of May and our ancestors used to dance around a Maypole in their day.'

'The kids will enjoy playing games at his party,' said Eliza. 'Mary will remember them and teach the young ones. I should imagine Simon and John will help as well.'

The rest of the day passed swiftly, although Eliza was puzzled when she did not hear from Olive – still, she was looking forward to seeing Jack that evening. He did not arrive until after she had put Alfie down to sleep.

As soon as he arrived by car, and with the sand tray and a sack of sand, she suggested that they go round into the back garden. She admired the sand tray and said they could tell Amelia about it later, as right now she wanted to tell him that she had come up with the name: Ada Jones. She knew she was supposed to be imprisoned, and she had been staying with Rosie a few months ago, which meant her fingerprints could have a perfectly innocent reason – although, surely, her fingerprints should have been found elsewhere in the house and they would have been there for a while? If that wasn't the case, it would suggest that they had been wiped clean, and the ones found were fresh and had been forgotten about. 'Do identical twins have identical fingerprints, I wonder?'

'An interesting thought,' said Jack, beaming at her. 'As it is, they don't have identical fingerprints. We already have Ada's on record. So, we took those of Glenys at the station and they proved to be different. Can you now tell me how Ada's fingerprints got there if Ada was imprisoned?'

'Glenys visited her twin, and somehow Ada overpowered Glenys's objections and changed places with her, but that raises the point that surely security would have spotted the likeness and checked out who left?' said Eliza. 'My thoughts on this are that Glenys did not go in as herself but disguised as her mother, with her mother's identity card and a ration book in her handbag, as well as a rail ticket from Conway.'

'You've had this idea in your head for a while.'

'Yeah, I woke early and was thinking about it even before Amelia mentioned it when she returned from London, but I thought I'd also mentioned it to you,' she said gravely. 'Unless I dreamed it.'

Jack drew her into his arms and kissed her. 'Have you any idea where Ada is now?' he asked, nuzzling her ear. 'She gave us the slip.'

'The Republic of Ireland,' replied Eliza. 'She most likely took a train to Holyhead and caught the ferry to Dublin.'

'Near enough in our opinion,' he said. 'If she'd caught the ferry from Liverpool, we'd have found her out.'

'So, do I get a medal?' asked Eliza.

'I wish,' he said. 'Anyway, I can't see the police over there handing her to us, even if they could trace her.'

'Is that the last we'll see of her, do you think?' she asked, snuggling closer to him.

'I hope so,' he said.

'So, do I,' she said. 'Now, let's go and tell Amelia that the sand tray is here.'

Amelia duly admired the sand tray and paid Jack's costs. Then they returned inside, and had drinks and conversation, which involved the evening post, which Eliza had not had a chance to read. Firstly, there was a letter from Olive's mother, saying that her daughter was no longer living at home, but asking if it would be all right for her to drop by on Alfie's birthday with a present. Then there was a letter from Dilys, saying that she missed them and maybe after the war she would come and see them; also, she was getting on with the kiddywinks and considering applying to train as a nursery teacher after the war.

Then there was a bulky envelope, which held two birthday cards: one from Alfie's grandmother with a cheque for five pounds. Generous, thought Eliza. The other card was from Glyn, Mairi and Gwen, and said they were all looking forward to the wedding, when they would bring presents for Alfie's birthday. The last envelope looked official and contained a card and a cheque from the Jones slate company. The cheque was for a hundred pounds for Alfie on his birthday to purchase whatever he needed.

'Goodness me!' exclaimed Eliza. 'I don't understand.'

'I'd open a bank account for him,' advised Amelia.

'Good idea,' said Jack. 'Unless there is something he needs right now? There's bound to be stuff in the years to come that we can't afford.'

'But I thought he wouldn't get any money until he's twenty-one.'

'You read what it said,' said Jack. 'It's for his birthday. Stop worrying and send a thank-you letter on Alfie's behalf.'

'Do I tell them I've opened a bank account on his behalf?'

'It wouldn't do any harm,' said Amelia. 'Have a saving account where his money will earn interest and a current account, which normally doesn't earn interest but from which he can draw out money when he really needs it. The earlier he learns how to manage money, the better.'

'Surely, he's too young,' said Eliza. 'I've never had a bank account.'

'I bet you've a post office saving account,' said Amelia.

She nodded. 'We used to be able to buy saving stamps in school and stick them in a card, and when the card was full, we took it to the post office and paid it in, and they gave me a book with the amount written in. Dad used to give me the money when he came on shore leave. He gave Mam money, too, but she bought a new bike. She ran up a bill at the corner shop one time and she wanted me to hand over my post office book, but I wouldn't give it to her because Dad had told me that he wanted to see what I had in it when he was back. He was furious when he came home and she asked for money to pay off her bill, and then he saw the new bike and they shouted at each other. She loved cycling, did Mam.'

'She should have got herself a little job,' said Amelia.

'She told me that I held her back because she had to be at home for me and that she'd be damned before she'd take in washing.'

'But she went cycling,' said Jack.

'Mam told a neighbour that was for company and that it was good for her health to get out into the country,' said Eliza.

'Who looked after you?' asked Amelia.

'Holidays I stayed with Dad's mam and dad.'

'And during school days?'

'A neighbour was supposed to keep an eye on me before and after school, until she came home.'

'Interesting,' said Amelia.

'I have another name for it,' said Jack. 'But times change, and Alfie's going to have a party that we can also enjoy.'

'I've never had a party,' said Eliza, 'and now there's two to look forward to.'

'Shall we empty the sand into the sand tray?' said Amelia.

'Let's,' said Jack. 'I bet, though, some of it will end up in the paddling pool I bought the other day as a surprise.'

The next two days were busy, and Eliza was glad to put her feet up by the evening, but on Alfie's birthday she knew that the work had been worthwhile, because the party was a great success. Olive's mother had brought candy given by Olive's American boyfriend and told her that they would be at Eliza's wedding, if that was acceptable. Alfie had made a new friend in Irene Evans and so had Eliza in the girl's mother, Grace, and she told her that she believed it was her husband Ben who had helped rescue her during the May Blitz. Grace's eyes shone but she told Eliza that Ben had left the army training camp in Wales for the English south coast, where he would be a gunner, watching for the enemy, so she wouldn't see him any day soon, but would write to him with that interesting piece of news.

CHAPTER THIRTY-SEVEN

The rest of May passed, and the war went on with what appeared to be deadlock in Europe, but Japanese advances in Asia. June was welcomed in by Eliza and Jack, and their friends and family, all looking forward to a happy time at the wedding. Eliza still had her wedding dress to sort out; she had used some of her precious clothing coupons and savings on a silk and lace nightgown, as well as some pretty underwear, but she was torn between buying a dress she could wear afterwards or a full-length gown in white brocade and lace that she had seen in the Bon Marché window, which would take all her clothing coupons and the rest of her savings. Eventually, she bought neither, but was lent an evening dress in ivory satin that Amelia had bought before the war for a Romantic Writers event in London and which she had put away. It needed to be taken in and Amelia suggested adding some silver sequins around the neckline, which Eliza sewed on herself after going shopping with Milly and her daughter Mary for the matron of honour and bridesmaid dresses. Then, using Mary for a model, she also bought a dress for Gwen. She had used some of the money sent to Alfie to buy a romper suit with navy blue bottoms, and a navy blue, white and palest green striped top. She made a veil and headdress from a lace curtain runner and artificial flowers. She had already ordered a wedding cake from the local bakery, and talked bouquets and buttonholes, as well as flowers for the church, with the local florist on the corner of Edensor Terrace and Breck Road. Catering was to be done by some of the church members, as they were accustomed to doing so at church events, such as the harvest festival evening supper and barn dance in the church hall, which she had booked for the wedding breakfast and dancing afterwards. She prayed that all would go well.

–

The big day finally arrived and although the sky was cloudy, the weather forecast on the wireless had promised that it would clear in the north-west and there would be some sunshine later. Eliza prayed for safe travelling for all that day.

Glyn, his mother, daughter, and radiant, blooming wife had arrived yesterday and all, except his mother, were off to feed the ducks in the park early that morning. Theo hoped to be there by one o'clock, later than hoped as, unable to get enough petrol, he was coming by train.

He had been planning on picking up Dilys but would be unable to do so now, so their original numbers were down by two, as Glenys had been invited in the days when she was staying under Amelia's roof.

Eliza pitied Glenys but when she set eyes on Theo, she felt even sadder for him. It was obvious he was doing his best to put on a brave face, but he admitted to her that he was still having trouble coming to terms with Glenys breaking his trust and her being such a fool over that sister of hers, who was obviously off her head. 'Even though she's been able to prove that she is Glenys and not her sister, she'll be had up for aiding and abetting a prisoner. Although Ada made the excuse of wanting to see her daughter, Glenys gave her twin freedom to murder again. I haven't mentioned the latter to Dilys when I phoned her, as I didn't want to upset her. I also feel miserable because I have let Dilys down, as she had really been looking forward to coming to Liverpool and seeing us all at the wedding. Besides, she would have been good company on the journey. Maybe we could all meet up again when the war is finally won.'

'You truly believe that we'll have the victory?' said Eliza.

'Yes,' he said firmly. 'Eventually, and at a cost, but we can't let Hitler win. He must be stopped. The Russians are having a

273

rotten time, but they'll beat the Germans back eventually... and in case you haven't heard, at the beginning of May there was a sea battle in the Coral Sea between the Japanese navy, and America, Australia and other Allies, in which the Japanese suffered a great defeat. Anyway, enough of the war. You're getting married, so don't be worrying, but enjoy your day.'

She eventually left him talking to Glyn, who was looking after Alfie while the women visited the hairdresser. On their return, the bouquets and some buttonholes had been delivered, and then they had a light lunch before getting changed for the wedding ceremony.

Once ready, Milly viewed Eliza's appearance with her head to one side. 'You've made a good job of the alterations and the silvery sequins. I'm not so sure about the veil but I'm sure Jack will consider himself a lucky man.'

'I think she looks like a princess,' said Gwen. 'But I'd have liked Alfie dressed in peach like me.'

'What you'd like doesn't matter,' said Milly. 'He's a boy and boys don't wear peach.'

'No disagreements,' said Eliza, smiling at Mairi, who was holding Alfie's hand. 'Now we're all going together to church, and the milkman doesn't want his horse frightened by loud voices.'

'But who's giving you away?' asked Gwen, remembering Glyn and Mairi's wedding.

'I'm giving myself away,' said Eliza, wishing her father was there to do so. She gazed at the milkman and his horse and cart, which he'd decorated with ribbons and crepe paper flowers, and said, 'You've made a good job of the decorations. Thank you.'

He replied, 'I was thinking of the Horse Parade when I decorated her up, plait ribbons in her tail and the like. She's getting old now and I'll have to retire her. No more Dolly tiring herself out dragging the cart with crates of milk. I'm going to get one of those electrified milk floats. I'll keep her and offer penny rides up and down the street for the kids during the holidays. That will pay for her hay.'

'What a good idea,' said Eliza, watching him help the children into the cart, which had shelves both sides that would now serve as seats. Then he helped her up onto the long driving seat behind Dolly, took hold of the reins and said, 'Walk on!'

They waved to those watching their progress and Eliza knew she would never forget this journey and old Dolly, who had delivered the milk to the doorstep without fail. They arrived at the church and, on the pavement, and in the grounds, stood well-wishers who cheered as bride and attendants descended from the cart. They stood in the church entrance and had a couple of photographs taken, and then in they went, but waited at the top of the aisle as the organist launched into Mendelssohn's 'Wedding March'. Tears filled Eliza's eyes and she threw back her veil, but even then, she could only see Jack and his best man. As she arrived beside him, he reached out a hand and she grasped it. The organ stopped playing and they both gazed at the vicar, who was smiling at them. They smiled back and the service began.

'Dearly beloved, we are gathered here to join this man and this woman in holy matrimony...'

This is reality, she thought, as she and Jack repeated the promises that made them husband and wife, and which finished with the words: 'Let no man put asunder... And you can kiss the bride.' Then they were signing the register and walking up the aisle, and to her surprise, outside there was an archway of policemen cheering them on and the photographer was there again taking photographs. She felt Alfie tugging her skirt and when she lifted him up, he noticed the shiny golden ring on her hand. She had removed Bryn's ring a good while ago. Then after Jack took Alfie from her, she threw her bouquet into the crowd, and she never knew until years after the war ended who caught it. Then it was off to the church hall, where a good time was had by most, despite a few tears being shed.

When the cake had been cut and the bottom tier sliced, Eliza, Jack and Alfie went home to change. It was as they left the house that a jeep pulled up at the kerb and a man in uniform climbed out. 'Is this where Eliza Griffiths lives?' he asked.

'No longer,' said Jack. 'Today she became my wife and is Mrs Molyneux. We're just off on our honeymoon but can we help you before we go?'

'I'm Josh Armstrong and I'm obviously late. I was to give my friend Joe Jackson's apologies to Olive. Fresh orders meant he couldn't make it and I got lost trying to find my way here. I went to the wrong park and then past the wrong football stadium.'

'I didn't see Olive,' said Eliza. 'But that doesn't mean she wasn't at the wedding, there was such a crowd. She might still be there.'

'The church isn't far away,' said Jack and gave him directions.

They watched him drive off and then Jack put the suitcases in the boot, and Eliza climbed into the back with Alfie, who immediately fell asleep as she sang softly, 'We're off, we're off, we're off in a motor car. Sixty coppers are after us and we don't know where we are.'

'That's daft,' Jack said. 'I wonder when it was first sung.'

'Maybe it was during a Keystone Cops film.'

'Perhaps, but I don't really think so,' said Jack. 'Do you remember the rest of it?'

'No, I just remember singing those words in a charabanc on the way to Blackpool with the other kids. We mustn't forget to take Alfie there when the war's over.'

They both fell silent and were soon through the Mersey tunnel and as far as Bebington, and then after passing a church, they reached the turn-off to Wales. At that time of the evening, the traffic wasn't too bad, and Eliza dozed off. She was woken by Alfie pressing a sloppy kiss on her mouth and she opened her eyes, feeling she could not breathe. She tried to move him off from her lap, only he seized a strand of her hair. 'Ouch!' she cried.

'You might as well stay awake now,' said Jack. 'You've missed us crossing the Menai Bridge. We'll be at the hotel in about half an hour.'

'I must have been more tired than I realised,' she said, catching Alfie as he almost slipped from her lap.

'You've had a busier day than I've had,' he said. 'Now, are we on the right road to the hotel?'

Eliza stared out of the window for a while and then said, 'Just carry straight on. Eventually, we'll pass Valley Junction. RAF Valley has a base there. If there's trouble at sea, the coastguards get in touch with them or the lifeboat station at Treader Bay, where the hotel is. Depends on how serious it is.'

'That's good to know,' said Jack. 'At least it's still light.'

'We'll see the sunset then,' she said. 'We should have a walk by the shore after we've unpacked.'

He agreed.

It wasn't long before they arrived at the hotel, signed the register and were shown to their room on the first floor. They changed and had a drink, and then left the hotel and within minutes had reached the seafront, where they could see the sun dipping to the horizon, as its light sent an orange path on the surface of the water. They both sighed contentedly.

After walking for a while with Alfie perched on Jack's shoulders, Eliza said, 'What about getting up earlier tomorrow and going to Love Island to catch the sunrise while the weather is fine?'

'Let's give it a couple of days,' said Jack. 'I'd rather sleep in and have breakfast in bed after our first night,' he added.

'I suppose you're tired after the drive,' she said.

'Not too tired to make love to my beautiful wife,' he retorted. 'The sun could rise just as we're going to sleep. Maybe around four o'clock.'

'I wouldn't be surprised,' she said, a flush in her cheeks. 'It is midsummer.'

'We should be going back, anyway,' said Jack, glancing at his watch. 'It's getting late and past time this young man was in his cot.'

She agreed, as she was ready for bed herself and, as there was a slight cool breeze off the sea, she needed warming up in Jack's arms.

Their lovemaking was all that she had hoped it would be, and she felt so safe and satisfied as they lay in each other's arms, their legs tangled up afterwards, that she was convinced that he was right, and they should not hurry to see the sun rise over Love Island that morning, which was a few miles away and had a proper Welsh name which she could not pronounce properly. They should linger and then take Alfie down to the nearest patch of sand and build a sandcastle and fetch water for a moat and paddle in the sea. The day passed pleasantly, and they decided over dinner that evening that they would take things easy for the next couple of days but make time to visit South Stack, near the lighthouse, and Holyhead, and go round the shops. South Stack was a high cliff where many seabirds nested, and Alfie could find them interesting. Eliza also thought about Holyhead being a port where the ferry left for Dublin and how odd it would be if they unexpectedly caught sight of Ada Jones having decided to return to Wales. She voiced her thoughts to Jack who said, 'It's far too early for her to do so.'

'Do you think she might do so one day?' she asked.

'I suppose it's possible but don't let's start thinking of that. I'm on my honeymoon and just want to think about making love.' He kissed her slap-bang right outside a fish and chip shop, and they went in and bought some for their lunch. Then they sat on a bench overlooking the sea and frowned at the sound of a plane zooming along the coast.

'One of ours,' said Jack, his eyes following the flight of the plane.

'They probably do watch for the enemy planes, ships and U-boats from the air, and warn Merseyside and Belfast defences, as well as Welsh ones,' she said.

Suddenly, she was thinking of Grace Evans, whose husband Ben had rescued her and was now down south, coast-watching. She wondered if Jack knew this. She had not thought of asking him before, but now she did.

'Jack, do you know that Grace Evans's husband Ben has left the training camp in Wales?'

He looked thoughtful. 'Is he now back home?' They lived in Saxon Street, which was the street next to Milly and Jimmy's.

'Grace told me he's been transferred down south, coast-watching. I wonder if he was near the coast then, training to spot enemy planes and shoot them down.'

'Could be,' said Jack, getting up. 'But before then he was in the Civil Defence on rescue work as you know, repairing houses that weren't too badly damaged as well.' He paused. 'Anyway, I sense Alfie's falling asleep and is in danger of over-balancing and falling off my shoulders. Help me to stop him hitting the ground?'

She did so and carried him until they reached the car. Then they drove back to the hotel, went up to their bedroom and, after laying Alfie in his cot, they lay on their bed and dozed off curled up together.

That evening there was a dance at the hotel, so they attended it with Alfie, who was wide awake – and they even managed a couple of dances themselves when one of the receptionists offered to mind him where he could watch them.

The days passed too fast and almost before they realised it, the day they were to return home arrived and they hadn't visited Love Island, so they rose early, made love, had breakfast, paid the balance of their bill, and departed, intending to visit Love Island on the way home. The sun had risen, and it was a lovely morning, with streaks of apricot and yellow in the sky. They were surprised to find a few cars, as well as motorbikes, in the car park at Newborough Warren and they quickly collected what they considered necessary for a dip in the sea, sandcastle making and a walk on the island.

They decided to take the path through the woods, where it was very pleasant, and they saw a fox. It was not until they came out onto the beach that they realised that the tide was in, and they would have to put their cossies on, and wade to the island, which was only cut off from the mainland when the tide was in. As it was so early, the water was cold, but they still managed to reach the island safely and read the information board, which told them the island was called Ynys Llanddwyn. Not pausing to remove their wet garments, they raced along until they arrived at the chapel.

They entered stealthily and changed in a corner where two walls met.

'Should we be doing this in a holy place?' said Eliza, rubbing herself with a towel, having already seen to Alfie.

'You're not rubbing hard enough,' said Jack, taking her towel and rubbing her vigorously until her skin glowed. Then he helped her dress and, when dry, he accepted his clothes as she passed them to him.

'I thought I heard someone coming,' she said.

'You're imagining it, and anyway we're married,' he said. 'Tied in holy wedlock.' He lifted Alfie from a block of stone that he had scrambled onto, and said, 'But now we're here we could repeat our vows before heading home.'

She nodded. 'I'd like that.'

So, they repeated their vows. 'I'm glad we made it here eventually and the saint blessed us,' she said.

'I'm not sure about the blessing,' said Jack as the sky darkened. 'We'd best move before it rains.' So, they left and were soaked through by the time they reached the car and tumbled inside on the back seat in a heap.

'I suppose it was a daft idea,' said Eliza. 'We must look like drowned rats.'

'Speak for yourself,' said Jack. 'How often will we behave the way we just did?'

'I suppose never again,' she said. 'Now we'd best get home.'

'I'll get one of the suitcases and you can take out some dry clothes,' said Jack. 'We can't travel all the way home soaking wet.'

Within moments Eliza was rooting through the suitcase, which fortunately was a jumble of mixed clothing, as she had packed in a hurry, so there were dry garments for each of them. It was not easy changing in the car and there were parts of them that felt damp even after they had on dry clothes. The wet ones were stuffed in a bag to deal with tomorrow at home. Then off they went and after they had left Anglesey behind, they caught each other's eyes in the mirror and started to laugh. 'We'll never have such a time again,' said Eliza.

'It was a honeymoon never to be forgotten,' Jack said.

'Do you think Alfie will remember it?' she asked, a hand to her mouth.

'I should think he's too young,' said Jack. 'But he could think he remembers when we return and make sandcastles in the future after showing him some photographs.'

The future, thought Eliza, wondering what lay ahead and when the war would end.

CHAPTER THIRTY-EIGHT

The pavements were gleaming wet in Liverpool when they arrived back and Eliza, who had been hoping for warm, dry weather to get their sodden clothes washed and dried, worried about using the coal they bought in summer and generally hoarded for the cold winter days.

Amelia was glad to have them safely back and handed her a letter from Olive, who apologised for not catching her at the wedding but had needed to hurry away. Eliza had expected to be told something about the American, but there was nothing.

Within days she had settled into a new routine, which included not seeing her husband at regular hours, for he could be called out on a case at odd hours. Still, he had told her that sometime after the war they would be given a new police house. But the war went on, and in September she and Alfie went to Colwyn Bay to spend a week with his grandmother, Glyn, Gwen, Mairi and the new baby, who was a boy and named after Glyn's father, Daffyd Glyn. Eliza was asked to be a godmother and the baptism took place while she was there. A happy event that, naturally; Mairi's mother attended, but there was no mention of Glenys and Ada from her – only of their mother, who had left the neighbourhood and gone to live with her son's family.

Back in Liverpool, Eliza often met up with Grace and asked after her husband Ben, coast-watching in the south. The war news was hopeful: British troops under General Montgomery had a resounding victory over German troops at El Alamein and the enemy had retreated further into Tunisia, away from the border with Egypt. Eliza recalled that the Suez Canal was in Egypt and that it was vital to Allied ships taking a safer route to Asia rather than round the coast of Africa. During the following days, the prime minister, Churchill, issued a bulletin from the mayor of London's mansion house during a banquet, stating that the victory at El Alamein was not the end of the war. It was not even the beginning of the end, but it was the end of the beginning. It took Eliza a few minutes to get her head around what he meant, but his words gave her hope, and she realised that this Christmas was going to be a lot happier than the last one after the Japanese attacked various British bases in Asia, as well as making a surprise attack on the American base at Pearl Harbour.

There were more goods available that Christmas and 1943 was welcomed in with a real hope that this might be the year that the war ended. But although during January there was news of German troops withdrawing from parts of Russia, the struggle went on. In Libya, British troops launched an offensive to capture Tripoli, while in Asia the Americans and Australians retook part of New Guinea, and there was an uprising in the Warsaw Ghetto in Poland by the Jews. The enemy continued the fight but as spring approached, there came news of victories. Tripoli was taken by British troops; the Germans surrendered at Stalingrad to the Russians; and the Japanese retreated further in New Guinea, and some of the Solomon Islands were freed by the Allies.

As summer approached, there was news that the Allies were taking the offence into Germany, with long-range bombers attacking ports, industrial sites, Berlin, and other sites of import-ance. But despite all their efforts, the U-boats still caused havoc to ships in the centre of the Atlantic, so long-range bombers took on the task of destroying them, and the Battle of the Atlantic soon ended in victory for the Allies.

This meant that Simon, Grace's stepson, was appointed to another ship which, as it happened, was a troopship that was sailing within a couple of days, destination unknown.

Eliza met him the evening after she heard the news and he had a note for her, which he handed to her, saying, 'I'm meeting Barbara outside the Paramount to see the second showing of the film *The Adventures of Tartu*. It's a spy film. She's coming straight from the hospital. A few weeks ago, we saw *Tarzan Triumphs* at the Trocadero. It's a great cinema but it's expensive. The film was fun, though – I'm a great fan of Johnny Weissmuller. He's a brilliant swimmer and makes a smashing Tarzan.'

Eliza said, 'I hope you enjoy it, but I've just heard your news and I want to say I'll be thinking of you and praying for you every day.' She kissed his cheek and squeezed his hand, and returned to the house, blinking back tears. She had become fond of Simon in the short time she had known him because he was often at Angus's mother's house, where Barbara lodged with her widowed mother.

The following week she went to visit Grace and decided to leave the pushchair behind, so Alfie could get more practice walking, but she carried him across the road.

When they arrived at Grace's, and she had taken out some toys and placed them on the rag rug for the children to play with while the mothers had a cup of tea, Eliza was surprised that Irene wouldn't play with Alfie but wanted to sit on her mother's knee.

'Is Irene sickening for something?' asked Eliza.

Grace shook her head. 'She's missing Simon now, as well as her daddy. I think she's scared I'll be the next to go.'

'The poor love,' said Eliza.

'She'll probably get used to him not dropping in, but I know how she feels. I miss him already, myself,' said Grace huskily. 'I wish this blinking war would be over.'

'It can't be much longer,' said Eliza.

'A week is too long for me,' Grace said. 'It was bad enough when he and Ben were out during the Blitz, with buildings collapsing. Simon was caught by flying debris once on his bike. He took messages to various groups.'

'An unsung hero,' said Eliza.

'Not by me,' said Grace. 'I love him as if he was my own son. You know what his being on a troopship means – he'll be heading for a danger zone: Italy or Asia.'

'Most likely Italy,' said Eliza. 'The British and the Americans have taken Italian prisoners, as well as some Germans during the

Desert War. Jack reckons the Italians don't have the heart for this war. I'd bet Simon's troopship will be bringing back prisoners of war.'

Grace smiled. 'You could be right. Anyway, this one can get down and play with Alfie.' She eased her daughter off her knee, and soon Irene was chatting to Alfie and building a brick tower with him.

At eleven o'clock Eliza left to shop for food for that day's meals. The worst of the queues had shrunk, so she did not have too long to wait before she reached the counter and then, after purchasing some sausages, she went straight home.

Within a short space of time, it was known that British forces had invaded the isle of Sicily off the south of Italy and the Americans had invaded the mainland in the north. German troops poured into Italy, so the fighting was fierce, although the Germans fought mostly without the help of allies.

Jack had been right and soon thousands of POWs were being taken off to camps in various parts of Britain and the Isle of Man. Simon was only home for a short time before he was off again. Eliza did not get to see him because there was an unexpected visit from Theo and Olive, who broke the news to Amelia and Eliza that they were married. They had not wanted a fuss, so had kept it quiet.

They explained that they got talking at Eliza and Jack's wedding and enjoyed each other's company – Eliza would have liked to have known more about the romance, but the couple were not stopping, so she realised she was going to have to wait until another time. But when she told Jack about the visit, he did not appear that surprised at the news, even though he swore to her that he had not known about the marriage. 'It's no romance in my opinion,' he said. 'But a marriage of convenience.'

'What do you mean?' she asked.

'Consider their situation: Theo, who had been messed about by Glenys, and Olive, who had been let down by an American. Both unhappy at a wedding, so they found comfort in each other's company.'

'I suppose you could be right,' she said.

'I wouldn't be surprised,' said Jack, 'if we hear that she's pregnant in a couple of months.'

She stared at him, eyes wide open, wondering how Glenys would feel when the news reached her, although that could be some time, as the last she had heard was that Glenys was still behind bars. 'I'd like to have another baby,' Eliza said, feeling broody.

'Me, too,' he said. 'I'd like us to have our own home first. A house to ourselves.'

She punched his arm. 'You should have told me. It's a decision we should talk over. We don't know for sure when you'll get the police house. What if it was decided to give it to a returning soldier? We could end up waiting too long and I'll be too old to have more children.'

'You're only young,' he said, taking her in his arms.

'I'm twenty-eight and I don't want to wait any longer,' she said. 'Amelia loves having us here and she'll be happy if we have another child.'

'Not if the baby is a crier like our Jean was,' he said.

'How do you know you weren't a crier?' she asked.

'Because my mother said so,' he said teasingly.

'Naturally, she probably thought you were perfect,' she said.

'Just like you believe Alfie is perfect.'

'No, I don't,' she said, sticking her tongue out at him. 'Anyway, enough is enough and we'll leave it to God to decide when the time is right.'

'Agreed,' he said. 'Shall we go to bed now?'

She smiled and nodded.

'We're fortunate, you know,' he said.

'I do know,' she replied. 'There are so many people in the world who don't have any choices and time is passing them by, like Glenys still in prison.'

'She made her choice,' said Jack. 'A pity, but there's nothing we can do to help her.'

'I'll never understand her,' said Eliza. 'But then, I never had a sister.'

'Nor I a brother,' said Jack.

They had reached the top of the stairs and he paused.

'What is it?' she asked.

'I was wondering if Grace had told you about Ben's brother?'

'What brother?' she asked.

'Obviously, she hasn't,' said Jack. 'His elder brother Martin, who was declared missing presumed dead in the Great War. Soon afterwards, because his mother wouldn't believe her son was dead, Ben, who was only a youth, went over to see if he could find him, but didn't.'

'Why are you telling me this?' Her voice quivered.

'Because not so long ago, Andrew Fraser, a journalist from Liverpool working in London was approached by a French woman. But she was different to the women from the French Resistance who he was interviewing at the time. She lived on a farm with elderly parents, and she did most of the work. She came across a man who was obviously in need of help during the Great War. He had a head wound and could not remember who he was or where he had just come from. She took him home to the farm, bound up his wound and soon realised that he was blind. There was no money to take him to see a doctor and, besides, despite his blindness, he was of help to the family. Then, after the war had ended, there was a football match on the radio and Liverpool was mentioned, and it seemed to strike a chord with him. I can't remember exactly when, but at some point, they were married and had a son. He wanted to name the boy and he wanted to call him Ben. They did not have the money to go to England and, besides, the Germans had invaded France. Then as time passed, she heard from a cousin who had joined the recently formed French Resistance that she was being taken to London by aeroplane and, somehow, both cousins were brought over here, where she met Andrew Fraser and told him her husband's story as far as she knew it.' He paused. 'So, Andrew arranged a meeting between Ben and the French woman, who claimed to be his brother Martin's wife. He believed her story and promised, by hook or by crook, to meet her husband and see if he was his brother. It was not going to be as simple as it might sound and could not take place immediately. Despite Ben being stationed on the south coast, it would not be easy for him to sneak away and cross the English Channel.'

'Milly and Jimmy know Andrew from when he lived in Liverpool and also Jimmy's aunt lives next door to him and his wife, but I never met them,' said Eliza. 'Anyway, what do you think will happen next?'

He shrugged. 'There are millions of soldiers training on the south coast for the invasion of Europe. None of them know where or when, but they are preparing for it. Ben might have thought it would be simple just to join those men to get to France or to be dropped in by plane but, of course, it won't be. But he has another plan, which he is going to tell his commanding officer about, along with his brother's story. He wants to bring him home and have him see a specialist at St Paul's Eye Hospital.'

'That's some story,' said Eliza. 'So, what's happening now?'

'The brothers wait for the right moment,' said Jack.

'Who told you the story?' she asked.

'It doesn't matter who told me and you must not speak of it to anyone else,' he said.

'Who would I tell?'

He only said, 'Don't even mention it to Grace. Remember: careless talk costs lives. Just be a friend to Grace. Perhaps you could invite her here with Irene.'

Eliza thought about that and said, 'She could play with Alfie in the garden. Grace doesn't have a garden and the sand tray is still in the garden here.' She paused. 'I hate this war. I wish it could be over now.'

'Remember what Churchill said. He knew we'd still some way to go after the invasion. The Germans will not give up any country they took easily and will fight every inch of the way.'

Eliza shuddered and Jack's arm tightened about her. 'Pray and remember we're not in this alone. We have allies, as well as a navy and an air force, who will be supporting the soldiers. Now let's go to bed and get some sleep. There's work still to be done on the home front.'

Despite not getting much sleep that night, Eliza had taken to heart all that Jack had said, including the home front, and recalled what she had read in the *Echo* about those involved in the Civil Defence and other branches of the war effort: boat builders and dockers, those making weapons and keeping the nation fed, and those keeping the home fires burning, farmers and land girls, miners and the police, hospital workers, builders repairing buildings, entertainers and those who brought the news – and she mustn't forget the furniture makers and shopkeepers, and those in government doing administration work. She thought of those in Colwyn Bay, which led her thoughts to Jean and the young Polish soldier, wondering where he was, praying for him and those in German prisoner-of-war camps and in Japanese camps, for families parted, parents and evacuees, and for the church. She thought of buildings which had been damaged or destroyed and those that still stood, of Coventry. Then she prayed for the Jews, and pleaded for deliverance and peace throughout the world, and then she prayed for the Royal family, her own family and friends and herself, and that she and Jack would have a baby.

PART THREE

1946

CHAPTER THIRTY-NINE

Eliza glanced up as Jack entered the bedroom with Alfie, who would be going to school in September. Alfie scrambled onto the bed and gently touched the baby's rose-petal-soft cheek.

'So, what are we going to call her, Mammy?' he asked.

She glanced up at Jack, who was perched on the other side of the bed, and he smiled down at his wife and daughter. 'Let's call her Beth, and then your name and hers put together shall make Elizabeth, the name of a princess who drove an ambulance during the war.'

'When will she be christened?' asked Alfie. 'Will it be before my birthday?'

'Hopefully,' Eliza said. 'You were christened just after Christmas so your uncle Glyn and Grandma Gladys could be there.'

'My first daddy couldn't be there because he was killed in the war,' said Alfie. 'Grandma told me he was a hero.' He hesitated. 'And she said I wasn't to cry when she died because she was old and would be joining him in Heaven.'

'And you didn't cry,' said Jack.

'And neither did Gwennie,' said Alfie. 'But Aunt Mairi did, but she has a little boy to make her happy and they have a big house by the sea to live in. Will they be coming to the christening?'

'I should think so,' said Jack, thinking that was another phone call he would have to make.

But Eliza was remembering Gladys's funeral and how surprised she had been by Mairi's tears, and how at the time she had envied her the baby in her arms, because she and Jack were desperately wanting a baby of their own. Still, she had been pleased for Mairi and Glyn for having the son they both had longed for. And she had known even then that envy and jealousy weren't good for a person. There was a knock on the door, and Amelia and her niece Dilys entered the bedroom. 'Is it all right for us to come in?' asked Dilys.

'You're already in,' said Alfie with a giggle.

'Smart alec,' said Dilys, who had returned to Amelia's just after the war ended a year ago. Her mother had run away with a travelling salesman and, unable to cope living with her father after the children had left to live with another aunt, Dilys had applied to a teacher-training college in Wales. Eventually, she got a placement at a school in Liverpool and a home with her aunt. There had been little time to talk about intimate matters, so Donny's name had seldom been mentioned, but she had been a great help during Eliza's pregnancy, especially when it came to looking after Alfie.

Gwen had returned with Eliza, Jack and Alfie to Liverpool and was staying for several weeks. This morning the two children were playing in the back garden and Dilys was peeling potatoes, while supposedly keeping an eye on them, as Eliza was feeding the baby in the lounge. Amelia was in her writing room and Jack was out on a case. Eliza looked out of the window every now and then.

After she finished feeding the baby, she looked out of the window again: one minute the children had been there and then a few minutes later there was no sign of them. She rushed into the back kitchen, but Dilys was not there. Eliza remembered that Angus and Donny's ship was back; she knew that Dilly had not passed her, so if she had gone out anywhere it must have been through the back garden door, which meant the door would not be bolted. The fear that had never completely left her filled her and she went into the writing room to ask Amelia if she could put Beth in her cot, telling her what she feared. She rushed out into the garden, which was empty, ran down to the door and opened it, and then went outside and onto the length of grass and trees that separated the houses from the main road. She glanced left and right, but there was no sign of Alfie and Gwen. However, there were some children playing and she remembered having seen them before, playing at Robin Hood and his merry men, and she had spoken to them.

She shouted to one of the boys, 'Have you seen my son and a girl with a woman?'

He signalled for her to come towards him. She hurried and he said, 'She was dragging them along and the girl said, "Let us go, Mam. Why couldn't you have stayed in Ireland?" Me and Bert followed them: she went along Orphan Drive and up Donkey Hill by the railway and towards Lister Drive, and then they vanished up one of the streets which had been bombed. I told Bert to follow them but keep out of sight while I came back here to see if I could find you. I suppose I should have gone into the police station, but I thought they wouldn't believe me.' He paused, out of breath.

Eliza was dithering. Her worst fear had come true, but she was hopeful and sent up a quick prayer and told herself not to panic. She had to find them and rescue them. There was no time to waste. She asked the boy, who was called George, to go to the police station and ask for Sergeant Molyneux and tell him that Alfie and Gwen had been abducted by a woman that Alfie's mother believed to be Ada and that she was on their trail. As she was talking, they were hurrying in the direction of the police station and Orphan Drive. They separated and, having got her breath back, Eliza ran along the drive and up Donkey Hill and walked swiftly along Lister Drive, where she saw a boy waiting on a street corner and she hurried towards him. 'Are you Bert?' she asked breathlessly.

He nodded. 'The children escaped her and are hiding in one of the bombed houses. She's looking for them. The little boy bit her hand and she was about to hit him when the girl grabbed him, and they made a run for it. I thought I'd better stay in hiding and keep my eye on things, as I'd be no match for the woman.'

'You did right,' said Eliza. 'Have you anything else to tell me? And then you'd best point out to me where the children are hiding.'

'I heard children whispering and a slithering noise, and I hid behind this wall. The woman had stopped but now she has a dog with her. I don't know where it came from, but she sent the dog ahead and it was sniffing around this gap in the rubble.'

Eliza stopped him. She knew she was going to have to make a move. Maybe draw the dog's attention towards her and away from the children. She whispered to Bert to go back towards the police station, hopeful that some men might be heading their way now. She stood straight and watched as Gwen's head appeared: she was attempting to shoo the dog away. But the woman had seen her and, shoving the dog out of the way, she dragged the girl out despite her struggles.

Eliza waited no longer and shouted for help, before running towards Gwen and her mother. She would have faced Ada alone, if she had not turned back and reached out for Alfie, even as Gwen was hitting her with her free hand, screaming, 'Let me go, Mam!'

Then Eliza saw Alfie disappear back through the gap and she heard a man's voice, but Ada wasn't giving up. Eliza saw her disappear down the hole and heard her say, 'Bloody hell!' and then she screamed. The scream was cut off suddenly.

Eliza reached the site and saw Gwen flat on the ground on her back. The dog was sniffing at her. Eliza shoved it away and, after checking Gwen was still breathing, she gazed down the hole. Although it was quite dark, she could make out Ada sprawled backwards on a hillock of rubble, which shifted beneath her. At the foot of the hillock Eliza could make out a man clutching Alfie to his chest.

'Eliza,' he gasped. 'Here, take your laddie, while I try and stand up.'

'Donny!' she gasped, scarcely able to believe her eyes as she gingerly stretched down, trying to avoid Ada's body, and reaching out for Alfie, who was reaching up to her. She took hold of his wrists and managed to hoist him through the air towards her and clutch him to her bosom. He was whimpering but soon stopped as she soothed him and told him that he was safe.

Donny said, 'Here's where I lived with Mam and Dad. They were killed when the house was bombed.' He paused. 'I come here every time I land, to pay my respects. One of you will have to go and get help.'

'I've sent for help and Jack should turn up if Bert doesn't get lost,' Eliza said, her head feeling muzzy.

'How's me mam?' asked Gwen, attempting to see her mother by peering around Eliza, who was blocking most of the opening.

'She slipped and then fell – she was in a helluva rush,' Donny said. 'She could have banged her head on one of these clumps of brick and mortar. I couldn't reach her. I didn't want to put Alfie down in case he slipped.'

'I'll go and see if help is coming,' said Gwen, over the barking of the dog, signalling that help might have arrived.

'I think she's dead,' said Eliza, her emotions confused as she felt for a pulse but could not find one. Of course, she was relieved that she would never have to fear Ada again, but at the same time she thought, what a waste of life. Ada spent a large part of it hating and bitter, with a desire to punish those that she thought deserved to suffer and that in her mind stood in the way of her having what she wanted. Poor woman! How she had suffered.

The feel of Alfie's hand on her neck and Jack's arms around her a short while later brought her back to herself and she was thankful that two of the persons most precious to her were here close and safe. After numerous kisses and hugs, Eliza gazed about her and saw that Jack had not come alone, but had a couple of policemen with him, as well as George and his gang. He was standing beside Gwen and was whispering to her; Eliza wondered what he was saying but was relieved that she had company. She had almost forgotten about her. The poor child. She must ask Jack to telephone Mairi and Glyn to take her home. She would be better off there. A fire engine and an ambulance were summoned, and, within the hour, Ada's dead body was recovered, and Donny was rescued. He was taken away in the ambulance, as he had a suspected broken ankle, which happened when he had first entered his former home earlier that day and had been unable to get out, due to the pain.

Dilys couldn't apologise enough when they arrived home and told their story. She would have rushed to the Royal Infirmary to see Donny if Angus had not already gone to the hospital intending to bring him home, having told her that she was not to come round to see him as soon as he was back, as he would need rest and quiet after spending so many hours in a cold damp place in pain. She would be informed when he was fit to see her. Dilys was put out by his words, but nobody was prepared to listen to her moaning, as she was in the doghouse still. Besides, the children needed warming up, feeding, and being comforted.

It was to be sometime before Eliza had a chance to talk to Jack about phoning Mairi and Glyn, but she need not have worried, as Jack had already thought about it and been in touch with them, but they could not come and collect Gwen, so it was decided that something would be sorted out tomorrow.

In the meantime, Dilys made a jug of cocoa and jam butties, which the children wolfed down. Angus gave Eliza a sedative, as she was still shaking, and advised her not to breastfeed the baby but to give her a bottle of National milk until the effects of the sedative wore off.

'I'll see to that,' said Amelia.

Eliza thanked her and was glad when Jack ushered her and the children upstairs and helped them into bed. They snuggled together and were soon asleep.

A short while later there was a knocking on the front door and Jack went to see who was there, to find Milly and Mary standing on the doorstep. 'Can we come in?' asked Milly.

Jack hesitated. 'What is it you want? Eliza and the children are in bed.'

'I've something to tell her and Mary wanted to see the baby.'

Jack stared at her. 'So, you're not here because you've heard about the kidnapping?'

'What kidnapping?' Milly asked, a tremor in her voice.

'You'd best come in. Alfie and Gwen are back but they've had a shock and so has Eliza, who found them, thanks to the help of Robin Hood and his merry men.'

'You are joking?' said Milly.

'He's not, Mam,' said Mary. 'He's talking about Jeffrey and his gang who play at being Robin, Little John and the rest.'

'You're going to have to explain,' said Milly.

'Come back in the morning and Eliza can tell you the story,' said Jack, 'but not this evening. Angus has given her a sedative, as she's still a bit shaky, and she is in bed. Alfie and Gwen are with her. Mary can see Beth, though. Amelia is giving her a bottle.'

So, they went into the lounge and were welcomed by Amelia, and Jack explained that Mary had wanted to see the baby.

'Oh, she's beautiful,' said Mary.

'And so small and dainty,' said Milly.

'She's got lots of black hair and it's curly,' said Mary, reaching out and placing a finger in one of the curls. 'I wonder if it will stay curly.'

'We'll have to wait and see,' Jack said.

'Her eyes are blue,' said Mary.

'Lots of babies are born with blue eyes,' said Amelia. 'But they don't always stay blue.'

'How odd,' said Mary.

'Was there anything else you want to say, Milly?' asked Jack impatiently.

'I just want to tell you one thing and then we'll go.' She paused. 'Jimmy's aunt phoned him and told us that Andrew, the journalist who lives next door to her, had told her that Ben's brother has arrived in England with his son. His wife had to stay on the farm with her parents, but as soon as she can get someone to take her place for a while, she'll come over.'

'I'm sure Eliza will be interested,' he said, thinking it had to be more than a year since he had told Eliza about Ben's brother and to keep quiet about it, but there was no need for secrets now.

'Oh, and by the way, Kyle's back, and with his wife and two children, for good.'

'I'll tell her that, too,' said Jack, ushering them out of the room and to the front door. He waved them off and then, taking the baby from Amelia with thanks, he went upstairs.

He placed *Squirrel Nutkin* on the bedside table and gazed down at his sleeping wife and the children, and his heart was filled with thankfulness.

He smiled and touched the dark tendril that curled on his daughter's brow, and then he left, walking cautiously, and closed the door gently after placing Beth in her Moses basket.

The following morning Alfie woke up first and cried, 'Mammy!'

Eliza heard the panic in his voice and struggled to rouse herself, but eventually managed to open her eyes and slowly the horrors of yesterday came back to her, and she reached out for her son and hugged him close. 'You're all right,' she said huskily.

At that moment she saw Gwen stir and then her eyes opened. 'I was having a horrible dream,' she said.

'It wasn't a dream,' said Eliza. 'But you're safe now and will be going home to Colwyn Bay soon.'

'I remember Robin Hood helped to rescue us,' she said. 'He told me I could be Maid Marian and join his gang. He was coming to call for me this morning.'

'You can see him when he comes but you have to tell him that you can't play because you're going home today,' said Eliza.

Gwen looked disappointed. 'Couldn't I stay here for another day?'

'Let's think about it,' replied Eliza. 'Let me speak to your uncle Jack first.'

Gwen nodded. 'I'm hungry,' she said.

'Me too,' said Alfie, picking up the book he had noticed on the bedside table.

Gwen glanced across at it. 'Squirrel Nutkin,' she said. 'I've seen that in the library when Mairi took me.'

Alfie glanced at the red squirrel on the cover and handed it to Eliza. 'I like squirrels but…'

'But you like bears better,' she finished for him. 'Daddy will buy the next one when it comes out, but in the meantime, I thought we'd give this lady's books a try because she's written a lot and they're set in a real place that we could visit one day.'

'Where's that?' he asked, cuddling up to her.

'The Lake District.' She opened the book and they gazed at the first picture, and she began to read, determined to concentrate and not to let her mind wander. Concentrate, Eliza.

'Mammy, what do you think Squirrel Nutkin has in his sack?' asked Alfie.

Eliza searched her mind for an answer. 'Acorns, of course,' she said.

'I like his raft,' said Alfie. 'Can I have a raft with a pole, Mummy? Perhaps Daddy could make me one.'

'We'll see,' said Eliza.

'Beth wouldn't be able to go on a raft,' Alfie said. 'She's only a baby and a girl.'

'Girls can do lots of things that boys do and the same when they grow up. Think of Gwen and how she helped when you went down that gap where Donny was trapped with a broken ankle.'

'She was brave,' said Alfie. 'And so were you, Mammy.'

'Let's get back to the story,' said Eliza.

She still had not finished the story when Jack returned with Beth.

They were eager to talk. Alfie got in first, with a request for Jack to make him a raft. Before Jack could reply, Eliza was asking what Beth had in her hair.

'It's a pink rosebud,' he replied. 'I couldn't resist picking it for her. There are no thorns that could prick her on this bit of stem,' he added reassuringly.

'It looks very pretty but some pink ribbon could be tied round the stem, so it doesn't fall out,' said Eliza. 'Now there's something I want to ask you.'

'I'll buy some pink ribbon,' he said.

'That wasn't the question,' she said. 'Amelia might enjoy buying the ribbon.'

'All right,' said Jack. 'What is the question?'

She told him about Gwen and Robin Hood, and her asking if she could stay another day.

He told her about Milly calling, and what she'd said about Ben and his brother.

'Could we visit Grace and Ben in a few days? If his brother is here from France, not only do I want to hear his story first-hand, but I also need to talk to Ben to thank him for being one of my rescuers.'

Jack raised his dark eyebrows. 'Are you absolutely sure?'

'As sure as I can be without speaking to him,' she replied.

'All right, as soon as you feel up to it,' he said. 'Now, is there anything you want? A cup of tea? Dilys has made a pot.'

She nodded but added, 'I'm getting up. The three of us are hungry.' She continued, 'I suppose we have to forgive Dilys.'

'It's the creed we live by,' he said. 'Thinking of creeds, we have to think about Beth's christening.'

'Which will be when?' she asked.

'As soon as possible. A fortnight, if that's all right with the vicar,' he said.

At this point Alfie repeated his request for a raft. 'Show me a picture and I'll let you know,' said Jack.

'And you can finish reading the story of Squirrel Nutkin, Daddy, if Mammy is going to make breakfast,' said Alfie.

Robin Hood called round at half-ten and by then the decision had been made that Gwen would stay another day. After Jack had spoken to the police superintendent to discuss further the kidnapping and what to do about Ada Jones's body, it was decided that it would be best for her daughter Gwen to be back with her father and his wife when Ada's mother and son arrived in Liverpool to arrange Ada's funeral. Due to Glyn's inability to drive, and since Mairi couldn't leave him and their baby, Jack would drive the girl home. He and Eliza decided that she, Alfie and Beth would go with him. When told about this decision, Gwen asked if Robin could come with them, with his mother's permission, as a reward for his help in their rescue.

After much thought, it was decided that he could go with them. His widowed mother, who worked as a cook in a school's kitchen, agreed. He was to sit in the front passenger seat while Eliza sat in the back with the baby on her lap, and Gwen and Alfie either side of her.

Glyn and Mairi welcomed them with open arms. Mairi fussed over Beth after having heard the whole story of the kidnapping from Gwen, who was occasionally interrupted by Robin, and then she wanted a chat with Eliza. The women suggested the men took the children down to the beach.

It struck Eliza, as she and Mairi talked first about Ada and her funeral and then about rationing and shortages and money, that Glyn's house could make a perfect B&B with a bit of altering and a good lick of paint to brighten the rooms up. They would need some staff, of course.

So it was that Jack, Eliza, their children, and Robin said their ta-ras and returned home to Liverpool, leaving Mairi to put ideas into Glyn's head about their future. Mairi had told Robin that he and his mother could come and stay for a holiday at reduced rates next Easter.

CHAPTER FORTY

Ada's funeral was a few days later and took place in the chapel of Anfield Cemetery. It was a brief service and sparsely attended. The atmosphere was charged with a strange air, as the police had managed to keep it quiet. Her mother and brother were there, and so were a pale-faced Glenys and a man who was a stranger to Eliza. The only hymn was 'Guide Me, O Thou Great Redeemer', which was sung lustily by the Welsh. Prayers were said, as was the 23rd Psalm.

Then the coffin was carried out, led by the priest, and followed by the family to the burial plot. Jack and Eliza remained behind, leaving the chapel only when all had gone. They left the cemetery as quickly as possible and drove straight home.

'I wanted to say hello to Glenys,' said Eliza, leaning back in her seat.

'I know, but what could you say to her that would be appropriate?' asked Jack.

'I did wonder if Theo might have turned up,' she said. 'Dilys might have told him about the funeral.'

'He's in London. He wasn't going to come all this way. He had no love for Ada.'

'He did for Glenys,' said Eliza.

'She let him down.' Jack sighed. 'Let's put it all behind us.'

'I wonder who that strange man was,' said Eliza.

'I reckon he was Ada's Irish chap,' said Jack.

'You could be right,' said Eliza. 'Glenys might have wanted to know how Gwen was getting on,' said Eliza.

'She'll know she's with Glyn and Mairi. As far as I know, Gwen has never asked about her aunt,' said Jack. 'Now shush and think of something nice.'

Our special place, she thought.

When they arrived home, they answered Amelia's questions about the funeral, and then they had slices of game pie and salad with whisky, for Jack, and sherry for Eliza and Amelia. Dilys had gone to see a teacher friend.

A fortnight later and Eliza, after a conversation with Milly and then Grace on the telephone, was pushing the new Silver Cross high pram with Beth inside and Alfie walking beside it, holding on to the side of the handle, to Grace and Ben's home.

The front door was not opened by Grace but by a dark-haired man with attractive weathered features and of strong build, who greeted her warmly with the words, 'We meet at last, Eliza. I'm Ben and I believe you wish to talk to me and my brother Martin, but come in – shall I help lift the pram into the lobby?'

She thanked him and followed him inside with Alfie by the hand. Grace appeared with her son Peter in her arms; he had been born nine months after Grace had gone down to Oxford to meet Ben in the spring of 1944, so he was a few years younger than Alfie, but they played well together.

Grace gazed down at the sleeping baby and said, 'She makes me feel broody.'

'Now, none of that,' said Ben. 'We have our hands full as it is. Peter's not even fully potty-trained yet. Besides, Simon and Barbara are getting married soon and I bet it won't be long before they hear the patter of tiny feet and we'll be asked to babysit.'

'I suppose you have a point,' sighed Grace. 'Anyway, come and sit down, Eliza, and have your talk with Ben while I make some fresh coffee. Martin makes the best coffee – his wife showed him how, her being French and them drinking lots of coffee – so he's told us how to make it the French way.'

'Martin is having a rest in the best armchair in front of the fire, drinking a mug of coffee,' said Ben. 'So, we'll have our talk first. What is it you want to ask me?'

303

'I think you might have an idea as Grace might have mentioned it.' She paused. 'In May 1941, I could have died when the house I lived in in Norwood Grove was bombed and caught fire. I was on the ground floor, as I'd just entered the house and was partly buried. I received a head injury that led to temporary amnesia and for a long time I could not remember anything. I was also pregnant and went into labour. I came to in Oxford Street Maternity Hospital, where I gave birth to Alfie.'

Ben smiled. 'So, what makes you think I could have been involved?'

'When I first heard your name mentioned by Milly, something clicked in my brain, but then it went until mentioned again by Simon... Grace also mentioned you and Simon in connection with rescue work and what came back to me was a man calling Ben and talking about having found two dead bodies and a young woman who was still alive. He sounded quite desperate and needed your help.'

'That was Jimmy, and he was on the verge of a breakdown: he had broken a bone and couldn't get you out from under the rubble,' said Ben.

She stared at him, aware of a mixture of emotions.

'How was it he didn't recognise me?' she asked.

'Your face was filthy with dust and ashes from the burning building. So was his and mine,' said Ben.

She reached out and shook his hand. 'I've been wanting to find you since I gave birth to Alfie to thank you. We wouldn't be here now, and neither would Beth, if it weren't for yours and Jimmy's bravery. It's been a long wait.'

'Jimmy couldn't talk about it. His nerve had completely gone. That's why he wasn't accepted for the Forces,' said Ben. 'Angus recommended that he get completely away from Liverpool.'

'Coffee and cake,' said Grace, interrupting them. 'Then you and Martin can tell Eliza his and your story.'

'We've talked our heads off all the way here after leaving the farm in France.' He paused. 'Besides, I've just remembered I

304

promised I'd take him to visit Mam's grave this afternoon. He's bought flowers.'

Eliza said, 'It's sad he won't be able to see where your mother is buried, Ben.'

'Smell, touch and sound are what's important to him,' said Ben. 'If he hadn't lost his memory, I suppose he'd still hold a picture in his mind of the grave from when we buried Dad. Martin was made up when I told him Mam believed he was still alive, so she never gave in to despair.'

'You were a comfort to her, though,' said Grace.

'You and Martin should have a chat, what with both of you losing your memory, Eliza,' suggested Ben.

'I wonder if his loss of memory and his loss of sight were caused by the same thing,' Eliza said.

Ben stared at her and then blinked and said, 'Now, there's a thought. He never did see a doctor, what with wandering away from the battlefield. Maybe he has a bit of shrapnel inside his head that caused the damage that's blinded him.'

'It's no use guessing,' said Grace. 'You must take him to see our doctor, explain the situation and have him arrange an appointment at St Paul's Eye Hospital as soon as possible.'

'Martin and I have already discussed him visiting St Paul's,' said Ben.

'Don't go wasting time,' Grace said, agitated. 'I wish he would see Angus. He's had a lot to do with war wounds.'

'What about Barbara? She's a nurse. She might have heard about such things.'

'Whatever you say,' murmured Eliza. 'You have to consult your GP, as he's the one who has to refer Martin to the hospital.'

'It could cost a lot of money,' said Grace.

'Why don't you get in touch with the *Echo*?' Eliza said. 'Big headline: "Missing soldier from the Great War turns up suffering from loss of memory and blindness and needs to raise money for medical fees". They'd start a fund and ask for donations. It's the sort of thing newspapers like.'

'Even better was Jane's idea about getting in touch with our friend Andrew down south and him writing the piece,' said Grace. 'After all, it was through him meeting Martin's wife that Ben discovered his brother was still alive.' She turned to Eliza and added, 'Andrew started out working for the Liverpool *Echo*, before getting a job on a national daily and moving south.'

'Perhaps he could also write an article about the gap it leaves in the lives of those who have been injured on the home front,' said Eliza. 'I don't remember anything about arranging the wedding to my first husband.'

Ben and Grace stared at her in amazement. Then Ben said, 'But surely you asked your husband, and he told you?'

'It's not the same as remembering it for yourself,' said Eliza. 'He's dead now so I'll never get the chance to speak to him. Even so, he told me he arranged it all, and then it turned out that he'd deceived me and was still married to his first wife.'

'Don't incidents from the past pop into your head seemingly from nowhere?' asked Grace.

'You mean like déjà vu, when you have a strange feeling that you've met someone and can't remember where or been somewhere before and done something but can't remember when?' said Eliza.

'That sort of thing, yes,' said the voice of the man who had just stuck his head around the kitchen door.

'How long have you been listening, Martin?' asked Ben.

'Since I heard an unfamiliar female voice talking about memory loss,' he replied. 'I remember marching to the Front and being in a trench, and the sound of the big guns and the stinging of the gas in my eyes – and that's all. I don't remember getting hit on the head, but I do remember darkness and the cries of wounded men, and my stumbling about for what seemed ages and the cries fading, and then I blundered into a tree and just dropped to the ground and drifted into unconsciousness.' He paused. 'When I came round, my head ached like billyo, and it was still dark, so I thought it was night. Until I stumbled over a fallen log and realised that surely, I should have been able to make out some outlines, even during the night hours...' His voice tailed off.

Silence.

Grace said, 'Let's go and sit down, and have coffee and cake.'

They trooped into the parlour, and all sat down, Ben guiding his brother to the chair that Martin had occupied earlier. Eliza was able to have a better look at him: she guessed he was in his fifties and most likely had been in his twenties when he went to war, so thirty years since last he was in Liverpool. If he had been able to see, he would have found it very different.

'Have you ever been, Eliza?' asked Ben.

'Been where?' she asked. 'I was near to remembering something, and felt it was important.'

'The Grand National,' said Martin.

Ben said, 'The racecourse was occupied by the United States Army during the war, so the stands haven't been used for years and now it's being discussed whether they're safe for the paying public when the big race is on for the first time in years.'

Suddenly, Eliza was thinking about how she had met Bryn. She had been with Olive, whom she hadn't heard from since Olive and Theo's daughter had been born. Time to get in touch and see how they were getting on.

'I never expected him to get serious, so when he suggested we get married before he left for the Middle East, I said, in what I thought was a jokey voice, "Oh, yeah, but we'll have to get the banns read." He laughed and so I said, "You are joking? Aren't you?" But he replied, "No time for jokes."' She paused. 'So, we were married in a registry office and Jack was a witness pulled in from outside. I can't remember much of what happened afterwards, until I came round in the hospital with a wedding ring on my finger and my wedding lines in my handbag and was informed that I had been rescued from a bombed house and that my baby was okay.' She paused again. 'I should have asked him more, but I never thought of it and there wasn't much time. He was killed in the Middle East.' She wrinkled her nose. 'I'm so glad

307

I met Jack again and we are a family, with Alfie and Beth. Now tell me, Ben, how did you get over to France?'

He grinned. 'Soldiers were needed, not for fighting, but to follow the troops over later with replacement weapons, food and other necessities, unload them on the beaches and load them onto lorries, and send them on to where they were needed. I volunteered. It was hard work, nonstop. We slept on the beach, and I didn't take my socks or boots off for a month. Eventually, I managed to get a lift on a lorry that would take me near to where I needed to be. I met Josephine's cousin there and she took me to the farm, and there was the brother I hadn't seen since he marched off to war. The French Resistance managed to get us picked up and flown back to Britain with young Ben, and here we are,' he said.

Eliza could not wait to get home and tell Jack what Ben and his brother had told her, and he was as pleased as her to know who had saved her from a nasty plight. He did not appear as surprised as her that she had not heard from Olive and suggested that she should talk to Amelia and ask if she had heard from Theo.

Eliza asked her the following morning and Amelia looked uncomfortable. 'Theo's living in London, as you know. The marriage broke up and although they haven't divorced, they have separated, and I believe Olive and their daughter have moved back to live with her mother in Aintree.'

Eliza felt sad and was sorry for the little girl. She decided to write to Olive's mother about the situation and see what she had to say. She also asked Jack to write to Theo, asking whether he had heard anything about Glenys.

Theo's only reply was, 'You're a detective, detect.'

Eliza was shocked by the reply as much as Jack was and took it to heart. Meanwhile, Olive's mother had answered her letter, saying that she had not heard much from Olive since she left and joined the Women's Royal Air Force, during the war, but that her granddaughter was living with her. She congratulated Eliza and Jack on the birth of their daughter, adding that she would love to see Eliza, Jack and Alfie again, as well as the new baby.

Eliza showed the letter to Jack, and he suggested that they think about what to do. In the meantime, Dilys and Donny were friendly again, but there was no sign that they planned to get married. Eliza decided not to get involved. She agreed with Jack that marriage wasn't for everybody. Besides, Dilys enjoyed her work as a teacher and Donny didn't want to give up the sea, so she accepted that their feelings could have changed.

EPILOGUE

'Well, what do you think?' asked Jack, gazing at the shiny new burgundy-coloured Triumph Mayflower.

'It's beautiful,' said Eliza. 'But can we afford it? I know you've just been promoted again, Chief Inspector. But what happened to your wanting a house to ourselves?'

'I like living opposite the park and I like this house, and I think Amelia will be lonely if we leave.' He turned away from the car reluctantly and said, 'I've been thinking of how she would cope if we moved. This house would be far too big for her and it's old and needs looking after as much as she does.'

'What are you suggesting?' asked Eliza who liked the house and living opposite the park as much as he did and cared about Amelia who was more of a granny to the children than Gladys could ever have been.

'I think we should ask her to sell it to us and she carries on living here that way I'll be responsible for repairs, etc.' He placed an arm around her. 'What do you think?'

'I love the idea but what about the money and buying the car?'

'I take out a mortgage on the house and say goodbye to the car until next year,' he said. 'After all I'm already paying rent.'

'But she has Dilys living not far away.'

'I know, in those high flats,' said Jack.

'She likes the view high up and has friends to stay whenever she wants,' said Eliza. 'And she likes everything modern.'

'So, if Amelia had thought she had to leave the house to her niece and nephew, she would know they would sell it and she would hate that thought. This house is where she shared many happy moments with her Thomas and us. But there could be ill-feeling if she simply left it to us.'

At that moment Alfie came and stood next to Jack. 'Are you going to buy the car, Dad?'

'I've been considering it. I've never had a brand-new car.'

'You could drive us to Blackpool in it to see the lights,' said Alfie. 'The war's been over for years. You promised we could go after the war.'

'The lights have only just been switched on this year,' said Jack. 'What does your mother say?' He winked at Eliza. 'Promises have to be kept, love.'

'But we didn't promise to go in a brand-new motor car,' she said, 'besides we can't afford a new car and to buy Amelia's house.'

Alfie looked thoughtful and then said, 'But Dad's car is old and beginning to struggle up hills. We need a new one. I could buy it and he could teach me to drive when I'm old enough. I've all that shares money just sitting in the bank and I'm going to need to drive once I join the company.'

Eliza stared at her son doubtfully as he waited hopefully for her reply and suddenly, she was remembering singing, *we're off, we're off, we're off in a motor car, sixty coppers are after us and we don't know where we are.* 'Yes, let's do that and go,' she said. 'We'll need to speak to the other trustee. But for how long do we go? A day or a weekend?'

'A week,' said Alfie. 'It'll give us plenty of time for me to show Beth how to build a sandcastle.'

'You can build sandcastles in New Brighton,' said Jack, looking dazed.

'Or we could go to Anglesey,' said Alfie. 'Beth's never been to Anglesey.'

Eliza thought, it's true! And she felt a yearning for that special place where the war had been forgotten, and she and Jack had felt free to act as young lovers. Everybody needed a special place that would rouse happy memories. She thought of Jean and her young Polish soldier. Lots of Poles and Italians had stayed or come to Britain after the war, including George. His mother and sisters had taken to the mountains when the Russians invaded, as they were feared as much as the Germans. George had met up with them in Austria, where the Americans had a camp and had needed interpreters to cope with Polish refugees, and George had volunteered. His English was good after the time he had spent in England. His sisters and mother had decided they wanted to go to America, so he wished them well, as he was heading for England. In Liverpool he had met up with Jean and they got engaged and were planning a Christmas wedding.

'We'll go to Blackpool for one day to see the lights next weekend and take Amelia with us,' said Jack.

'And to Anglesey for a week during half term, just the four of us. You do have school, young man,' Eliza said, tousling the fair hair that he had inherited from his father, along with shares in the slate company that would come in handy for his future. 'We could call in on Uncle Glyn and Aunt Mairi and Gwen. But we won't stay. I just want to see how the B&B plan is working out.'

'We'll be able to see Robin and his mother,' said Alfie.

Eliza smiled, thinking about Robin and his mother, who had accepted the offer of employment as cook and general handyman, respectively.

So, the car was bought, and a mortgage was applied for and the following weekend they set out for Blackpool, where they dug sandcastles, paddled in the sea, ate fish and chips out of newspaper, sprinkled with salt and vinegar, and sucked Blackpool rock and went around the fairground, before returning to the car as twilight came and the main thoroughfare was lit up with many coloured lights.

'It's magic,' said Alfie in a rapt voice. 'Irene and Peter's uncle really should see this.'

And it was possible, thought Eliza. Because it had been diagnosed that Martin had cataracts, which could be removed, and there had been no need to open a fund for the operation because the National Health Service had come into being three years ago and was a blessing to so many of her friends who had been damaged by war. She had not heard from Olive, but her mother had told her that she was still in the Women's Air Force, and her granddaughter, Joanna, lived with her. Occasionally, the girl saw Theo, and he sent her cards and money on her birthday and at Christmas, but she seldom saw him and Olive together after they were divorced. Eliza accepted that Joanna and her gran were fine together.

Although, she did wish that she and Olive were more in touch with each other. She wondered when she would leave the forces or whether she enjoyed the life. It suited her to leave her daughter with her mother; after all, Joanna had been company for her since her grandfather died. She could not also help wondering why Theo had not taken on the responsibility of his daughter. Could it be that it was because, just like Bryn, he wanted a son, and he did not care enough for Olive and his daughter to want their company?

Maybe, just like Bryn, he would find someone else to marry, although he was divorced so the marriage would be legal. Thinking about Bryn, she had forgiven him his deceit. As much as it had pained her, without it, she would not have Alfie, and she might never have met Jack and have such a happy life now.